The
SACRED POOL

BAEN BOOKS BY L. WARREN DOUGLAS

The Sacred Pool
Simply Human

The
SACRED POOL

L. WARREN DOUGLAS

THE SACRED POOL

This is a work of fiction. All the characters and events portrayed in this book are fictional, and any resemblance to real people or incidents is purely coincidental.

A Baen Books Original

Baen Publishing Enterprises
P.O. Box 1403
Riverdale, NY 10471
www.baen.com

ISBN: 0-671-31956-6

Cover art by Larry Elmore

First printing, January 2001

Library of Congress Cataloging-in-Publication Data

Douglas L. Warren.
    The sacred pool / by L. Warren Douglas.
        p.   cm.
    ISBN 0-671-31956-6
    1. Provence (France)—Fiction.   2. Lost children—Fiction.   I. Title.

PS3554.O82627 S23 2001
813'.54—dc21   00-045542

Distributed by Simon & Schuster
1230 Avenue of the Americas
New York, NY 10020

Production by Windhaven Press, Auburn, NH
Printed in the United States of America

10   9   8   7   6   5   4   3   2   1

Dedication

For Sue E. Folkringa, my wife, my friend and companion on all the trails and byways of Provence, and wherever else the endless quest may lead us.

Acknowledgments

Poul Anderson, Dave Feintuch, Leo Frankowski, Cornell W. Lugthart, Jr., Sara M. Ormerod, W. F. "Bud" Potts, and Ron Sarti, for reading the manuscript, criticizing it, and making suggestions. Judy Green, for typing great chunks of it.

Leo Frankowski, for all the discussions of history and time.

Alain Bonifaci et Nathalie Bernard, Hotel Cardinal, 24 Rue Cardinale, Aix-en-Provence, France, *pour une chambre jolie et confortable, et un gai "bonjour" chaque matin.*

Martine Lattouqoux, archaeologist at Entremont, where I saw my first Portal of Skulls, for the after-hours discussion.

The Granet Museum, Rue Cardinale, Aix-en-Provence.

The French people for the preservation of so many antiquities among which we may, on certain magical occasions, part the Veil of Years.

Sue, as always, for everything. Celeste Anne and Emma Sue, of course, just for being warm and furry.

Table of Contents

Part One ∾ *Infans*

Long before Romans made this land their Province, its forests, lakes, plains, and mountains were home to men who fashioned tools of stone and ate roots, wild seeds, and small creatures of the bogs. The early folk feared the spirits bound in brooding rock, lurking in shadows of great oaks, leaping in hares, bears, great stags, and wild bulls.

Somewhere in the vast sweep of years they began to generalize their awe, and to understand the underlying unities among stones, bears, stags, and summer thunder. They called such universal spirits *gods*. *Ma* meant "breast," and also "Goddess." "Man" meant the folk of Ma. In such ancient syllables lie the beginnings of wisdom, the capacity for awe and worship, the great reality sensed only dimly, never proven, that we call Faith.

This is a tale of a daughter of the land, a child of Ma.

Otho, Bishop of Nemausus
The Sorceress's Tale

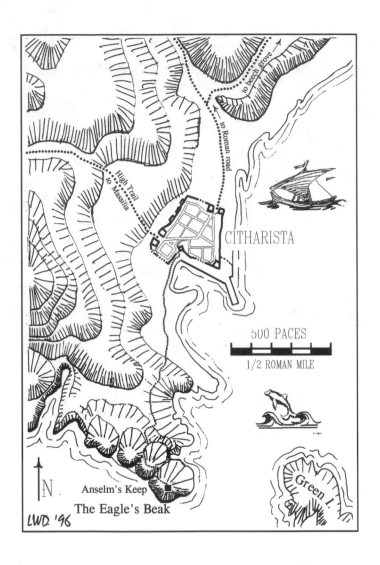

to beech grove

to Roman road

High Trail
to Massilia

CITHARISTA

500 PACES

1/2 ROMAN MILE

Green I.

N

Anselm's Keep

The Eagle's Beak

LWD '96

Chapter 1 ∿ The *Masc*

The moon shone bright upon the ancient stones of Citharista, lighting young Marius's dash to the chapel. "P'er Otho! *Pater!*" he shouted. "Come quickly. The *gens* are pursuing the witch Elen onto the rocks. Bring the *Sancta*. Come!" He had to stop, to take breath.

Father Otho rose from his knees, his face more drawn and angry than the boy's unseemly babbling could account for.

Marius shrank back, averting his eyes from the priest, and from the reliquary where the holy bones lay, in their tiny gabled house of gilt cedar encrusted with garnets and gold. He did not understand Otho's anger, because he was too young to remember the revelation of the saint's remains, or to know what was between the priest and the woman who fled.

The moaning Latin chant was a distant dragon growling up the winding path from Citharista. Villagers' torches curled like a glowing serpent from among red-tiled houses and Roman warehouses.

The fleeing masc's eyes, wide with terror, reflected the red and gold of serpentine flames, and when she turned her head toward the dark, wooded path, she stumbled, blinded by torchlight. The roots of twisted cypresses tripped her, slowing her headlong flight. Her twisted ankle felt as if a knife blade pried between the bones.

The moon had withdrawn its light. Had she angered the Goddess, begging for a male child to quicken in her womb? Had the Virgin Huntress abandoned her to that other Virgin, whose torchbearers even now drew close?

3

She drew her skirts about her knees and stumbled onward in darkness and pain. A refuge lay ahead, the old Saracen fort at the tip of the cape. There dwelled the magus Anselm. The Christian villagers would not pursue her within those walls—but she did not think she could reach them in time.

Pressing on, she fended off stiff, scrubby oak branches grown malevolently hard and sharp, branches that clawed at her eyes as she passed. Abruptly the moon emerged from behind its veil. The path branched. One trail ran south to the cape, another eastward across the headland, where cliffs plunged a thousand feet to the sea.

She let her sash drop on the southbound trail, then hid in the feathery shadow of a tamarisk bush. If the villagers reached the fort without finding her, they would believe her already safe within. Then, later, she would limp around to the fort by a goat path.

"Cado! Wait!" she heard a distant villager call. "We'll never catch a masc here by the sea, where the old devils rule. Wait for Marius to come with the priest and Sancta Clara's bones." The witch smiled then. Father Otho would not come. The *gens*, townsfolk, would wait, but young Marius would return alone. Otho would not allow his saint's relic to be so ill-used.

Otho sighed. "I'll go with you," he told the boy. "We need not disturb the Saint."

"P'er Otho, the castellan himself commanded it. You must bring her."

Commanded? Otho bristled. Only the bishop commanded him, not the Burgundian soldier.

Otho himself had discovered the holy bones protruding from the cut earth where the Burgundian horseman had ordered a fortification built. The priest's nocturnal vision had revealed the holy one's tale, which he told to the villagers and the Germanic soldier.

Sancta Clara. A name or a description? Clear and holy: Saint Claire. He envisioned her on the road from Massalia, fleeing the Roman hundred with their bloody arrows in her back. There at the edge of Citharista she had died, but her death provided a vital distraction that allowed the Magdalen to escape to the north, to the Saint-Baume and the holy

cave where she remained, preached, and prayed for yet
another thirty-three years. Thus here in poor Citharista had
the life of Mary Magdalen, patron saint of all Provence, been
saved.

Otho's fiery inspiration had daunted the big yellow-haired
German knight, and he had moved his proposed walls twenty
paces north. The shrine now stood over holy Clara's grave.
Thus Otho's interest was proprietary, and he did not take
kindly to the boy's demand to jostle the saint and carry
her bones on a fool's errand.

"Saint Claire was hounded by the Roman hundred," he
told Marius coldly—perhaps even a trifle pompously; there
was no proof of the tale, only the vision he had been granted
during his vigil over the newly exposed bones. "It's not right
that she, the hunted, be used to track down another woman
wrongly pursued. Her bones are for healing. You have seen
me wash them in balsam and oil. Didn't the drink cure your
own constricted throat, a summer ago?"

Young Marius scuffled his feet uneasily. "Elen is a witch,
Pater, a masc who doesn't worship God."

"Ah, Elen," the priest murmured. "See what your pagan
mischief brings?" Aloud, he said, "Wait, boy, while I pray."
He knelt again, unhurried.

Elen crouched low as footsteps crunched stones on the
path. She plucked a willow twig and urgently whispered an
incantation over its lanceolate leaves. For a moment they
gleamed like the feathers of a white hen or a gull.

The magics of the world are not evoked in silence, but
with words. Elen's words were not in an old, magical tongue,
but were mere Latin overlain with Visigothic, a musical
tongue that would someday be named for a single word,
"yes," which was "oc." The *Langue d'Oc.*

"Oc," said Elen, satisfied, as the moon again withdrew
its face. Her spell had come from the fairy Guihen generations past: Guihen the invisible, who stroked his white hen
and disappeared at will. Guihen the Ligure, who righted
wrongs and won the daughter of a *dux* as reward, and a
Roman villa, and a chest of gold. She watched her hands
fade to invisibility as the moon disappeared.

The footsteps on the trail were quick and light, no heavy
farmer's tread, but Elen did not dare raise her face from

the curtain of her dark hair until she heard one pursuer speak.

"Look! It's Mama's sash." Appalled, the masc recognized her eldest daughter, Marie. "She must be near. See? She dropped it on the path to the cape."

"The Eagle's Beak? Will the *gens* follow her there?" That was Pierrette, her second child.

Elen's heart sank.

"Let's trick them," suggested Marie. "I'll move the sash to the other branch of the trail, and they'll think she fled east."

Marie and Pierrette had outdistanced the townsfolk. They would "save" her by undoing her own deception. Elen was torn between bidding them leave the sash and remaining hidden. Once undone, Guihen's spell would be difficult to renew. Magic failed oftener than not, or took strange turns.

Otho's knees ached on the unyielding stone. Tonight, his prayers took strange form, a reminiscence of a time that he held close in his heart. . . .

That summer, he had been but thirteen. Elen had been a year older, a dark forest sprite tiny as the fairies from whom her ancient folk had sprung. She had been to Otho a fairy indeed, and he had fallen in love with her by the tiny spring her folk held sacred, the Goddess's breast from which they drank. The day he met her, Otho had hiked miles in search of game for his father's table, and the water in his leather pouch was warm, stale, and sour. When the dark-eyed wood spirit had offered him water fresh from the rock, in a clean beechwood cup, he had drunk greedily, and had fallen utterly under her enchantment.

In truth, the spell had been his own, sprung not from the waters but from the life that pulsed in his groin. Similar magic had flowed in the girl, unchecked by Christian inhibition.

That summer his hunting trips all took him near the Mother's breast, and he never again carried his water pouch. He felt the urge to hunt whenever he felt the swelling of his maleness in the heat of the summer nights, as often as his heart and mind sweetened with the memory of dark eyes, lithe limbs, and the warmth between them.

But summer did not last forever. Even before the last leaves

fell from the oaks, before the mossy ground grew too chill
for revels with the Goddess's child, his brothers discovered
the game he hunted. His father bundled him off to the abbey
at Massalia, where he had remained for two years.

Returning to Citharista, he bore about his neck a bronze
cross, and upon his heart a weight heavier still. Elen carried another burden, for even then little Marie swelled within
her—Marie, the daughter of Gilles, a fisherman who also
tended a grove of olive trees outside the town.

In two years a second daughter was born to Elen, and
Gilles approached the young priest with an odd request. Elen
had lost two sons before their birthing, and it was likely
the new child would be her last. He did not say that Elen's
old Ligurian magic had determined so. Otho suspected Gilles
was but a messenger, and that Elen herself had sent him.

Gilles was then thirty-two, and had lost many teeth. He
might live another five years or twenty, but without a son
to aid him, their Burgundian defender would press him to
sell the olive grove to him, and Gilles's family would suffer.

Gilles fished also, as had his father, but his old boat was
frail, and he was afraid to sail all the way to Massalia, the
only market for his sea urchins, a delicacy among rich folk
of Greek and Roman descent. He told himself he was a
cautious man. Thus he must have his olive grove.

"I need a son," Gilles said. Otho protested that he was
no *masco*, and could not change the sex of a daughter born.
"Then I need only your silence," Gilles replied. "We will
raise the child as a boy and call him Petros, which means
'a stone.' The Burgundian will not know of the deception
until I am dead."

"Petros? I can't perform an unhallowed baptism using Saint
Peter's name."

"Then don't baptize the child. Merely keep silent for Elen's
sake, and we'll call him Piers." In the vernacular tongue
it meant the same thing, a stone. Otho did not ask its deeper
meaning, suspecting it was Elen's secret reprimand: the stone
she had borne beneath her heart, since her first love had
left her and taken the cross.

The "boy," Piers, was now five, and no one suspected he
was not merely small like his mother. Otho speculated that
Elen had cast a small glamour over the child, causing the eye

to slip past Pierrette's delicate features and focus upon the boyishness of her clothing and short-cropped hair.

Yet whether or not Elen had done so, she had not relented in her effort to bear a son. Her small forest magics failed, but there were others. She visited the magus Anselm in his Saracen keep, and was heard speaking words in a tongue no man could fathom. The pagan witches of the hills were tolerated, for they sprang from the same roots and beliefs as Christian townsfolk, but this new sorcery was not. Folk had talked harshly of Elen and her foreign magics. . . .

"P'er Otho?" At Marius's tremulous query, Father Otho's reverie faded. As smoothly as an aging man could, an elder of twenty-seven with streaks of white in his hair, he got to his feet.

No need for haste; either the *gens* would catch the poor woman or they would not. He was too far away to affect the outcome. If Elen was caught, they would beat her, perhaps even to death, and he would cry shame and heap penances upon them; if they lost her on the rocks and forest trails, or if she reached Anselm's stronghold, he would meet his flock on their way back, and shame them for their murderous intent.

Then he reconsidered his resistance to the castellan's command: the Burgundian could request a more docile priest. He sighed, picked up the reliquary, and held it reverently on supine palms. There was surely no harm in carrying it forth; the saint, herself a fugitive, might even take pity on Elen and cast confusion over her pursuers. Surely she would do Elen no harm.

The rough voices of the villagers neared. Elen heard a curse as someone fell. "Hold! Wait for the priest and Saint Claire. Marius says they're coming!" Elen lost herself to despair. Even gentle, loving Otho had at last completed his transformation, his rejection of her. He would bring his magical bones to sniff her out.

"They're closer," whispered Pierrette. "What shall we do?" But the decision wasn't hers. As villagers, priest, and holy bones drew near, Elen felt the Christian magic overpower Guihen's pitiful spell, driving off her hard-won obscurity with its baleful might, with unforgiving Faith. The Moon's round disk again emerged, and the light that shone on Elen was not the Huntress's visage, but a cold, bright, silver lamp that belonged to Otho's celestial God.

"Mother!" gasped Marie, seeing Elen. She ran to her, with Pierrette close behind. Both girls, one seven and in skirts, the other five, clad in a boy's tunic and small Frankish trousers, clung to her arms as she tried to rise. "Mother, we must flee! Listen—they come."

"Marie, hear me," Elen said desperately. "They mustn't find you with me. Run to the Eagle's Beak. Stay with Anselm. Go!" The moon was bright. Even the stars seemed unnaturally intense, and she knew there was no hope—but the children must get away.

"Mother, come!" But the sharp crack of Elen's palm on her cheek cut off Marie's words.

"Obey! Go now. Take your sister." She pressed a small, soft leather sack in her youngest daughter's hand. "Take this, my sweet. Give it to Anselm."

It was not her mother Marie saw then, shedding the two girls from her skirts; it was the masc Elen, the witch, and Marie was suddenly cold with fear of sorceries, unnatural moonlight, and darkness among the trees. With a tiny, despairing cry Marie fled, pulling Pierrette after.

Alone, Elen waited, now hearing the priest's sweet tenor joining the chant, guiding it, inspiring it to ever greater volume and power.

Chapter 2 ~ The Strange Ones

The Eagle's Beak, a broken crest of red rock west of Citharista's small harbor, was almost unclimbable on its gentlest side. It sloped like a steep roof. It was a soft, crumbly matrix of red marl encompassing rounded pebbles. As climbers struggled, fragments broke off and rolled beneath their unsteady feet.

Below, shallow caves pocked the three scarps, which looked, from Citharista, like bulging domes of bare, brown rock.

From the sea, the "roof" could be seen as an overflung edge, undermined by waves gnawing at its base four hundred feet below. A pebble dropped from the scarp would fall well out beyond the surging waves, in water as deep as the cliff was high.

The few faint trails to the summits were clogged with thorny-leaved scrub oak that clawed at skin and clothing, and tangles of finely branched evergreens. Where rock had crumbled to make soil, the spreading parasols of pines shadowed and obscured the narrow ways.

Otho, Bishop of Nemausus
The Sorceress's Tale

Pierrette had seen the Eagle's Beak from her father's fishing boat. Riding the swell, she'd looked up not to the sky, but to a looming roof of stone.

Now, on the slope, their way obscured by stubborn pines,

it was not surprising that two little girls should take a wrong turn, and then, in dismayed confusion, find themselves tantalizingly near the mage Anselm's stronghold, but on the wrong side of an unscalable scarp, with the enraged townsmen between them and safety. They huddled in a dank cave, hoping not to be seen.

They were close enough to hear shouts, and the thump of clubs on human flesh—but thankfully not near enough to hear their mother's agony, which was wordless, except for a murmur, perhaps her daughters' names.

Whether or not Elen spoke those names, they were what Cado the fisherman heard as he knelt close to verify Elen's dying. "The brats," he growled. "She's saying something to them. Where did they go?"

"What does it matter?" Someone—a faceless shadow under stark moonlight—raised a club for a last, killing blow.

"Never mind," Cado said, seeing the spreading stain on Elen's garment. "She's dead."

"Where are the whelps?" the other man said again—a harsh devil-face, Cado saw, one that ordinarily belonged to Jules, a carpenter who repaired boats.

The other villagers crowded around the inert masc. "They didn't pass us," someone muttered uneasily.

Otho, last to arrive, bearing his holy bones, pushed through the huddle. He knelt, and gently closed Elen's staring eyes.

He arose.

The *gens* backed away, and none would meet his bleak, baleful gaze.

"Murderers," he grated. "Would you kill the children too?"

Those who could, slipped away. Among them were Cado, Jules, and the others who had wielded clubs. Otho lingered, alone with Elen for the last time. At last he covered her battered face, and headed down the narrow defile.

From the shadow of the shallow cave, the two children had heard enough to fear their mother was dead. Marie spun away, covering her face. Little Pierrette stood like chiseled stone, unwilling to turn from her dismay. . . .

And then she saw . . . him . . . just within the cave.

His hair was white as moonlight, yet his face was a boy's. It had a stiff little nose, and lips like those of the tumbled Eros marble half-buried inside the ruined walls of a Roman edifice. Violet eyes seemed to glow from within, like none

Pierrette had seen, in that land where most were brown or black.

His ears were huge. They wiggled.

"You may laugh," he said. "It doesn't bother me." His voice was youthful, yet hauntingly familiar, with inflections like Elen's—who had grown up speaking the old Ligure tongue.

"They'll hear you," Pierrette whispered, her eyes shifting toward the cave mouth behind the strange apparition. He laughed, a sound that carried echoes of tiny bells. Moonlight wafted over his clothing. Pierrette gasped.

His garments—a puffy moon-white shirt, green pantaloons, and floppy-toed shoes—all seemed to be made of willow leaves. Or were they feathers? The shirt glowed like nacre, the short trousers like magpie feathers, first russet, then azure, then green. "They'll hear only the sighing of wind among the pine needles," he said. "They'll see only moonbeams and the flicker of a bat. Not me, and not you."

"How can that be?" the girl queried the apparition.

"Once you knew that," he replied oddly. "Once you knew me." Pierrette had ten fingers, and knew she had fewer years than digits. Her confusion showed. "Later, I'll explain," he said with a touch of sadness. "First we'll win free of this place."

Marie, the older girl, had hardly lifted her face from her sheltering hands. Now, she peered up at the odd little man. "Mother is dead, isn't she? Are you the devil, come to take us as well?"

Pierrette shook her. "Mother can't be dead. And the devil is Pan, with his horns. This is only . . ." She turned hesitantly toward him.

"I'm your mother's friend, and no devil—not yet. My soul is my own."

Marie rose, shrugging as if she did not care if their guide was a devil, or whether their mother still lived. Together, they climbed down from the cave. No townsfolk were in sight, though their cries could be heard among the rocks and twisted pines.

"They won't see us," said the feather-clad boy-man. He led them through gullies and up long, rough slopes. Red rock gave way to bleached limestone, scrub oak and pine to sharp-twigged, sticky-leaved brush, then to taller oaks with large leaves, thick boles, and heavy shadows that hid the moon and stars.

"We won't find Mother here," Pierrette complained. "Look—the Eagle's Beak is far away." At the extreme tip of the cape, high on the rock, but far below where they now stood, were the geometric shadows of the fort people said Saracens had built long ago.

In the shadow of those walls, something moved, low to the ground, humping from one dark place to the next, visible only when it crawled across a patch of moonlit ground. As it moved, it groaned like a soul tormented, and left behind a faint trail of scuffled pebbles, and dark wetness that glistened momentarily.

Its progress was erratic, yet it moved inexorably toward the wooden gate at the end of a narrow footpath. On either side of the path, the red rock plunged downward. Disturbed pebbles tumbled free and rattled down into silence long before they splashed into the sea.

Humping itself up, the apparition took on almost human shape: a head with hair that hung in rootlike clumps, arms like branches twisted by sea-winds.

"Aaa . . ." it croaked. "Aaa . . . Anssselm!" Again and again it uttered the cry, in wet, broken tones that bubbled up as from a depth of mud.

With a rattling of chains and the thump of a heavy bolt, the fortress's door opened. The yellow light of a candle flickered across the pebbled path. "Who calls? Show yourself!" The voice was high and querulous.

The flickering light revealed an old man in a gray nightshirt that matched his long, tousled hair and beard. A halo of frizzy hairs waved like seaweed across his pate as the breeze rushed past him, up the stairs, to dissipate in the maze of mysterious rooms beyond.

"Anselm . . ."

The mage gasped. "Elen!"

"Help me!"

"Poor girl, what have you done?" His skinny arms fluttered as he hovered about the broken shape on his path. "Oh, Elen, I warned you. Why couldn't you listen? Look what's become of you."

"My children . . ." The masc Elen saw the mage through

a red haze of blood. The pain of her broken legs, wrist, and ribs was as nothing. Death would free her, but her daughters . . . "Help me!" she moaned, her words a wind among bare, dead branches.

"I can't," wept the mage. "I don't control the magic that destroyed you."

Elen, knowing full well that the *gentes*' clubs, not magic, had broken her, shook her head. The creak and groan of her neck-bones was loud in her ears—and she could not see herself as the mage saw her. She had not noticed the stiff, gray bark that wrapped her wrists, fingers and bare forearms. She could not see the beech leaves in her hair.

Beech leaves, on a windswept seacoast? Beech trees grew in the sheltered valley of the Holy Balm, where Magdalen's bones lay buried, and by the sacred pool, not by the sea.

Yet Anselm saw them, and realized they weren't merely clinging, but growing. The tips of twigs shaped themselves from clumped strands of bloody hair. "You've destroyed yourself, girl," he murmured sadly. "My own weak magic can't undo that."

"The children," Elen pleaded, her voice dry and rough as branches rubbing against stone.

"What can I do? They aren't here, and if I leave this place, I'll fade away. Perhaps they'll come to me . . . I'll do what I can." He hesitated "I don't know what help I may be."

"Teach them."

"Hasn't there been enough horror? Look what my magic did to you."

The masc, with sounds of agony, drew herself to her knees and examined her hands. Where fingernails had been pushed small, green leaves. Smooth, gray bark stiffened her fingers and obscured the joints. Nubs and knotholes scarred her arms, and a spur pushed itself from her elbow, a woody protuberance that ended in twigs and swelling buds.

Then Elen knew her destiny—and what must be done. "This is not your magic," she said, though speech became more difficult; beech leaves rustled where her tongue had been, and her lips were stiff and gray. "This is older. It's Mother's. The children, Anselm. Promise."

The mage nodded. "If they come to me. But you can't stay on this dry path. What's to become of you?"

"Take me to my Mother," she wanted to say. "Take me

to the spring called *Ma*, far up the valley past the old Roman
fountain." She tried to say that, but her voice was only the
whisper of a breeze among her leaves, the rattle of stiff twigs,
of insects upon her gray, smooth bark.

Marie huddled near the small campfire, silent.

Pierrette pulled herself closer. "Mother said I must go to
Anselm."

"Elen was distraught." Their big-eared guide fed a twig
to the flames. "That's no place for a child."

"Take me," she said, as if he hadn't spoken.

"When you're older and wiser, go yourself. I'll never take
you." In his lap, between his skinny knees, was a plump
white hen. Neither grief nor the darkness of the deep woods
could still the growling of Pierrette's stomach as she imagined
that succulent bird turning on a spit. She could taste it
already.

When she said as much, the long-eared fellow reacted with
voluble horror. "Eat my hen? Ignorant, nasty girl! Would
you kill and eat me too? As well if you did—without my
little friend, I would die anyway. Shame! Horrid carnivore!"

Only her tears, when he made as if to leave her by the
flickering fire, seemed to stay him. "She is the source of
my magic," he explained. "I stroke her feathers, and I become
invisible." He made a show of stroking the bird's wings.
"Watch," he said. "Now no one can see me."

"You're right there, in front of me. How could I not see
you?"

"Oh, mud!" he said.

Pierrette giggled, her misery forgotten for the moment.
He was so foolish, with his feathery clothes, his wide,
crooked grin, and ears that wiggled as he spoke. His
manner—boyish, yet as if inside his skinny frame lurked
a grumpy old man—drove away her fear. "Why shouldn't
I see you?" she asked.

He scowled. "Didn't your mother tell you who I am?"

Mother had said many things. She pondered for several
moments. Feathery clothing, and a white hen . . . "Guihen?"
Her voice was hesitant.

"You *do* know me!" he crowed.

Pierrette frowned. "I know of Guihen," she said, "but I'm
not sure you're him."

"Oh?" He seemed crestfallen. "Why not?"

"My mother said you were old—or even dead. She said all the forest spirits were old, and had gone away to die. Besides, I still see you."

"Wait, let me try again." Once more he stroked the hen's feathers. For a moment, Pierrette thought he wavered, as if heated air from the fire had blurred his image. For one long second she saw, instead of a ridiculous feather-clad man, a small willow, the undersides of its leaves white, the tops rich and green as magpie feathers.

"How wonderful!" Then she smiled mischievously. "But you weren't invisible."

"What?" His features drooped. "What did you see? Sometimes my ears . . ."

"I saw a willow bush."

He brightened. "Well, then, I was invisible after all. You saw a willow, and I am not a willow. Q.E.D."

"Kewayday?"

"Q.E.D., child. *Quod erat demonstrandum.* 'Thus it has been shown.' The conclusion of a mathematical or geometric theorem. It means I was right: you saw a willow, not me, therefore I was invisible. Q.E.D."

"I don't know what 'mathematical' means," Pierrette confessed, "but yes, I saw a willow, not you, and you aren't really a willow tree." Her words were slow and thoughtful, uttered with unchildlike precision.

Guihen grinned broadly. "You have a talent for logic. Someone should teach you."

Pierrette thought of the priest, P'er Otho, who knew much. Then her face twisted in painful memory. He had climbed into the hills with the vengeful townsfolk. She looked away. She dared not think of her mother, yet she could not keep from thinking of her.

"What's wrong, child?" asked Guihen. "Why the dried-fig face?"

"The *gens* caught my mother. What will happen to me?"

Marie emitted a throaty wail like a terrified cat. "Now see what I've done!" Pierrette cried. She threw her arms about the older girl, muffling her wet, burbling sobs. "There, Marie," she crooned, stroking her sister's tangled hair. "Soon we'll go home to Father." She did not believe that, but giving comfort allowed her to lock her own torment in a cellar, deep within the edifice of her mind.

Marie lapsed silent, and her breathing became soft and regular. Across the dead ashes, Guihen sat, illuminated now by the first, rose-petal tendrils of dawn weaving themselves among the trees.

Pierrette asked him, "Is my mother dead?" Dawn took the edge from emotion. Someday, Pierrette knew, she would weep. . . . But not in the ashen light of this new, empty day.

"Am I dead?" he retorted. "I'm a thousand years old, yet still a boy. Perhaps I'm the oldest boy alive—or dead. I suspect there's something in between the life ordinary folk know and the death they fear, because I am here—or so I believe."

Time and place were abstractions in the damp woods. In the aftermath of emotion, gray light made whimsy of forbidding things and permitted one not to care. "I will believe Mother is dead," said Pierrette, "when I see what remains of her. Not before." *And not unless*, said the voice deep in her personal cellar, hoping it would not happen, and that Elen would continue to live, saved by the ignorance of a five-year-old child.

Gilles, Pierrette's father, was hiding.

The skinny peasant's breath whistled between gapped brown teeth, and he clenched his jaw to prevent them from rattling against each other. Not that anyone would have heard, for he was too afraid to venture near the *gentes'* campfire. Were his children there? Had the townsfolk found them?

Gilles was not brave. "Cautious," he said when villagers chided him for refusing to take his sea urchins to Massalia for the best price. "The coast is gray and dangerous," he told them. "The currents are treacherous, the fogs constant, and any cove might hide a Saracen pirate."

Yet tonight he could not justify cowardice as caution. Any man worthy of the name would have rushed from his hiding place to fight the torch-wielders who had killed his wife. A *man* would have died if needs be, with the mother of his children, but Gilles had watched Elen die. What then was he?

He watched the distant firelight. If the children were there, he would see them when dawn illumined the camp.

A short distance from Gilles's hiding place, Marius slumped against a flat face of limestone, which reflected the flicker of firelight. The bludgeons, the murder weapons, had long since been consumed by the flames. Now Father Otho and several townsmen huddled close, sheltering the embers from wind that swept over the bleak heights, feeding the fire with twigs, stretching their meager fuel, praying they might make it last the endless hours that held away impending dawn, and the return of God to this forsaken place.

The townsfolk were afraid of ghosts and their own guilt. Yet Otho was not afraid; he was sickened, grief ridden, and worried about two small girls, huddled alone and cold in that hideous night.

"I saw beasts out there," Marius muttered, his teeth clattering as with intense cold. "I saw a terrible, starving man. And two pairs of eyes as big as limes glowed in the shadows. I saw them! I did!"

"Bears," said Cado the fisherman. "*His* bears! Yan Oors."

"John of the Bears is only a story," said the priest, annoyed that Cado was further agitating the boy. "We've no bears here. The Romans killed the last of them, and are themselves dust. The boy saw the old hermit, Anselm, and the glowing eyes were deer, startled by our thrashing about."

"They weren't deer," Marius said sullenly. "And the old magus has white hair, and never leaves his fortress. This man had a fat staff, as tall as a doorway."

"Yan Oors has an iron staff," said Cado. "He rights wrongs and protects the innocent."

"Who here is innocent?" snapped the priest. "Have you no blood on your hands?" Elen's blood, he thought. Elen, whom I and Saint Claire failed to save.

"That's not what I meant," Cado said. "I fear he has come . . . for us."

"Then pray. If anything walks the night it is Satan, not some long-dead Gaul. Fear for your soul, not your bald head."

"That too," grunted the fisherman.

Otho knew what he was thinking: Cado had been caught up in the townsmen's rage. Otho had felt the power and elation of the mob. Even the night, realm of devils and beasts, was no proof against the villagers' frenzy to catch the masc, Elen, the pretty witch who had spurned all of them, who had married Gilles-bad-teeth, and had birthed his brats.

Whether Satan or Yan Oors trod the rocky hills made no difference, thought Otho. Neither would save them from what they and their bloody clubs had done.

"Careful! Careful!" warned old Anselm. "Her tender roots."

"She has reached between the rocks," said his tall, gaunt companion, leaning on a heavy staff. The cudgel—liver-colored like rusted iron—was wedged in a crack. "I must free her from them."

The two men stood on the narrow causeway to the fortress. A strong breeze blew from the open sea westward of them, and over the glittering waters of the fjordlike calanque east of the ridge, yet it disturbed neither the smooth drape of the mage's robes, nor his tall companion's rough-woven, patched cloak. Their task concerned a small beech tree, a slender, muscled trunk the same silver-gray hue as the sky, which dawn and impending sun had not yet quickened to blue. Small leaves not darkened by day's burning heat fluttered at the ends of tender stemlets.

"The sun comes!" the oldster hissed. "Hurry! You must carry her to the spring, *Ma*."

"Shall I hurry, and damage her roots?" rumbled the tall man.

"Bah! Do as you will. Don't stop to converse."

"Then put your breath to work by removing the stones I have loosened." For some time thereafter the only sounds were the rattle of red marl and quartzite pebbles falling, and the iron clank of the big man's staff working loose rock for his companion to drag away.

At long last the work was done. The big man removed his frayed cloak and spread it. Both men gently lifted the small uprooted tree and placed it on the cloak. They packed pale, exposed roots and clinging soil with soft pine needles, and wrapped the cloak tightly around all, binding it with twine from the mage's sandals.

Carefully lifting the bundle, the gaunt one turned to depart. The mage nodded and turned away toward the yawning darkness of his fortress's gate. Then, as an afterthought, he said, "Be careful; the *gens* of Citharista will be returning home. Don't allow them to consummate their murderous intent."

"They won't see me," said the other—sadly, or so it seemed. "I almost wish they would." He didn't explain, but the mage seemed to understand, and replied, "I too yearn for the old times, but that is not to be." Did tears glisten in his eyes, or was it a reflection from the bright blue-green waters far below?

The big man—call him John—strode purposefully down the long rough slopes, making his own path. If men saw him, they averted their eyes, concentrating on their own precious footing, or pretended that they recognized him as someone safe and familiar—the priest, perhaps, in his dark garment—or saw merely the shadow of a scrub oak disturbed by unfelt movement of the air.

He walked along the narrow trail south of the town, and those townsmen who might otherwise see him turned aside into the brush to relieve full bladders, or bent to relace sandal-strings that had been snug a moment before.

The hairs on the necks of such villagers stood on end as they urinated or fiddled with their footgear, because they felt eyes staring at them from brush and shadow, eyes that— without their looking up—they knew to be green, as large as limes, and belonging to no wayward deer.

Striding softly despite his purposeful pace, John carried his bundle across the sandy spit south of Citharista port, and past old stone wharves, built in Roman times. He walked on gravel, but beneath the rattling stones was Roman pavement, limestone quarried high on the slopes where white dragon bones protruded from the bleak, fearsome hills.

None saw him as he passed through Citharista. At the pool where the crumbling aqueduct ended, women bent low to fill their jugs with extra water. Their burdens, walking back to their houses, would be heavier than usual, but they would excuse their excesses. "It's a good day to dye that cloth I wove last winter," one might say. "I have roots to color it as yellow as sunlight, and a jar of old wine to set the dye. It's a fine day for it."

"Today promises to be dry," another woman might say. "I'll need more water than usual. Octavus will be thirsty when he returns from the hills . . ."

Other folk, other rationales. John continued out of the town unseen. The road widened between fields of scruffy grain, vegetables in crooked rows, and grapevines on frames of split poles. North of Citharista he left the last cultivated plot behind. Sheep grazed on the slopes where the valley narrowed. He crossed a tiny stream once captured by the aqueduct and led downward to the town, now freed to make its own way, or to be soaked up by the thirsting soil, evaporated by the relentless sun.

He passed a last ancient olive grove, planted five hundred years earlier. John had not seen that particular grove since it had been young, but he remembered it and assured himself that, for all the changes the centuries had wrought, he was on the right trail. It wound over increasingly rough ground, among ancient trees far younger than he—who remembered an earlier forest there, one long-since cut for ridgepoles and ships' timbers.

At last he neared his destination. Obscured by trees and a tumble of eroded rock were the cut stones of a Roman fountain long dry. The channel that had fed it was clogged with roots old as the forest. The spring that welled up from *Ma*, the mother of folk more ancient than he (who considered himself a Gaul), was ahead, restored to its ancient place.

There, amid beech trees that thrived in the shelter and shadow of hills north and south, amid maples and broad-leaved oaks entirely unlike the seaward kind, he set his burden down. He contemplated the grove, the upwelling spring and the great, mossy stones as if seeking instruction from them. Then, with an inaudible sigh, he plunged his staff into the soft mold to loosen it. Gently pushing aside pine needles and moist soil, he unwrapped his cloak from the small beech tree's roots. He held the sapling upright in the hole, and sprinkled crumbles of soil over the tender roots. As the hole slowly filled, he tamped them with prodding fingers.

At last, he was finished. He brushed detritus over the disturbed soil. From a rock exposed to afternoon sun he rubbed dry moss, crumbled it further in the palm of his hand, and blew it over the dirt. Moss would grow from the fine powder, and in a year or two there would be no hint of what had transpired there.

Yan Oors, John of the Bears, then cast his eyes upward at the barren peaks to the north. No one saw him, of course, when his feet followed where his vision had gone ahead.

He almost wished someone had—some shepherd, perhaps, who might have hailed him, hoping for news from the town. But though there was a shepherd, he saw only his sheep, for he sensed the presence of wild beasts, and was afraid. He hailed no one—for in truth, no one was there.

"In truth," a dispassionate observer might have said, "Elen died upon the path to the Eagle's Beak, and someone—likely her husband Gilles—carried her poor remains away and buried them. That a spindly beech tree now grows in the ancient sacred grove means nothing, because the logical place for young beeches is where their parent tree's seeds fell. If indeed Elen is buried there, then the new seedling merely found the freshly turned soil hospitable." But no such observer had been on the Eagle's Beak that night, so who was to say what really transpired?

Far below—though high above Citharista, and in a forest also—Pierrette gently nudged her sister awake. "Guihen says it is safe now, Marie. We'll return to town. Papa must be terribly worried."

Marie's eyes, always dark, were lost in shadows her sister could not fathom. Would she ever smile again? "I want Mama," Marie said without inflection.

"Later, child," said their elfin companion. "She is resting, and must not be disturbed." That seemed to satisfy Marie, who was easily led down the trailless slope and out onto open ground.

"Why did this happen, Guihen?" asked Pierrette. "Why can't Mama come here right now?"

"She made a choice long ago, child," said the odd man, his ears hardly moving at all, as if they were leaves that had wilted in the sunlight. "Someday you'll remember, and will understand."

"How can that be?" asked the child—who knew that whatever choice had been made, it had surely been more than five years ago—and knew, though without training in mathematics, that she herself was but five. She explained that to Guihen.

He shook his head. "It's true that you are only five," he said, "but I remember when you were a great sorceress with magic in your eyes and flames dancing on your fingertips. That was very long ago, when I was not so young as I am

now—or is it old? Oc, I think so. I was not then so old."
He looked around himself, as if confused, his expression
conveying dismay.

"What's wrong?" asked Pierrette, frightened by the change
in him.

"I must go," he said. "I begin to fail. I've been away too
long."

"Don't leave us alone."

"Look below. There are the red roofs of Citharista. You
can find your way. I must go. Do not ask me to die for
your loneliness."

"Where will you go? I'll find you someday."

"The Camargue," he said, edging away as if she might
compel him to stay, "where the great river meets the sea—
where the white horses roam free and salt lies in drying
pools." The Camargue, the delta of River Rhodanus, was
unimaginably vast and far away.

"Good-bye!" Pierrette called out, though he was already
gone. Had he rubbed his hen's feathers, to disappear so
abruptly? She looked for a willow bush, for leaves that
fluttered where no breeze impelled them to move, but saw
only oaks with leaves the size of her small fingernails, and
pines, and stony ground.

The *gentes*' passion was gone, and in its place were bland,
sheepish faces that wore a burden of unexpressed guilt. The
Burgundian knight, Reikhard—baptized in his youth as
Jerome—was as close as anyone to being a magistrate. He
had demanded that P'er Otho take several men and recover
Elen's body. When they came back and announced their
failure to find it, the knight announced that without evidence of murder he could not establish guilt. The *gens*
collectively breathed a great sigh of relief, and went back
to their occupations.

Elen's children were mostly ignored in the weeks and
months that followed. Marie hardly spoke to anyone, even
Pierrette. The younger girl—the boy Piers as far as the
villagers were concerned—seemed to recover more completely. Of course, said the common wisdom, boys are
resilient, and Piers's tender age helped too. Likely the child
would forget everything in a year or two. The villagers were
content to pretend that nothing had happened. Later, as their

natures dictated, they would be overly kind to the half-orphaned children or would continue to look past them as if they—and the reason for their orphaning—did not exist.

Thanks to the intervention of Guihen (who might, of course, have been a "just pretend" creation of the girls' imaginations), neither child had witnessed their mother's demise, and their last memories of her were less horrible than were their father's. They only knew she was gone, and many years would pass before Pierrette began to understand the connection between the townsfolk's silence about that night's events, and her mother's absence. Marie, older, scarred by her sketchy yet terrible comprehension, chose not to remember anything at all, and no one was wise enough, or cared enough, to worry that such denial might sow the seeds of madness within, to sprout when conditions were right for them. . . .

Pierrette hid the little sack her mother had given her on top of a rafter, and let it slip from mind. She did not, though, put her mother's memory aside. "I will someday be a powerful witch, and I will put terrible spells upon those who hurt Mama."

"Oh, no!" exclaimed Marie (who was the only person Pierrette confided in). "That would be a terrible sin. I will pray to Mary that she turn your heart from un-Christian revenge."

Pierrette did not protest. Marie was her mother now, and she would not gainsay her. Of course, Marie was only a child, and ill-fit the maternal role, but it was enough for Pierrette. Despite Marie's growing piety and Pierrette's lack of it, the two sisters would grow ever closer as time passed.

Gilles, the girls' father, didn't forget anything, but being a quiet, gentle man, consumed by his own guilt and cow-ardice, and being of little importance among his fellows, his mute agony meant little to anyone, because they didn't see it.

A niche in the front room held a leather-wrapped bundle, old and cracked. Within was an ancient sword, a Roman spatha, that had belonged to an ancestor of Gilles's. When the olivier's eyes fell on it—far too often for his peace of mind—he imagined himself unwrapping it, and running to stand astride the torchlit path to the cape, defying the murdering *gens*. Yet it was too late for that, even had the

Roman blood not run thin in his veins. Gilles left the sword where it was. But there was another reminder of his wife and his personal failure. He packed up Elen's little sacks and jars of herbs and powders, and pushed them into a tiny cellar between sloping bedrock and timbered floor.

Pierrette, with a strange, distant expression, watched her father hide the wooden box. Despite Marie's prayers, she dreamed of being a masc like her mother. Those dreams would have frightened Gilles.

She had another dream, a recurring nocturnal one of a lovely, secluded calanque where she lived with . . . the Golden Man. He was taller than anyone in Citharista, and his hair was the color of late-afternoon sun. He wore only a fur skirt, so she knew that the hair of his chest was gold against the darker bronze of his skin.

The Golden Man laughed when she told him of Citharista. There were no towns in his world. His laugh was kindly, though, and if she had been older she would have put her arms around him as women did with men they loved. But she was a child, and did no such thing—and she told no one, not even Marie, what she had dreamed.

Pierrette had her Golden Man. Gilles had his own dreams, but while hers came in her bed, or dozing in the shade of an olive tree, or even while her head nodded in sea-reflected sunlight on her father's fishing boat, Gilles dreams came only in one place—the sacred grove of beeches and maples, beside the pool called Ma.

"You were gone all night, Father," said little Pierrette, close to tears. "I looked for you in the olive grove, and at your boat." Gilles laid two loaves of bread on the stone hearth and enveloped her in his long, skinny arms.

"There is a place, a long walk from here," he explained, "where I go when I feel lonely and old." Where I go when my yearning for Elen, and my inability to be both father and mother to my children, overwhelms me.

"I don't feel old," Pierrette mused, "but I am sometimes lonely. Will you take me there?"

"It's a long walk, and you are too big to be carried." In truth, Pierrette was small for six or seven years, even for a girl, but Gilles didn't wish to burden her with concerns over his health. He could not chew a thick crust of bread without soaking it in oil or wine, and he often left the table half-satisfied. In the olive grove, the children did most of the work.

"I'll wear thick sandals. I can walk a long way."

Gilles didn't agree at once. The spring Ma lay almost five *milles*, one thousand Roman paces, up an ever-steepening, rock-strewn valley, a long walk even when the sun's heat didn't drain one's strength, when the hard *Mistral* wind didn't blow down from the mountains like a great, cool hand pushing him back. Several things had yet to occur before Gilles would consider his daughter's wishes. Even he was not aware what they were.

Chapter 3 ∾ The Logical Child

As a village priest I observed that children's capacity for language is greatest in their early years. Yet there is no fixed age when it becomes possible to reason.

"In the beginning," children learn, "was only God." Yet God created an Earth and a Universe to surround it. From what font did He gather the materials? For a child, remembering its amazed pride of creation when it first grasped conscious control of its own bowels, it is no great step to assume that all matter sprang from the bowels of God.

Pierrette's logic outpaced most children's. *Foeces* demanded food, and in God's beginning, there had been none. Logic was not satisfied. "Someday I will figure it out," she promised herself, but for the time contented herself with lesser logical exercises.

Her restraint, had anyone known of it, would of itself have defined her as a very logical being.

Children who are different often isolate themselves. By the time Pierrette was ten or eleven, her separation was conscious and deliberate. No doubt discomfort with the deception she was required to practice contributed. Her small stature and inability to compete in boyish striving limited her, too. But I suspect it was mostly natural inclination.

Some lone children become merely strange. Those with God-given resources may become observers of the human condition, practitioners of solitary arts like painting, philosophy . . . and magic.

> Pierrette, spurred by innate intelligence, by vague comprehension of her mother's arrested ambitions, contented herself with developing her logical mind far beyond what might be expected of a child of her years.
> Otho, Bishop of Nemausus
> *The Sorceress's Tale*

In the tiny cellar, Pierrette dipped her fingers in water. She dribbled the fluid on a pinch of tinder in another bowl, while a dun snake watched with silent stare. It was a viper, subsisting on occasional mice, but she imagined it a friend.

Touching the wet tinder to the candle's flame didn't ignite it. Yet tinder dribbled with olive oil burnt with sputtering and black smoke.

"The essence of fire," (she didn't frame her thoughts in quite such mature words), "is in tinder and oil, but water is heavier and stronger, and drives it away."

Flames fascinated her. Were they alive? Were the flames of a burning log the escaping soul of the tree? Was steam the soul of water, rising until the pot boiled dry? Was a person's soul a fire within?

She dared not discuss such speculations with anyone, even Father Otho.

Perhaps her preoccupation arose from memory of the *gens'* bonfire, the night she and Marie hid in the cave, or of the torches the villagers had carried, a snake of lights creeping into the hills. Perhaps it was the flames that lit the almost-forgotten face of their rescuer, of whom Pierrette remembered only feathered clothing and mobile ears that grew larger in her memory as months, then years, passed.

The hidden wooden box gave new scope for experimentation. She recognized the aromas of some powders: rosemary and thyme gathered on the unforested hills, other herbs from woods and garden, white ashes and black, powdered charcoal. But there was also red powder that smelled like spoiled liver, and white crystals that puckered her tongue. Some burned easily, giving off strong odors. Others didn't burn at all, or smothered flame.

Liquids didn't burn, having—as she thought of it—watery souls. Then she found the tiny bottle, blue-green glass with a stopper so carefully ground that no essence had escaped in two years' storage. That liquid made tinder burn fiercely. It even burned all by itself in a bowl, and the flames pooled like water, filling it, then overflowing onto the bedrock floor. Had Pierrette known the word, she would have announced to herself that fire, like water and air, was a fluid, and that those three elements were unlike the fourth, which was earth, and which didn't flow.

Her curious play, limited to the selection of materials in the box, inevitably involved substances in various combinations. Always, the unifying element was fire.

One particular melange, when dampened with the liquid essence of fire, burst with a loud *poof!* into a ball of flame. Acrid, rolling smoke forced her outside. Her eyes streamed, so she didn't even see the smoke that crept up between aged floorboards and out through the house's loose shutters.

But Gilles, ascending the steps to the house, noticed, and saw his small daughter wiping tears with a soot-blackened hand. He pulled her away from billows of foul smoke.

"Oh, not again!" He knew the source of the poisonous stuff. In his child's wet, blackened face, he saw what he most feared.

Elen's eyes, streaming tears.

Elen's face.

What now? He should have destroyed Elen's powders, but he had so little that had been hers. He sat rocking his child, bewildered and hurt.

By the time Marie returned from her stall in the marketplace the smoke had dissipated, but an acrid stink clung to walls, clothes, and bedding.

She too knew what the odor meant. Unlike Pierrette, Marie had become devout in the aftermath of death and terror. "I'll find Father Otho," she said, and her set face—a Roman face not at all like Pierrette or Elen's elfin visages—allowed no disagreement.

Otho squatted in the dusty street, and Gilles, more stiffly, did the same, bringing their faces level with Pierrette's. P'er Otho looked sad and amazed, as if she were a spirit from some far past. Gilles's eyes held fear and anger. The men looked from her to each other, knowingly, with resignation.

Elen, thought Otho. Elen, before I knew her. He should

rise up, red-faced, and threaten her with God's wrath, denouncing her pastime, but he did not, as he had not chastised her mother.

Otho wondered if Gilles knew of his long-past dalliance with Elen, by the spring Ma. Unlikely, yet in that triangle of figures, two large and one small, Otho sensed a common love, a shared loneliness evoked by the elfin-faced child.

"I promised to take her about," Gilles said. "I should have shown her more work in the grove, and taught her to pull in my nets."

"She shouldn't be left idle." Otho pondered. "She has an agile mind. Perhaps I should help occupy her. But how?" Again, silence reigned.

Pierrette stirred. "Teach me," she said firmly. "Teach me to read."

Thereafter the child found no idle hours for her cellar.

From Gilles she learned how best to prune long, green shoots that bore no fruit. He showed how such shoots, packed with moss, could grow roots. "The new trees will bear fruit for a lifetime or two," he said, drawing upon ancient lore transmitted through generations, "and then they'll die. It's better to plant the olive pits. Trees grown from them will live forever."

Perhaps "forever" wasn't attainable, but the thickest, most gnarled trunk in the grove had—though Gilles didn't know it—been grown from a seed planted by a Greek settler from Massalia, when Rome itself was a collection of mud huts on just one of its seven hills. The tree had died the same year the Christ had been hanged on the wood of another tree.

Gilles knew none of that, but he knew olive trees, and he taught Pierrette to fish, too. He did not, for many weeks, lead her to the sacred pool, though he yearned to spend a day with his bittersweet memories, where he felt closest to Elen.

Father Otho filled Pierrette's remaining hours. Books, of course, were so rare that Otho had not one. But he chalked letters for her on the chapel's red tile floor. Often he sent her with a sanded plank and charred grapevine to copy inscriptions from the Roman funerary steles, amid grazing goats that belonged to Marcellus the Dacian.

"What does this say?" she asked one day, her smooth

board filled with odd letters copied from a stone washed out of the bank by winter rain.

"Is that Celtic? Where did you come on that?" His tone was wrathful. "Erase it! I'll break the stone."

"What does it say?"

"I forbid you to think of it."

He might as well have commanded the hills to dance to a shepherd's flute; Pierrette could think of little else. Not only were there Latin and Greek, but another sort of writing, in a tongue with its own mysteries.

That night she dreamed of a deer-horned man dancing about a deep grave-pit, a dark place like the cellar. His chant was familiar, but she could not understand the words. The tune she remembered hearing from someone who held her. It brought memories of warm softness, and something that tasted like goat's milk, but thinner and sweet. She awoke with damp cheeks and stinging eyes, and an urgent need to go to the hills.

Though it was hours before dawn, Pierrette rose and dressed. She carried her sandals until she reached the outskirts of the village, where dust, sand, and ancient cobbles gave way to gravel and sharp stones.

The wind was off the land, not the warm sea, and she shivered, even though her exertion on the steep upward trail should have warmed her. Ghosts of memories arose with each step.

Here had wound the glitter-scaled dragon, the winding line of torches, that had hunted her mother.

There was the cave where she'd hidden, abandoned by mother and father alike. Beyond, as she turned southward beneath tall pines, was the barren cape, plunging on either side to the sea, narrowing to a natural stone span that led outward . . . to a dark wooden doorway now closed.

She hesitated near an odd willowlike bush. Where had she seen one like it? The upper surfaces of its leaves were rich green, their undersides pale and silvery.

She stared, as if the very force of her gaze would penetrate its illusion. Gradually, limned with light and shadow, she saw what she suspected was waiting for her to see.

"Ha, child!" said Guihen. He wiggled his overlarge ears. "That didn't take you long. Are you growing stronger, as well as more lovely? Or am I losing my touch?" His grin was toothy. "But then, you always saw through my illusion."

Pierrette wasn't sure what he meant about growing stronger. And more lovely? She was a small, bony-kneed child of seven. Later, she would think about that, and wonder.

"What are you doing here?" she asked.

"I came to warn you."

"Of what?" Wisps of fine hair at the back of her neck stiffened. "You're only a willow bush, and I'll push you aside." She was angry. She wanted her mother.

Guihen sighed. "Elen is not here, child. She lives in a green and lovely vale."

"She's not in heaven. P'er Otho said so."

"No, her place is of this earth, but you won't find it on the Eagle's Beak. But here, beyond that gate, is the magus Anselm . . . and a terrible fate for a little girl."

"Mother said to seek out the mage."

"She was distraught. She didn't think. Go back to your father and sister."

"Don't try to stop me!"

"If you knock on that gate, you won't return to Citharista unchanged." Guihen's ears flapped, as if agitated. "Would you deny yourself an ordinary life: husband, children, a place to call home?"

Pierrette hesitated.

"Go back, or be doomed to make your bed in strange places. Go back, lest time itself bend about you, and you not find what you seek for a hundred hundreds of years!"

Pierrette was too young to value the prospect of a husband and children. And her own bed was not the secure place it had seemed before that terrible night she first had met Guihen.

The sprite's speech gave her pause, but the dark gate ahead beckoned. "Are you sure Mother isn't there?"

"Elen rests in the arms of her own mother, and her mother's mother, beside the pool called Ma. Seek her there, if you must." The gentle pressure of Guihen's spidery hand on her shoulder turned her. "Go home," he commanded. "Enjoy what little you have, for it is sweeter by far than what awaits you here."

Pierrette felt the soft branch brush against her shoulder, a willow branch, not a hand. The downhill trend of the trail quickened her steps, imparting a false eagerness to her pace.

She did as she was told, and made her way back to the village. But Citharista, her father and sister, her lonely, motherless house and bed, gave her heart no ease.

Chapter 4 ∿ A Dark Vision

The first folk were slight and dark. Elsewhere, on the high plains, yellow-haired folk forged long knives of bronze and tamed horses. Between horizons unbroken by trees or mountains, only the sun stood higher than they themselves atop their steeds. *Ma*, the earth was dirt beneath their hooves. Their souls turned with fear and adoration to the vastness above. Is it any wonder that when, with long blades and horses, they entered into *ma* of the dark, quiet lands, it was as conquerors?

New men and old found differences to ponder: earth gods and sky god did battle in their faculties. To survive, the earth folk resorted to slyness, theft, and lies; inevitably the sky folk lumped those faults with the old ways and customs. They coined new words, and with the words were born the realities: Evil and Good.

Otho, Bishop of Nemausus
The Sorceress's Tale

"I miss my mother," Pierrette said, after Marie had left for the marketplace with her jars of oil.

Lonely pain crossed Gilles's face. Must she remind him? The child's uncanny resemblance was hard enough. Then, chiding himself for his selfishness—and indulging himself as well—he sighed and said, "I'll take you to a place your mother loved."

Her motherless state was more his fault than Elen's. Her

quest for a spell to give him a male heir had driven the villagers to fear and murder. He could not give the child her mother, any more than he could restore his wife, but perhaps the shimmering pool, where water upwelled in bubbles from its sandy bed, would ease her pain as it did his.

For him, the pool Ma assuaged guilt as well as loneliness.

Citharista lay ringed by rocky hills, open on the southeast to the Middle Sea. The rough ridge of the Eagle's Beak sheltered it from west winds. Atop the southernmost of the three scarps forming the Beak, at the sea's edge but high above it, stood the mage Anselm's keep.

North of the scarp, hills swelled so high that the Beak seemed no more than reddish fragments of broken pottery at the sea's edge. One trail followed the coast west to Massalia, and another led north, where it joined an east-west Roman road. Only one other led out of the town, Gilles's chosen path; it led northeastward and up into an ever-narrowing valley. Only a few shepherds ever used it.

When they passed beyond the last house, the last fig and olive tree, Pierrette fell a few steps behind. Her eyes missed no detail of rock, tree, or silhouetted mountain; she engraved in her mind the way to their destination.

Once arrived, tired, thirsty, and footsore, father and daughter drank like deer on all fours. They tossed sandals aside and laughed as they plunged dusty feet into the clear, icy pool. Then Gilles stretched out to nap, his mind more at peace than at any time since his last pilgrimage here.

Her thirst slaked, Pierrette looked about. Sunbeams wound their way downward between wide, flat leaves, and turned dark moss to a green like the water of the sea.

The spring Ma created about itself a strange foreignness. She knew nothing of how seeds blew from faraway places, how trees and flowers responded to water-soaked ground, to hills that sheltered them from drying winds. The tiny, moist cleft seemed a world unto itself, open to them only by cosmic accident, God's oversight, or . . . magic.

Pierrette wandered about among the odd trees—beeches, Gilles called them. Their gray, rippled bark reminded her of Father's thin, muscled arms as he pulled in a net or strained to reach a high olive branch.

"Oh!" she exclaimed, muting her voice with a hand. "How beautiful." Sunlight illuminated dry leaves spread about the base of a small beech no thicker than her slim wrist, making a hollow much like the lap of a woman clad in a heavy woolen skirt. A ring of tasty-looking mushrooms grew around it.

Pierrette lowered herself amid the leaves, curling up in the sunbeam, and rested her cheek on a closely folded arm. Warm sleep was only moments in coming, drifting on air as soft as a blanket made of sea-bird's down.

She only slept for a little while, yet she felt rested. Her feet no longer tingled. Father slept, oddly silent; at home he often snored.

As she got to her feet, something fluttered from her shoulder—a magpie feather with a black vane on one side of its central spine, and bright green that shifted to indigo, then to russet, on the other. Pierrette picked it up and spun it between thumb and finger, delighting in the shifting colors.

Watching, spinning the feather, she hummed a tiny tune. Unbidden, her lips moved ever so slightly, shaping half-remembered words, staccato consonants, vowels that rubbed against them like oily fish in the net. "*Mondradd in Mon,*" she crooned. "*Borabd orá perdó.*" Words flowed, dancing within the tune, never repeating themselves, yet always almost the same. "*Merdrabd or vern,*" she sang. "*Arfaht ará camdó.*"

She dipped the feather in still water. How had she gotten to the spring? She didn't remember walking. With the wet feather, she dribbled a pattern on white limestone that was bare of moss. A beak, and wings. A long, long tail that seemed green, rust, and blue, but mostly green.

"Magpie fly," she sang, "Magpie chatter. Where will the road go . . . and does it matter?" Silly words, she thought. What do magpies know of roads? She tossed the feather, and it fell upon the stone. Feeling dizzy, Pierrette shut her eyes, and raised an arm to steady herself—yet she found no support. She fell . . .

She fell, and fell, and at last spread her wings. With a thump of speeding air brought up short, she swept upward, her tiny body teetering on long feather-clad wings, her tail streaming stiffly behind, trembling in the rush of fluid air that buoyed her. Below, vast black hills spread, and past a wingtip was the sea. A dull, leaden sea, no sunlight upon it.

Pierrette the girl would have felt a sudden chill, though Pierrette the magpie did not. What land lay below? Where were the trees, the open sea, the sun? No clouds billowed or promised rain. The sky and sea were dull as old, musty cloth.

Where was Ma? Where was Citharista?

As if someone . . . something . . . heard her silent plea, she found, along the brown, unlit coast, several familiar narrow bays. At the head of one, she saw great, spidery towers that concealed the waters beneath them: Citharista, seen with magpie's eyes. She recognized it from the distinctive shape of the Eagle's Beak.

Yet it was unlike the town she knew. The towers were topped with wheels threaded with ropes like ships' rigging, brown and orange as rust. The towers themselves were built of spidery timbers. Beyond were dark, windowless stone boxes high as the cliffs of the Eagle's Beak, that pushed out into the sea beyond the last wide, black road. Of the red-rock fortress that crowned the Beak there was no trace. Below the cliffs, waves thick as honey oozed over the rubble.

Her magpie's eyes traced dark lines eastward and north. Roads with no carts, donkeys, or men's feet upon them. Gaunt walls of broken houses large as Citharista's forum marched up steep hillsides where trees should have grown.

Where the valley grew narrow, she spotted a glitter of water, as if a single sunbeam had momentarily broken through the moss-thick sky. Magpie eyes marked the spot. Magpie wings tilted her toward it.

She landed in a rattle of stiff feathers upon the rotted shell of a great tree. Devoid of bark, it retained a hint of muscular texture that proclaimed it to have once been a beech.

Pierrette trembled. With hands no longer wings she reached down and lifted a tiny green feather, the only color that brightened the dead landscape.

Beyond an oily swirl of water that stank of dead things, her father should have lain asleep, but only bare rock the color of old bones protruded from powdery ash.

Sinking onto sooty dust that should have been crinkly leaves, she covered her face with her hands. Dry, wracking sobs shook her shoulders.

✧   ✧   ✧

Beech leaves rustled. Leaves fell upon her dark hair. Amazed, she peeked through dampened fingers.

Spread before her was a wrinkled brown cloth, homespun, with patches where it had been torn, or where wool-worms had eaten it. A skirt . . . and within it, legs. Her gaze moved upward.

Odd, fey blue eyes, much like her own, gazed sadly. "Pierrette." The voice was like hers, too. "My little stone."

If Pierrette had known what madness was, she would then have thought herself so. In her relief, delivered from her magpie-dream, she didn't question the strange woman, or note that their two voices had not awakened her father, or that the woman knelt exactly where the smallest beech tree should have been, but was not.

"It was a terrible place," Pierrette whispered. "All dead, and I was lost."

"It's well you were afraid, my child," the woman said, in words neither Roman nor common speech, but clear to Pierrette. "Terrible it is—and worse, it's not entirely dead. Evil reigns there, and the living howl in torment unending. You saw a place of tears and wailing, where laughter is unknown."

"Don't send me back," Pierrette pleaded.

"The spell you spoke sent you, not I." The woman's brow furrowed. "Do not seek to see ahead—or else endure again what you saw."

"But I don't know any spells."

"You know enough. I sang the words when you suckled at my breast. How else could I leave them for you? I, unlike you, didn't learn to write on wooden boards or the skins of sheep."

"I don't understand," Pierrette said, almost weeping.

"Oh, child! Remember this: When your confusion gives no peace, when the questions burn and will not be answered, seek the mage Anselm in his fortress, as I once bade you. I taught you what I could with my milk and lullabies. I've nothing to teach you now, that you don't already know."

The woman shook her head, jostling long, black locks as laden with dry leaves as Pierrette's own. "Come, child, finish your nap. See? The sun has not moved. There's still time." She smiled. "Yes, there's still time." She guided

Pierrette's head to her lap, stroking leaves from her hair. "But time is not so sure of itself as the gods might think."

Pierrette slept.

When she awakened, her father also stretched, with a mighty sigh. He glanced at her and saw nothing amiss—a small girl nestled in a heap of leaves, beneath a small beech tree hardly as tall as himself.

"You didn't breathe the dust from those, did you?" Gilles indicated the fat mushrooms ringing the tree. "That kind is poison." That kind, he reflected, your mother gathered, and ate. Elen said they helped her grow wings like a magpie, and fly so high that the days of yore were visible as far as the veil of night.

"I didn't breathe the dust," she said truthfully.

Her father turned away. "We must go, or spend the night here. See how the sun has flown?"

Pierrette glanced toward the sun, far to the west now. Its glare wiped away the image of a ring of mushrooms, incomplete, and turned-up moss where one had been plucked from the ground.

She brushed pale crumbs from one corner of her mouth, then glanced again at the small beech tree. "I'll see you again, Mother," she said. Though her words were strange and staccato, they were yet slick as fish scales.

"What's that?" Gilles said, startled. "What did you say?"

"Nothing, Father. The words of a song. I don't remember where I heard them."

Gilles was silent. He didn't speak the tongue of the most ancient folk, but he had heard it on Elen's lips.

Hiking home through darkening hills, Pierrette tried to understand. One long-unasked question had been answered. Her mother's body had never been found, so there was no grave. When she asked P'er Otho where her mother was, he said, "I don't know." Had it been anyone but Elen, he might have said, "In heaven."

Now Pierrette knew, and would not have to ask.

"Goodnight, Mother," she whispered.

Chapter 5 ∾ The Olive Grove

Citharista enjoyed a summer of peace. Provence rested between the bouts of devastation that kept its population low, its valleys untilled.

No shark-sailed Saracen vessels ranged the rough seacoast. The Franks ruled from their damp northern cities, and the Church sent bishops to tend men's souls. But neither Franks nor Church bought goods or traded. No Frankish silver marks wended their way south, and no Moorish *solidii*, minted to the full Roman measure, found their way to Citharista.

The trading cities of Arelate and Avennio lay devastated, their bid to keep Mediterranean trade alive by alliance with the Moors overthrown by Frankish Carolus's brutal conquest.

Elsewhere—in the crowded ports of Sicilia, the Levant, and the African coast, ships offloaded Egyptian cotton, gold from Senegal, fine horses from Andalusia. But without trade, outlets for Provence's figs, apples, wine, and salt were gone. Salt pans in the Camargue lay untended, until spring floods claimed them. Men worked their groves and vineyards, harvesting enough for local trade alone.

The land was at peace, but Pierrette was not. Even years later, she would speak uneasily of the dream-within-a-dream that haunted her. Raucous magpies taunted her by day, and visions of a dead future tormented her nights.

Otho, Bishop of Nemausus
The Sorceress's Tale

"Your soul wanders because you remain unbaptized," said Father Otho, when she told him of her torment.

"I'm afraid of magic." She sounded wise and old.

The priest had an eerie sense of having sat on the half-fallen stone wall in another time, of having the same conversation with someone much like Pierrette, many years before, and with no more success.

"The rite is not magic," Otho wanted to say, but he kept silent. He knew he was right, but couldn't explain it, even to himself, and as he had failed to convince Elen, so he feared to fail with her daughter.

Gilles also knew no peace. Branches fell from his olive trees, and when he poked and pried at the dead wood, white grubs and black beetles tumbled in a dismaying rain. One tree, an old one named Pelos, put forth a final meager crop, then died. The other trees were miserly as well, and one day the Burgundian knight Jerome visited Gilles in the grove, eyeing the sickly trees with ill-concealed scorn.

"What a shame." Jerome tugged at a branch that had kept only a few forlorn leaves. "Such a grove is too much work for one old man and your little Piers. You need someone strong to maintain it."

Gilles, with sinking heart, knew the German's desire. The grove had been in his family beyond recall. A Greek ancestor had planted some of the first trees; a Roman one had expanded it and built around it the now-falling limestone wall. Conquering Goths left the grove in his family's hands, claiming only the first pressing of oil as their due, recognizing that the trees didn't love them as they did Gilles's ancestors.

Now a Burgundian lord held a throne in Aquae Sextius, in fee from the Frankish king. His vassal Jerome ruled Citharista—a light yoke for the villagers to bear, as Jerome's horsemen gave security in return. No brigands or bands of homeless soldiers raided Citharista. Yet in the new order, slaves often prospered more than free men.

Gilles was a free landowner, yet he was poor. His neighbor Jules, whose forefathers had been senators of Rome itself, was nominally Jerome's slave. Yet Jules prospered, and Gilles did not. Jules had sold his trees, his sons, his wife, and himself, to the Burgundian, in exchange for Jerome's soldiers' help at harvesttime and a promise that he and his family would never go hungry. Now Jules wore white linen, and Gilles contented himself with an old homespun shirt.

If Gilles pledged himself to Jerome, and sold his grove for a silver mark or two, he too might prosper. Yet he balked. "It's only evil winds," he told the knight. "Next year they'll be warmer. Then there'll be no rot in the crotches of my trees."

"Next year you'll have no crop." Jerome dangled a small purse. "This would tide you over."

"I will think on it," Gilles said grudgingly.

But he thought instead that the grove had once flourished with little labor on his part, that the trees, for all their thick-trunked age, had given fruit so full of oil that even the final pressing was rich, green, and sweet.

But in those times, he'd had Elen.

He'd pretended not to notice when she had crept from their bed. Once, only once, he followed her, and saw her toss off her night-shift at the edge of the grove. With a fascination almost erotic, he watched her glide gracefully, entirely nude, from tree to tree, embracing this one and that as if they were lovers, gnarled old men, yet not without dark, woody desire.

Gilles understood why the grove no longer flourished. Only a week before, he had found cloth-wrapped herbs in a rotted crotch—a bundle dark with years of decay. Elen's magic. No harvest aid from Jerome would restore his trees.

Pierrette overheard Gilles speak with the knight. Losing his trees would kill her father; he was far more devoted to them than to his boat and nets.

She, too, felt the tie to his small patch of land, fine, rooty tendrils that reached from her most remote ancestors to wind themselves about her heart.

How could she allow harsh-tongued foreigners to harvest her trees? She gritted her teeth and strode away.

Her steps took her along the harbor toward the cape. Guihen had warned her of risks beyond that dark gateway, but . . . Her mother had bade her do so. She weighed choices as if they were pebbles and her mind a balance scale. Mother said that when Pierrette's confusion gave her no peace, the mage Anselm could give her solace. Hadn't she? Was it solace, or was it knowledge Elen promised?

A breeze sprang up, cooling her forehead. Pale leaves of a wild olive flickered with dappled sunlight.

"Guihen?" she whispered uneasily. Quickly as it had arisen, the wind died.

Guihen had warned she would be denied husband, home, children if she went to Anselm the mage. Yet if Gilles lost the olive grove, what would she, in turn, have to pass to her children? If Gilles allowed himself the security of servitude, then she, her children and their children, would be *servii*.

She looked down on the town. Was the Golden Man of her dreams part of the future she would be denied?

Her child's reasoning was not clear like P'er Otho's; her weighing of choices was not exact. Hers was a battle of facts and emotions, not sedate debate: Guihen's voice and her mother's, arguing inside her head.

She clenched her fist. There was no way to decide.

Her vacillating footsteps took her to a path that led into the high, thin forest above the cape. The rough terrain gave her only one choice: retrace her steps, or continue on and perhaps become lost.

"Come," a faint zephyr breathed.

"Guihen? Is that you?" There was no reply. Pierrette pressed on. The air was sullen and still, its silence portentous.

Between two white limestone slabs she stepped on a low, grasslike growth, and a sharp spiciness wafted up from the crushed plant. Rosemary. She plucked the damaged sprig, recalling the rich melange of similar scents from the wooden box in the cellar.

The tiny leaves rustled. "*Now* you understand . . ."

Her heart thumping as if she had run a great distance, she tucked the sprig in the waist of her boy's pants, and climbed farther. From the stump of a long-dead oak she scraped red-brown fungus into a little sack made from the hem of her shirt.

Cheerily now, she hummed a strange little tune as she tapped yellow pollen from white starflower blossoms, and plucked dry, brown petals and swelling, reddening hips from a tangled rose.

It was as if the odd words and melody came from somewhere outside herself. As if it were her mother's voice, not
Guihen's, not hers. With newfound resolve, she set foot on
the faint trail back to Citharista and her father's grove.

The eighth winter of Pierrette's short life promised to be
severe, and she was grateful for the fat bundles of dead
branches she and Gilles gathered in the olive grove.

"Wait, Father," she protested, as Gilles fingered a prom-
ising branch. "That one may not be dead."

Her father examined the tips of the twig, looking for the
first swelling buds of midwinter. "Not a single new bud on
the tree." His tone was bleak. "If I had a good axe, I'd split
the trunk for firewood."

"We don't need that much wood, Father. The nights are
less cold than a week ago." She needed time for what she'd
done to have its effect. Too weary to argue, Gilles shrugged
and climbed down from the tree.

Spring came, and winds no longer blew bitter in the
mountain valleys. The few clouds were high and puffy, and
under the strengthening sun the ground dried.

Gilles and Pierrette surveyed the grove. "You were right,"
he crowed, cradling a leafy branch in both hands. "The tree
lives! Look at those buds. Next year, we'll harvest a whole
basketful from this branch alone." Olives do not bloom or
put forth fruit every year. This year's rich foliage held a
promise of something more.

As they walked home, Gilles rehearsed to his daughter
how he'd rebuff Jerome the Burgundian when he came again
to buy the grove. Pierrette, never really talkative, said little.
Gilles saw nothing unusual in that.

Gilles's good cheer stemmed not only from the tree's
rebirth, but from the shattering of a belief he had held for
several seasons now: that the grove's decline began with
the death of his wife, and that it was irreversible. Now he
could speak with true conviction when he told Jerome that
its ailment had been only a fluke of the weather.

The summer passed slowly.

At the marketplace, Marie's preferred spot to sell pots
of last year's olives and jars of oil was at the end of

the stone-paved square, where the columns of the Romans' forum shaded the cobblestones from the afternoon sun.

Behind the crumbling brick arches was a weedy open space, from which issued a wooden clatter. "They're swordfighting again," Pierrette said. "I'm going to watch." Marie, who seemed to have no interest in anything except olives and oil, shrugged.

Pierrette was—in the eyes of the *gens*—a boy, Gilles's son Piers, so it was only natural that she should gravitate toward boyish things. As a girl, albeit disguised, she considered boys pretentious little imitations of men, who puffed and postured in a manner she could not imitate without an inward laugh.

Her ready smile served a purpose: the genuine boys—most of whom were taller than she was—seldom pressed her hard. Her thin arms were hardly capable of wielding even a wooden sword, should she be invited into the game. She was neither a leader nor a scapegoat. As if by some unremarked magic, she was never really noticed at all, unless she made a point of it.

She peered through an irregular doorway. Of the boys with wooden blades, she only had eyes for one: Marius, whose father owned the largest boat at the wharf. He was tall, with curly hair and a long, straight nose. Older and half again her height, he seemed manly and mature. As always, he was getting the best of his opponent.

"When I marry," Pierrette promised herself, "it will be to Marius." Then her face twisted. She would marry no one. She was, as far as they all knew, a weak, ineffectual boy.

When, if ever, could she reveal herself as a girl? Would she ever get over the teasing, the laughter, when the townsfolk learned her secret?

Avoiding Marie's notice, she slipped down a narrow street, and away from the market. How unfair life was. Marie, who didn't care whether boys noticed her or not, drew their attention with her quiet, indifferent gaze, her ethereal smiles and downcast eyes.

The street opened onto the empty place between the last houses and the half-fallen town wall. Pierrette gazed outward and upward—to the three domelike rocks that formed the Eagle's Beak. Guihen, on those very heights, had warned her away from Anselm.

But what difference would that make? She had no real friends and no prospect of a husband, anyway. Why not continue westward right now, to the mage Anselm's?

The long, upward trail daunted her, and it was past noonday. She let her steps take her instead to her father's flourishing grove. Best if she spoke with Gilles, make him let her end the charade, let her wear skirts and bind her hair with bright yarn or a ribbon. If they did it now, the boys might in time forget her father's deception.

She found Gilles under the tree he had believed dead. He stood, stiff as a crow-bane, his face immobile and pale, staring at a small, brown object in the palm of his hand.

Pierrette's steps slowed as if beneath her feet was sticky mud. A confrontation was at hand. Better here in the grove, she decided, than at home where Marie might hear.

Gilles stretched out his hand. She glanced indifferently at the twist of once-white cloth, stained where rain had soaked powdered leaves and burnt bone within. His glance was accusing, yet overlaid with something resembling grief. "You are too young for witchery. Who showed you?"

"Mother did."

"How? You were only five when . . ." He could not, even now, speak of Elen's death. "She sang words in the old tongue. Did she teach you those too?"

"She came in a dream. The spells were hidden in her lullabies."

"Dreams lie, child!" He swallowed, summoned his courage. "Have you been to the Eagle's Beak as well?"

"I can't go there. Guihen says . . ."

"Guihen?" Gilles's eyes widened. "Didn't Otho tell you such creatures are Satan's tricks? You risk your soul!"

"I don't know about souls. Only about olive trees, and powdered blood, and . . ."

"Don't tell me!" Gilles backed away, his eyes troubled. "P'er Otho says the nuns in Massalia will take lost children. That's where I'll take you."

"Those hags with long noses? They'd beat me." She saw the nuns as pale wraiths with red and knobby knees and harsh raven voices, haunting a windowless warren.

Her father seemed obdurate.

"Father," she coaxed, "who'll help with the harvest? All the trees—all the olives . . ."

Gilles glanced uneasily toward his grove, realizing the reversal of his fortunes wasn't due to his skill as olivier, or to favorable weather. Elen had wandered among his trees, talking to them as if they were house cats or children. The little bundle in his hand was not the first such fetish he had seen. Pierrette, whether through innate talent or witchery from beyond the grave, had taken up Elen's task.

Gilles was freshly ashamed. He had risked and lost his wife for a rich crop and a male child, but he would not so use his daughter. "After the harvest," he mumbled. "I'll speak with P'er Otho. After the harvest feast, you'll go to the nunnery."

Despite his words, Pierrette knew she'd gained a respite. She would not be bundled off to Massalia in someone's oxcart, not right away. Yet she felt no joy, no victory. Silhouettes loomed across the harbor: the Eagle's Beak, and the mage Anselm's keep. "I should have gone there today," she whispered. "Perhaps the sorcerer might teach me to be wise."

Chapter 6 ～ The Gaunt Man

Marie flowered at eleven, not uncommon in warm Provence. Even light-haired northerners bloomed early, often at the end of a mild winter.

For almost the first time since their mother's disappearance—Pierrette would not say her death—Marie laughed. She laughed often, until the sound no longer startled Gilles, Pierrette, or the women in the marketplace. Though no breasts stretched the fabric of her chemise, her walk became less the motion of a young goat, all knees and elbows, more the sway of a tall pine in an offshore breeze, the dip of sails on a ship far out on great ocean swells.

Marie, returning from the market, regaled her sister with talk of babies, and of boys who stopped to ask the price of a jar of olives or a bottle of oil. The family purse was now fat with coins—Frankish pennies, worn silver *obols* from which the faces of forgotten emperors were almost effaced. "Someday I will exchange them all for a shiny silver *denarius*, and later my *denarii* for a gold *solidus* from Byzantium. . . ." Marie's enthusiasm grew with her imaginary fortune, and after years of silence, neither Gilles nor Pierrette thought to quiet her.

Bertrand, the smith's son, brought her wildflowers. Neither parent nor sister saw fit to reflect aloud that Bertrand was fat (though strong) or that he was not very smart (though a hard worker). Marie's happiness was a fragile bubble that could be punctured by a sharp word or a returning memory.

49

For Pierrette, Marie's rosy projections of Bertrand, domestic and carnal bliss, and children at her breast, were like thorns pricking her own tiny bubbles. No boys noticed her. How long could Gilles's deception continue? With the grove so happy, was it necessary? Yet Gilles refused to discuss it, and she remained Piers in the eyes of all. Others knew of the charade, but few villagers associated with our Burgundian overlord, so the secret was safe from the only person who mattered.

Pierrette's loneliness, her motherless state, and her self-enforced isolation drove her to long walks eastward up the valley past the ruins of the Roman fountain . . .

Otho, Bishop of Nemausus,
The Sorceress's Tale

Again, Pierrette lay amid the folds of her mother's leafy skirt—for what was "ma" but "mother," her mother Elen? She drifted into sleep. . . .

"Anselm!" murmured the soft, motherly voice, the rustle of beech and maple leaves. "Anselm! Within his magical walls, where the sun always stands at high noon, you will find what you seek."

"Guihen warned me away." Pierrette's voice was like the dry passage of a preening magpie's beak along its feathers.

"Guihen!" Beech twigs rattled their annoyance. "What does Guihen know? You cannot remain a child. You must grow, and feel pain. Did Guihen explain that?"

Guihen had not. Guihen had given her a choice between two futures so alike as to make no difference at all—between being childless, husbandless, and alone in the village, or equally childless and alone somewhere else. The spangle of sunlight descending through high branches became Marie's smile as she contemplated Bertrand, as she planned the fine two-room stone house he would build for her. Pierrette's hands formed tight, jealous fists.

"I *will* go to the cape," she murmured. "I *will* learn magic from the mage. I'll wear a long skirt, and a ribbon in my hair."

Pierrette arose from slumber, brushing dry leaves from her sleeves. "I'll do as you say, Mother." The gray trunk seemed thicker than before; the silvery branches reached outward in silent benediction.

Gilles was angry. "In a month, the bishop will arrive to bless the harvest. Must an old man do everything, while you frolic afield?" Gilles treated Pierrette as if she were indeed Piers, a strong boy, and berated her when she failed to measure up.

There was another facet to Gilles's anger. Pierrette was free to visit the pool Ma, yet Gilles was not—or so he told himself, citing work always uncompleted. There was an element of self-inflicted punishment to Gilles's denial: when he slept in the moss and leaves, in the shade of the great, sheltering trees, the pains of age, labor, and guilt were wiped away. Yet Gilles had used his wife's fairy-magic for his own ends, to her destruction, and now used his daughter similarly, for the rich harvest of his grove. He didn't deserve solace, so he denied himself.

For a week, Pierrette also denied herself, carrying baskets of fat olives from the grove to the great press, shared by several growers. The press bed was a basalt slab with a groove around its edge for oil. Atop it rested a loose-staved cask with a lid that fit loosely inside, forced downward by a weighted beam that magnified the force of the rock's weight.

The oil that dribbled into the waiting pots was thick and rich. Before the harvest was pressed, they would run out of vessels to contain it.

Gilles would never allow Pierrette to wander off until the last of the crop was pressed, and they would be lucky to be done before the festival, her father's imposed deadline. There was no time to hike to the cape during daylight hours. She sighed, and made up her mind to leave as soon as her father and sister were asleep. If the mage would take her in, her father's threat would be moot. If not, she would lose only a night's sleep.

The moon was half full. Pierrette's steps were light. She imagined herself dressed in white Egyptian cotton, a red leather belt, and shoes to match. She pictured a room with ten lamps, a long shelf of scrolls and books.

Stumbling over a fallen branch, her fantasy shattered. She had come almost all the way up the crevice between the northernmost scarps. Ahead, something moved. She became as still as a startled hare. No concealing brush or trees grew on the rough rock. Nothing could hide there.

No moving shadow occluded the stars, yet the prickly sensation didn't abate. Two stars seemed to swell as she focused on them, to blur and become fat and green-hued, like staring, unblinking eyes. Across the starry cleft, high on her left, were two others.

Those star-specks, exaggerated by her narrow perspective into great, glowing eyes, turned her to stone. Ahead was a dark presence unseen. Behind, she heard her mother's voice, soft as rustling leaves. "Anselm will give you what you need. . . ."

"Go back!" said the hollow wind blowing over the cleft. "Go back, or wander forever."

". . . Only where the sun always stands at high noon. . . ." promised the voice from behind.

Unable to push forward or to flee, Pierrette's helpless terror changed to the anger of a cornered beast—and with rage came clarity of thought. Behind, her mother's voice urged her forward. Ahead . . . Guihen! The wood-sprite played tricks to frighten her away. With forced bravado she stood with hands on skinny hips. "You can't make me go, Mother." The sound echoed hollowly from the rocks.

"And you!" she spat, facing about, "you can't scare me away, either. Both of you stop it. I'll do exactly as I please."

The sense of presence behind evaporated, as if her mother's spirit had withdrawn. She thrust herself upward. Another step, then another . . . Her head and shoulders were above the enclosing cleft. Limned against the moonlit sea were the black walls of the mage's keep—but between her and that destination was a darker mass, not part of the rock. "Guihen, let me pass."

The blackness shifted, stretched upward in the shape of a man. A man . . . but not Guihen. Pierrette shrank back, her heart thumping. He was dark, and no feathery willow leaves glimmered on his rough clothing. He towered over her. A crudely woven kilt ended short of knees gnarled and twisted as old olive trunks, calves thick with coarse black hair, and knotty feet with long, yellow toenails.

This was not Guihen. She forced her eyes upward, fearing what she would see. . . . P'er Otho's Satan, with his bronze helmet and deer's horns, passed before her eyes, wavered, and faded. It was an ugly face—but not a demon's. She met his eyes—blue like her own, beneath bushy eyebrows. His nose twisted like an old root, and his cheekbones flared. Deep crevices delimited the corners of his narrow-lipped mouth, then lost themselves in a tangled black beard.

A frightening face, but not Satan's, for there was no evil in it, only pain long denied, and unrelieved fatigue. "Go back, child," the man said. "Seek happiness, for there is no joy in wisdom."

No joy in wisdom? Was there joy in foolishness and ignorance? Then she envisioned Marie and her sweetheart Bertrand, gazing into each other's eyes like placid sheep. "I don't care about happiness," she said. "I wish to learn mathematics, and magical words in strange tongues, and how to mix charcoal, brimstone flowers, and bitter salt without them going *poof!* in my face."

The gaunt man nodded. "Anselm's magics do that, sometimes. Spells don't work the way they used to. The nature of magic has become twisted—that's why he's trapped in that stone-heap, and can't visit your village any more." He sighed. "But yes, Anselm can teach you," he admitted reluctantly, "if that's what you really want."

"It is," she stated—but his words were hardly reassuring. "Will I lose my soul, as P'er Otho says?"

The gaunt one grinned, displaying large, yellow teeth with gaps between. "That frightens you? Good. Fearlessness and foolishness are one. Listen to your fear. Go home. I'm not going to let you pass." He spread his arms, and splayed his fingers, which were long and gnarly, with huge knuckles, covered with a mat of black hair.

Pierrette's eyes darted. On the left, she saw something massive that humped up as big as a cow. Great yellow-green eyes glowed unnaturally. On the right eyes also glowed, a sickly hue, a dull phosphorescence. There was no way she could get past the man and those . . . things . . . too.

"I'll come back," she said. "I'll come back in daytime, when you're not here."

"What makes you so sure I'm a creature of the night?" he rejoined. "When you have answered your own questions—about your soul, and all that—then I won't stop you."

"I will," she said. "Good-bye." He didn't answer. It was as if once she turned from him, he just faded away.

Pierrette did think about it. She thought about P'er Otho's Christian heaven, which appealed to people whose lives were pointless repetition and grueling work. There should be more to eternity than refuge from the unendurable. Did she really care if she was denied entrance to a tedious Heaven?

Yet if the mage's spells were no more successful than her sooty experiments, what was the use? Can't I just go on as I have? she asked herself. That, she decided, was what she would do, at least for now.

Chapter 7 ∾ The Black Time Foreseen

The last of the olive pulp was discarded in a heap. Cool air had speeded the work of carrying baskets of fruit to the press and heavy jars of oil to Gilles's storehouse.

Pierrette's thoughts had a similar pace. The olive grove was real. The warm ache in her arms at the end of a hard day was genuine. Was Guihen as real? What of the voice of the spring Ma, whom she thought of as her mother? Was reality determined by effects? She had never touched sun, moon, or stars—yet they illumined day and night. She had never touched a cloud, but had felt rain and tasted it.

She stayed awake long after Gilles and Marie slept. Her struggle was real, too. Had she known how to phrase her question, she might have asked if something with measurable effect needed a real cause, and if her confusion proved that the cause—Guihen, for instance, and the gaunt man— were also real.

P'er Otho pleaded that his years in Massalia had not prepared him to resolve such things.

There was only one person who might help—a person no more "real" than Guihen or the gaunt, hairy man. She would demand that Ma defend her own reality, as justification for Pierrette risking her own (however nebulous) soul.

It could not have been the same magpie feather, lying there among the contorted roots, because Pierrette had left that in the box where she kept the little sack her mother had

55

given her. She twisted the feather. The musty aftertaste of mushroom clung to her tongue.

"*Mondradd in Mon. Borabt orá perdó . . .*" She waited for the dizzying fall, the sudden snap of magpie wings. Nothing changed. Frustrated, she stepped away, intending to kneel at the pool and wash the foul taste from her mouth.

She swayed, dizzy, feeling light as the magpie feather. She saw that her hand was empty. She gasped.

There, unmoved, still holding the feather, she stood. Yet here she also stood, looking at herself. Which one was she— the Pierrette who had moved, or the one who had not?

"*I* am real!" she said, perhaps aloud, though she felt no air in her throat. "*That one* is illusion." She could see through that other Pierrette. She could also see through the little beech tree, and where it stood was a shadow image, not a small tree but a great gray stump.

"I'm real!" she cried, frightened, because all around her were doubled images—young trees and old, rocks covered with moss and the same stones half-buried in ashes, under great, dead branches that bore no twigs or leaves.

If the dead trees, and the oily, scummy pool were illusion, then the Pierrette she felt herself to be, the one who moved in that bleak world, was also, and the Pierrette who stood as if frozen beside the little tree was real. But if not . . .

She slumped to her knees. Tears blurred her eyes. "Which am I?"

The dull water's reflectionless motion caught her eye. An old woman waded ashore.

"Who . . . ?"

"I am Ma-who-is-not," the woman said. Thin lips covered a gap-toothed mouth. "Just as you are Pierrette-who-is-not. The spell has twisted, child."

"The spell? I don't understand."

"*Mondradd in Mon,*" the crone said. " 'The Parting of the Veil'—a divination spell that used to allow a glimpse into days ahead—days of the masc's choosing."

"I didn't choose this black place," Pierrette protested.

"You cannot choose, child. The spell leads always here— to the far end of all time. Or so I believe, because here all I have is memories of times past." The old woman sat on a bare rock, and squeezed water from her shapeless dress.

Pierrette saw, beneath yellow, wrinkled skin and brown age spots, the mother she remembered.

"Why am I here?" she asked, almost weeping.

"You must know of it . . . to prevent it. You are the last—but one—who can. You must choose the path to the Eagle's Beak, to knowledge wherever it leads, or this place will be all that is."

"Guihen says I will lose everything. The gaunt man says I will lose my soul."

"Guihen?" She spat. "What does a wood-sprite know? And Yan Oors—the dark one—once earned a kingdom and a king's daughter for his bride. Now look at him. The old scarecrow. His great bears are wraiths without substance who steal starlight to fill their eyes. Choose."

"I can't! You goad me, but they bar my path."

The old woman sighed. "I suppose I'm being unfair. Here, look into the water. . . ."

The crone swirled the oily surface with a thin, spotted hand. "This is your first choice . . ." she said, and an image appeared. . . .

A young woman cradled her boy-child in the crook of her arm. She laughed at the antics of her daughter, who had put chicken feathers in her hair and waddled in the dust, clucking. "Elen! You're scaring the *real* chickens." The child looked up. Its face was Pierrette's own . . . and her mother's.

The old woman again swirled the water.

The young woman had aged, though no white strands marred the blackness of her hair. "Never go to the cape," she said to her daughter, perhaps ten years old. "You will lose your soul and be denied heaven."

"But I must, Mother," the child replied in a voice like Pierrette's. "I must go, because you did not."

"Who have you been talking to?"

"To Guihen and old John, the hairy man—and to Grandmother, by the pool up the valley. . . ."

"No! Remain in the village, or you will be destroyed." She held the child close, sobbing.

"Was she my mother's mother?" Pierrette asked the hag. "The first woman?"

"Oh no, child. I didn't show you what was, but what will be. You were that woman, weeping for the fate of your daughter, Elen."

"If I don't choose the path to the cape, then my daughter must face the same choice?"

"She'll have no choice. You'll go, or she will, and she'll fail, for Evil will be stronger then—just as it will be harder for you than for your mother."

"But Mama chose to be a masc."

"She chose to seek a male child. Before that, she chose to give her maidenhead to the boy Otho, by this very pool." Each time the old woman said "chose," spittle sprayed from her stiff lips. "The way narrows, girl. If you wait until springtime, it will be too late. Even now *Samonios*, the winter festival, approaches, and the mass for Christ's birth soon after."

Pierrette resented the crone's criticism of Elen. "Is maidenhood important to a masc?" she asked softly.

"To a backwoods herbal woman? Hardly." The old woman's lips drew down in scorn. "But for a great sorceress, as for a goddess, it is vital. Diana, Selene, Epona . . . virgins all."

"Is that why I would have no children? Not because of the curse?" Despite herself, the words "great sorceress" had piqued more than just curiosity.

"A curse? Who told you that? Guihen? Starved John?"

"I'm not sure anyone actually said it, but . . ."

"Don't assume. Know!"

"Know what?" Pierrette had overcome her fear of the crone. "I'm confused. Are there no other paths?"

"I hoped you wouldn't ask. I hoped duty would move you—that glory wouldn't be necessary."

"Show me."

The crone roiled the scummed water with skinny fingers. "See what will become of you. . . ."

Black clouds mounted the horizon, swirling, twisting, darkening the foam-tipped waves of the world-river Oceanos. The young woman's fingers tapped a rhythm on the gilded arms of her throne. "Come, Taranis," she said. "Thunder, come." She laughed, and raised her fingers. Storm-winds whipped her long black hair. Lightning glittered from her fingertips, and leaped toward the swelling clouds.

Beside her was another throne—and a man. Black curls tumbled to his shoulders and intermingled with gold about his neck. Flashes from the approaching storm highlighted his features. "Enough! Send it away." He laughed.

She waved a hand as if dismissing a servant. Winds abated, the sky lightened, and distant currents of air tugged at the tops of the anvil-clouds, tearing them to wisps.

"There! Your Fortunate Isles are again at peace. See what a terrible disruption I would be?"

"Better storms with you than sunshine without. Marry me! Rule with me!"

He gestured. Pierrette saw a ring of black mountains above harbors, wharves, rich green fields, and waterways. Had the jagged peaks continued upward they would have joined in a single, enormous volcanic cone, larger and heavier than the earth's breast could support. "All this," said the king— for such she knew him to be—"will be yours until the last day of the world."

"Who was he?" Pierrette asked the crone. "Where?"

"The king? Ask Anselm. Once his kingdom, the Fortunate Isles, were on the sea-route to Egypt. Some say they stood in a great marsh—the Camargue, or near Tartessos in Iberia. Now, who knows? They aren't ordinary islands."

"Are those visions my only paths?"

The next visions the old woman stirred up made her wish fervently that she had not asked. In one, she saw herself floating facedown in the pool Ma. She didn't need to see her face to identify the bloated corpse. She simply knew.

In another, she saw Gilles in rags. He had no teeth, and his cheekbones were sunken with starvation. "Bread!" he pleaded. "Please, a morsel of bread." His right leg was missing. The pedestrian—who ignored him—was little better off, except for having two legs. The place was Citharista— but the buildings she remembered were crumbled heaps.

"No!" she breathed. "Not that!"

"This?" asked her guide, rippling the pool. Pierrette saw Gilles, Marie, and herself sitting at a polished wood table, on a terrace tiled in a mosaic of dolphins and boats against a rich blue sea. Behind them reared the smooth walls of a fine stone house.

Pierrette-who-watched saw her father gesture toward new

warehouses far below, by Citharista's harbor, and knew they were his. Fat merchant ships waited their turns to offload goods. Her father's arm was sleeved in silk. That vision was more comforting.

Again, as the pool's surface quieted, Pierrette saw herself dressed in furs and red wool, peering from a window. Beyond were tall steep-roofed houses with wooden shingles, snow-blown plains, and a great river. Kiev. The name came to her out of nowhere.

Window and high palace dissolved, and she was atop a pyramid of stairstepped stones. A green blanket of trees stretched to the horizon, broken by patches of fields and rooftops. Around her stood hawk-faced men draped in bright robes made of songbirds' feathers. They looked to her with awe, but she saw also fear in their eyes—and hatred.

"Enough!" said Pierrette, grasping the crone's wrist. "They can't all be real. What good are such visions?"

The old one laughed, a brittle, harsh cackle. "How many choices in a lifetime, child? Nothing is sure—except if you do not choose. See what indecision will entail. . . ."

Pierrette saw the dead pool, the blackened stumps, and the dry, ashy ground.

Chapter 8 ✀ The Horned God

Plow followed sword. New folk tilled the soil, raping
and impregnating Ma, harvesting as their due. It was
fearful rape, so in the spring priests and priestesses went
into the plowed fields and futtered there to appease angry
Ma, that their coupling might quicken the sown land.
The priest, incarnation of the male god, wore the horns
of the aurochs, or the antlers of the great stag. The folk
knew that plowing was rape, not consent, and each year,
to mollify Ma, they slew the priest, and watered the
tillage with his blood. In time, the two folk, Celts and
Ligures, merged, and when the Romans came, they called
them all Gauls.

Otho, Bishop of Nemausus
The Sorceress's Tale

She did not know which visions to believe—if any. Visions
within visions, for was not the black future where the crone
dwelt itself unreal? It had not felt so—that bony wrist she
had grasped had been solid, the skin papery dry. That vision
was not false; it had not happened yet, but it was no less
actual than Citharista, whose roofs she could see from the
trail.

The water visions were like the paths over bare mountains to the north, or westward to Massalia. Perhaps only
one route could be chosen. Perhaps one, then another, if
her life was long enough. . . .

When Pierrette entered the town, folk had donned festive garb. The marketplace was crowded with folk who had brought a sampling of their harvests for the bishop to bless. Marius was with his father, proudly displaying dried and salted fish, arrayed like the wooden shingles of the houses of Kiev, unimaginably far to the north and east, further in years than in miles.

She could not imagine such expanses—years or miles. On the way home from Ma, she counted her paces. One pace was two steps, left, then right. She was not as long-legged as a Roman soldier, so a thousand of her paces was surely less than a mile.

The counting-letters Otho taught her were cumbersome. One, two, three—those made sense. She could count them on her fingers. I, II, III, each stroke a finger. One hand was V, representing five fingers, but four was IV. It should have been IIII.

She got to XXXIII, thirty-three, before she lost count. Between thirty-three and the magical M—one thousand paces, one mile—were several Cs and Ls. Those did not make sensible words, either. The Greeks said "Khee" for the letter "X," and P'er Otho said "Zzz," which sounded like a bee's wings. One thousand and nine was "Meeks," spelled MIX, wasn't it? But one thousand and eleven was "Mksee," MXI. Impossible.

She did not see the knight, Jerome, until she bumped into him. "Ach, boy! Are you blind? The bishop has already blessed your father's oil. You will only be in time to help carry the jars home."

"I'm sorry," she replied. "I was . . . I was . . ."

"Celebrating the day in your own way?" he grinned, displaying a full set of big teeth, which made him look much younger than his jowls and hairy ears. "As did your mother?" Cold eyes gave menace to his smile. "You aren't alone. Many will ask blessing of the long-armed one on this day." He gave her a light push between her shoulder blades. "Hurry now," he said. "You can still make it to mass."

Pierrette hurried away. The long-armed one? *Lamphada*, in the old Celtic tongue, was a euphemism for the light-bringer, Lugh. Some folk of Gaulish blood still acknowledged Lugh, and Epona of the Horses, and made secret sacrifices to Taranis when they heard the rumble of thunder—Taranis, whom she had commanded, in the vision where she sat beside the handsome island king. But this feast day was *Samonios*, when ancestors were honored. Lugh's had been months ago.

She reveled in the wondrous sense of power she had felt, when lightning's fire had danced on her fingertips, but that vision was fading, here in busy Citharista. So Jerome thought her mother worshipped Lugh? But that was not so. This was only another day for Ma, the goddess of the pool.

She shrugged the encounter off. Jerome was Burgundian, not Gaul, but gods were much the same—except the Christian deity, who bore little resemblance to the rest. It was not important what the town's protector believed—or so she thought then.

Marie berated her. "You left me to carry everything." To pacify her, Pierrette slung four heavy jars, and made it halfway home before Gilles took pity on her and lifted two from her chafed shoulder.

Pierrette barely had time to rub oil on her raw skin. She scrambled after her father and sister.

The chapel, yellowed limestone in the round-arched Roman style, was a barrel vault wide as three carts and three times that long. It could not hold half the population of Citharista, let alone the country folk who came on special days. The bishop would celebrate mass on the broad top step, in front of the chapel doors.

Arriving late, Pierrette had to stand on tiptoe in the chapel's forecourt. Smaller than anyone else, she saw only the broad buttocks of some shepherd's wife. She wanted to see the miraculous transformation. Would the bishop's loaf gush salty blood when he broke it? Would the thick crust hold not soft, white bread but meat—the flesh of Jesus? Would he eat it raw, as if he were a dog? Perhaps, because bread was baked, so the meat would be. Was there a bone in the middle of the loaf? Would he gnaw on it?

Unbaptized, she was forbidden the sacrament in the chapel. If she did not see it now, she would have to wait a whole year.

She edged past the fat-bottomed woman. Placing one foot on a projecting cornerstone, she lifted herself, leaning against the shoulders of people in front of her.

There was Father Otho, and the bishop, resplendent in

a robe so white she squinted. All she could see of him was
dark hair beneath his tall, white hat. When he moved from
one side of the altar-table to the other, she caught the
glimmer of gold. She was too far away. She would not see
the bread become flesh.

Beside the bishop, another man moved as the cleric
moved, imitating his gestures. His dark clothing absorbed
light as if it were coarse, nappy fur. The altar boy? No, he
was too tall, and wore a funny hat with candlesticks on
it. The harder she squinted, the less clear the scene was—
and the more uneasy she became. Something was terribly
wrong.

She wriggled between the tangle of knees, the herdlike
jostling of fat and skinny hips, the rooty impediments of
sandal-clad feet. Working her way forward as an adult could
not have done, she at last peered out at the table, and the
feet of the white-robed *episkopo*.

She was too late for the miracle; the part with the bread
came before the wine, didn't it? The bishop held a shiny
cup in both hands. He drank, with obvious relish. It must
be wine, Pierrette decided. Had it been blood, wouldn't he
have grimaced the least bit?

She was so close she could have touched the bishop's
fine-sewn hem. . . . Where was the dark man? There—in back
of the bishop, hands raised as if he too held a shiny cup.
When the bishop dropped his hands, so did he. When the
churchman nodded, he nodded, at exactly the same moment,
as if he were the bishop's shadow.

Was he part of the ritual? She looked over her shoulder
at the gathered *gens*. Their solemn faces betrayed no surprise. They didn't see anything unusual. Was she the only
one who saw the dark man?

She slipped to one side, where he was not behind the
bishop. Being short, she saw first his dark legs, covered not
with trousers, but with coarse, goatlike fur. His joints were
all wrong, like a goat's, with "knees" facing backwards,
fetlocks analogous to human heels, and . . . and shiny black
goat's hooves.

Deer antlers grew from his head. His nose was long and
sharp, his bushy eyebrows pointed. His teeth gleamed
unnaturally white, and his eyes were a wild animal's, like
the orbs of Yan Oors's companions.

Cernunnos, she breathed. The Celt god Teyrnon, the "father of animals." She stared with horror at his midsection, where a huge . . . thing stood out from him, bloodred and gleaming wetly. Pierrette had seen male goats ready to mount, and had not been disgusted. She had seen her father, and had been only mildly interested in an organ that neither she nor Marie possessed. But what she saw now, like a goat's, but on a man . . .

She turned her head—and almost missed seeing the creature's grin, as he looked directly at her. It was a terrible, knowing, evil grin. Yet as she looked into his yellow-brown deer's eyes she saw not evil, but pain, as if behind that leering visage was trapped some gentle, doomed forest spirit. She backed into the crowd. She saw red fire rise up in those eyes, engulfing the suffering spirit with a hot, malevolent glow.

Long before the crowd dispersed she reached home, and hid in the cellar until she heard Gilles and Marie overhead. She crept out, and peered through the open door to make sure that the third voice she heard belonged . . . to a human being.

She had seen the man before, when his fat vessel put in to Citharista. A Greek from Massalia, he owned a fleet of merchant ships. He was rich because, for some unexplained reason, Saracen corsairs never attacked them.

Why was he in their humble house? She slipped in, and sat next to Marie on the hearth. The men leaned over clay cups and a wine jar at the table.

"I can supply everything," Gilles said, waving his hands expansively. "Ten casks or a hundred. I'll hire coopers, and . . ."

Casks? Coopers? One stored oil in clay jars, not wooden barrels. Knotty scrub oaks were hard to split into staves, and imparted a sour taste. Pine was too light, and swelled when wet. The only wood for barrels was beech, and the nearest beeches were . . . in the moist, sheltered vale of Ma.

The Greek, Theodoros, clapped his cup on the table. "We have a bargain, then." He departed.

Gilles rubbed his hands with glee. "We'll be rich. Who would have thought it? Water casks for his ships . . . and for other ships as well." He was thinking that Theodoros of Massalia was not only safe from Muslim warships, but that he traded with them on the sly, and that barrels of Ma's clean, fresh water would soon be stacked in Muslim holds.

"I'll send Parvinus and Mercio to cut trees and shape them into staves. Old David can fetch and carry, and fill barrels." He turned toward his daughters. "Who has a strong cart and an ox? Not any old dray—I'll be hard pressed to keep Theodoros supplied, without broken axles and barrels smashed alongside the path."

"Father—you can't cut the beech trees. They belong to . . ." She was going to say, " . . . to Ma," but thought better of it, and said only, " . . . to the spring."

"Who owns the spring?" Gilles snapped angrily. "Your mother, and her mother before that. They left no kin, so it reverts to me." He stared defiantly, as if daring them to contradict him. Marie would not, but Pierrette sensed a flaw in Gilles's reasoning: the spring had passed from mother to daughter, not wife to husband or mother to son. It should pass—if such a place could actually be owned—to Elen's daughters, not Gilles. And since Marie had no interest in it, it should be hers.

Something in Gilles's eyes stayed her protest. A yellow glint from the low sunbeam in the doorway made his eyes look evil, like . . . Her gaze strayed upward to the sides of his head—which bore no deer antlers—and then below his waist, where she saw only the coarse fabric of his trousers.

When Gilles poured himself a celebratory cup of wine, she slipped outside, unnoticed except by Marie, who was lost in a dream of fine clothes, a house high on a hillside, a terrace where ships and dolphins shared a blue ceramic sea.

∞

The Sorceress's Tale

I was sweeping the small forecourt when I saw the troubled child's face—more like her mother's every day.

"Does Satan have goat's feet?" she asked.

I had never considered the Lord of Evil's feet. "I don't know, child."

"Does he have horns on his head?"

Why would a child concern herself with physical aspects of Satan? His existence was terrifying enough. The Gospel said little of the Tempter's aspect—or did it? I could not remember the text word for word, and written books were the property of bishops or abbots.

Had the Evil One sought her out? Had he some design upon her?

"Pan," I said at last. "The old Roman god—the Greeks' Dionysos—was portrayed as half-goat. Such 'gods' are deceivers who lure men from true Faith." Was it much of a stretch to consider deer-horned Gallic priests as the Devil's tools—even as aspects of him? I would not know for several years how wrong I was— or how right.

"Perhaps I saw deer's legs, not goat's," Pierrette responded. "Perhaps I saw nothing at all." She bade me good night, leaving me puzzled and concerned, but without suspicion that she would not go straight home. Darkness had already fallen.

Thinking the child had chanced upon worshippers of the old gods, I set off in the gloom for the castellan Jerome's house. Rufus, the elderly soldier on duty, passed me within. Jerome sat at his long table near the smoldering hearth. He offered wine, which I accepted gladly—though I did not delay getting to the point of my visit. "The horned one has been seen in the town," I stated.

The knight peered from beneath bushy brows. "I don't wear the god's horns, but perhaps some other man . . ."

I didn't believe him. "Are you truly Christian, Jerome? Will you recite the 'Credo' with me?" He had been born pagan, and his Christian baptism did not fit comfortably— as his infrequent confessions revealed.

"I believe in the Father and the Son," he said, "but tonight is Long-Arm's."

"You can't serve two princes without betraying one, or being crushed between them. It's the same with gods."

"It's easier to choose between what I believe and what I do not, than between two gods who call me with equal voices."

"There is only one God," I replied.

The Burgundian shrugged his broad shoulders. "Let them decide that. Don't push me into their battle, priest."

"Ah, Jerome," I said sadly, setting my wine-cup on the table, its contents hardly touched. "You misunderstand. You yourself are the battleground."

Otho, Bishop of Nemausus

∾

Unbeknownst to Otho, Pierrette did not go home. Gilles was going to destroy the beech trees. He would bring about her terrible vision of ashes and stumps. And hideous evil stalked the streets, mocking the Christians' rite. How could she stay? Yet where could she go? The Goddess could not succor her, could not save her trees or herself. There was only one path open to Pierrette. With slow, hesitant steps, she turned westward, toward the Eagle's Beak.

Part Two ❧ *Discipula* (Student)

One hundred and twenty-odd years before Christ, the Roman Calvinus defeated the folk of old Ligurian and Celtic blood at Entremont, and garrisoned the countryside.

Romans were in turn overwhelmed by Goths. Vandals left devastation in their wake. Visigoths lingered, and were conquered by Moors. Then came Franks and Burgundians, bringing myths, gods, and folktales of their own.

Others came one at a time, from more remote and stranger places. One of those called himself Anselm Girardel. For more ages than are easily contemplated, he kept his secrets and his counsel, and was not of the land at all, until at last . . .

Otho, Bishop of Nemausus
The Sorceress's Tale

Chapter 9 ∿ The Reluctant Magus

By moonrise I was on the path to the Eagle's Beak.
If I did not do my mother's bidding, father would cut
down the trees, beginning the vast devastation I had
seen through a magpie's eyes. I had no choice. If I
remained in Citharista, my soul would be forfeit to the
hideous beast that had mocked the bishop. The Church
protected the baptized, but not me. Only then did I
know fear.

Pierrette teetered on the narrow path to the gate. Wind from
the east threatened to blow her into the yawning chasm on
either side, into the dark waters of the calanque; lovely, in
shifting blue and green, in the day.

Her father's prosperity would come not from God the
Father, or His Son. It would not come from Teyrnon, whom
the Gauls believed was husband to Ma, nor from the more
ancient, unwed Ma whose visions Pierrette had shared. It
would come from Satan, who consumed the world and
turned it ashen.

Several thoughts gelled. P'er Otho said goat-legged Pan
was Satan's deception, to entrap men, but had it always been
so? Otho speculated that Cernunnos was also Satan but
hadn't the deer god been a benefactor, before his worshippers
accepted the Christian God?

71

Once Pan had been good, she decided, and so had
Cernunnos. They were not guises of P'er Otho's evil deity,
but his captives. She remembered the pain in the apparition's
eyes, the look of a wild thing caught in a snare, unable
to escape even as it heard the heavy tread of the trapper
approaching.

The keep lay ahead. This time no Guihen appeared to
warn her off, no Yan Oors—yet she saw the flutter of willow
leaves among the scruffy oaks, and low-hanging stars swelled
and glowed atop the rocky scarp. Were they really there,
just at the corner of her eye, powerless to stop her?

Where bedrock met stone wall was a door black with age,
so engraved by wind and sunlight that it skinned her knuckles when she knocked. She heard the tapping of sandaled
feet on the other side.

Iron hinges red with rust squalled protest. "Pull it open,"
a querulous voice said. "Must I do everything myself?" She
tugged, until the opening was wide enough. "Are you going
to just stand there? Most people who knock wish to come
in." She entered the darkness.

First she saw only an oil-pot's miserly flame. Then, behind
it, she made out a flutter of draped cloth, the fuzzy outline of an unkempt white beard, lank hair, and dark, hooded
eyes, oddly familiar.

"Are you the mage Anselm?" she asked quietly.

"Who else?" snapped her host. "More to the point, who
are you?"

She told him she was the daughter of the masc Elen, who
had sent her, and proffered the small leather sack her mother
had given her long ago. "This is for you."

"What's in it?" he snapped.

"I don't know," she replied. "It's from my mother."

"Hmph. Took you long enough to deliver it." Pushing the
sack inside his garment, he went ahead of her, ascending
a staircase in near darkness. Somewhere, she hoped, the
stairway would end. She saw a vertical line of blue—the
sky, seen through a crack between doors? But no—it was
still night. What could it be?

"Squint!" the old voice commanded.

"What?"

"Are you deaf? Shut your eyes."

She squinted—unwilling to trust the crotchety old man.

The doors swung open. The glare was like coming out of a cellar at midday. She opened her eyes, blinking.

"Come." The mage grasped her wrist. "It's a lovely day. It always is." He led her across a red-tiled floor, through a square-lintelled arcade into the full sun of a summer's day. Blinking only occasionally, she looked out over a broad vista of blues and greens—the sea. A white stone parapet marked the edge of . . . of everything. Beyond, the scarp dropped so steeply that she saw none of it.

"Well?" he said, sounding neither old nor cranky. "Do you like it?"

She turned to look at him . . . and drew back, shocked. No old man stood there. His hair was black. It hung in curled ringlets. The white robe was gone. Only a brief cape draped over one broad, bronzed, muscular shoulder. Gold glittered at his throat, and bright sunlight made mock of its ornate details. He wore a kilt longer in back than in front, and no tunic. Sparse black hairs were strewn down the center of his chest and around his prominent nipples.

A child, with few sexual leanings, she was still discomfited by his beauty, his full lips and heavy-lidded dark eyes. Pierrette drew back from him—and from her conflicting emotions. She knew this man.

"I thought I looked fine. What's wrong with you?"

"You . . . you are the king—in my dream, by the pool of Ma."

"A king? Me? Oh no, child. Look around—is this tiny patio a kingdom?"

"I saw you on the island with the black mountain . . . the Fortunate Isles . . ."

His eyes narrowed. He gestured to a bench. "Sit. Tell me what you saw."

Pierrette sat. Despite her confusion—having stepped from midnight into noon, and having the old man she had seen in the darkness become the proud ruler of her dream—she managed to give a reasonably good account.

"I suppose I overdid things a bit," her host murmured apologetically, when she finished. "I wanted you to see me as I should be . . . not as I am. Vanity, I suppose. Being old before my proper time is hard. I wanted you to see me as . . . as I want to be." He shrugged. "Ah well, I'll remedy that—but first . . . are you thirsty?"

Pierrette grasped the opportunity to collect her thoughts. The breeze off the ocean was balmy, little puffs like her sister's breath at night, barely stirring her hair. The stone bench was warm, and felt like a well-stuffed pillow. Shadows pooled like cool water. She leaned back, and the sun danced redly on her shuttered eyes.

When her host returned, she viewed him from beneath half-closed eyelids. He was again as she had first seen him, robed from head to foot in white cloth. His hair and beard were long and white, his wrinkled face as old as Ma-who-was-not. "Now you see me as I am," he said sadly. "I didn't frighten you, did I?"

"I wasn't afraid. But I don't understand. You said you *should* be as I saw you before."

"True," he said, nodding, his beard flat on his thin chest. "I'm not as old as I look. Why, only a few centuries ago . . . A few? Oh, drat! I've lost track of time again. What year is it?"

Pierrette did not know. "I know that the last man in Citharista who remembered Charles the Hammer died last year."

"That doesn't help. Let's see. That Calvinus, the Roman, whipped the Vocontii in 124—that's B.C., the way you'd reckon it—about 800 years before Charles Martel. I suppose I'm a bit over a thousand. How old do I look?"

"About eighty," Pierrette said hastily. "Or ninety?"

"Ninety, you say?" His grin split his beard. "How kind." Pierrette did not try to correct his misapprehension. Eighty or eight hundred, he was very old, and looked it.

"You said you're Elen's child. Why are you here?"

"My mother wanted you to teach me."

"Teach you what?" His eyes shaped a challenge. "Not magic!" he said. "That's what *she* wanted—my spells. As if they work any more. I won't teach you magic."

Pierrette suppressed her disappointment. "Arithmetic?" she suggested. "Greek and Arabic?"

He crossed one skinny leg over the other, beneath his voluminous garment. "Arithmetic! Of course. Geometry, and the new Saracen numbers. Greek, Latin, and Minoan for sure, and Etruscan, just for the fun of it. Wonderful poets, those Etruscans; it's a shame nobody reads them any more." He nodded repeatedly, rapidly, like a hoopoe bird bobbing its ridiculous, crested head at a puddle. "History too? I love history. I have scrolls and scrolls of history. Herodotus . . ."

He stopped in mid-thought, as something occurred to him. "What will you pay me?"

"Pay?" She had not paid her father for teaching her to prune olive trees, or P'er Otho to read tombstones. The crone had not demanded payment. Was knowledge a commodity like oil or apricots, sold by the pound or basketful? "How can I pay?"

"I suppose you're right," he agreed. "I can't trade history for oil. We'll work something out."

"I'd be glad to bring oil—but I can't go back." She spoke of her father's plans, and of Satan, who waited for her return.

"You have to go back," he said, putting a gnarled hand on her knee. "As for your father, I can fix that, but you'll have to deal with that Satan fellow yourself. My advice is to ignore him like everyone else does. He can't be all that powerful, if no one but you can see him." That made sense. Even P'er Otho, who was terrified of Satan, had never actually seen him.

"But if I go back, I'll have to work with Father, and I'll have no time to learn things," she protested.

"Time?" His belly laugh seemed to issue from younger lungs. He gestured. "See the sun? What time is it?"

"It looks to be noon," she replied. The sun was overhead, a bit south.

"And where was it when you arrived here?" he asked.

"I don't know," she replied. "It was wherever the sun goes when it is night."

"No, no! Where was it right here, when you came through that door?"

"It was . . . right where it is now," she concluded. But that could not be so, could it? Always, the sun moved, or there would be no day or night, no time at all.

"It has not moved," she said.

"Not a finger's width," he agreed. "And, it will not. Do you see why you have to go back sometimes?" He looked miffed when Pierrette shook her head "no."

"You can't remain a child forever. You'll get tired of being no taller than a wheat stalk, and peering under the sheep's tails whenever you're in the pasture."

"We have no sheep," she said stubbornly, not wanting to acknowledge what she was beginning to understand—and not wanting to go home.

"Fah! Who cares? Don't you want to grow up? No one ages here."

"You do," she replied, unwilling to admit defeat.

"When you've learned arithmetic, you'll understand. I have been here nine hundred years—give or take a century or two—and you said I look ninety. Do you want to wait a hundred years to grow breasts?"

Considering the complications of womanhood (not least the moon's influence, as Marie complained), Pierrette thought a century not nearly long enough. Yet the reminder of arithmetic—she might learn what a "century" really was—forced her to agree. She would go home—and grow up a bit at a time—and would visit the mage between times.

"Father will ask where I go, and will worry."

"How will he know? Tell him you're going for a walk. If you don't grow older when you're here, then he's not worrying—not doing anything—while you're here, see?" Pierrette did not, but she decided to test what he said, the first time she went home. She would ask Marie how long she had been gone.

"Is everything settled?" she asked, rising. "When can I start?"

"Contain your eagerness. What about payment? Remember? How about an apprenticeship? I'll teach you everything—except magic, of course—and you'll sweep my floors and cook delicious meals, and will bring me a bottle of oil once in a while."

He too got up. "Tomorrow, you'll go home and verify that I have kept my part of our bargain. But right now, it's the middle of the night, and I'm sleepy. Your room is one landing down, at the end of the hall. Take this lamp—I know my way in the dark."

In the morning, the clatter of Anselm's sandals awakened her. "Come," he said, "there are figs and bread on the terrace." She recognized the great lumpy loaf as one Claudia had made, right down the street from her house, and she wondered how the old mage had gotten it. It was fresh.

"I'm not entirely isolated," he explained. "People want things from me—people like your mother, and the baker. They don't come empty-handed." He must have seen her disapproving look. "Well, it's only tit for tat," he said. "After all, if I starved, I wouldn't be able to give them what they want, would I?"

"Can't you use magic to make a loaf of fresh bread?" she asked. "Or at least a sack of flour . . ."

"Magic! Don't speak of magic. You're my apprentice, and must do as I say." Then he relented. "Magic is unpredictable, though it was not always so. I think it gets used up. I used to be able to do wondrous things, but now . . . I live in terror of the day it's all gone, because without magic, this place would fall into the ocean."

"I see. Would teaching me use it up faster?" Clearly the old man was speculating, but if magic was indeed a personal attribute . . . might she offer him some of hers in exchange for lessons in using it?

"I don't know," he moaned. "It never seemed like that, at home—but this world is different. Storms! I never saw a storm, before I left home."

"I don't know where you are from, Master," she remarked politely.

"You don't? But you thought I was a king. You mentioned the island, and the black mountain."

"The Fortunate Isles?" she asked, remembering what the crone had said.

"Of course. You thought I was Minho." He smiled reminiscently. "I'm related to him, though distantly."

Pierrette wanted to know more about the Fortunate Isles— the place where, according to her vision, a handsome king would entreat her to marry him—but Anselm would say no more. "It pains me to talk of it, because I can never go home."

"Why not?" she asked. "Are those Isles further than Tartessos, in Iberia?"

"They haven't been there in a long time. Perhaps they're off the coast of Armorica. The Phoenicians had a city, Ys, there once." He shook his head. "That's nothing to me. I can't leave here. When I go out the lower door, the further

I go, the older I get. By the time I reached Massalia, I'd be dry, dead bones."

Pierrette wanted to offer sympathy, but he preempted her. "Enough. The day wears on, and you must return to Citharista." He grasped her arm and led her toward the long series of stairways, where he lit an oil lamp with a spark that seemed to come from his fingertip. "Can you do that?" he asked, with a superior grin. "It doesn't take much magic, one little spark like that."

"I don't know," said Pierrette, who very much wished to know how.

As they went down the stairs to the exit at the base of the fortress's wall, the darkness thickened, until only the wick's tiny flame illuminated them—just as when she first arrived. She heard the groan of rusty hinges, and was shocked to see that it was dark outside. There were stars, and in a moment the moon came out from behind a cloud. Hearing another creak, she turned, and saw the door pulled shut from the inside.

"Master!" she cried out, but no one answered.

Chapter 10 ∾ King of the Fortunate Isles

It was night on the cliff-flanked path outside Anselm's keep—but what night? The magical sun that hovered always at zenith had disrupted Pierrette's subtle body rhythms. She felt as if it were morning.

By the time she slipped past Citharista's ruined gates, only the brightest constellations were visible. Would Anselm teach her to read the stars? Her mind roiled with things she wanted to learn, whole disciplines she had no names for. The most important was magic, and the mage had adamantly insisted he would not teach it—but life was long. She would find a way around that.

When she lay down on the pallet she shared with Marie, her sister hardly moved. Pierrette lay awake, listening to her sister's light breathing and the heavy, wet sounds her father made as he rolled back and forth.

With first light, Marie awakened. She put a finger to her lips. "Father got drunk last night," she whispered. "After you left, the merchant Theodoros returned. A ship had put in at the wharf, and something its captain said caused him to change his mind. He told Father he had a better source of casks. When he left, Father drank two whole jars of wine." Gilles had not done that since the year the olive trees had sickened.

There it was. Anselm had upheld his end of his bargain with Pierrette. The beech trees and the pool Ma would be spared. Pierrette resolved to ask Anselm to teach her law, as it applied to the tenure of land, so that she could do something—though she had no idea what—to prevent further threats to the precious, tiny valley.

Yet something Marie had said stuck in her mind. "That was last night?" she asked. "Not the night before?"

"What are you talking about? The night before last, Theodoros's ship wasn't even in port. He only arrived in time for mass."

"Of course," Pierrette replied with a crooked smile. "I slept soundly. It only feels like I slept through a whole day and an extra night. Only yesterday the bishop held mass, and Theodoros talked with Father last night."

She had indeed slept a whole night on the cape (and her visit with Anselm had not been a dream), because even at that moment, she picked a fig seed from a crevice between her teeth. She had eaten two figs with Anselm, but none at all the week before that, and the seed that now rested on her fingernail was still hard. She rolled the telltale bit between thumb and forefinger, and let it fall silently.

"So life will go on as before," she mused. "We won't be rich, and won't have a fine house up on the sea-cliff where the air is always fresh, nor a terrace of blue tile with ships and dolphins on it."

"Sometimes you sound just like Mother," Marie said. "'Ships and dolphins' indeed. Don't you even care that we're poor?"

Pierrette was pleased by Marie's allusion to Elen. Had Mother too had visions like hers?

She put her arm over her sister's shoulder. "Don't be sad. Everything will work out, you'll see." She couldn't explain her own happiness. Marie was her best friend and her stable foundation in that insecure world, but her piety was a weak joint in the edifice of their relationship. Pierrette's pagan affection for things magical, for forgotten goddesses who lived in sacred pools, was a wedge that might drive them apart. Pierrette said no more about dolphins.

∽

The Sorceress's Tale

Days passed as if nothing out of the ordinary had occurred. Folk confessed their trivial sins. The docks remained empty except for fishing boats. Occasional Saracen vessels were sighted far out, but the days when those were a threat to small, poor towns was past.

Gilles worked in the olive grove, and when the sea was calm took his boat out—though never for long enough, or far enough out, to get much of a catch. The grove prospered, but that meant little to either Marie or Pierrette, for Gilles diverted much of the profit to the taverner, Germain. He no longer visited the pool of Ma, whom he had intended to betray, but sought surcease in the wine-cup.

Marie grew tall like a Celt, from someone on Gilles's side. Her hair lightened to red-gold, which entranced Bertrand—who was wholly besotted with her, and paid little attention to other girls.

Anselm kept the rest of his bargain; no horned men or gods appeared in shadowed streets or from behind limestone outcrops. Memory of the repulsive Satanic organ still haunted Pierrette, especially in the seasons when rams or goats rutted, but gradually, through a summer, a winter, and the springtime that followed, such memories rose up less and less frequently.

To all outward appearances, her life seemed placid and normal. Pierrette grew taller, though she had long since abandoned hope of becoming as willowy as her sister.

Whenever her work was not pressing, she retraced her route up the narrow pine-shadowed defile to the cape, to the polished table in her room, where her days were spent with books, scrolls, and her charcoal-board. The cloth covering her small, hard buttocks gave a fine polish to her bench. As for sleeping (only drawing her curtains made it resemble night), there was the bed, made of feathers and very soft.

Her outward appearance was little changed, because she did not age within the timeless spell that enveloped the cape. But because her mind did not slow down or stop, she grew erudite, if not wise.

Was she becoming a woman, hidden within a skinny child's body? She was more knowledgeable, but if she never ventured outside, would she remain forever a child at heart? Only experiences gave maturity. Whether she slept one time or seven on each visit to the cape, she did not believe her mind matured any more than her body did. She might be a well-informed girl, but only in the world outside could she grow to womanhood.

Otho, Bishop of Nemausus

༄

Pierrette's Latin expanded, because it was like ordinary speech, and because P'er Otho's lessons had provided a foundation. She found Greek not unlike Latin, with cognate words she already knew. She had to struggle with Etruscan. Anselm's native tongue, Minoan, was most difficult of all.

"One must be born to it," her mentor said. "But you aren't going to learn magic, so it won't matter if you mispronounce things." Of course once she realized that most of the spells written in Anselm's special books—ones he had forbidden her to touch—were in Minoan, she studied that language harder than ever, until at last Anselm said, "Amazing! Are you sure you have no Minoan blood?"

She did not know where "Minoa" was, so she could not say. "Minoa?" Anselm laughed. "There's no such place— and never was. Once my language was spoken on all the islands of the sea. My people controlled the trade from Crete and Egypt, before the Phoenicians learned to build rowboats."

The Minoan capital—the name derived from Minho, or Minos, the title of their priest-king—had been the island called Thera. From the north, aboard a ship from Athinai or the Isle of Pelops, its profile resembled a hornless cow.

Thera was not the largest of the eastern isles but it provided the best harbor, and grew from a trade center to the seat of a mighty king.

Two pointed towers built at the western end of the island changed its aspect from polled cow to straight-horned bull— and it was as a bull that Minos appeared before his people— a man with a bull's head wrought in silver, electrum, and gold. "Minho-tauros," he was called. Minos the bull.

"In my grandfather's father's time," Anselm told her, "before the magical event that made Thera into the 'Fortunate Isles,' Minos was the greatest king in the world. The pharaohs of Egypt kissed his feet, for he was a mighty sorcerer who could drink the Nile dry from his own wine-cup, without leaving his palace."

All might have remained unchanged, Anselm said, but for two events unrelated except by fate. The first was a human event. Two of Minos's wives gave birth to sons on the same day. Which one was to be heir? The king reached into one child's cradle, and pressed its cheek with his thumb. The babe turned, and grasped the digit with strong lips and gums, sucking so hard that Minos's thumb tingled. He laughed loudly.

When he repeated his action with the other child, the babe did not suck. He gazed at his father with clear, gentle eyes, and he smiled.

"It is clear which one will be king," Minos said. "That one, who could suck blood from a stone, has the drive. He'll inherit my throne and learn the ways of trade and war."

The king pondered the other child. "This one looks beyond me to the heavens. He'll be high priest. I'll teach him how the earth moves, the secrets of tides, and all my spells and magics. He'll wear the mask of the bull."

Dividing the roles of priest and king was unprecedented. People mumbled uneasily that no such change could be without consequence. They were right.

When the old king died, the aggressive son took the name Minos, and was king. The placid child, calling himself Minho, dealt with gods and the hidden powers of the world, and everyone prospered.

But the child who sucked did not become less greedy with age. When his ship-captains had bled the Egyptians dry in hard trading, when the Greeks groaned to see his vessels sail into their harbors to collect tribute, Minos's half-brother remonstrated with him, because the people were unhappy. The island folk were not immune to Minos's sucking, for the stones of his new palace came from their quarries, and the food to feed laborers from their pastures, fields, and orchards. But Minos continued to suck, just as when he was a baby.

"The second event," said Anselm, "was a change in rocks beneath the sea-bottom ooze. Have you read Strabon's thesis on the nature of rocks?" he asked his pupil. She nodded. She studied everything he gave her to read. "Then you know that rock flows deep in the earth. Beneath Thera lay a great pool of flowing rock, and like water beneath a spring, it yearned to push upward, and to become . . . a fountain."

"A volcano," said Pierrette.

"Just so. And Thera had been a volcano before. Weaknesses in the seabed were already there. The island of Thera, home of the high priest Minho, was doomed."

"Where did Minos, the king, live?" she asked.

"His palace was on Kriti, at Knossos, a town without streets, of buildings without corridors."

"That must have been confusing," Pierrette commented. "How did they get from place to place?"

"People went from room to room—from courtyard to kitchen, to get to the granary, or through a bath or winery to get somewhere else. Because the king's symbol was the *labrys*, a two-bladed axe, they called his palace the Labyrinth.

"Minho," Anselm continued, "knew the way of rocks and gods alike. He knew Thera was doomed, but took no measures to get people off the island. Instead, he sent agents and priests to all parts of the kingdom to seek out men who loved peace more than profit, and to bring those men—and women, and children—to Thera.

"The hope of becoming rich means more to poor men than placid poverty. Yet though nine hundred and ninety-nine out of every thousand stayed away, Thera was crowded with those who came. Profit-seekers and the discontented departed, and in a few years, none but the contented were left on the isle.

"Avaricious Minos could not believe Minho meant him well. All his priests and philosophers went to Thera. His fat chef had gone, and his mapmakers and goldsmiths. Among those who left Thera were soldiers and tax collectors—men useful to Minos, had they remained."

Anselm sipped wine, his voice hoarse from unaccustomed speaking. But he pressed on to the end of his tale. He told how Minos suspected his brother of using his own wise men and advisors against him. "Minho the Usurper," he named him, and called his generals together to plan a military campaign.

Within months Minos's fleet sailed, and the sailors witnessed what became of the island. A half-day away they saw smoke as of a riot or conflagration. They approached, believing that unrest in the streets would make conquest easier. The smoke column expanded tenfold, twentyfold, laced through and through with fire.

Black clouds obscured the sun. Yellow fog billowed across the unnaturally quiet sea. Captains ordered their ships turned about, for the wrath of a god was at hand, but there was no wind. Then the fog was upon them, choking crewmen, captains, and soldiers with poisonous vapors.

Few survived to report. When the deadly yellow air dispersed, the great humped bull was no more. Remaining were shoals and the toppled remains of one hornlike tower. Island and city, wharves and rich fields, scholars and farmers, were gone. In their place a single, fresh volcanic cone jutted from the water, gouting black ash, fiery stones and terrible vapors.

Anselm sighed, drank deeply, and finished the tale. "Minos celebrated his brother's demise, but not for long. I won't repeat that tale, because I'm sure you already know it."

Pierrette did. She knew how the writhing earth had tilted the distant island of Kriti so harbors on one side were high and dry, miles from the coast, and ports and cities on the other side were miles out, beneath the ocean. Perhaps the kingdom could have survived that blow to its commerce, as well as the loss of its fleet, but it did not survive what came next: for months, clouds spilled their burden of gray ash on Kriti. The fertile fields were hidden beneath a gray, rolling blanket. Where no ash fell, crops wilted from acid, sulfurous rain.

Minos's empire starved. Men said it was destroyed by an angry god, and perhaps it was. Other empires were shaken, too. An angry God sent plagues to Rameses's Egypt. The skies turned black and unspeakable substances fell. Enslaved Hebrews waited in their houses for the manifestations to fade, then fled across the narrow sea into Sinai, where they wandered for forty years.

Storytellers made much of Minos's end. Shorn of imagination, it was this: a hostage at Knossos, Theseus of Athinai, raised a rebellion. The king hid in his palace, donning the bull-headed mask of a priest to disguise himself. But Theseus recognized him, and slew him. The rest was history—or a fanciful tale.

Pierrette was not satisfied. "What really happened to Thera, Master?"

Anselm twisted his face into a caricature of a frown. "You should know that, child. Minho was a sorcerer. He took his island out of the currents and winds, and out of ordinary time—where it still lies."

Now she understood why her avatar, the woman who called the storm, had jested with king Minho of the Isles about allowing strife to return. Still, she was no closer to finding that king and his island, because Anselm did not know where they were.

The tale spurred Pierrette to new efforts. She needed to become not a masc like her mother, but a great sorceress. Anselm's refusal to teach her became only an obstacle, not a finality. She used her time—hoping he would relent—in preparing herself for that day.

She needed to know where the Fortunate Isles were. They were the site of her wondrous dream, and she suspected they held the key to becoming the enchantress in that vision.

Too, she had developed an affection for the old curmudgeon, and though he appeared to have given up hope of going home, she was still young, and had not discovered how to give up. Among Anselm's collection were not only travellers' tales and scholars' treatises, but maps that amazed and tantalized her. She studied where the Isles had been, and where they might be, and learned geography in the process.

The world, she discovered, had once been a marble slab held up by four turtles, and had been small. In the remote past it had changed, according to the maps, and had become grounded in the mud of the world-river Oceanus. Later still— perhaps just as a chip of wood floats from creek to still pool—it had drifted into a great sea. The ancients had not sensed its movement. Thinking it still in the river, they continued to call the sea Ocean.

Beyond the Pillars of Herakles, on Ocean's Iberian shore, had been Tartessos. Further north, off a rocky point where tides made froth of the waters, had been Phoenician Ys, and the Isle of the Dead, from which none but druids could return.

Was the Isle of the Dead what she sought? Several scholars placed the Fortunate Isles there, just south of other islands called Hibernia (the winter land), Brittania (which might have been an island, or the mainland peninsula later called

Armorica), Albion, and Avalon. The accounts were confusing, because Albion meant "the white," and may have been Hibernia.

Geography was confusing because the names of places changed through time, and men's understanding of the shape of the world changed too. It expanded. Did that mean only that people had explored further, and recorded new places, or that the world itself grew, accreting new lands at its edges, just ahead of the explorers with their measuring staves, their pens, and their maps?

Pierrette studied. She also swept floors, prepared meals, and washed Anselm's clothing, spreading his white garments in the ever-shining noonday sun to dry. Seasons passed outside, but within Anselm's keep it was always the same—late spring, she decided, never quite sure.

Outside, down the rough slopes and along the sinuous coast to Citharista and her father's house, Pierrette continued her domestic duties—sweeping, preparing meals, laundering her father's garments and bedclothes, and working in the grove.

She continued her lessons with Father Otho, who was amazed at her progress. How had she learned words even he did not know? Her manipulation of the clumsy Roman counting-letters surpassed his own fumbling efforts.

Because Pierrette was in Citharista for all but the stolen hours to walk to the cape and back, she grew apace. Few noticed that her mind and abilities grew faster than her body, that as yet did not betray her masquerade as Gilles's "son."

At some time between her eleventh and twelfth year—her thirtieth or fortieth, perhaps, if time had been measurable within the keep—she began writing observations in a volume of blank pages. There she confided her sometimes-cynical reflections, and snippets of magical lore than she gathered from the many sources at hand.

Chapter 11 ∽ The Theorem

Pierrette's Journal

In the years since my mother's death at the hands
of the Citharistans, I have learned the Church's Latin,
Greek, and the language of Minho of Thera, long forgotten, yet rich in magical incantations. All are here,
in Anselm's books.

I am obsessed with visions and auguries, magics to
pierce the veil of time. Perhaps I am simply impressed
with Anselm's claim to have been alive since Rome was
a cluster of huts. Perhaps, seeing my mother's face in
the full moon, I fear having my life shattered because
I was unprepared.

I know a few spells, like "Guihen's Deception," the
one my mother cast to hide herself. In the oldest tales,
Guihen the Ligure used it to win a governorship, a
Roman *castra*, and a rich, pretty wife. I have studied
the Guihen tales' many variations, and I am not sure
what they portend. Guihen the Ligure, a wood-sprite
of my mother's lineage, has become in some devout
households a Christian boy, the stone fort he governed
a kingdom, and his pretty Roman wife the daughter of
a Frankish lord. How many such changes can his spell
endure? When the Guihen of ancient times is entirely
transformed into Guihen the altar boy, will the spell
become a prayer to the Christian God?

Anselm says few spells give the results the books
claim. "Plead for manna," he says, "and you will be

lucky not to be buried in poisonous toads." He complains of the inconstancy of magic, but I have no such complaint; with unfailing constancy all my divinations are of one place, one future, a dark time when all the gods and demons have been consumed, and mankind is enthralled within a great Evil that allows no magics at all.

I have dreamed of that dark time forty-three times since I came here to Eagle Cape. In my latest vision I knelt in water that reeked of rot and death, and peered over a heap of rubbish across a great flat plain of stone. The refuse stank, and glowed with sickly hues. No stinging insects swarmed, no frogs croaked; none could live in the poisonous water.

Across the plain, eldrich lights shifted like lusterless moonbeams, and huge demon-shapes growled and grumbled.

"Now it will come," said a voice I seemed to know. A hand took my wrist and drew me down into the foul water. The cold glow reached out like a stabbing sword. Baleful eyes big as platters sought me where I hid, and demonic roars battered my ears. I wanted to run.

"Wait! Watch!" my unseen companion commanded. The roar became shrill. It was upon us! I buried my head in my arms and felt its breath in my sodden hair. I could not look up even when the demon's voice fell off into the distance behind me, diminishing, like summer thunder that brings no rain. Yet I still breathed. The demon had leaped over me. I was not consumed by its fiery breath.

"Take me from this place," I begged the spirit I had invoked. "I want to wash away this filth." I envisioned the cold freshness of the pool of Ma.

A voice bitter as untimely death snarled: "*This* is the Mother's breast!"

Awake, I am not sure that the visions portray the future, though that is what I seek when I cast herbs on the fire or peer at glistening entrails. Could Evil could so entirely vanquish Good? Would not a world so lacking in beauty and goodness destroy itself in one vast spasm of hatred and horror, or drown in its own foul flood?

When I awakened, I crawled beneath Anselm's plump feathery coverlet, and took what comfort I could from the negligible warmth of his old bones. Perhaps he misunderstood. Though my breasts are small, I am no longer a child, and he suggested I reconsider my intention to remain virginal, and seek a lover—some shepherd boy who does not know me as the boy Piers. I will not do so. I wish to remain virgin as huntress Diana, which my mother did not. I wish to become . . . a sorceress.

Sometimes my dreams were pleasant, when I visited the Golden Man at the end of the undiscovered calanque. We ate mussels steamed in seaweed, tossing the shells on the great heap that had accumulated there. Still I had not held him, or even touched him. I often wanted to, but one does not dictate the terms of dreams.

By Marie's fourteenth summer, her breasts and hips swelled to womanhood. She and Bertrand approached Father Otho for instruction in the mysteries of marriage. Pierrette was quite happy for her. Even though Marie would move out of the house someday, and Pierrette would have no one to whisper with when the darkness was thick and close, she was (so she told herself) outgrowing such childish needs. Their deep friendship would endure. Nothing could change that.

That night Pierrette and Marie lay whispering and giggling. "P'er Otho was so funny," Marie said, wrinkling her face like a dried fig. "When he spoke of the 'marriage bed,' he became red as a pomegranate. 'The marriage bed,' he said, 'is joyous.' He kept saying things like that—the 'marriage bed' this, the 'marriage bed' that—as if he was not speaking of me, or of Bertrand, but only of some for-nickating bed."

Both girls laughed, imagining the impersonal "marriage bed," all by itself, fulfilling God's plan, bouncing and jouncing with no one in it. "Poor P'er Otho," Pierrette said. "What does he know of such things?" Neither knew what carnal memories Otho cherished, of a time before either of them was conceived, or whose lovely face and small breasts came to mind when he thought his hidden thoughts.

Pierrette could not imagine being kissed by Bertrand, but was not immune to the generalized attraction of such things. . . .

Only the week before, hearing a soft cry that had not sounded like boys swordfighting with wooden sticks, she had slipped through the crumbled portal in the marketplace. There she saw Marius lying with the baker Claudia's daughter, Marcella.

Marcella's skirt was bunched up around her waist, and Marius's hand covered her dark fluff. He rhythmically rubbed his trouser-clad midsection against her plump thigh. She arched up against his hand, emitting little squeaks.

Pierrette turned away, burning with ill-defined emotion. It should have been her with Marius, not Marcella. Yet it looked ridiculous, uncomfortable, even disgusting. She was glad Marius did not want to do that with her. But why would he? She was not even a girl, to Marius. That made her angrier still.

Marius saw her. "What are you looking at, Piers?" he growled. "Go find your own girl."

Marcella tugged her skirt down. "Yes!" she snapped. "A *little* girl!"

Humiliated, Pierrette withdrew. Days later, the memory burned still, augmented by a fresher one: she had blushed, and whispered to Marie. "Do you ever . . . touch yourself . . . down there?" she asked.

Marie answered with a giggle and a mischievous leer.

The next morning, a Sunday, Pierrette would ordinarily have gone to the Eagle's Beak, and spent long days studying with Anselm. He had introduced her to the nine Saracen numerals and the strange symbol that meant "one less than one." Once she had memorized the characters and the simple rules for combining them, she was able to count to one hundred with ease. Now she really knew what a "century" was.

Yet the questions that burned in her head did not concern numbers. Anselm's suggestion, recorded in her diary in letters of lampblack and oil, did little to ease her mind. She intended to remain a virgin, as Ma insisted. Why had he suggested otherwise? Had he felt manly stirrings? Had he pushed her away so she would not tempt him to use up his dwindling magic by making himself young for a night? Or was it simply that if she gave up her claim to the Virgin

Goddess's beneficence, she would cease to importune him
to teach her magical spells?

She could not go to Anselm feeling as she did. Instead,
she turned eastward and onto the path to the Roman fountain—and beyond.

Pierrette did not eat the fungi that ringed the small beech
tree. She did not wish to fly as a magpie or peer into future
time. She needed to talk to someone who would not laugh
at her childish ideas. She wanted her mother.

She may have dozed. When she jerked her head up, the
woman of the spring was there, dressed in brown homespun the color of dry leaves, but she was not old, except
for crinkles at the corners of her eyes, and minuscule grooves
between her dark eyebrows, that hinted at suffering.

She put her slender arm around Pierrette's shoulders.
"You're far too young for such a troubled face."

Pierrette told her how Anselm had pushed her away, and
what had happened behind the marketplace, and how those
things made her feel.

"Perhaps Gilles's deception, fooling people to think you
are a boy, is not so bad," the woman mused. Something
in the way she said "Gilles" alerted Pierrette—warmth and
amused condescension, the way Pierrette herself might say
"Marie" when her sister was being silly.

This was not just the woman of the spring, Pierrette
decided. This was truly . . . Elen. She sighed, and settled
against her, smelling old wool, the ozone tang of windblown
hair, and the musky aroma of a woman's skin.

"As Piers, you are less tempting—and less tempted—than
Pierrette would be," Elen said. "Gilles has made it easier
for you to remain virgin. I was not so lucky."

"Do you wish you had not married, *Maman*?"

"Oh, child, how can I answer? Had I done so, I would
not have you. Yet had I not, I might have done what needs
doing, and not left you to bear that burden."

"What must I do?"

"If I knew, I would tell you. You'll know. Until then, enjoy
what you have—your father and sister and P'er Otho,
and . . ." Her words dwindled, as if she regretted them—
and regretted all that she herself had lost.

"I'm twelve, Mother," Pierrette said. "I'm no longer a child.
At least . . . I should not be."

Elen laughed softly. "That? Never wish for that, little stone. The moon does not command you. You won't suffer its pull until you have abandoned your quest—or have completed it."

Pierrette was overwhelmed with troubling thoughts, but was afraid to destroy the moment by voicing them. When she finally drew breath to speak, it was too late. She was alone. It was afternoon. The little tree was again just a tree, and her mother's voice was only the soughing of a soft breeze in leaves and branches far overhead.

Pierrette trudged back through Citharista—and beyond it. She was tired and her feet were sore, but she pressed on toward the cape. It was always impossible to predict, from the course of the sun or stars "outside" what it would be "inside." She did not think the old man himself knew—he just declared it "night" whenever he felt need of a nap— and that made it so. She hoped that when she got there she could sleep, and not speak with Anselm until she had rested.

Crossing the natural stone bridge, all that remained of the old roadway, she noticed that another chunk had fallen from the span, leaving a raw, red scar. What would happen when the rest fell, leaving the gate a mere hole in a bare cliff, impossible to enter by? Would Anselm starve, without bread and oil, when the last of his magic died?

"I must find out why the magics have changed. I don't want to lose another person I love."

Her first opportunity had not long to wait. Anselm (who was not sleepy, and did not give Pierrette time to rest) wished to teach her a whole new way of looking at the world.

"Geometry!" he announced. "You'll be able to measure the height of a tree, a cliff...the moon and stars themselves . . . without lifting your pretty little bottom from your bench."

Pierrette was not sure how she felt about such allusions to her body. She was pleased that Anselm was aware she was a girl, almost a woman, and was flattered to be called "pretty," "delectable," even "succulent"— which sounded grown-up and slightly dangerous. But Anselm's words stirred uneasy feelings she did not wish to acknowledge; had she read Ovid, or certain lascivious Saracen writers, she would have called them erotic. She had spent more years inside the keep than outside, but was less comfortable with womanly things than any other girl her physical age would be.

Anselm did not press his unconscious suit beyond occasional words; it was easy enough to let them pass unremarked. Besides, his enthusiasm for his main topic was contagious. "We start with a point," he was saying, "a spot that has no size, only position."

"Like zero!" Pierrette blurted.

Anselm looked strangely at her. "I never thought of that," he remarked. He made a charcoal-dot on her smooth board. "That is a point." He made another. "Another point," he said. "Now what have we?"

"Two points."

"That's not what I meant," he said, annoyed. "What is between the points?"

Pierrette stared at the two dots, but saw nothing.

"Well then, how many points can I fit between those dots?"

Pierrette almost said, "About fifty," after estimating the size of the dots, but instead asked a question. "The dots have no size? I mean, your dots only symbolize much smaller dots? Infinitely small ones?" He nodded.

She had only heard the words "infinite" and "eternal" a week before, and the concepts—foreverness, something without limits, a whole universe of tiny, perfectly real numbers all crowded between zero and one—made her head spin.

"Then," she said, "there are an infinite number of . . . of points." Only fifty dots or so, but an infinity of tiny, sizeless points. She took the charred grapevine and drew all the points at once, with one sweep of her hand. "There they all are," she said. "All infinity of them."

Anselm drew her from her chair, then capered around her room, holding her hands and pulling her along. "You're brilliant," he said. "You understand."

Of course she did. It was self-evident, once you knew about zero and infinity.

"Now—what is that?" Anselm asked, leaning on the table, panting, pointing between the two original dots.

"It is an infinity of . . . no, it is . . . a line. A line of points."

"Exactly!" he blurted. "And this?" He took the charcoal—

which broke in his hand—and made two more dots. She said it was both two dots, an infinity of invisible dots, and also a line.

"A postulate!" he crowed. "Two points define a line. Now three points, like this . . ."

"Three lines—a triangle . . . and three infinities of dots . . . can there be three infinities?"

"You may have as many as you want, child. An infinity of infinities."

Pierrette's first geometry lesson was off to a grand start. The core of what she learned that first day was less obvious to Anselm than to her: that all knowledge and understanding is related. Not just zero, learned in one context, and dimensionless points in another; every fact, every possible observation, was linked in some way to every other.

Over several working and sleeping periods she learned how postulates—initial assumptions like the existence of points—could be combined, and manipulated into proofs or theorems, grander statements of derived reality. "Kewayday!" she exclaimed when she had proven, to Anselm's satisfaction, the number of points required to define a circle.

"What?" he blurted.

"Kewayday. *Quod erat demonstrandum*," she said. "That is like 'amen' at the end of a prayer, or 'abarakat' after a magical spell."

"Bah! What makes you think so? Nonsense! This is a logical proof, not a prayer or . . . or a spell." He eyed her suspiciously. "Have you been dabbling with prayers? Spells?"

"Only those my mother left me," she replied, "and I haven't 'dabbled.' I studied them and wrote them down."

"Well, cease doing so. They won't work right, and you'll get hurt."

"Prayers and spells and mathematical theorems aren't so different," she mused. "I'm not sure they're not exactly the same."

"Nonsense! Have you been eating mushrooms? If you're going to waste time with crazy daydreams, do so in your father's grove. I'm trying to teach you worthwhile things."

Pierrette did not bring the subject up again, but she did not stop thinking about it. The geometry of Euclid seemed little different than well-written incantations.

When she progressed into trigonometry, she upset Anselm

no end. "The sum of the angles of a triangle," she said one day, "must be at least 180 degrees."

"At least? That's wrong. The sum of a triangle's included angles is always 180 degrees. No more, no less."

"It's immutable? Just like magic, Master? Is that what you mean?"

"It is not! I mean that if a geometric postulate changed, everything that proceeded from it would also, and the proofs would have to be redone, with new conclusions. That's nonsense. The universe would fall apart."

"That's what I mean," Pierrette insisted, carefully forming her argument as did philosophers in books. "Just as a difference in one basic tenet of a faith—as bishop Arius discovered—can create two faiths at war with each other, so one change in a magical premise can create two kinds of magic, in which identical spells produce entirely different results."

"Bah! Nonsense! Unicorn feathers." Anselm was so angry he sprayed spittle on her charcoal-board and on smooth linen paper she used for her final copies of theorems. "Religions are not magics are not geometry."

"I can show you triangles with more than 180 degrees, Master," she said, very quietly.

"Good! And I will show you a four-legged chicken."

"I mean it. Will you let me show you my proof?"

Anselm eyed her suspiciously, alerted more by her ominously quiet voice than had she bellowed as he did. He nodded.

"I have prepared my proof in the tall courtyard." The tall court was a light-well between the east wall of the keep and Anselm's library. At one time he had experimented with pendulums, and a great basalt ball still rested there, its rope rotted. Pierrette picked up a lump of chalky limestone and proceeded to demonstrate, on the surface of that ball, how a triangle, when projected onto a sphere instead of a flat surface, did not have precisely 180 degrees among its internal angles, but always at least 180. She then proffered several pages upon which she had written the theorem proving her contention—which he brushed angrily aside.

"That's cheating!" Anselm expostulated. "A special case of no practical value doesn't change the fact that a *plane* triangle has 180 degrees." That, of course, was the flaw in Pierrette's case. She had not shaken the foundations of the universe by changing an essential premise. Anselm praised her cleverness, but did not accept what she intuitively knew to be true.

∾

Pierrette's Journal

Someday I will devise a theorem based on postulates of magic. I will leave those based in Faith to priestly theologians. Anselm will never accept my proof, but if I show him results, perhaps I can save him from the fate he foresees, as he fades slowly, and his keep crumbles into the sea.

I have had small successes. My mother's magics can be expressed thus:

I. There are four elements: Earth, Air, Fire, and Water.
II. Each element is absolutely different from each other one.

Those are postulates. It is easy to see that a change in one would change any spell that depended upon them—and I have found such a change. Because of it, no spell that depends on the second postulate works as intended. These are my new postulates, that reflect a changed reality:

I.   There are four elements: Earth, Air, Fire, and Water. (This is unchanged.)
II. Two elements are fluid at all times—Air and Fire.
III. Earth and Water can be solid or fluid. (I have never seen molten rock, but I know of it.)
IV. Fluidity has two substates, liquid and vapor.

In Anselm's workshop (though not when he was awake) I condensed fire in a bowl and bottled it in glass. It lights this page as I write. I captured a raindrop and induced it to become a diamond that I wear around my neck. Those spells are so simple I hardly need to write them to remember them.

I suspect that the spell that holds the sun at midday is based in some fundamental premise, yet undiscovered, that remains unchanged, and that the failing of the spell that kept Anselm young has, somewhere in its written lines, a premise that no longer reflects the universe as it is.

I cannot stop my master's decline, because he will not allow me to search his magics for the flawed assumptions within each failed spell. He does not have forever. Somewhere, an infinity has been assumed where a zero exists. Did Anselm's aging begin with the discovery of zero, when something that had been infinitely small suddenly ceased to exist?

∾

Pierrette shuddered, and put down her pen. She often scared herself, as though the floor her bench rested upon might not be solid, and she might fall through tile, earth, and bedrock when some hitherto stable premise changed: when a word in some ancient prayer was replaced by another, and some god heard, and did something new.

It was late. She had drawn the curtain because she preferred to write dark thoughts by the glow of liquid fire in the blue glass bottle. It reminded her that the universe was not truly out of control, only changing, and that understanding was the way to confront change.

She draped a scarf over the bottle and, because she wished to visit the *oubliette* before sleeping, lit an oil lamp with the flick of a fingertip. Smiling as the tiny spark took hold, she went out into the dark, unwindowed corridor.

Chapter 12 ∾ The Castellan's Lust

Pierrette fingered the wedding dress that lay across the bed like the rich coverlet of an emperor. It was not new. Gilles could not make enough silver in a lifetime to buy its like. Soon Marie would wear it, as had Gilles's mother, and Elen. Soon thereafter Bertrand, the smith's son, would remove the yellow silk sash and the gilt clasp set with garnets. Pierrette tried to imagine herself as Marie, her husband's hands lifting the linen dress over her head, but no image came. She shook her head in annoyance.

At twelve, Pierrette's courses had not yet flowed and, if Elen of the beech trees were to be believed, they would not, for a long time. Her breasts were rose-tipped, and cast a slight shadow when the sun was full overhead. Marie promised to fill out the dress more than their mother had. Marie took after Gilles's family, Pierrette after her mother.

Carefully, so she would not tear the old fabric, Pierrette put on the dress. She grimaced when she discovered how long it was, how she had to tug it up and tie the sash so it would not drag. An old bronze fibula sufficed to tighten the fabric across her chest.

The two-room house had no windows, only a door that Pierrette had closed so no one could see. Now she opened it enough so she could look down at herself in the fine clothing. There was no mirror. Ah, how beautiful! The silk sash shined like gold in the sunbeam, and the linen, for all its age, was white as a cloud. Pierrette twirled on bare toes. The skirt billowed, then wrapped fetchingly about her ankles.

She giggled—but her laugh turned to a cry of dismay as the door was flung wide, blinding her. Gilles shut it again, and looped the thong over its peg to secure it.

"Pierrette! Remove the dress immediately. It's for Marie."

"I haven't soiled it, Papa," she protested, hanging her head. She had no mother to teach her womanly things, only Anselm's books, written by men. She could not chatter with girls, or imitate their gestures, for she was Piers, not Pierrette. Even her father accepted the deception as real, and frowned when she pouted like a girl.

"What if someone saw you?"

"The door was mostly closed. Besides, it can't matter much longer."

Gilles could not stay angry. She was like her mother, and he had fond memories of Elen in that very dress, tucked and pinned in the same manner—Elen had been no larger than Pierrette, and the dress was too valuable to alter.

"People would know you're a woman, not a boy. And what won't matter long?"

They would know she was a woman? Pierrette's eyes glowed with the unintended compliment. "Papa," she said gently, "you must decide. Girls no older than me have suitors already."

Gilles shook his head. "They are all . . . fuller . . . than you. In a year we'll speak of it, but not now. Take off the dress."

"Father! Look at me."

Gilles turned. The dress hung about Pierrette's waist. How long since she had played bare-chested with the boys? How long since she had become shy and covered herself in his presence?

"You see?" she said, blushing hotly. "How long before everyone knows?"

Gilles sighed. "At least wait until after the wedding," he said. "Bertrand will work with me at harvest time. The castellan will not press me to purchase my grove."

"Promise we'll speak of it before the harvest."

"I promise," her father agreed, not unkindly, but with a sadness Pierrette could not fathom. He stepped outside. It took only moments to slip into her boy's tunic and trousers, but Gilles was nowhere in sight.

He had not wanted his daughter to see. Instead of turning right toward the town, he had taken the path up into the hills. It was not the loss of the grove he contemplated.

With Marie wed, he and Pierrette could live by his fishing. The sight of her young breasts had forced him to acknowledge a stronger motive for keeping her a boy and at home; she was so like Elen, and he was so alone.

Ah, wife! Why? Why had Elen continued to practice sorcery once it was sure she would bear him no son? Why did she not call down a demon upon her pursuers? Why did she give him a daughter so much like herself?

He had never asked if Elen loved him. Enough, that she was his. She had not come virgin to his bed, and he had heard the gossip when Otho's father sent him away, but Elen bore his children, and never spoke of what had been.

Gilles walked far. At the spring-fed pool he drank from cupped hand without praying. Elen's Goddess had not heard her pleas. Why would she do more for him, who had planned to cut her trees?

In the marketplace, Marie sold oil from the last pressing. Pierrette hid under Granna's awning, behind her baskets of wool. Marie was talking with the castellan, Jerome. A gold chain trickled like liquid sunlight between his splayed fingers. Marie turned her head away as if shamed. Pierrette strained to hear.

"It's too fine," said Marie. "I can't wear it."

"I'm not *giving* it to you, girl. Wear it now, then return it to me—before you seek your husband's bed." He grinned broadly.

"It's not a proper image," she protested. "The priest would not allow it at mass."

"You speak of proper images? This is the face of the horned god your mother worshipped."

Pierrette understood the Burgundian's misunderstanding. The horned god, the old Celts' deity, who ruled for a year at the Mother's side, and then was slain for his presumption, had no place in Elen's rituals, where reigned Ma, the land alone. "They rape with the plow, then think the Goddess is soothed by the rapist's blood. We take only what Ma offers. There is too much blood, and fear of blood, in that warrior religion, and in the Christians' too." Elen's words? Ma's?

The land was an onion with many layers. The oldest folk feared neither a woman's courses nor shedding virgin blood, but warrior peoples saw a curse and a wounding, and thus

evil. Only the strongest dared take on a curse of blood—
and thus to chieftain and priest fell the initiation of women.
The castellan was long removed from such chieftainship,
but the custom endured as a right and a pleasure.

The lust in the big foreigner's eyes sickened Pierrette. She
strode forth looking as if she had rushed there, out of breath.
"Marie! Did you forget you must speak with the priest? Come
with me." The Burgundian gave the impetuous boy an
annoyed glance.

"I remember now," Marie said. "He wants to counsel me
about my vows." She looked around. Only a few jars still
had oil. "Help me carry these," she asked briskly.

As Marie and Pierrette straightened up with their arms
full, the Burgundian draped the chain and its medallion
around Marie's neck. "Don't forget," he admonished her.
"This was my grandfather's. I will have it back on your
wedding night."

"We'll ask Father Otho about it," said Pierrette

∽

The Sorceress's Tale

The low wall held sunlight even after darkness fell,
warming my buttocks. I was growing old, to need such
comforts. Yet when I saw the young woman and the
boy, I forgot my age. I say "boy," for even knowing
what Pierrette was, my mind shifted from thinking about
her sex, because I would inevitably think about Elen,
and would curse the day I took vows. She might have
been my own child.

Marie's hair caught the evening sun and turned red-
gold, like a halo. She was a woman—the years had
flowed swiftly.

The second child held my eye longer. Even had I not
known she was not the boy she seemed—with her ebon
hair cut short and her rude trousers bagging—I would
have known she was Elen's child. Her face had nothing of Gilles in it.

Otho, Bishop of Nemausus

∽

Marie dipped one knee as she approached the priest. Pierrette—the boy Piers—did not. "Father Otho," Piers said, holding out something that glittered. "The castellan gave this to Marie."

Otho's expression hardened. "You know what this is?" They nodded. "What do you wish of me?"

"Tell him to leave Marie alone!" Piers blurted. "Marie is no fat Burgundian cow for him to mount." She thought of the horned god, and her anger swelled.

Otho sighed. "What he contemplates is a sin, because he is a baptized Christian," he said without heat. "I remonstrate with him about his affections for the old ways, but he's stubborn."

The irony of it: had Marie been less pious, she would already be swelling with Bertrand's child, and the problem of the randy Burgundian would never have arisen.

"It's rape," Pierrette spat angrily.

The priest winced. There was nothing he could do. Did Jerome no longer straddle the fence between his Christian baptism and the call of his tribal gods? Otho realized the irony of what he was about to suggest. "Have Bertrand carry your basket to where wild rosemary grows. If you come back without a certain thing of value . . ."

"Then the horseman will have no pretext," said Piers, delighted with the priest's cleverness. "Yes, Marie. We must find Bertrand immediately."

"But Father," Marie protested. "Isn't that a sin too?"

Otho sighed. "Do you have two jars there, one empty and one full?" Marie nodded. The priest took them and decanted half the contents of the full one into the other.

"There," he said. "This one has all the evil in the world, and this other all the goodness. You see?" His visitors nodded. "There is never more, nor less, but only this much. Now . . ." He poured a few drops of oil from the jar in his left hand into the other. "Now is there more evil in the world? Have I transmuted something good into something bad?" He poured some back, and hefted the two jars. "Ah— now this one is heavier. Is there more good? Tell me child— if I poured all the oil into goodness's jar, would all evil be banished?" He shook his head. "Of course they are only jars of oil. Would that the world were so simple."

Marie did not understand, but Pierrette was quick to

comprehend, though his example was not quite to the point. "If you and Bertrand go beyond the town, and if you come back . . . as a woman, not a girl . . . then you may have sinned. But if you do *not*, then the Burgundian will have his way with you, in the horned god's name, and that would be a greater sin." According to the Church, it would. It was only a sin for the baptized, like Marie. The girls' mother had never accepted Christian baptism, nor had Pierrette. Was it different for them?

"You're our priest," spat Marie. "Just tell him to forget his sinful demand!"

"This is Provence. The Holy Father's hand rests lightly here. I can't command a Burgundian lord pledged to the Frankish king." He again sighed. "Go child. When you confess before the wedding mass, your penance will be light."

Pierrette stood. "Come on, Marie. Let's find Bertrand before it's too dark to go out after rosemary."

Bertrand's forge was hot, and he did not want to waste the coals. "Have Piers carry your basket," he suggested. "I have work to do."

Pierrette rolled her eyes toward the charcoal shed. Marie took the suggestion, and withdrew a distance.

"Don't you know anything about women, Bertrand?" Pierrette used her best "man-to-man" voice. Bertrand shrugged. Women's ways were the least of his interests.

This is the man my sister is marrying? It would be a long, long time before she herself married, if she couldn't find anyone better. "You want to marry her, don't you?" Bertrand's eyes lit up. "You'd better do as she asks. Today at market, she spoke with another man. I doubt they talked of forges or charcoal, either, and he bought no oil. He gave her a gift."

"Who was he?" Bertrand demanded, now quite attentive. "Was it Marius? I told him to stay away . . ."

"It wasn't Marius. Why don't you ask Marie, while you gather herbs?" Bertrand grunted, and pushed ashes over the hot coals.

Pierrette sidled over to Marie. "Don't tell him about the castellan right away," she suggested. "Have you decided where you're going?"

Marie's eyes lit with a mischievous light. Fearing that her

sister's curiosity would impel her to spy, she would not say where.

"Well, where's your basket?" Bertrand demanded.

"I left it at the gate."

When they turned the corner, Pierrette peered after. Indeed she intended to spy. She would not have to guess where they would go—to the soft ground and moist coolness of the pool sacred to Ma. . . . There was a quicker way than the path, if one were agile.

Pierrette hid beside the Roman fountain. Marie and Bertrand would be coming along soon. When she heard their feet on the dry pebbles, she would dash ahead, and hide among the beeches. Now she would see what men and women did, that boys speculated about.

She jerked her hand from the warm stone. A beady-eyed snake tracked her movement, but did not strike. Thick as her wrist, it had the geometric markings of a viper, but Pierrette was not concerned: like the snake that had shared her cellar hideaway, its kind seldom struck creatures it could not swallow whole. "Sorry, friend snake," she whispered. "Just let me share your hiding place." The snake only stared.

She heard footsteps—but they were coming down the path, not up. She could not run toward the Mother's breast without revealing herself, and could not go the other way without running into Marie and her betrothed.

It was her father! If he met Marie and Bertrand on the path, their opportunity would be lost. "Father!" she exclaimed. "I've been looking for you." She tugged on his sleeve, attempting to turn him toward the fountain, out of sight of the path.

"Why this way?" he demanded. "This leads to an old ruin."

"If we go the other way, we'll meet Marie and Bertrand. Come. I'll explain as we walk." Pierrette regretted she would remain uninformed about the rite they would perform by the Mother's breast, but that was the lesser loss. She explained what had transpired in the marketplace, and what Father Otho had said.

"The priest can't command Marie to sin!" Gilles protested. "I must stop this folly!"

"Father! They'll hear."

"They'll hear anyway—I'll tell them. That Bertrand! I warned him!"

"No, Father! You don't understand. The castellan . . ."

"I understand all too well. What will Jerome think, if Marie allows herself to be had, just to spite him?"

Gilles reddened with shame when he realized what he had revealed. The castellan had approached him a month before, dangling that fat purse that jingled with silver . . . "Ah, Gilles," he had said, "it must be difficult, with no wife to keep an eye on your daughter."

"Indeed," Gilles agreed.

"Perhaps she and her sweetheart slip away. After all, you're often at sea, or working in the grove . . ."

"Marie has not been with any man!" Gilles protested indignantly.

"Good, then," said the castellan. "See that it remains so." He departed, leaving the purse. It seemed to beg to be picked up. Gilles turned away in horror at what he contemplated. Silver coins jingled, as if the purse held some malevolent life of its own.

He understood what Jerome intended, but perhaps Marie was not virgin, and would say so when the time came. Father Otho would not allow it, anyway. He would mention it to him.

Time passed. Gilles did not speak with the priest. He hid the pouch. Now, confronted by Pierrette, he was forced to look at what he had become: a whoremaster. Had he been of the same blood as the castellan, there would have been some excuse; it was, after all, a matter of ancient religion. But it had little to do with old rites, only modern lust.

Whoremongering. He could not look Pierrette in the eye. His only recourse was age-old: rage. "Bertrand! I see you. I warned you what I would do . . ."

Bertrand dropped the basket and fled, leaving Marie to face her father.

"Whore! Sneaking off with any man! Were you going to have him by the spring? Have you become a priestess like your mother? You, a baptized Christian?"

Marie was as pale as the moon that had betrayed their mother to her slayers. Treachery! Only with difficulty could Pierrette accept that she had not misheard, or that Gilles had not misunderstood. "Father," Pierrette essayed at last, "don't you understand . . ."

"You encouraged this! I'll send you to the nunnery after all. Do you want to starve, when we have no oil to sell?" He had forgotten his decision, made only that morning, that they would not really need the grove, for just the two of them. As he had no true son to inherit it, his family would be better served by another sack of the knight's silver. Two such purses would last his lifetime. Women, whose husbands took care of them, had no need of such things.

There was no reasoning with Gilles. Perhaps later Pierrette would bring him a pot of wine. Then he would listen to reason.

Marie did not speak all the way back to Citharista. The priest could not protect her. Her father would not. Her husband-to-be fled almost before Gilles had opened his mouth.

Gilles did not wait for his daughters to prepare his meal. "Piers! Fetch me wine—two pots." Marie gave Pierrette the purse she carried at market.

When she returned, Gilles gulped the first pot unwatered. She silently offered him the second. Marie moved silently, preparing bread and cheese, with a bowl of olives saved in sea-brine.

Gilles shook his head. "I'm not hungry." His eyes filled with tears. "You understand, don't you? Without the soldier's favor . . . It's such a little thing. One night with Jerome, and then you'll be with Bertrand. Isn't that what you want?"

Marie turned away.

"Damn you, then! I'll watch you like a sow watches her litter, until you're safely in the Burgundian's bed."

"And you!" he snarled at Pierrette. "Go live with your mother's sorcerer friend." He spat on the floor. He rolled onto his bed, knocking a wine pot over with his foot. His snores were the full-blown ones of heavy slumber. Pierrette would not speak with him that night.

Gilles arose early. Pierrette sat up on her pallet. "Father? Wait . . ."

Gilles shook his head. "We have nothing to talk about. What do you know of such things? Do you think your mother was virgin when she came to me? Why should Bertrand be luckier?" He slipped outside.

Marie awakened. "Pierrette? Is he going to talk to Father Otho?"

"He is not. He won't change his mind."

"The old drunk! I won't go to the castellan's bed!"

"There's one person we haven't spoken with yet. I'm going to visit the castellan myself."

Gilles sat on the worn Roman quay, staring at his boat as if watching it decay splinter by splinter. "If I were less despicable than I am," he told himself, "I would sail straight toward Africa, and seek a great storm. I would do that if I were not so . . . cautious." Yet had he not been "cautious," he might have done good where he had done nothing—surely a sin itself. He spat, but could not rid himself of a foul taste. The best wine would not wash it away.

MA - TA - RO   RE - KA   : NO - SO - JO
(Matr reka nosyo)

MA - TA - RO - SO - JO   MI - KO
(Matrosyo mykos)

MA - TA - RO - SO - JO   MA - E - DO
(Matrosyo maedoum)

PA - QO   DO - NO   E - NA - PA - NE - TE - JA
(Bhagos dono infantia]

MA - TA - RO - SO - JO   PA - QO
(Matrosyo bhago)

Prayer in variant Indo-European
dialect, transcribed using
Mycenaean Linear B syllabary.

Chapter 13 ∾ The Spell

Pierrette had never been inside the Burgundian's house, though she had watched the soldiers practice on the wide, sloping field in front. Mounted soldiers were practicing when she arrived. When she heard the clatter, she almost laughed: their swords were only wooden staves, like Marius and his friends used behind the marketplace.

Seeing the slender "boy" at the edge of the field, one soldier turned, kicking his horse's flanks. He raised his wooden slat as he charged. Had Pierrette been a boy indeed, she might have looked for a rake or other "weapon." Instead, as the scruffy horse and its straw-padded rider bore down upon her, she stood as if made of wood herself.

"What's wrong with you, boy?"

"I . . . I must speak with Jerome."

"Then mount up here." He was strong, for all that his face was as worn as her father's. Swept up, she barely thought to swing a leg over, so she did not end up draped across the horse's rump like a sack of grain.

"I haven't seen you with Marius and the others," he commented over his shoulder.

"I'm Gilles's son Piers," she said. The horse's stiff gait made her lower teeth clack against her upper ones.

"Your sister's marrying the smith's son, isn't she? About time, I say—Jerome's been a hard master these last weeks." He guffawed, and jabbed her in the ribs with a padded elbow. "Well, don't say I said so," he said as he swung her

111

down in front of the tall open doors, "but we'll all rest easier when your sister's in her own bed at last."

Did everyone know what was planned for Marie's wedding night—and did no one care? Her errand was doomed.

A shed leaned against the inner wall, where fat brown rats scurried beneath open barrels of grain.

"What are you looking for, boy?" It was Jerome, just come—by the thick odor that followed him—from an *oubliette*, shaking his red wool kilt down from his waist. She glimpsed hairy calves and knobby knees. His uncombed hair stood in rumpled spikes.

"Please, Master Jerome . . . There is a terrible misunderstanding."

"Indeed?" he replied, lifting a bushy eyebrow. "Then tell me. Come. I am about to eat."

Beyond a narrow doorway lay a kitchen, with strings of onions and fat sausages hanging from pegs. A long table dominated the room. The remains of a crusty loaf lay atop scattered crumbs. Jerome sat.

"What brings you here, not your father?" he asked, tearing a chunk of bread and stuffing his mouth.

"The goddess Ma is not wife to the horned one," she blurted. "It's wrong for Marie to celebrate his rite. She is baptized in the Church. She must go with her husband on her wedding night."

"Is that so?" Jerome gulped wine. Red dribbles darkened his garment. "What does Father Otho say?"

"That doesn't matter. It's wrong to worship someone else's god, or to force her to."

"Are you a theologian, child? The god's blessing can do no harm—if indeed he lives, it might do good. Blood will be shed. That's my trade; Bertrand's is iron. Blood is a curse, and takes a strong god to purge it."

The strands of his mussed hair seemed to darken, to thicken, and the knight's breath was hot, sour wind. Pierrette tried to back up, but her legs failed to obey. Sunlight from the doorway flickered across Jerome's red clothes like flames. The air thickened with their heat.

"I'll show you what god rules here, boy," he said, pulling the cord at his waist. His garment fluttered to the floor in a shower of sunlit flame.

Pierrette could not move or speak. Spiked, branching

antlers grew from Jerome's head. His chest and shoulders were a mat of coarse hair. His skinny legs performed a jittery little dance, and she heard the clatter of hooves on stones.

"No!" Her voice was thin and reedy, as if it never actually escaped her mouth. "You are not a god!"

"Who am I, boy? Who wears these horns now?" Hot light emanated from crimson eyes. "You know me, child. I consumed Lugh, and Teyrnon, and Pan. I've eaten the old gods, and soon the priests will feed me that tortured one who hangs on a cross. Who am I?"

"Satan!" she cried out. "That is who you are." A billow like thick smoke rose between her and the demon. Her head felt light, her arms and legs as if they did not belong to her at all. She felt herself falling. There was no floor, only a hole that went down and down, without a bottom.

"What's wrong, boy?" someone said. "Drink this." She felt a splash of coolness on her chin and chest, and tasted sour wine.

"Your father is wealthy now—doesn't he buy meat? A boy needs meat, you know." The voice was Jerome's. "You'll never be a soldier—you're skinny as a girl."

She felt the coarse rim of the pitcher against her lower lip, and another gout of wine splashed into her mouth. She choked, and pulled her feet beneath herself.

Backing away, coughing, she opened streaming eyes. Jerome stood there—not Satan. "Better now?" he asked. "Good. Tell your father to feed you. You can't be fainting in an olive tree."

She backed away until she was outside the door. "What's the matter with you?" the knight said, annoyed. "You look like you saw the devil himself."

Pierrette released an inarticulate cry, turned, and ran.

"Tell your sister she'll be happier with me than that pudgy smith!" Jerome called out after her. "She'll be sorry it's only one night."

Pierrette ran, the narrow streets a flickering of shadowed doorways. She ran, stumbling over loose cobbles, until she could run no more. Her breath came in gasps, and tears streaked her cheeks. She let herself fall against a wind-smoothed rock, and wiped her eyes clear.

The red tiles of Citharista's roofs were lost behind a screen of pines. Her feet had found a familiar path. Ahead loomed Eagle Cape. On her left a cleft led to Anselm's keep—the one place where she might resolve the terrible doubts that threatened to drive her mad . . . if she were not already so.

There was no need for hurry. The wedding was not until tomorrow. She could spend as long as she wanted with the mage, and still return in time for the mass.

What had really happened in Jerome's kitchen? Had she fainted? Had her own fears—her anger with Otho and Father, with gods and their adherents—overcome her?

Whether Jerome's transfiguration had been fleshly or only shifting sunlight and red cloth, it had been no pointless illusion. "Real" and "illusion" were only words. She was here on the path to the red scarps of the Eagle's Beak. *Something* had caused her to run. Where there was an event, there was a cause.

She distanced herself from terror by shaping an intellectual exercise, like a mathematical proof.

Gaulish priests had taken the burden of virgin blood on themselves to spare husbands its curse—yet neither Teyrnon nor Lugh was a god of war, reveling in blood shed with metal weapons. There was no one Celt war-god, only long-forgotten name-gods of each tribe. "Teutatis," from *teuta*, which meant "tribe."

Yet Jerome—or Satan—claimed the allegiance of *all* who shed blood. And had not Father Otho called war "the devil's work?" Anselm's histories told of Mithras, god of the Roman legionnaires. Had Mithras faded away, or had Satan "eaten" him too, and grown by the sum of his puissance? Was that what she had seen in the horned god's eyes during the mass? Satan's fires consuming the essence of the gentle Father of Animals?

The demon had seemed smug. How could he consume P'er Otho's Christ? Can evil consume good and not be sickened? It did not seem right. The image of Father Otho pouring oil from one jar to another passed before her eyes.

She was reminded of that other vision, seen by a magpie flying over a devastated landscape: the Black Time, as she had come to call it. Was there a connection between Satan's victory over the gods, and the degradation of Ma's earth?

Pierrette pushed on, her mind aswirl, as she considered one small possibility she might yet bring about. If Anselm would not help her save Marie, could she steal one of the mage's spells and do so herself? Was there time for her to study them, to discern just what ancient postulate no longer held true, and . . . and to rewrite one?

What kind of spell? She hardly dared trust the molten fluids of the Earth to obey her like fire caught in a jar. Would they consume just one evil Burgundian, or all Citharista, all Provence? She needed a smaller spell, one she could be sure was right *before* she tried it.

Yet would it matter—in the greater sense, considering Satan's burgeoning influence and the Black Time's approach— whether she, Pierrette, could save one insignificant village bride from a night with the . . . the Evil One? She did not know. Nevertheless, she had to try.

With new resolve strengthening her steps, and dark fears pushing her on, she reached the door to Anselm's keep in what seemed no further time at all.

∾

Pierrette's Journal

Some places have more magic than others—ruins, woods, bogs, and lonely beaches. Places unworn by events cling to the past, when great magics were in the air. Perhaps, having changed little, they exist outside of time itself. That is what Anselm Girardel claims for his homeland, the Fortunate Isles. Walking in uninhabited places, could I actually pierce the fabric of time, and step into another age?

That day, sick at heart for my sister, I wonder if I did not push momentarily into some future when the stones of Anselm's stronghold are almost worn away.

The approach is forbidding; the cape narrows to a path, with steep, rocky cliffs plunging on both sides, like walking atop a wall. The fortress itself is as if carved from a wave-cut pinnacle. There is a single gate.

Townsfolk say it was built by Saracens, but tapered columns with fat capitals like round loaves are not Saracen, and the Moors were not fond of the black and vermilion pigments that still remain where the stone is protected from sun and weather.

The fort clings to the southernmost point of a hostile land. Waves have gnawed at the cliffs, and the path is barely wide enough to put one foot beside the other. Had it deteriorated even since my last visit? How much longer would it be here at all?

∿

On that day the path seemed especially precarious, the painted pilasters even more weathered. Pierrette remembered black and vermilion, now weathered away. A silver bell rested in a niche. She rang to let Anselm know he had a visitor. Once she had just gone in, and had startled him atop the parapet. He had almost fallen.

"Ah, child," Anselm said. "Have you come for another lesson?"

"The castellan wants Marie!" she blurted. "Tomorrow she'll marry Bertrand and my father has sold her maidenhead to the Burgundian for a sack of silver and P'er Otho says he can do nothing and Jerome has turned into a devil and . . ."

"Slow down, girl. One thing at a time. Let us broach a bottle of cool wine, and sit in the sun atop the keep." She followed him. A narrow stone stairway wrapped itself around three walls of the small entryway, with landings at the corners, and doors that led to the further rooms. Just below the topmost level, she glanced into the room beyond. There! The forbidden books. She did not hesitate, or give the mage any idea of her budding plan.

From the shade of the parapet the magus drew earthen cups and wine. Had he seen her coming? She could see the roofs of Citharista, and the brilliant blue of the calanque, but the trail was hidden in trees. Magic? If Anselm had known she was coming, did he know what she planned? She still had to try. She told him everything—the Burgundian's lust, her father's betrayal of Marie, and the priest's indifference. Perhaps if he offered a solution to Marie's dilemma, she would not have to betray him.

Anselm nodded, jiggling the white curls that ringed his head. "If the castellan were here, I might dissuade him. But beyond the portal, I'm helpless. My magics don't work."

"Is there anything?"

"There's so much I would do, if the rules allowed. Let me tell you how it was . . ."

Pierrette had heard some of his tale. She knew she was about to hear more. Each telling lent insight or birthed new speculations. She was desperate, but the old mage would not be rushed. She forced herself to listen while he talked of ancient days, and poured more wine into his cup. That was part of her stratagem.

Anselm had not always been known by that name, he said, but the one his mother had given him sounded odd. He had changed when he was trapped in this savage land.

"I was arrogant, full of the wonders of my master's kingdom, trained in magic, but not common sense. The Isles had been moved many times since the great catastrophe that had freed them from time's erosion, thirteen centuries before my birth, and I don't know just where they were, not long after the crucifixion of the Christians' Jesus . . .

Rich tones of a sounding brass wrapped around the palace's vermilion and black columns. Ansulim knelt with his brother initiates in the presence of the Bull, their faces against the hard stone.

Had Ansulim dared look up, he would have seen Minho, priest of the bull-god, wrapped in the spotted cape, his human face hidden beneath the great helm of the Bull— the Bull of Minos, Minotauros. The master's voice echoed hollowly, amplified by tubes and chambers within the mask. Mask, cape, and ringing brass were not for boys like Ansulim. They had attained their twentieth year, and had worn the god's likeness themselves. The symbols were for the folk gathered at a distance, awed by the manifestations of Minho's wisdom, not knowing the wisdom itself.

When Anselm reached for his cup, Pierrette dutifully filled it. "You say Minho was—is—kind," she remarked, "and that his disagreement with the king at Knossos began over cruel taxes and sacrifices. Yet the result of his spell was still more suffering."

"It would have happened anyway." Anselm set his cup on the parapet, and she filled it, though it was but half emptied.

"I don't understand."

"The earth's might cannot be denied. Thera had been formed from fires beneath the land. Had Minho not acted, they would have burst forth anyway. The same ash would have fallen. The folk of Thera would have disappeared anyway—burned to foul steam in the catastrophe. Minho's spell saved the isles from that fate."

"Where did they go?" she asked. "And where are they now?"

"That is two questions," said Anselm, once Ansulim of Thera. "And there are two answers . . ."

Ansulim felt a hand on his shoulder, and looked up . . . into the golden eyes of the bull. "I have a task for you," said the hollow voice. "Follow me."

Trepidation warred with pride. He alone had been called. Within the palace, blue dolphins sported on stylized waves, the painted sea a wainscot on plastered stone walls. Ansulim's eyes absorbed the splendor.

"Lift this from my shoulders," said Minho, ruler of Thera. Ansulim leaped to take the bull's head. "Now sit. Listen.

"You know the Jew called the Hermit?" Ansulim nodded. The Hermit had been a follower of the prophet Jesus. Following the holy man's death or transfiguration, he had sprung from obscurity to influence among the disciples. He had not witnessed the multiplication of loaves and fishes, the healing of Cedonius's blindness, or the raising of Jesus' friend Lazarus from the dead. His talent came to the fore after Jesus departed: he was a planner and organizer with contacts in Rome, Damascus, and caravan towns on the route to the East.

The nascent Church was scattered across the Roman empire. Years passed between visits by those who had sat at Jesus' feet. Confusions arose. "Jesus was the son of a carpenter, a carpenter himself," one Christian might say. "This hammer is sacred to him." Confusion could lead to grievous error. Hammers were hammers; there was no physical symbol of Christian worship. The Cross, representing both sacrifice and resurrection, was not revered until later.

The Hermit was a scribe. He wrote letters to erring communities, extolling the simple virtues of Jesus.

Among the Jews of the diaspora men called *apostoli* collected money for support of the Faith. Their visits were not always welcome, for few Jews felt themselves wealthy. The *apostoli* were thus hard men who did not take "no" for an answer. "We Christians can learn from the *apostoli*," the Hermit said.

"We don't need money," said one disciple. "The Master taught that what we needed would come in our time of need. We had a money-man once, and look what happened."

"This is not the old days," said the Hermit. "We are scattered the breadth of the empire. I envision a new kind of *apostoli* to guide our far-flung believers." Those disciples agreed that something was needed, but there was no central authority. Each followed the mission of Jesus in his own way.

Minho spoke: "I dreamed that in a hundred years the emperor himself would bow before the Hermit's priest-apostles. That was a nightmare.

"I dreamed next of carpenter-priests in Galatia who wielded hammers of gold, and shepherd-priests in Iberia who bore crooks decorated with crimson silk. I foresaw fisherman-priests in Ionia, and winebibbing charlatans in Gaul. I dreamed of the Christians fragmented, nothing in common except their Book—and that soon rewritten, retranslated, until each sect had its own. There was no Hermit in those visions. They were the ones I preferred."

"I don't understand, Master."

"I believed that without the Hermit, that last dream would transpire. As for why—we exist here only as long as folk outside believe, but Christians deny my magic. They name me sorcerer, in league with demons." He snorted. "Demons! Superstitious nonsense. . . . But they believe in demons, so demons there will be. I do not wish to live in a world with demons, so I tempted the Hermit, and had him brought here. Do you know what happened then?"

"What the Hermit would have done, the Apostle Paul did instead."

"Saul of Tarsus, Paul, was a nobody. He had not known Jesus, yet he united the Christians. Where he did not go in person, he sent letters . . ."

Ansulim nodded. Saul of Tarsus had been an enemy of the early Church, until he was converted—by a miracle, some said—on the road to Damascus. The bright, shiny threads of his words and letters had created a Church of tighter weave than anything the Hermit had envisioned, a tapestry in which the dark warp, the words of the Nazarene, were obscured by the brilliant weft he threw over them.

Warned by his dream, Minho removed the Hermit from the world of time, but what then transpired was even more damaging to the sorcerer-king's cause.

"So there you have it," said Anselm. "Saul of Tarsus was my mission. I was to draw him to the Fortunate Isles before martyrdom put the final fringe on his weaving. Had I succeeded—or so Minho believed—the entire fabric of his Church would have unravelled. I encouraged new thinking, new rituals and dissensions, but I failed in Corinth, in Thessalonika, in Galatia, Iberia, and Rome. The weave of Jesus and Paul was too sturdy, and my pickings and snippings were repaired, adding new strength and texture.

"And where am I now? Here on this forlorn cape, unable to find my way home to report my failure. I can't even beg Minho to free me to marry, sire children, and then die in good time."

Pierrette filled the mage's cup. "I'm sorry for you—but still, through this tale, you're saying 'No, I won't help save Marie from the castellan's lust.' "

"How can I?" Anselm muttered, slurring his words. "I don't trust myself to utter words of change, for fear I'll create further turmoil."

"I understand," said Pierrette.

"Do you?" he replied. "Do you understand that I fear to disturb the fabric of things because the bubble of timelessness that surrounds this place could be pricked? You aren't asking for a simple manipulation, like stirring anxiety in the soul of an avaricious Greek to save your precious beech trees. I can't fight gods and demons."

"I understand, Master," Pierrette sighed. "Here, let me fill your cup."

Pierrette tucked a cushion under the mage's head. She draped a corner of his robe to shade his eyes. A guttural snore rattled in the back of his throat.

She tiptoed to the doorway, and snapped the lamp wick into flame with a spark from her fingertip, hardly having to think the words of the spell, let alone voice them. She descended the first staircase, then stopped to listen. When he snored too loudly, his roars startled him awake—but not now.

She had memorized the location of every tome and scroll on those shelves without touching one of them, afraid that the mage might have set a spell to warn him if she broke her promise.

Now that did not matter. If she failed to find a workable spell and to "repair" it, he would be angry about her meddling, and would probably ban her from the Eagle's Beak—but if she failed, she suspected he would not last much longer. She herself might not survive. How near was the Black Time? How powerful was the Eater of Gods?

She lifted a scroll and unrolled it, weighting it with polished onyx blocks. Anselm would not sleep in the hot sun for more than an hour, yet she dared not rush: the crabbed entries were written in Minoan characters; the ink had faded even as the parchment had darkened; it would be easy to miss what she sought.

She skipped over complex spells. The one she sought would be short and simple, not so powerful that it would disrupt the fabric of things if she got it wrong.

She did not find it on that first scroll or the fifth. Halfway through the eighth, she was successful. It was only seven lines entitled "Sweet Earth from Sour"—but she sensed that the principle it embodied lay at the root of powerful phenomena: it was a fertility spell.

The characters were Mycenaean, representing not vowels and consonants, but syllables. The words were not Minoan, but something was strangely familiar, when she muttered them aloud.

She repeated the first two lines over and over, not daring to pronounce the spell in its entirety. "Ma-ta-ro re-ka no-so-yo . . ." The language was her mother's, her ancestors'! "Matr' reka nosyo," she pronounced. "Matrosyo mykos." Mother who judges, mother of mushrooms. The words were truncated and distorted because Mycenaean characters could not express the sounds exactly. Even the scribes of Agamemnon and Menelaus, of Achilleus and Odysseus, had been forced to spell "Knossos" as "Ko-no-so." But once Pierrette knew she was reading known words, it was not hard.

She continued. "Ma-ta-ro-so-yo ma-e-do." That was Matrosyo maedoum—"Mother of strong drink." Mother of . . . of confusion? Of fermentation? Of course—the change from honey to mead, from waste to rich soil. Mother of mushrooms, mother of . . . compost.

Why had speakers of the ancient tongue written the spell in such clumsy characters? Because they had none of their own?

The last two lines were "*Pa-qwo do-no e-na-pa-ne-te-ya* and *Ma-ta-ro-so-yo pa-qwo.*" *Pa-qwo*? *Bhago*, the beech tree. *Bhagos dono infantia, matrosyo bhago*. The incantation, in its entirety, was: "Mother who judges us, mother of mushrooms, mother of mead, beech tree's children, mother of beech trees."

The simple, wholesome prayer seemed clear: first an address to Ma, who gives life to the soil; then a gentle reminder that she was the giver of fruits, the mother of trees. Ancient words that did not beg the goddess or command her, but set one image after another in the hope that she would understand what was needed, and would give it freely. The spell was all postulates, with only an implied conclusion.

Yet Anselm had marked the spell as dangerous. How could that be? He would not sleep forever. She had to figure it out. What had the ancient sorcerer presumed that was no longer true?

The part of the scroll where the spell was written was darker than the sections above and below, the ink more faded. Had the scroll lain open to this exact spell long enough for light and air to affect it? How long had Anselm pored over it? Hours? Days?

That was a clue. She was the mage's student, and thus might be expected to think enough like him that when they considered a single problem—the erratic working of magic—they might gravitate to similar sources. And if Anselm had studied this spell . . .

She rushed to the forbidden shelf, and lowered a heavy bound volume: Anselm's notes. A flurry of dust motes filled the air. How strange. How could dust gather where time stood still? She flipped through pages of dense Minoan interspersed with Latin and Greek. The notes represented years of work. How could she find what she wanted in the time left?

She had to assume that she thought enough like her

mentor that he would also have come upon the spell early on, near the beginning of his work—and of the book. She looked for key words—soil, rot, and fertility.

There! "The spell does nothing!" he had written. "I observed no change in the sour soil. I will get back to this when I have bathed and changed undergarments. The itch I contracted from these dusty experiments is affecting my concentration."

Below, he had appended a copy of the spell in the Roman alphabet, seemingly from a later scroll.

NETROS REX NOSIO
NETROSIO MIKOS
NETROSIO MEDEOM
BAGOS DONO INFANTIO
NETROSIO BAGO.

That was all wrong. *Matr'* was "mother." Netros meant "snake." And *reka,* "she who judges," was misinterpreted as *rex,* "king." The whole spell was rendered meaningless . . . Or was it?

The Latin abruptly took on sinister meaning. Think not of the gentle mother, mediator and judge, but of the Gauls' Taranis, a thunder-wielder with the lower body of a snake. With a snake between his legs. Think not of a sweet, white mushroom for soup, but of red amanitas that erupt after rain like erect penises—like the member of Cernunnos/Satan. Amanitas, that drive men to fatal, erotic madness.

Snake and mushroom, the banes of women who fall asleep in the woods and find themselves with child—the trees themselves great wooden stiffnesses—NETROS BAGOS, wooden snakes . . .

She understood. As language, perception, and religion had changed, someone had substituted "na" for indecipherable *"Matr',"* or *Ma.* "Judge" became "king." Furthering the confusion, *"Netr"* was "king" in Egyptian while *"ma"* was represented by a hieroglyphic sword, and meant "to destroy."

The new spell—no longer a prayer—had three postulates and a conclusion. Still a fertility ritual, it commanded a male god and the male member. Manly madness. No wonder it had made poor Anselm itch.

But dangerous? She studied both versions, prayer and spell.

When she saw it, she laughed—a crone's cackle, not the musical ripple of a young girl's delight.

The unwritten postulate was that serpents, male organs, and mushrooms functioned similarly. Anselm's reference to undergarments informed her of the locus of his particular itch. Had she been male, it might have affected her too.

What god did the spell entreat? What had happened to him? She remembered Cernunnos, his eyes glaring with fire that consumed from within. Had this god too been . . . eaten? Were the last lines of the spell now directed to a different power?

She wrote the spell again, changing a word in line one, and another in line five. Now it would work—though differently.

She folded her page. From a storeroom she took powdered mushroom from a clay jar. She glanced up the stairs. Something seemed odd about the light that diffused down to the landing, but she had no time to think about it.

Hurrying down the rough trail, she snatched a pinch of dry soil and a sprig of a succulent herb: earth and the life that sprang from it. She was driven by an undefined sense that something was wrong.

Nearing the Burgundian's residence, her sense of wrongness intensified. She felt displaced, as if this were not the Citharista she had grown up in but some almost-identical duplicate in which cobblestones, differently placed, made her stumble where ordinarily she would have unconsciously avoided them. Yet she herself, not Citharista, was out of step.

She approached Jerome's gate, and heard the castellan's voice raised in anger. Close against a chalky limestone wall, she peered around the corner.

Jerome was berating his soldiers for something. It was as good an opportunity as she would get. He was in view; the materials for her spell were ready. She whispered the first line. As she spoke the second line she sprinkled dry earth, and throughout the third and fourth crushed the succulent sprig and rubbed it with dirt and mushroom spores until it formed a dark ball. She broke it into crumbles, then scattered it before her feet.

Her breath caught in her throat as she uttered the final line, and she had to begin again. Ugly words rasped across her tongue like coarse sand, and the name of the god she commanded was not some forgotten deity, but was . . . Baalzebab, Moloch, Satan. Pagan god or demon, usurper or master, it was too late to draw back the hideous names.

The knight did not collapse nor cry out in agony. Had she failed? The rebukes he heaped upon his soldiers did not change in tone or content as he scratched idly at his crotch.

Pierrette's shoulders slumped. Had it been for nothing? Had she overlooked some key element of change? Her tongue felt coated with foulness, and smeared dirt on her palms itched as it dried. Jerome turned on his heel and disappeared.

Gilles's house seemed strangely altered too, though Pierrette could not say why. She mounted the stairs cautiously, unsure of the origins of her feelings. The door was latched from the inside, and she had to knock.

Not Gilles, but Father Otho, opened it. "Pierrette." He closed and latched the door after her.

"Where have you been?" her father whispered angrily.

"I went for a walk," she replied. "I haven't been gone long."

"A day and a night and a day? That's not long?"

His face reddened, and Father Otho put a restraining hand on his shoulder. "Hush—remember Marie!"

Two days? Of course it seemed like that to Pierrette, but she was used to the timelessness of the Eagle's Beak.

Then with a terrifying rush, the small oddnesses she had seen and felt all came back to her: the faded crumbling paint on the gate pilasters, dust on the books in the library—and not least, her own sense of displacement as she walked through the town. Anselm's spell of timelessness had failed. And that meant . . .

"Marie? What happened?" she blurted. If she had been gone two days, then today was the day after the wedding.

"Come," Otho said softly. "I'll take you to her. Perhaps your presence will have some good effect." He took her arm.

Marie lay on father's bed. She still wore the glorious wedding dress, but the hem was brown with dust, and the fabric was blotched, as if she had fallen. Her bare knee was exposed by a rent in the skirt.

Her eyes were open, but she stared fixedly at the wall, where Pierrette saw nothing but plastered stone.

"Dear sister," she murmured, dropping to her knees. Marie's hand was cold and stiff. Pierrette recoiled.

"She's not dead," Otho said. "Look—her chest rises and falls. She blinks once in a while, too."

Again Pierrette lifted her hand. It remained raised when she let go, then slowly lowered itself to the bed, like a candle sagging in hot sunlight. "Oh, Marie, what's wrong?" She turned accusing eyes on Father Otho.

"She seemed resigned. I performed the rite, not knowing the hidden depth of her distress. Afterward, the knight led her away. She was smiling, so I thought . . ."

"That she had resigned herself to whoredom?" Pierrette spat the words angrily, without a care that she might disturb Marie—who was beyond mundane concerns.

The Greek physician Galen had written of "a quiet madness of women," stating two possible outcomes: that the patient recovered, retaining no memory of events leading to her deathlike condition, or that the waxy semblance of death continued until the victim wasted away and died of starvation and thirst.

What else had Galen written? She berated herself for having skipped blithely over words now vitally important for Marie.

"She must be removed from here," she said at last. "Perhaps in a place where nothing she sees reminds her of what has transpired, she'll decide that it's safe to return to this world."

Otho eyed her strangely, because her words were at odds with her appearance: a slight child, wavering between girlish- and boyishness. His eyes focused on her tightly drawn, delicate face, and then on her boy's garb. Perhaps he reacted because she spoke as if she understood Marie's condition in a way he could not.

Where could Marie be taken that would not remind her? Every wall and stone in Citharista would evoke images that eventually led, by whatever circuitous path, to the moment when she had withdrawn her consciousness.

At last, Otho spoke. "The convent in Massalia," he said. "The nuns can spare someone to feed her and . . . and change her undergarments."

As he said that, Pierrette became aware of the stink. "Bring warm water and cloths," she said to Gilles. To Otho she said, "Find a cart and an ass. We must leave as soon as possible." He nodded, not questioning her authoritative tone at all, and left the house. Gilles brought tepid water and rags, then backed away from Pierrette's glare.

What little she knew about rape had been written by men, who dismissed it as inconsequential. She could not imagine it without injury—but Marie showed no bruises, no scratches, only deathlike repose.

"You withdrew to your deep refuge before anything happened, didn't you?" she murmured. "Where are you now, sister? Will you come back? Will I hear you laugh again?" Bathing Marie and struggling to remove the torn, stained dress, she continued to talk, though Marie did not respond.

She bundled the dress and laid it on the embers of the fire Gilles had made to heat water. He stirred as if to protest—then thought better of it. The old cloth smoked briefly, then burst into flame. In hardly any time it was consumed, and only fluffy ash remained. Had Pierrette's subvocal incantation sped the fire's course and encouraged the completeness of its consumption? The flames had perhaps been unnaturally bright, but Gilles's eyes and hers had been blurred by tears. Perhaps his had been tears of regret, seeing the dress burned—the same dress his wife, mother, and grandmother had been wed in. Perhaps they were tears of guilt for his inaction, that had led to the burning.

The carter Augustus, whom the villagers called Gustave, refused to leave before dawn, afraid of spending one more night than necessary on the high trail to Massalia. The valley road, with remnants of the Romans' limestone paving, was less steep, but farmers became brigands when they saw strange faces, and though he feared the ghosts of the dragons who had left their bones in high places, he feared robbers more.

Pierrette slept on her pallet. Gilles made do with a coverlet by the hearth. Once Marie cried out, a wordless keening. Pierrette climbed on the bed and held her as she writhed and moaned in some terrifying internal battle. Her eyes darted about, seeing things Pierrette could not.

When the shaking ended, she was as before—skin cold

as tallow, body stiff. Pierrette had to pull her eyelids closed as if she were dead, but they fluttered as if in true sleep.

In the morning, Gustave arrived with a clatter of iron-tied wheels and the bawling of his donkey. Marie got up by herself, walking hesitantly as if blind, yet without stumbling. She stared straight ahead, even on the steep stairway.

She climbed into the cart. "She's getting better," Gilles stated. Pierrette scowled, but hid her expression from her father. "Perhaps by the time we reach the edge of town, she'll speak, and bid us turn around." He, no less than Gustave, dreaded the journey ahead, and grasped any sign of improvement hopefully. Yet had Gilles not been "cautious" he might have suggested that he and Pierrette take Marie to Massalia in his boat—braving that tortuous coast to get his daughter there sooner.

Pierrette knew Gilles's rationalizations for what they were—and she knew Marie had not taken one step toward recovery. Once seated, she made no attempt to pull her shift down over her thighs, or to keep the folded blanket between the hard planks of the cart and her buttocks. Something within had commanded her steps from bed to cart, but withdrew when no longer needed, leaving her unwanted body unprotected against slivers, grit, and the jolts of the cart as it rolled over rough cobbles and unpaved streets.

As they passed the soldiers' practice field, someone at Jerome's gate cried out, and Gustave halted the cart. The knight himself approached, waving an unsheathed sword and shouting. He was clad in a nightshirt that fluttered about his bony knees. Pierrette cringed, remembering the last time she had seen those hairy legs.

Otho sprang between Jerome and Marie. "A pox!" the knight howled. "The dog's brood gave me a pox!" Otho wrested the sword from his hand. "She has unmanned me!" Jerome wailed. His garment was stained with blood and other fluids. "This is what she has done!" he cried, pulling the hem of his nightshift up. Pierrette covered her eyes, but not before she saw his swollen member and the fat, wet boils that covered him from navel to mid-thigh.

She did not hear P'er Otho's words, but when she peered

between her fingers, the priest was leading the stricken knight away.

Cold bumps sprang up on her skin. The spell had worked. It had produced just what she had intended—yet she was not elated by her success, because it had come far too late for Marie. Perhaps later she would contemplate the transposition that linked snake and mushroom, that caused Jerome's poor useless member to appear not as the red prong of a horned beast but as the white-flecked, poisonous red amanita mushroom instead.

Perhaps someday she would write in her journal her discovery of why the spell had changed in the first place, as spellsayers themselves grew in understanding that fertility was not wholly the province of females, but of the snake, the male, as well.

Otho drew Pierrette aside, and they spoke heatedly for several minutes before returning within earshot of the others. "I must stay," he said to Gilles, "but here is a letter to the abbot in Massalia. I hope he'll recommend that Marie be taken in until she is healed."

"*If* she heals," Pierrette said silently. Gustave lashed the ass with his long cane, and soon Father Otho was out of sight. Pierrette held her sister as the cart jounced and clattered over the cobbles, then onto the softer gravel and grass of the road leading upward and away.

When they reached a branching trail, Pierrette leaped from the slow-moving cart. "You go ahead," she told her father. "I'll catch up tonight." Gilles did not protest, and Gustave did not care. The donkey snorted, as if to say "good riddance." One less human meant one less he had to keep a perennially suspicious eye upon, and a lightened load as well.

It felt good to be away from brooding Gilles and silent Marie, though she dreaded what she might find, if Anselm's spell had failed completely. Would she find only dry, old bones in his bed? She could not help but suspect that her attempt at magic had caused the time-binding spell to go awry. She was half-convinced that Marie's condition was her fault too.

She scrambled up the final leg of the trail to Anselm's door. The vermilion and black paint-flecks were there.

Actually, she could see pigment even where the stone had always been bleached white. Despite that optimistic sign, she picked up the handbell with great trepidation. What if Anselm did not answer?

"Ah, child," he said cheerily, swinging the door wide. "It seems like only minutes ago we were drinking wine and I was telling you of—"

"Master! You look . . . different." She stared. Having experienced negative change in Citharista, she was in no mood to anticipate that some change could be positive—but the dark strands in Anselm's once-white beard could not be interpreted otherwise. "Won't you use up your magic, making yourself look younger like that?" Deep lines in his face had smoothed, and the tip of his nose seemed less red.

"Do I look younger? I feel it. I have no idea why, but I woke up without an ache. Do you know how long it's been since I couldn't find a sore spot?"

Had her spell something to do with it? How could that be? But if Anselm were well, she could hurry to catch the travelling party. "What's your hurry?" the mage asked her. "Rest first."

"Then the time-binding spell is not awry?" she asked.

"Why should it be? See for yourself. The sun is at high noon, as always." And so it was. Seeing her delight at what should have been of no consequence, the mage became suspicious. Before long, he had the whole story, and he put her fears to rest.

"Marie's curse lies within her own mind," he said confidently. "It is not magical, but escape from something unbearable. She'll hopefully—with time and peaceful surroundings—recover entirely."

He shook his head then. "As for your purloined spell . . . I feel no pity for the knight. He deserves what he got." Then he scowled. His moods changed so fast that Pierrette couldn't keep up. "Satan? You took a great risk, uttering that Christian deity's name. I haven't met him, but he seems to be doing all too well for himself. You must promise not to do that again."

That was not hard to promise. "But he's not a god, Master. There's only one Christian God."

"Is that so? You could have fooled me. Don't people avoid dark places and graveyards for fear of him? Just because smart ones don't pray to him doesn't make him less a god. Since Christians insist their God is entirely good, they needed somewhere to put the evil—and that is their other god."

Pierrette, who had heard Father Otho's explanations, was sure there was some distinction she was missing, but she could not explain it.

After a long "night's" sleep and a meal of crusty bread, cheese, and juicy figs, Anselm accompanied her down the stairs, carrying a cloth-wrapped package. He had thrown a black woolen cloak over his shoulders, and wore the kilt that was longer in back than in front. His sandals were so new they squeaked. "I'll walk a way," he said. "I have too much vigor to be contained."

"Is that wise, Master? If your strength fades as you get farther away from this place . . ."

"It may. Yet something has changed, and I wish to test the limits of my confinement." He smiled indulgently. "Besides, I may be able to contribute to your sister's welfare, now that your meddlesome priest is not around to watch."

At that moment, Father Otho was thinking of the mage also—if there was any way to define "that" moment which, for the mage and Pierrette, stretched on forever in the world outside. Perhaps the moment did not occur until Anselm stepped outside his gate into Otho's world.

Strange things had occurred. Not just Marie's ailment or Jerome's—though the knight's pox defied remedy. It was no ordinary pox; it was far too horrible.

Did the hermit mage have something to do with it? Once a week, sometimes twice, Pierrette walked to the cape, yet never lingered. He had been curious.

He spoke with an old woman. "We bring the old fellow bread and fruit in exchange for powders an' such—things hard to find hereabouts." She smiled, as if a priest had no need to know what "and such" was. "Always at noon, too. He never opens his gate any other time." In all her years, the old man never aged a day.

Pierrette never took a lunch or drink, yet never returned hungry or thirsty. Otho reached conclusions of his own. She did not go there for nothing. She had learned things far beyond his ability to teach, which took time. Much time. And the old women had been welcome only at noon. What would they have noticed if they had been allowed to stay? That it was always noon there? Otho's conviction came slowly, but was all the more firm for that.

What other magic did the old man practice? Otho should have written to his superiors in Aquae Sextiae or even to the archbishop, but he had no evidence of evil—no evidence of anything except that the old man had been there as long as living memory, and perhaps longer.

Jerome's pox put things in a different light. New red swellings appeared, spotted with pustules, as soon as old ones scabbed and healed. Jerome's agony continued. Otho drew two conclusions: *primus*, that the lore the old mage taught was not innocuous, for Pierrette had surely caused the pox; *secondus*, that she had not ensorcelled Jerome to prevent his taking Marie, but only afterward, as revenge. That was evil.

He had begged her to exercise Christian charity—even her pagan mother would not have objected. She said only, "The pox is not mine. It belongs to one of yours—to Satan." Otho still shuddered at the conviction behind her words. "You Christians created him by pouring all the oil but a drop into one jar. Pour half back, and Jerome's boils will dry up." What had she meant? Otho did not then remember his own poor explication of Good and Evil, when he had poured oil between two jars.

∽

Pierrette's Journal

Otho was wrong; the lapse of Anselm's time-binding, and my failure to recognize it, caused me to cast the spell too late. Only later did I clear myself in his eyes. Only later did I realize also the effect his speculations had upon the reality I inhabit: his reasoned belief in Anselm's sorceries rejuvenated my mentor at the very time when his continued existence was in doubt. The unquestioning belief of a lesser person than a priest, unsupported by doubts and skepticism overcome, would not have turned the ebbing tide.

But that was before I had begun defining the changing

nature of magic, my life's work, and I did not know why Anselm suddenly felt strong enough to leave his fortress and accompany me. My experiences on that voyage to Massalia set the stage for that realization, and others . . .

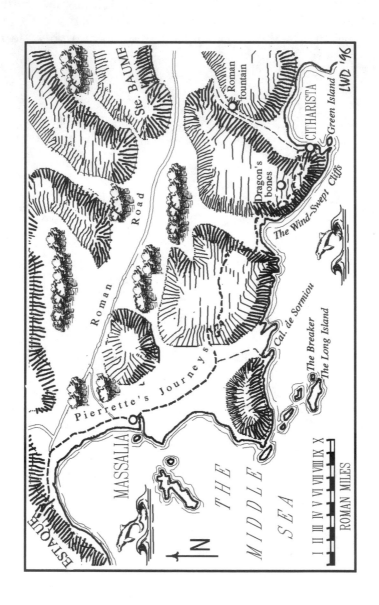

Chapter 14 ∾ The Vow

"We're not going to find Father and Marie tonight," Pierrette stated as they crested the high slope. The sun's passing had left a dull mauve glow. "We should stop before we leave the trees behind. Here, there is dead wood for a fire."

They dragged branches to the lee of a rusty beige outcrop. Pierrette reached out with an extended finger—but no spark flew to the tinder. Again she tried, carefully whispering the exact words of the spell—with no better result.

"Try this." Anselm proffered flint and a steel-bladed knife.

"I don't understand," Pierrette said. "That spell always works."

"Always? You have more faith than I do." He made as if to return flint and knife to his pouch.

"Master—give me the flint and steel. I meant only that it has worked, until now." She stroked the dissimilar materials, guiding sparks toward the tinder, then blew gently upon the dry shavings. A puff of fragrant smoke rewarded her. Soon they were settled with a fire between them, sharing bread and olives, washing them down with wine from a skin bag.

"I wish I knew why the spell didn't work," Pierrette mused.

"All magic is unpredictable. Remember that, or you'll be in trouble when it betrays you, and you've prepared no alternative."

"If I understood *why* it didn't work . . . I've gone over the words and the postulates, and nothing seems to have changed."

"Perhaps your postulates only apply to a limited case—some theorems only apply to right triangles."

"This isn't geometry, Master."

"Still, I suspect you have overlooked some greater principle. Perhaps it could be stated as, 'Magics will always work until you have come to depend upon them and have no other recourse.' "

Pierrette went to sleep thinking about it. Yet when she awakened before dawn, she was no closer to an answer—and the spell still did not produce a spark. She had to heap tinder around a surviving ember to start the fire.

"Why are you staring like that?" the mage asked.

"Last night you walked between me and the fire, and I saw the flame as if you weren't there. I've been trying to see if I can still see through you."

The mage stiffened. "And can you?"

"Stand between me and the rising sun." She peered long and hard, at first unsure if the dim, vaguely circular glow was a trick of her eyes. Then she nodded. "I can see the sun. You must go back, or you'll fade entirely."

He squatted, and shook his head. "Why are you so sure this has to do with my departure from the cape? My earlier recovery didn't have anything to do with distance. I'm going on with you, at least until we pass the dragon's bones. If I fade further, then we'll be reasonably sure . . ."

She was not convinced. "If you're fading steadily—if it isn't a matter of distance from your stronghold—it will still seem so if we go on. We should wait here and see."

"It doesn't matter. Either way, you must go on to Massalia."

The long slope was cut by enormous ravines. Tough greenery clutched scant soil not scoured away by the monotonous wind. "Ahead, a great battle was fought," Anselm told her. "The last dragons were vanquished. Their bones lie half-buried."

Pierrette pushed on, eager to see. As the trail wound past a craggy outcrop, the mage stretched out a hand. "There!" he exclaimed. "The battlefield."

The land tilted northeastward like an eroded table with two broken legs, scattered with white objects. Some stood alone, and others were broken lines of convoluted shapes. "Those are dragon bones?" she asked, disappointed. "They

look like white limestone—eroded into strange shapes, but
still only rocks."

Anselm also seemed let down. There was a chain of white
vertebrae several hundreds of paces long—or so it had once
appeared to him, long ago. Now indeed it looked like an
outcrop of limestone. The great skull looked like a reptilian head, but the arch of its cheekbone was worn to irregu-
larity, and the single eye socket was only the mouth of a
shallow cave. "I don't understand. I remember it differently.
I was sure those rocks were dragon's bones."

Ideas tickled at the back of Pierrette's mind. "I can think
of several possibilities. One is that enough time has passed
for wind and weather to destroy a resemblance to bones.
Countering that, inscriptions on Roman *stelae*, surely almost
as old, have not weathered into unreadability. Perhaps your
imagination was once more vivid, and you saw dragon bones
where now you see rocks."

"I remember rib bones," the mage mused. "I remember
teeth. I find it difficult to imagine myself gullible enough
to have seen such details, where none exist today."

"Perhaps the world itself has changed, and what once were
immense bones are now only limestone."

"That's not elegant," Anselm criticized. "Your earlier
alternative is a closer fit: I am fallible. Perhaps my perceptions are in no better shape than my magic."

"I considered my fire-starting spell infallible, Master. Yet
as you pointed out, its failure may result from some principle I haven't envisioned. If these rocks were once dragon
bones, perhaps some equally grand principle lies at the heart
of the change." Yet what it might be, she could not say.
Only her uncomfortable sense that the universe was indeed
in a state of flux led her to choose her final speculation
over the others.

They picked their way between ambiguous formations,
cutting across the stony ground instead of following the
circuitous route the carter Gustave had taken. Shortly before
noon, they spotted the wagon, less than a mile ahead.

"I'll catch up with them, Master," Pierrette said. "You must
go back."

"I feel no worse than before."

Pierrette pointed at the ground. "What do you see?"

Anselm stared at the cobbles and gravel, the tiny growing things. Pierrette did not elucidate. He had to see for himself.

"I have no shadow!" he cried. Pierrette's shadow pooled about her feet as if darkness dribbled from her and stained the ground, yet where the mage stood, sunlight illuminated every pebble.

"You're right," he admitted at last. "Ah, how I looked forward to this trip. Do you know how long it's been since I stood in a marketplace and heard the bustle of a hundred people? Ah well—at least I have looked at hills and smelled the rosemary that grows on them."

Trying not to think hopefully ahead to a time when—if Anselm's strength grew further—he might dare venture beyond this distance, Pierrette set about one final task. . . .

"What are you doing?" the mage asked, watching her heap loose fragments of limestone.

"I'm building a cairn. You must return here in a few weeks. If your improvement continues, then at some future time you'll see your shadow here."

"Ah," said Anselm. "Then when I return home, I should also pause when I see my shadow again, and build a cairn. If I can't see it there when next I come this way . . ."

Pierrette was saddened by his pessimism. "That will define the lower limits of my hopes, though I truly expect you to build a third cairn beyond this one.

"Perhaps," said the mage, "but now I must go—if I am to journey in sunlight and be able to see a shadow at all." He held out the package he had carried. "Will you deliver this to the scholar Muhammad ibn Saul, in Massalia."

"A Saracen? In a Christian town? Or is he a Jew, as his surname indicates?"

"He's mysterious, but is as near to being a friend as any man I might name. We had wonderful conversations when he visited my keep—my prison. I sorely regret that I won't be able to enjoy his hospitality, for a change."

"I'll deliver it, Master. Will this ibn Saul be there to accept it?"

"He explores the fringes of the known world, and writes of the folk he meets, and their strange ways and beliefs. If he's away, his servants will see that my parcel reaches him—or will keep it until he returns."

Pierrette was happy to have an objective in Massalia besides delivering her sister to the nuns. Now she had an excuse to slip away.

Pierrette reached out and hugged Anselm. He made a strange, strangled noise and for a moment he stiffened. Then his arms encircled her, and they stood, swaying, between the distant, encircling arms of the Middle Sea.

"I never held a woman," he murmured softly. "I was a boy for a long time, and have been an old man longer . . . but I never had much chance to be young." He grinned. "I wanted to squeeze your bottom. I've never done that."

She smiled. He had called her a woman—not a girl, or worse, a boy—and had reacted in a way no one had, before. She suspected it was qualitatively different than the way her secret love Marius reacted to Marcella, or Bertrand had felt about Marie. . . .

Marie. The moving speck of the cart was no longer in view. Favoring Anselm with what she hoped was a womanly smile, she said, "Keep well, Master. Perhaps when I return we'll remedy your lack." Before she could see his reaction, she set off in the direction the cart had gone. She did not look back.

She decided that the fort on the Eagle's Beak was, to Anselm, much like the mysterious Camargue to Guihen and dark Starved John. Their magics were tied to places as with invisible cords, and they faded with distance from their anchor-point. Was Ma constrained in a similar manner, unable to wander beyond the narrow confines of her valley and her guardian beech trees? Yet once Ma had been everywhere—at least, everywhere that beeches grew.

That thought led to another. The prayer written in the Mycenaean syllables had specifically cited the "Mother of beech trees," but the corrupt version written in Latin letters said "Bagos," the ash. The Mother Tongue had grown into all the other languages. *Bhagos* became Latin *fagus*; in Greek it became *phagos*, "oak." What happened to spells and magics when the words changed? What unknown words restricted beings like Anselm and Guihen to their places?

Her mind thus occupied, she caught up with the donkey-cart when the others stopped to break bread just past noonday.

Someone had joined them—a small, bearded man wearing leather clothing. He leaned upon the most enormous pack she had ever seen. He was no taller than Pierrette herself. How did he carry it?

"Breb," said Gustave, "is a trader."

"How odd," she said, eyeing him askance. "I thought traders used the valley road, and travelled in caravans."

"Seeing is believing," the little man said. "I am a trader and I am here, so what you thought is not so." He tore a chewy crust from his bread, and seemed to dismiss her.

Breb, explained Gustave, was one of a score of folk who lived in a cluster of huts hidden in a mossy declivity. "They speak an unknown language, and appoint one of their number to trade with the world beyond—Breb, in this generation."

Pierrette thought that fascinating. She resolved to speak at length with the odd little trader. But now . . .

Gilles had not reprimanded her for her absence. In a flash of insight, she wondered how often he had suppressed his objections to her mother's disappearances.

"How is Marie?" she asked.

"She ate bread dipped in wine this morning," Gilles said. "She's improving." Yet when Pierrette rode with her in the cart, holding her hand, it rested with claylike heaviness in her own. She saw no change in her sister's condition. Halfway through the afternoon, Marie fouled her garment, and Pierrette ordered the two men aside while she wrung urine from the shift and rubbed sand on the cart. They had too little water for bathing, so she brushed oil on her sister's skin to lessen irritation.

When she led Marie behind a scrubby bush, she squatted obediently, with no more expression than a milk cow at a comparable moment. That dismayed Pierrette more than when she had urinated in the cart. Where had her sister's soul gone? Was it still hidden deeply within, or had that hideous entity that consumed gods devoured her poor human soul as well?

Pierrette ordered Gustave to get his beast moving. The carter and her father did not resist her abrupt authority. After all, the boy Piers merely commanded them to do as they intended to do. The ass, ordinarily requiring blows to get him moving, hardly protested. He did, however, roll his near eye at Pierrette, as if blaming her for his burdens.

Breb cautiously kept the cart between himself and the beast, who had already bitten him once. Could a donkey be jealous of a man who could carry a heavier load than he? Or could an ass be annoyed that another beast of burden walked unencumbered while he was required to pull that beast's load? Breb was content to avoid the donkey's resentful eye. So, for that matter, was Pierrette.

In any case, the two Citharistans were content for her to walk with the little trader. She had seen nothing of the world beyond Citharista. This opportunity to experience someone wholly different was important. She did not know what she might learn from unprepossessing Breb, but book-learning had no texture or aroma. A child who read about battle or babies was hardly prepared for war or motherhood. She was glad to walk with Breb. The trader's huge pack was in the cart with Marie and their supplies—which, she decided, was his reason for travelling with them in the first place. "It's hard to imagine you carrying a load that would stagger a mule," she commented.

"Seeing is believing," he said.

"Why don't you have a mule?" she asked.

"When mules eat, children starve. Mules eat when they are not working, and more when they work." He shrugged apologetically. "What you see is what you get."

"As you said, 'seeing is believing.' I saw you lift your monstrous pack into the cart."

Breb taught Pierrette a bit of his almost-extinct language. There were echoes of the old Ligurian dialect of her mother's incantations, but it seemed much older, without words for commonplace things.

"Only one of us may learn your speech," he told her. "In a year or two, my sister's son will come to live with me, and I'll teach him." Breb explained that knowing a "worldly" tongue was a sickness. Wherever he went, the world changed in unpredictable ways. Good food became inedible, and foul things tasted good. Thus he was a pariah among his own kind. A necessary pariah.

"I bring them iron needles made in Massalia," he said, "but I do not speak of blacksmiths, of making metal thorns from crushed red and yellow rocks."

"Why not?"

"If needles grow from ochre, then what will spring from clay? Dare I change their world so? Seeing, after all . . ."

". . . Is believing," she blurted. "And if they see only the needles, then . . ."

"What they see is what they get." As if what Breb's people believed not only shaped their thinking, but their reality. As if they intuitively knew what she had logically worked out—that their postulates would be dangerously changed if they were forced to accept a reality that contradicted them. If all Breb's tribe were as literalistic as he was, then their knowing that a mule could carry more than a man might incapacitate him.

The trail wound along cliffs at the western edge of the peninsula. The view was overwhelming. Pierrette clutched coarse red sandstone as if the slightest breeze might sweep her over the edge, and down . . . and down. Five paces from the edge she could hear waves breaking on fallen rock below, a mere whisper at this height, but she could not see them.

"How high are we?" Gustave did not know. She crept to the edge of the scarp and peered over. The carter slithered up beside her. "I won't fall," she said.

"I just wanted to see if Ant'ny's still there," he said.

"Antony?"

"See that bit of red about a third of the way down?"

"On that little pinnacle? What is it?" Pierrette saw a speck of red like a grain of russet sand at arm's length.

"Ant'ny—and his red horse blanket and cart. He was hiding under his cart, when the wind blew it over, and him and his blanket after."

"That tiny red patch is a horse blanket? And the wreckage of a cart?" That gave some idea of the terrible height of the cliffs—without some object to give them scale, the water might have seemed only fifty paces away—or ten thousand.

"I saw a Saracen war galley a hundred paces off the rocks, and it was the size of an ant—not even a big ant. These cliffs are a mile high, they say."

"Not that high."

"Who's to know? No one's going to climb down and measure."

"I'll find out," Pierrette said. She looked southward along the boulder-strewn coast, until she judged that her line of vision was close to forty-five degrees from the horizontal, and fixed a particular rock in memory. Then she backed up, and faced south. "I'm going to pace off the distance to the bottom of that cliff."

"You can't! You'll end up down there with Ant'ny."

"I'm not going down—just along the edge. Are you coming?"

"I better. Your Pa'll have my skin if you fall." Pierrette picked a fairly straight path south, making full strides. Her paces were shorter than the old Roman standard—she had once measured them between two worn milestones. Twelve hundred and two paces to the mile—to one thousand soldierly paces. A pace was two steps: left, right, or about five feet.

She counted two hundred paces, then crawled to the edge and peered down. The distinctive rock was still a bit south. She backed up, and walked fifty paces more. "Close enough. For a more accurate measurement, I'd need a graduated quadrant." Gustave did not ask what that was.

"The height of the cliff is one fifth of a mile," she said, "not a mile. Tell 'them' I measured it for you." It was the first practical use she had made of geometry. Assuming that her estimate of forty-five degrees, at her first location, was close, and that she was directly over the stone 250 paces on, then the angle between stone, herself, and the first position was ninety degrees, and the original sight line was the hypotenuse of a right isosceles triangle. The distance she had paced was thus equal to the height of the cliff. "*Quod erat demonstrandum,*" she said, with great satisfaction.

At nightfall, they made camp well back from the cliff. Marie neither improved nor worsened. Her clothing stank, but there was no water to spare.

While Gilles and Gustave gathered wood, Pierrette attempted to light tinder without flint and steel—with no more result than the night before. Did her magic, like Anselm's, depend upon proximity to the Eagle's Beak?

The chilly night passed uneventfully. Pierrette huddled close to Marie in the wagon, and wished that poor Antony's horse blanket had been eighty paces nearer.

In the morning, Breb shouldered his great pack. "Aren't you coming with us?" Pierrette asked.

"I dare not. The low air saps me. I will take the high road around."

"But that will take weeks. Leave your pack in the cart."

He shook his head. "I fear what I might see in the town below. Should I go there, I might not ever find my folk again. Besides, there are other valleys, other people who speak my tongue. I must visit them, or they will have to appoint one of their own like me."

She thought she understood why he could not go down to the fishing village. Who would believe such a little man could lift such a burden? As he said, seeing was believing. He might not be able to shoulder his burden at all, among so many people convinced he could not. So he would keep to the heights.

It took two days to reach the base of the cliffs. The ground sloped up from the north, dissected by ravines. The trail twisted back on itself time and again.

Halfway down, a small spring trickled from the rocks, and they filled their water-keg. Marie phlegmatically endured a cold bath, and stood naked, covered in goosebumps, while Pierrette washed her garment. Pierrette suspected that any discomfort she felt was nothing compared with what had caused her spirit to flee in the first place.

"The road to the village winds down that defile," Gustave announced, "but I'm not about to risk it in the dark. Those villagers keep heaps of rocks up above the trail, for bandits."

Gilles maintained his silence. Pierrette was still bitterly angry with his failure to protect Marie. If her sister had not been a constant reminder, she might have tried to draw her father out of his guilty reveries. Perhaps there would be time on the trip home.

Again Pierrette voiced her firemaking spell, and drew a quick, amazed breath. Had she seen a blue luminescence? The sun's afterglow made it difficult to tell. Again, she uttered the words . . . and a pale, cool glow suffused the air. A glow, not a spark. As quickly as it had formed, it faded, and she was reduced to kindling fire by ordinary means.

Would she ever understand? If a spell did not work, or worked differently, then, by her hypothesis, it meant one of its postulates had changed. In Citharista, the spell caused fire. On the heights, it did nothing at all. Now . . . a blue glow?

Her suspicion about distance from the Eagle's Beak was wrong. The spell was doing something. She decided to keep trying; if it changed again, that might provide further clues.

In the morning, Gustave went to the village. Pierrette dozed in a shady spot under some brush. Movement across her thigh alerted her, and she opened one eye. "Oh, aren't you lovely," she murmured. It was a ladder snake—so called for the linear pattern of its scales. She felt lucky. Snakes were sacred to Ma, for they lived close to her, never lifting their bellies from her. Even vipers were blessed, and as none had ever done Pierrette harm, she was not afraid. Ladder snakes were not poisonous, anyway.

The tiny copse was too small to support such a fat creature. "Have you come to encourage me?" The snake did not respond, except to look up at the source of the sounds. It slithered on its way, leaving Pierrette cheered by the encounter.

Gustave returned with stiff sun-dried fish, fat round loaves, and sharp goat cheese. Breaking a fibrous fish, Pierrette soaked the chunks in water to make stew. She tossed in fresh thyme and a few olives. Gustave produced clay cups and a small amphora of red wine. "There's no point in pressing on today, so we can take time to enjoy this."

As they ate, and afterward, Gilles and the carter drank cup after cup of sour wine. Gilles drank steadily, and Gustave matched him cup for cup. The carter attempted to sing, and enjoined Gilles to join in, but Pierrette's father did not drink for the joy of inebriation, but to reach an ideal (and unattainable) state of forgetfulness.

Pierrette again bathed Marie and saw to her needs, feeding her bread dipped in wine prudently set aside. Before retiring to the hard bed of the cart, she draped thin blankets over both men, hoping they would sleep through the night and not stumble about upsetting things.

During the night Marie awakened, trembling. There was no moon, and Pierrette could not see her face. She held up her hand and whispered the spell that no longer produced fire, and was rewarded with the bluish glow, enough light to see terror in Marie's wide, empty eyes. Shortly, they closed again.

Holding Marie close, suffused in magical light, Pierrette raged at the crazy unpredictability of witchery, sorcery, and all things magical, at the capricious greediness of her father

and the castellan Jerome—and above all, at the vast manipu-
lations of gods and demons who consumed each other and
any hapless mortals who stumbled while crossing their
unimaginable, unseen paths.

Carefully containing ire that boiled up hot as the lavas
of lost Thera, Pierrette rolled away from Marie, taking her
witch-light with her. She walked from the camp, and emerged
on a bare promontory. She could see the flat, starlit sea,
the black cliffs where she had played with geometry, and
on her right the looming shadows of hills yet uncrossed.

"I *will* understand!" she hissed between clenched teeth—
and her words seemed to fly forth as if she had shouted.
"I will!" She flung her arms upward and flailed at the
uncaring stars. The light that suffused her fingertips flew
away with the momentum of her gesture. Upward it soared,
coalescing into a sharp point of light, a fallen star returning to the heavens, then was lost amidst uncounted other
lights. Pierrette's challenge was given, her vow sealed, and
the very skies seemed no longer quite the same.

Part Three ❧ *Tiro* (Apprentice)

The student struggles to learn his chosen craft, and the teacher to guide his learning in profitable directions. Yet when all is said, much must still be done; some learning can only be accomplished with tools in hand, not books, and proficiency earned with bruises and calluses, when student becomes apprentice. This now becomes an apprentice's tale.

Otho, Bishop of Nemausus
The Sorceress's Tale

Chapter 15 ∾ A Christian City

Again, Gustave decided that the tortuous path close to the sea would be safer from human dangers than the relatively easy road through the valley. The outcrops turned more gray than white, more gray than brown, and even bright sunlight failed to remove their gloomy stain. The heights were a rock-strewn plain, unsheltered from the dry, dust-laden winds. Still, glimpses of deep sun-dappled inlets refreshed them: bright aquamarine in the shallows, and dark, rich blue in their depths.

The treeless, soilless plain had once been blanketed with tall pines, but a thousand years of grazing had stripped it until no single seedling was left to fight its way through bedrock. Was this a foretaste of the Dark Time? Would the last surviving men who looked upon it blame not consuming gods, but their fathers and grandfathers, who had stripped the world?

Pierrette performed a quiet experiment, unseen by Gustave or Gilles (who walked on ahead), and unremarked by Marie, whose eyes remained fixed upon the floor of the cart, and hardly moved.

She murmured the small spell—but even when she shadowed her hand under a blanket, saw neither glow nor spark. That was the sixth time she had uttered the words since leaving their low camp. The first time, the blue glow had been like the night before. She saw no difference the second time, but as the travellers approached that indistinct line where trees gave way to scrub, lush undergrowth to low, stiff-leaved plants, the glow weakened, and the last three

149

times there had been no visible result. She decided to wait until just before they started down toward Massalia before she tried again.

"Below is the last you'll see of the Middle Sea," said Gustave, pointing. The long embayment was broader than the narrow, water-filled fissures Pierrette knew. "When we cross to the far side"—he pointed northwestward—"we'll descend to the city. But tonight we'll camp here."

That night Pierrette awakened to the sound of many voices singing. She sat up and peered into the darkness, but the sound had stopped. She heard Gilles's snores and Gustave's rough breathing, and Marie also slept on undisturbed. Clearly, Pierrette had been dreaming.

A breeze stirred her hair, and she caught a whiff of wood smoke. Getting up, she walked away from the camp, until she could see the broad fjord. She was too far away to see the light of a fire along the rocky shore, but she stared until her eyes began playing tricks on her.

The way the starlit cliffs reflected on the bay, it looked almost as if the water was much lower, and the calanque narrower. In the illusory depths of that fissure, as if it were on an imaginary shoreline deep in the sea, she saw a flickering orange point like a distant fire. Again, she heard the rhythmic "hunh, hunh, hunh" of male voices and the higher, gracile notes of women, a wordless song that made her feel sad and alone—because she was not nestled by the warm, friendly blaze with the singers.

She snorted derisively. There were no voices, and the firelike glow in the water's depths was phosphorescence, as some sea creature roiled the mud at the bottom of the deep bay. Had it been otherwise—a reflection of a real fire—she would have seen the source.

She returned to her hard bed, and lay listening. The voices welled up again. "Come to us," they sang, "come back to when this land was new." For no reason she could define, tears sprang to her eyes, and when she awakened again, to Gustave and Gilles's busy clatter, she was stuffed up, as though she had been weeping.

As long as the northeast side of the calanque was visible from the road, she stared as if she could see those who had called her, but she was too far away, even had the

strange firelike light not come from far beneath the waters—
or from the depths of her own imagination.

Pierrette repeated her experiment as they descended toward
Massalia. They were halfway down a road that wound down
one narrow gorge after another. There was no spark, only
a diffuse ball-shaped glow—yet not exactly as before; it was
not blue, but clear and colorless. It became brighter each
time she tried the spell. Fearing it would be noticed, she
did not try it again.

"There's the abbey," Gustave remarked shortly later. He
pointed past a rocky dome and a notch in the coast. Lying
low on the south shore was a large church and a sprawl of
buildings surrounded by a wall. "They call the Abbey of Saint
Victor 'the key to the harbor.' Saracens failed to capture it
many times. Some say Lazarus is buried there."

"Where is the nunnery?" Pierrette asked.

"Outside the abbey walls—just east of the church."

The harbor was a calanque, a natural inlet, only in the
broadest sense. Its shores were lined with stonework in
various states of disrepair. On the north side—it ran eastward from its ocean mouth—were more buildings than she
had ever seen. They reached up three, four, even five stories; brown, buff, and white blocks topped with red, above
which thrust columns, ruins of ancient age. At the head of
the bay was a broad marsh of high, tasseled reeds.

"Stick close," Gustave cautioned Gilles. "There are thieves."

"Where is the house of the scholar Muhammad ibn Saul?"
Pierrette asked.

Gustave eyed her askance. "In the old city, above the ruins
of the 'Roman place."

"The Roman place?"

"A huge half-round of stone seats, where pagans cavorted.
It lies on t' harbor side."

Pierrette was uncomfortable. In Citharista, Christian folk
lived amidst a welter of older beliefs, and anyone might
secretly cling to family traditions, trusted rituals handed down
from Ligurian, Roman, Greek, or Celtic ancestors. Here in
the shadow of the abbey and the scattering of churches,
Pierrette sensed that such beliefs were buried deeply, perhaps entirely abandoned.

At the abbey Gilles, bearing Otho's letter, was invited

inside. He emerged shortly later. "The nunnery lies back down this street the way we came." The street reminded Pierrette of the eastern end of Citharista—run down, with rubble-humped vacancies between surviving buildings. The main town, across the harbor, was less deteriorated. There was a causeway across the bleak cane-marsh at the head of the harbor, and a gate with crenelated towers,

Pierrette imagined the city as it had once been: from a Phoaecean salt-traders' settlement, it had grown to a major port under the Greeks, who built pillared temples on the three northern hills. The northern hub of Greek trade with the Gauls, Massalia later allied with the Romans against fierce Celtic tribes. Along with its rival Arelate, farther west, it had remained prosperous through the long, sunny centuries of the Pax Romana, the Roman Peace, and had throbbed with the steady pulse of Mediterranean trade.

Centuries after the fall of Rome, Arelate and Avennio allied with the Saracens, caring less for Christian Franks than for trade with Africa and the Levant. That Christian hammer, Charles Martel, sacked both cities. Massalia played one power against the other, and remained undevastated—though the town shrank until the Roman gate lay well outside its rough new walls.

The nunnery was no fortress. In times of danger its women fled within Saint Victor's walls. "Wait here," commanded a hawk-faced woman in coarse homespun. She motioned to Pierrette to enter. "We don't allow men inside," she explained, "but as you are still unshaven . . ."

Slim, paired columns supported a shading overhang around the court. Vines twined, and red flowers as big as her hand gave off heady perfumes. Neat rows of thorny roses lay interspersed with fragrant herbs. "These are our medicines," the nun explained. "Rose hips, for the wasting disease and sailor's complaints, Frankish 'worts' that only grow in the shade . . ."

"And heart's balm!" Pierrette exclaimed incautiously. "I had seeds, but I couldn't make them grow."

"You know herbs, boy? A strange preoccupation—but I must fetch our Mother. Your sister's condition is new to me, but Mother has seen stranger things."

Left alone—for Marie, in her mute state, was no more company than a stone pillar—Pierrette pinched leaves to release telltale fragrances, and studied the shapes of each bush, leaf, and blossom. She knew many herbs by scent, from her mother's lost collection and Anselm's storeroom, but most she had only seen as dry, brown stuff in little pots. She wanted to recognize the plants if she saw them again.

"A curious child indeed!" crackled an old woman's voice. Pierrette spun about, and half rose to her feet. She knew that voice. She stared, wide-eyed. There in the shadow of the delicate colonnade stood . . . Ma, the old woman of the pool. There was no mistaking those furrowed cheeks, the high cheekbones, the knife-blade nose—and above all, the eyes, as dark and clear as the spring itself. Pierrette gasped.

"Don't be afraid, girl . . . you are a girl, aren't you, in spite of your clothing? We won't miss a few pinched leaves."

"I merely wished to smell them, Lady." The woman was Ma—yet she was not. She did not recognize Pierrette. How could that be?

"Keep your nose a safe distance away," the woman admonished her. "Only yesterday we killed a snake—a vicious thing with a ladder pattern on its back. It struck sister Julia, and we don't know if she'll recover."

"A ladder pattern?" Pierrette was about to remark that ladder snakes were not poisonous, but cautiously modified her words. "I didn't know ladder snakes were dangerous."

"They are serpents, stricken by God to crawl on their bellies, for having tempted Adam and his wife. Snakes are deadly abominations."

Pierrette was taken aback by such hatred of Ma's creatures—from the lips of one who looked like the goddess herself. "I won't smell the herbs again."

"Just be careful," the woman grumbled. "Why are you so interested in them, anyway?"

"If I see them again, I want to know them by sight."

"A girl herbalist, dressed as a boy . . . Perhaps later you will explain—but now, let me examine your sister. . . ." She guided Marie to a stone bench, and put a hand to her chin, turning her head from side to side.

Lifting an eyelid with a dry old thumb, she peered as if looking within the girl's head. "I need a brighter light," she murmured.

That familiar, trusted voice . . . Pierrette did something risky and foolish. "Here, Lady," she said, stretching out her hand.

From her fingertips emanated clear, pure light, a sourceless glow bright as a handful of candles, yet without smoke.

The woman methodically studied Marie's pupils, as if she had not noticed the light's source, but when she finished, her eyes widened. "Saint Mary's Light! Are you an angel come to visit?"

"I don't know what you mean, Lady," Pierrette replied, just now fully realizing her error. The glow disappeared.

"I didn't imagine it—it was the pure light of the Virgin, and it hovered by your hand. Tonight, when we've settled your sister, and have sent your men to an inn, you and I will talk." She stood. "Sister Agathe!"

The hawk-faced woman reappeared so quickly that Pierrette suspected she had been peeking around the door frame. "Yes, Mother?" she asked. The woman who resembled Ma was the abbess, herself.

"Help this . . . this boy," she commanded. "Take his sister to the south chamber on the third floor. See that both have baths—and don't gossip about them. In fact, say nothing at all, until I give you leave. Oh, yes—send the men to the Red Fish Inn, and have Sister Marthe prepare soft food for our patient. The other child will dine with me, later."

Sister Agathe, obedient to the letter of the abbess's command, said nothing. She guided Marie up narrow stone stairs to the third floor. Low afternoon sunlight angled across the chamber there, tinting the unglazed floor tiles rich, warm vermilion. Gesturing wordlessly, she indicated that Pierrette should undress Marie. She departed.

"What have I done?" Pierrette murmured. "The abbess is not Ma, though she looks and sounds like her. She is Christian, and has seen me perform a pagan spell." Yet the abbess had mistaken it for a mystical Christian phenomenon. "I have to make sure she continues to think that," Pierrette told the unresponsive Marie, "until I am safely away from here." She had no illusions. The old woman would not be put off.

Sister Agathe brought warm water and cloths. They bathed Marie and dressed her in a white shift. Marie looked more like an angel than Pierrette ever could. The nun spooned rich soup into her mouth, tilting her head and stroking her throat to make her swallow.

With Sister Agathe thus occupied, Pierrette washed herself, removing one garment at a time, putting her tunic back
on before removing her trousers. Watching Sister Agathe,
she felt reassured that, whether or not the nuns could cure
Marie, she would be well cared for.

Pierrette was glad when the nun left. She had something
to think about: snakes. Had Sister Julia truly been bitten
by a ladder snake? If so, how could she be genuinely ill?

She considered the abbess's vilification of legless beasts.
Stricken by God? Perhaps, here, ladder snakes were indeed
deadly. Perhaps the abbess had stated not an ignorant city
person's opinion, but a . . . a postulate. Uncomfortably, she
thought of the terrible spell that she had used against Jerome.
Snakes and sex. Snakes and temptation. Could snakes change
their natures as did a certain magical light, from one domain
to the next? How could she know, without risking being bitten
if she guessed wrongly?

Another nun came for Pierrette. Sister Agathe's eyes never
left Marie. Pierrette was hungry. Even her fear of the abbess's
questions could not quiet her grumbling stomach.

Pierrette thought the abbess's chamber too grand for the
simple wooden bed, the rough deal table and three-legged
stools. A single candlestick and two wooden bowls, with
brass spoons, were all the table bore. Yet within moments
a young woman brought a lidded clay pot, carried between
thick rags. Escaping steam filled the room with the aroma
of seafood, onions, and familiar spices. Pierrette's mouth
watered, and her stomach moaned.

The abbess laughed. "Sit down. We'll feed the lion inside
you before we talk." The stew that she ladled from the pot
contained whole mouthsful of redfish, chewy *langouste*, and
mullet. "Haven't you eaten boiled fish before, child?" she
joked—seeing how Pierrette hurried each bite from bowl to
mouth. Pierrette paused long enough to acknowledge that she
had—but never so deliciously spiced, and of such delicate
flavor.

"This is Sister Marthe's recipe," said the abbess. "She is
Massaliote, of the twentieth generation, and claims her secret
is as old. She doesn't know I've discovered her trick." She
paused. Pierrette, whose mouth was again full, raised a
dutifully curious eyebrow. "When the broth has simmered
well, she throws pine knots on the fire, and it boils over.

The others mock her 'forgetfulness.' The spilling soup quenches the flames, and only then does she remove the pot from the fire. Can you figure it out?"

Pierrette, swallowing, pondered. Was the question more than it seemed? She did not hasten to answer it. She envisioned the cooking process, the look of the simmering broth, and . . . "Of course!" she exclaimed. "When it boils over, the floating fat washes away, leaving the broth clear, not heavy with oils."

"I wasn't mistaken," the abbess said softly. "You don't accept the first explanation to come to mind, thus scratching an itch without ridding yourself of the flea. Let's sit on those pillows. It's time for other questions."

All too soon they were settled. When her questioner asked how Marie's condition had come about, Pierrette said only that the Burgundian knight had claimed the first night with her, and it had driven her mad.

Yet the tale lacked meat, like a weak soup. As the abbess tasted it, she was aware that something was missing. "Rape is not a treasured memory," she said reflectively. "Yet it seldom drives us mad." She spoke with confident authority.

This place, Pierrette realized, was more—and less—than a religious institution. The sisters were not all drawn here by abounding Faith alone. Some were novices whose eyes shone with holy zeal, but children's voices echoed in the courtyard. Their mothers were refugees, driven to holy vows less by conviction than necessity. But were they less sincere, for that?

The abbess was still speaking. . . . "Rape destroys innocence and trust, and sometimes drives us to seek God, but doesn't drive us so far from the world that we can't return. No, child. There is much you haven't said. If we are to guide your sister back to this world, you must risk telling me."

"I'm afraid, Lady," Pierrette murmured, eyes downcast. "I'm afraid of the clubs the *gens* of this city wield." She then told of her mother's death—and of the small witcheries that led to it.

Gently, the woman with the trusted face and voice of Ma pulled apart the tangled skein of Pierrette's memory, until almost all was told. Yet Pierrette had not once mentioned Anselm, her studies—or the fire spell that now gave cool, colorless light.

"Much remains unsaid," the abbess concluded, when Pierrette had told what she saw during the All-Saints mass, and described the visions beside the pool of Ma. Recounting the transformation of Jerome, she trembled, and the abbess gathered her close. Now she huddled in the woman's skirts, as coarse and brown as the beech leaves that rustled dryly beneath her beside the quiet pool.

"Some say 'Marie' derives from 'Marius,'" the abbess said. "I am called 'Sophia Maria.' Yet there's more to my name—and your sister's—than remembrance of a Roman general who fought a battle a day's march from here. Tell me what you know of words and names, child. No angry *gens* will hear."

Pierrette spoke. The names Maria, Marie, Mary, and Marius all sprang from one name: Ma. She hesitated to claim that Christian prayers to Mary were heard by the spirit who listened by the sacred pool . . . but Ma was also virginal, a mother, and her offspring died and were reborn.

"I'm not ignorant of the old ways, girl," said the abbess. "I sprang from the same rocky soil, the same clear sunlight, as you. Is it any wonder the three Marys who brought Jesus' words to this land were welcomed? Who were they but messengers of a deity we already knew—yet with a new message, indeed."

Pierrette had not heard how those Christian Marys had come to Provence—the Roman Province of Gaul. "They came on a boat without sails," said the abbess, "set adrift off the shore of the Holy Land, conveyed here by storm and current." She smiled wryly. "Or having decided upon their apostolic missions, they hired a fast galley.

"Perhaps," she continued, "they were blown ashore near a tiny village at the mouth of the Rhodanus; yet being aware of the political climate after Christ's crucifixion, they chose not to disembark in this busy port, whose officials might arrest them.

"Whatever the case, seven saints put ashore where the town named for them—Saintes-Maries-by-the-Sea—now stands. Mary of Magdala went north to preach in Lugdunum, a stronghold of Lugh, an older god.

"Martha, her sister, also named for Ma, went elsewhere to preach, and two Marys—one the mother of the disciple James, the other of James the Elder and his brother John—remained beside the sea, because both were old. Their servant Sara, an Egyptian, remained with them. Even today Gypsies, folk of her blood, make pilgrimage to her grave.

"Lazarus, brother to Martha and the Magdalene, is buried not a mile from here, beneath Saint Victor's church. Cedonius, born blind yet healed by our Lord, and Maximinus, went their separate ways."

The abbess sighed. "Now, child, we've come full circle, for the cave where Mary Magdalene spent her last years had long been home to another, to Ma, who made women fertile. So you see? Your worship, your mother's before you, is no sin. She who recites the litany of Saint Marie Madeleine prays also to Ma, who is hidden twice in the saint's own name.

"Child? Have you fallen asleep?" Indeed, Pierrette had. "Oh my." The abbess picked the girl up as if she had been a small child, and laid her in her own bed.

Pierrette awakened to the yeasty aroma of baking bread. The abbess raised her head from a pillow on the floor. "Ah, you are awake. I must have dozed, myself. I'm grateful that God left me my nose. Others younger than I can no longer rejoice in the scent of fresh-baked bread." She rose stiffly to her feet. "Come, girl—or shall I call you 'boy' outside this room? If God and Sister Sarah's cow have been kind, there may be warm, sweet milk to dip our bread in."

There was milk, and a compote of sweet figs. The abbess left Pierrette in the small refectory after a perfunctory sip of milk and a single chunk of bread torn from the center of a crusty loaf.

She returned shortly later. "Marie's condition is unchanged," she said. "Rest, care, and new surroundings may work with our prayers to heal her, but I promise nothing. If she weren't so weak, I'd suggest you take her to the shrine of the Marys by the sea, but that's an arduous voyage. We shall do what we can."

Pierrette thanked her. "Is my father here? I don't know the way to the inn."

"He'll be along. And Sister Clara's boy Jules will show you to the scholar ibn Saul's. But first, join me in the chapel, and we'll pray for Marie—and for you."

Pierrette hesitated. "I'm not baptized, Lady."

The abbess snorted. "I'm not a priest. We are two virgins,

one old, one young, who will beg that another take pity on her namesake, Marie."

Wearing her paganism like a dirty sack, Pierrette entered the Christian shrine.

The first thing she saw was the light. Rays of morning sun reached through glazed windows, and lay lightly across the carved and painted image of Mary, whose dress was white beneath a sea blue cape. Her sculpted face was sweet, her smile benign, with perhaps the tiniest lines of mirth about the corners of her mouth, as if the woodcarver had known something that books, scholars, and priests did not.

The abbess recited the litany. Pierrette nodded politely at every pause, because she did not know the words. Then the abbess turned to her. "Will you grant an old woman's wish?"

"I'm not a witch, Lady," Pierrette said, misunderstanding. "I have no power to grant wishes."

The abbess laughed. "Oh, you have power to grant mine. I wish to look upon the holy light one last time before you depart."

"Oh, Lady, I cannot! This is a Christian place, and the words of the spell are as old as the world. It wouldn't be proper, here."

"Let God—and Mary—judge. I think your 'spell' is a prayer. I saw that light before, remember, and judged it pure. Must I plead with you?"

Pierrette nervously stretched forth her hand. She did not speak the words aloud, only mouthing their shapes. For a long moment, nothing happened, as if this place was like the high country where the spell had been powerless, but then . . . The glow that hovered at the tips of her fingers was the same shade as the daylight coming through the old, violet-tinged glass, purified of the yellow warmth of ordinary sunlight.

The old woman gazed raptly. She grasped Pierrette's wrist, lifting her hand—and the light suffusing it—toward the image. "Watch over this one, Mother, for she is one of yours, though she does not know it." Magical light and sun's rays merged as Pierrette's hand rose, and when the abbess released it, it fell to her side, only a hand—but was the sunlight on Mary's face brighter?

It was not easy to leave Marie behind, to accept that the

nuns could give her care that her own sister could not, but Mother Sophia's warmth made it less hard.

Pierrette rode in the cart while her father, Gustave, and Jules strode on ahead. Pierrette was relieved to be out of there. For so long, she had considered Christians the folk who had killed her mother—who smiled at her pagan child, knowing they had themselves wielded clubs. Yet she trusted the old woman who looked like Ma. Perhaps, later, she could sort it out. Now she was too busy gawking.

Watchmen passed the party through the city's gate. The cart clattered down the broad Roman *decumanus*—the main east-west street. There was much to see. On a stony hill, temple columns jutted like stiff fingers into the clear sky. A church incorporated round, fluted column-segments into its patchwork, unplastered walls.

Massalia had been built, torn down, and rebuilt with the same stones. No edifice was of one era, but spanned decades and centuries. Pierrette wondered if this stone or that had been part of a Phoaecean warehouse, a Greek temple, or the great half-circular Roman theater—even now being quarried for its stone. The cart swung to the right, into the market square.

What a market! Cobbles of a dozen eras paved its sloping expanse, and merchants' wares formed aisles where folk of all descriptions jostled shoulder to shoulder, a moving, pulsing mass of white, dun, and occasional brilliant colors. Gustave was hard pressed to guide the cart through; their destination lay on the western side. She glimpsed peaches, red and gold in the morning sunlight, dark figs and olives, great pink amphorae of yellow and brown grain, bolts of cloth the colors of sunset . . .

Despite Saracen control of the sea lanes, the market's wealth came from ships—not all from Christian lands. One stall's Egyptian glass sparkled like sapphire, and another was draped with silk from beyond fabled India.

She breathed a sigh of relief—and disappointment—when they cleared the last shouting merchant. Passing beneath a lintel of megalithic proportion, they entered a quiet street just wide enough for the cart. "There's Muhammad ibn Saul's house," announced Jules, pointing past a tavern where men sat drinking from clay cups.

Pierrette would have known ibn Saul's house had the boy

said nothing. A colonnade from one side to the other butted against the plain walls of its neighbors, creating a haven of shade beneath a red tile roof. At the precise center were doors framed with blue-glazed tiles. Their motif foiled the eye's attempt to follow.

The doors were thick, dark-stained wood, hung on iron hinges whose leaves spread like dividing, protecting fingers. A bell cord led through a bronze grommet set in the wall.

Gustave guided his donkey into the shade beneath the colonnade. "I don't like this place," he said, eyeing the unusual architecture.

"Why don't you and Father wait over there," Pierrette suggested, looking toward the tavern. Both men were glad to follow her suggestion. She pulled the bell cord, and heard a silvery tinkling note. One door opened a crack. A single bright blue eye peered through.

"What do you want?" said a young voice laced with thick, Frankish overtones.

"I am Piers, apprentice to the magus Anselm of Citharista," she said, deliberately pitching her voice low, the voice of the boy she appeared to be. "I have a parcel for the scholar ibn Saul."

The door opened further. "My master isn't here," said the doorkeeper, a boy no older than Pierrette. But what a boy! His hair was the color of a polished brass cup. His nose was short, turned up, yet neither weak nor funny-looking. A more typical Mediterranean nose would have looked out of proportion on his pale, pink-tinged face.

"What are you staring at? Haven't you seen a Frank before?" She had not. Neither had she seen a boy with such broad shoulders, with a narrow waist drawn in by a belt bossed with shiny metal—gold? "Don't just stand there. Give me the package, or come in."

She was shocked by her reaction. It was not the boy's strangeness, but that she had—and did—look upon him as . . . as a man. She had briefly—but so intensely— imagined herself drawn close to his broad chest, his arm thrown protectively over her shoulder, her head against the soft, white fabric of his tunic. The laces of his shirt were loose, and fine, golden hairs curled in the V-shaped opening.

The door thudded shut behind her. "I'm Lovi," her host

said, unaware of her stupefaction. "That's 'Clovis' in my own language."

"It's a famous name," Pierrette responded vaguely. "Does the blood of kings run in your veins?"

"Has your master taught you history? Is he from a far eastern land like mine?"

Pierrette looked around herself, not answering. They stood in a tiny anteroom with an iron gate beyond, through which streamed bright daylight.

"Oh—I'm sorry," Lovi said. "Let's go within. Are you thirsty? I have wine, and ripe peaches. It's pleasantly cool in the courtyard."

The image of ripe peaches overrode caution and any thought for her father and Gustave—who would be tipsy before long, and would not care. Lovi opened the iron gate. "Find a spot in the shade. I'll fetch refreshments." Pierrette eyed him as he strode away. A small fountain trickled into a square stone trough, making wet, cool sounds.

"What's wrong with me?" she demanded of herself. "He's only a strange-looking boy." Yet she wanted him to like her. Her intensity made her desire for Anselm's approval seem weak and pale.

Had Marie been well, Pierrette would have looked forward to a whispered conversation beneath their bedclothes. Had her mother been . . . alive . . . she would have asked her. Yet in this great, tawdry city, the solace of Ma was far away, and she would have to handle these feelings with no advice at all.

"Why the sad face?" asked Lovi, returning with an amber-glazed jug and two cups, and a basket of peaches.

She told him about Marie. "The sisters will care well for her," he said, "but you'll never get her back."

"What do you mean?"

"Calloused knees and a voice hoarse from praying are better than babies, death in childbed, or a husband who knows the tavernkeeper's face better than hers." He grimaced. "I'm glad I'm not a woman. I can go adventuring with my master." He motioned her to sit on a wooden bench by the fountain. "If only he weren't so old. I hardly ever get to talk with anyone my own age, and I never meet any girls."

"I'm not so sure that women can't have adventures too." She really wanted to tell him that she was a girl. She imagined having a companion, this fine-looking young man, to share all the wonders of the world with. It was possible, wasn't it? If she really wanted to go adventuring, wouldn't Anselm write a letter to his friend ibn Saul for her? Impulsively, she rested her hand on his knee. "Not everything is as it seems. Perhaps there is a way for you—and for me— to have what we want. I have a secret I want to tell you . . ."

But Lovi brushed her hand away, and abruptly stood. "No! That's not what I want. I am not like that. Wait here. My master prepared a parcel for yours."

She had hoped he would sit with her. Why had he so suddenly cooled? If she had long hair, and wore a pretty dress, he would have, she thought bitterly. If he knew I am a girl . . . She snatched a peach from the basket, and bit into it. Juice dribbled down her chin. It was ripe and sweet, but she spat it with a loud, flapping sound. It fell into the water trough. She bit again, and spat. That seemed to dull the hurt, so she did it again.

She finished the peach, and stuck another in her shirt. She had just hidden it when Lovi returned. He went to the iron gate, and swung it open. "Here's the packet." His face was an expressionless mask. "Take it, and go. My master and I want nothing to do with boys like you." Before she was entirely out the door, he was pushing it shut.

"Boys like me? I don't understand. You don't understand." She had thought he had recognized her for what she was, but he had not.

"I understand all too well," he said, pushing the door the rest of the way shut.

She stumbled across the street, tears blurring her vision.

She tried hard to keep all expression from her face. When she stepped outside, she did not turn around. She heard the door hinges creak. She heard the bolt thump home. All the lonelinesses she had ever felt seemed to rush in on her at once.

She climbed into the cart, and pulled a blanket over herself, covering even her head. She wept long—but quietly. When drunken Gilles stumbled out of the tavern, he found her asleep. "Never mind," he mumbled, and returned to the tavern, where he found a himself place to sleep— under a table.

✧   ✧   ✧

If youth were not resilient, able to absorb the brunt of what the gods and other people threw its way, there would be few folk in Provence, for life is seldom without tribulation. But Pierrette was young.

The masquerade must end. She would have it out with Gilles when they got back to Citharista. Perhaps it would be embarrassing at first, but there was no longer reason for deception. Gilles was well off. The castellan could no longer press him to sell the grove.

Yes, she decided, I'll let my hair grow out, and when it is of sufficient length to braid . . . I'll become not Piers, but Pierrette. Should she step from the house wearing woman's clothing, and go to the marketplace with jars of oil to sell? Should she have P'er Otho announce it after mass, and save her explanations? There did not seem to be an easy way.

Without Marie to care for, Pierrette resumed her experiments with a will, drawing forth "Saint Mary's Light" several times on the way up to the high plain. She watched for any change in the light's quality, but it only faded as the cart ascended. Coming down to the broad calanque, that effect was reversed. The first glimmer was blue as sapphire. By nightfall, when they camped near the head of the small rocky bay, it had regained full intensity.

Pierrette again began to hear voices. She walked to the edge of the cliff, and peered outward. There, as before, was the glow of an impossible fire within the watery depths. Again, she felt indescribable yearning, a sense that somewhere below was companionship and warmth, laughter and friendship—that all she had to do was to pick her way among the jagged boulders and prickly oaks, and she would find fulfillment.

Her feet hovered on the edge of the slope, the edge of a decision, but at last she turned her back on the cove. Too much was unfinished. If she went down there, she would never return, would never know if Marie would heal, if Anselm faded, and his rocky keep fell traceless into the sea. She would never learn another spell, or read another book, for whoever or whatever was down there had no use for such things.

That night, as if her subconscious had decided to reward her wise choice, she dreamed of the Golden Man. They ate crisp venison by firelight, and he sang her a song without words, its simple rhythmic tune the one she had heard issuing from the depths of the calanque, where campfires had burned beneath the waters.

∾

Pierrette's Journal

I was right not to descend that slope, at that particular time—if indeed time has meaning in such places. Time was not my concern then, for I had just discovered the first principle of magic and sorcery: the boundaries between magical realms.

Mountains and windswept heights are boundaries, immune to even the greatest spells. Inconvenient for those who depend on magic to start campfires, they have advantages as well, for on the heights one is safe from the magics of others, and can choose which magical realm to enter, which watershed slope to descend.

Is there "Christian" light or "pagan"? I do not know. But even then, having decided not to descend into the enchanted depths of that disappearing sea, I began to formulate a second principle, a concept crucial to my understanding not only of the deadly fading that threatened Anselm, Guihen, and dark John, but to my understanding of the Christians' Satan and his consumption of the older gods—and, eventually, of the Black Time itself.

Belief was the key. In Christian Massalia—with its churches, abbey, and nunnery, its streetcorner shrines and catacombs—no older magic could endure. There, one postulate of my fire spell was based in a different catechism than in Citharista or Breb's wilderness—that admitted only one light, one darkness: Christian and Satanic. There ladder snakes became vipers, for Christian snakes partake of the first serpent's guilt.

In the low valley that descended to the calanque called Sormiou, with no town or human population, an older belief held sway, and a different light obtained.

In Citharista and its valley, from the sea to the pool Ma, Christian, pagan, and a mechanistic magic owing debts to Greeks and Phoenicians endured, and the spell brought forth not sweet sunlight or the blue light of stars on a cold night, but practical, usable fire.

But my discoveries were new and fragile then, and I had much to learn before I could apply them to my life's yet unknown task . . .

Chapter 16 ∾ An Experiment

Anselm had not faded away. He was delighted with the parcel from ibn Saul—an account of the Wendish folk of the far northern seacoasts. The Frankish king was concerned with Wendish expansion, and had financed the scholar's voyage to the Viking Sea.

Pierrette eagerly read of ibn Saul's voyage. One passage in particular entranced her. She did not know, on the first reading or the second, how important the knowledge it contained would be.

∾

The Wendish Women's Rite

I hid with the village men at the edge of the clearing. The priest stood on the rock. It was the dark of the twelfth moon. Women danced naked round the standing stone. "Run through water," cried the priest. He dipped a balsam branch in a blue-painted wooden bowl, and sprinkled water on them.

"Run through fire," he shrieked. He blew on a coal in a brass pot, igniting bark from the paper tree, and cast it among dry boughs. Three times around the stone the women leaped crackling flames. My companions claimed the smoke shaped itself as a fat woman stirring a pot with a stick. I myself saw only smoke.

"Run through blood," the priest next commanded. He sprinkled running women's hair with blood from a young goat. He mixed ash, water, and blood with secret elements from a leather sack, and marked their breasts with circles. He drew waxing crescent moons around their navels, and broken crosses upon their knees.

"Now flee," the priest cried, and the women ran toward the woods—and us. The great standing stone was no harder or more erect than were we men, as we awaited them.

We snatched them and threw them upon the ground. Such was our ardor—and theirs—that no man's seed was left unmixed with another's in any woman's womb.

That was in my first year among the Wends. I departed when the river was free of ice. Of the swollen bellies among the women, two or three at least would bear sons with fine noses and large ears not unlike my own.

The "magic" of the rite requires no recourse to the supernatural. From midwinter to midsummer those women had lived apart in a large hut made from elm bark. In such proximity, the moon worked upon all as if one. When one shed dark blood, so did the others. When the priest chose the night for the rite, he did not study the sun and the length of days, but the moon— and chose that time when all the women were most ready to conceive. Only then did he mount the stone with his bowls, branches, and goat's blood.

We men, after long abstinence, were preternaturally aroused by naked flesh long denied us. Did the shaman know that the mixing of seed in those eager wombs might have efficacious effect, when no man's seed, weak or strong, could be separated from another's? Did he know that it is most vigorous after long abstention, or that the fortress womb defends best against seed it knows well, and is most easily invaded by the soldiers of a foreign king?

I told my princely sponsor that the Wends' burgeoning population resulted not from magic but from the manipulation of natural processes, and could not be reversed by magical means. "You will have to fight them," I told my patron.

Years later, when my observations were put to parchment, when copies had been sent to sages from

Constantinople to Gades, I returned to the country of the Wends.

At the portage where Baltic and Euxine rivers meet, I again met the priest of the Women's Rite, and traded Black Sea gold for smoked deer meat. He was not happy to see me, for in the years after my departure, the Rite's efficacy declined, and few infants were born. Now he was priest no longer, instead supplying smoked meat for the long Varangian ships that ply the Dnieper, the great river to the Euxine Sea.

I protested that I had done no magic; Christian beliefs, the cult of the Virgin, had caused his women to forsake strict observance of the rite. Happily, my gold outweighed old grudges, and I proceeded northward unmolested and well supplied.

∾

Pierrette's hand trembled. In ibn Saul's pragmatic account was one more answer to her burning questions. "Your friend Muhammad is a powerful sorcerer, Master Anselm," she said. "Imagine! He destroyed the fertility of the entire Wendish tribe."

Anselm looked up, confused. "What are you talking about? He's a scholar, not a sorcerer."

"He's an intuitive sorcerer. He doesn't know it, but this manuscript is a well-organized spell. Its postulates, logical development, and conclusion devastated the poor Wends. No woods-priest's magic could stand against it."

"Nonsense! There's no magic in a simple account of what he observed."

Pierrette grinned broadly. "But it isn't simple, and his incantation is no mere account. Master, consider this: Ibn Saul's unspoken first postulate, is that he is—just as you said—a simple observer. Rephrasing that . . . 'What I can see is the truth, and what I cannot is false.' That's his first magical statement.

"That said, he describes the rite itself.

"Then he cites natural phenomena for its success. He postulates that synchronicity of the women's cycles made them ready to conceive, then that the mixing of seed allowed strong to supplant weak, and finally, that the womb has no defense against unfamiliar seed. That is ibn Saul's magic!"

Was the girl unhinged? Anselm saw no relationship between spells and ibn Saul's statements. "It would be self-defeating," he said. "Every such 'spell' he uttered or wrote would reduce the magics in the world, until at last . . . there would be . . ." His words tapered off as he realized what he had been about to surmise.

"There would be only one magic left!" Pierrette finished the statement. "One single magic based entirely upon what can be observed and parsed by logic as rigid as a geometric theorem. And doesn't that most elegantly explain your own diminishing abilities?"

The mage was pale. "There's no hope, is there? It's not fair. Even Minho couldn't prevail against such spells, but his isolation protects him. I'm caught, because the geas my master put on me was to complete a task, and I failed. Minho doesn't exist in this world of passing time, so no scholar can find him to debunk him. I have no such advantage."

"If I could find Minho," Pierrette mused, "I could ask him to free you. He can't be without compassion. But . . . would you want to live a few years as an ordinary man, and then to die?"

"If he gave me back my youth—or at least my manly vigor, and enough years to enjoy a wife, and a child or two . . ."

"I'll do what I can, Master," she said, saddened by his wistful bitterness.

He shook his head. "I won't hold my breath and turn blue while I wait."

"Where there is understanding, there is hope, Master. Some magics still work. Though no spell can survive rational explanation, the world is large, and skeptics are few."

"But powerful," he countered. "Sorcerers guard their secrets. Men like ibn Saul hire scribes to copy their . . . their spells . . . and publish them. They sow the seeds of my destruction."

"You mustn't give up hope. I've just begun to understand the principles underlying our vocation."

"That's a grand task, child," the mage said quietly, sadly, "and there's so little time."

"Time, Master? Time is an ally, not an enemy, for how can the skeptics weigh or measure it?"

"There are sandglasses, and water clocks . . ."

"How imperfect they are," she rejoined. "The glass in the library runs slowly when I memorize boring declensions, and fast when I read of heroes and generals, or the romantic verse of . . . No, Master. Time will be the last magic to fall to the pen of the observer."

"Here it's held at bay," he agreed, "unlike its swift passage outside this place."

"You see? You say it passes swiftly outside, but it doesn't. When I leave here, I haven't aged an hour, though I eat and sleep many times. To you, the centuries outside have flickered by in days. Time is the oldest magic, and the least rational."

"Then what do you propose?"

"I don't wish to say. There's one more experiment. As for ibn Saul, he's only one man, and there are few others. Many centuries will pass before the effects of their scribblings become widely apparent."

Pierrette's experiment needed only a white feather, a willow leaf, and half a mussel shell with a pearly interior. The spell was a simple calling and required, she hoped, no more than material similitudes, and a place to perform it, a place she remembered well.

The campsite in the high forest looked as it had that wan morning long past. Had she ever really been five years old, and innocent? Inconstant time! She was how old? Thirteen? Fifteen? How many ageless months and years had she pored over books and scrolls? Was she a crone, in a body preternaturally young?

She kindled fire, taking pleasure from the way her simple spell worked. She built the flames high with dry pine branches, then added oak for the embers it made. She placed leaf, feather, and opalescent shell across the fire from where she sat.

Only one element was missing: Marie had been here before. Now she was in Massalia, scarred by her encounter with . . . but she must not dwell on that, or the one who answered her call might be someone she did not wish to meet again.

Guihen . . . She stroked the feather, calling in a soft voice across sixty thousand Roman paces between this place and the mouth of River Rhodanus. The Camargue, channels and hummocks, tasselled rushes where salt sea and mountain creek intergraded in a balance that shifted with the seasons, with ebb of tide and springtime spate.

Her mind strayed to the boundaries that constrained magical realms. Bleak heights were simple places where few things grew and only birds frequented. Rivers might be boundaries, or might have some different quality. The sea must have a magical nature all its own. The Camargue was land and water too. Was it a boundary or—neither sea, river, nor shore—a place where all spells were unconstrained?

Guihen . . . She glanced across the fire.

"You've learned well, child," said the sprite in the old Ligurian tongue. His white tunic shifted between gold and red amber in the dying fire's light. "Your voice was a wind that bent reeds and rushes, and rippled quiet pools. Look at you. Despite your silly garb, you're the image of your mother."

"You haven't changed, Master Guihen," Pierrette responded, "though perhaps my 'great wind' has bent your ears a bit." She giggled, feeling about five years old. That startled Guihen's hen, whose disturbed clucking sounded like soft laughter. Guihen stroked the bird gently.

"It is good that you still laugh, child," said Guihen. "There's little laughter where I have been."

"Why is that?"

"The vast Camargue becomes lonely. One by one old friends fade, and their empty houses sink into the morass. Saint Giles's doe wanders alone—the old hermit was Christian, so I doubt he's been consumed, but others aren't so lucky . . ."

Pierrette had the feeling that she should know that tale. The sprite had brought other concerns to the fore, and she decided to leave the story of the Christian saint and the doe for another time.

"Consumed, you said?" If the Eater of Gods stalked the Camargue, where the old ones were safe from Christian dissolution . . . there might not be time to learn what she must. Would she—again—be forced to confront him unprepared?

"I haven't seen the stalker. If I had, I wouldn't be here."
Pierrette envisioned Guihen's eyes no longer moon-pale,
tinged violet, but lit with hot, red flames. She gasped, then
stared into his face to assure herself that his eyes were as
they always had been.

"We must strengthen you against such an onslaught," she
said. "You, and your friend with the iron staff—and my
master Anselm, too."

"Strengthen us? How? The tide of mystical wondrousness
ebbs, and the world becomes hard and logical. Salt mills,
churches, roads, and canals ring the watery plain, and we
who survive become constrained."

"You must break out of your confinement," Pierrette said
thoughtfully, thinking of what she had learned from
Muhammad ibn Saul and the Wendish priest. "Bishops in
Arelate and Lugdunum may come from Rome, Ravenna,
and far Constantinople, but only Per Otho preaches in
Citharista, and old grannies still tell tales and gather herbs."

"What's that have to do with me?"

"You must re-create yourself in the world beyond the
Camargue," she stated. "You must no longer hide while people
tell tales that mold you into an orphaned Christian boy."

"What's that matter? I am what I am."

"No, sprite, you are not," she said emphatically. "You are
what they believe you to be. That or—as you fade away—
you'll be nothing at all. You must do as I say."

"You're right," Guihen said, no longer cajoling a preco-
cious child. "I don't understand. Perhaps you're right about
this other thing as well. Perhaps it's time to taste the fruit
of the seed I planted, when I saved you from the angry
gens."

Pierrette nodded. "There's a woman who lives outside
Citharista's fallen wall," she said. "Her baby wails all night,
and doesn't eat. You must make him laugh—and then he'll
sleep. When his eyes close, leave this feather stuck to his
forehead with honey."

"Is that all?"

"Oh, no. You'll be busy indeed. There's milk to be soured,
and yarn to be tangled; there's a lost boy to be found, and
returned to his parents' doorstep with a feather in his hand
and a little song in his head. There are pranks to be played,
and good deeds to be done . . ."

Pierrette's list was long.

"By the time I do all that," Guihen protested, "I'll have faded away."

"By the time you are half done, you'll no longer fade. That . . . or you'll have drawn the attention of one whom we both fear . . ."

"I'll be careful! None but little children will see my face."

"That's wise. Now go—and we shall see if I'm right."

On the way down from the forest, Pierrette felt cold, as if no heart beat within her chest, no warm blood pulsed in her veins. This experiment was no small manipulation of light or fire, no affliction of boils on a lecher's groin. She now tinkered not only with the very existence of poor Guihen, but with the lives of innocent folk, for her own ends and edification.

Was she wrong? Should she have constrained Guihen—who seemed to take pleasure in perverse prankishness—to do only good deeds among the *gens*? But no. The Christian boy-hero Guihen—the diluted, approved version—might do that, but it would only further attenuate the poor sprite. Prankishness and quirks were as much a part of the ancient Ligurian spirit that motivated him as his ungainly ears. Without them, he would not be Guihen.

She had touched upon another truth of magic and the nature of the world, but months would pass before she thought of it again, and years before she fully understood.

She made fists of her fingers, but the cold was inside her. Ice in her veins merely reflected the state of her mind: a manipulative mind that would risk good and evil, guilty and innocent alike, in furtherance of her sorcerous education.

There were three soldiers in her battle, and Guihen was only one. She had no tokens to call John of the Bears, only a place, and a process. The place was the trail to the Eagle's Beak, where Starved John had turned her away as an unready child. The process? That was no more than mounting the path, looking for two pairs of greenish, luminous stars—his faded companions. As she climbed, she called his name, and looked up at the narrow band of stars.

There! A pair of lime-tinged stars glimmered behind a veil of sea-blown fog. "Yan Oors! I see your bear. Where is its mate?" Two more dull stars resolved themselves on the opposite side of the trail . . . and starless blackness filled the place where the trail broke out on the stony crest. Yet no words answered hers, and when she looked closely, faint stars appeared on the other side of the looming shadow.

"Oh, poor John," she murmured sadly. "Are you so diminished that the light of a distant star pierces your vitals?" Was the gaunt one that far gone? But she felt no pity, only purpose—and she was not to be thwarted. Whatever wisp remained of the Celt god, embodiment of the terror men felt when they invaded the hostile wood, she would use it. She might yet stave off his complete dissolution.

"Hear me, Yan Oors," she commanded. "Hear me, and do as I say . . ." As with Guihen, she gave him tasks to perform. A shepherd must awaken in terror, finding his sheep scattered and his fire trampled out. He must find the outline of a bear's foot pressed in his fire's ashes. Was that too much for a faded wraith?

Could a certain young boy—slipping from his bed and out of his father's hut to urinate—be frightened by eyes that glowed green, too widely spaced for foxes' eyes?

No affirmation rewarded her as she listed the tasks she wanted done, but the paired stars continued to glow, and the shadow still blocked the outlet to the crest.

Finished, she sighed breathily. "Good luck," she wished the dark spirit. "May we meet face-to-face, when all is accomplished." The blot obscuring the stars disappeared, and when she looked for the eyes of the bears, she saw only the twinkle of ordinary luminaries.

"And now," she sighed, again scrambling upward, "for the most difficult of my recruits . . . my master, Anselm."

Chapter 17 ∾ The Mage Reconsiders

"No! I'm no Ligure fairy, no Celtic wraith. You can't command me. In fact, as your sworn master, I command you to cease these importunements." He glared at her woeful face. "Yes—that too. No more sad eyes. Become cheery, and get about your studies. I'll hear no more of your 'experiment.'"

"I'll obey, Master," Pierrette said humbly, "but may I beg one simple thing?"

"What?" Anselm snapped.

"If my 'experiments' with elf and specter succeed, will you listen? Then—if so moved—will you consider my plea?"

"I'll listen," the mage agreed. "I'll promise that much, to buy silence now."

And so it was.

Pierrette returned to Citharista. The knight Jerome did not trouble her; in fact, he was not seen much, and rumor had it his illness kept him to his bed. Pierrette was not sure she could have looked at him without running away.

She took up Marie's duties in the marketplace.

She insisted that after a day's work with trees or nets, Gilles take his evening wine in the tavern. "When you're sleepy, I'll come help you home to bed." That was well by Gilles. Didn't he deserve to drink in company, where the conversations of other men would distract him from thoughts of poor Marie?

Being a simple man, he thought nothing of his daughter's prattle as they walked from house, marketplace, or grove to the tavern. "Are there bears in the hills, Papa?" she might ask, or "Has anyone ever seen a wood-sprite?"

Gilles had seen neither bears nor sprites, and he laughed at such innocence—but when the subject of bears came up at the tavern one night, he remembered enough to recount it to Pierrette. . . .

"It was a bear!" Marius protested. No longer a child, he was a stolid young man with a reputation for veracity. He pointed at the smudge on his tunic. "It stepped on me." Gilles and several others laughed. The smudge, paw-shaped, was where Marius had wiped his dirty hands.

One somber fellow, Parvinus, did not laugh. "Something set my dogs to howling, two nights ago," he mused. "When I took my stick and went to look, I found my oldest cow fighting to pass her calf. The calf was wrongly placed, and was killing her. If the dogs hadn't barked, I wouldn't have found her in time to turn the calf."

"You think they were barking at a bear?" Gilles guffawed.

"There were tracks in the dust. Big ones."

"Bear tracks?"

"I couldn't tell, but I know anyway. It was not a bear. It was . . . Yan Oors."

That old name had not been spoken often, in Citharista, but even old men had once been children, and remembered their grannies' stories. Yan Oors broke the heads of malefactors with his iron staff, and chased malingering children back to their tasks. Some claimed he had slain the dragon whose bones littered the bleak heights.

"Yan Oors, eh?" mused another man, grinning mischievously. "And what evil thoughts were you thinking as you lay dozing?"

Marius reddened. Indeed, he had been thinking of Sarah, whom he was to wed—carnal thoughts, indeed.

"I hear," said Germain—for so everyone called the tavernkeeper, Germanicus, "that other spirits have returned to these hills. Last week a man brought a two-headed white hen. I didn't buy it, of course. I told him to kill it with a copper blade, and to hang it in a willow tree."

"And?" prompted Parvinus.

"The next morning the hen was gone from the tree, and

he found a silver Frankish mark among its roots. I saw the coin myself."

A genial argument had ensued. Someone—Gilles did not remember who—speculated that the man had the coin all along, and made up the tale to cajole a free cup of wine from Germain.

"Still," Gilles told Pierrette, "such birds were once properly sacrificed to the sprite Guihen, as Germain prescribed, and most of us agreed that he had left the silver."

Pierrette agreed it was probably so. "If there are more stories, Papa, I hope you remember to tell me."

In the months that followed, he did. A man's ox yoke swung as if someone had brushed it while walking by. The stable door closed behind him, though there was no wind. "He found a white feather," Gilles said, "though his chickens are all brown and red."

Pierrette heard tales in the marketplace. Granna, who sold wool, was a font of gossip and events unexplainable in the light of day. Pierrette inched her jars of oil closer to Granna's stall each day, until she could converse without raising her voice.

"Claudia leaves a loaf of bread on her doorstep each night," Granna recounted. "I tell you, boy, the old ways don't just fade, no matter who goes to mass and who doesn't. P'er Otho saw the loaf, but he's smart enough to turn a blind eye."

"What of the bread?" asked Pierrette.

"Every morning, it's gone."

"Couldn't some passerby be taking it?"

"Could be, could be," Granna said, not believing it for a minute. "Yet have you bought Claudia's loaves lately?" Pierrette nodded. "Then you know how light and fair they've become. It's the sour—the yeast. She says she came down the stairs one morning, smelling something wonderful, and her sour pot had overflowed—bubbled up and pushed aside the wet cloth she covers it with. That feisty sour gives her bread the flavor and lightness."

"Perhaps it was a wild strain brought in on her clothing. That happens."

"Ah," Granna said knowingly, "that could be. Indeed it could. But one day, Claudia sold all her *boules*, and had none to leave for the spirit, and . . . can you guess what happened?

"The morning after," Granna continued, "her yeast pot was dry as old bones. Ha! She made no bread that day. Now she leaves a cup of milk with the loaf, and it's always empty in the morning."

Pierrette asked about the missing part of the story—how Claudia had rejuvenated the dead yeast, in order to make bread, so that she had a fresh loaf to leave on her door-step again. Granna grinned, and raised an eyebrow. "She must have done something to make him happy, eh?"

"Who is 'he'?" Pierrette asked.

"You know! You don't want me to speak his name, do you? But I'll tell you this—when Claudia did right by him, there was a fluff of white chicken down in her proof-loaf that day."

Marius's tale, and Claudia's, were not isolated. Pierrette's strange acquaintances were following her instructions.

At first, she wished she had told them to exercise restraint, to do only good deeds, but the more she heard of their activities, the more right they seemed. Neither Guihen nor Starved John were "good," nor were they "evil." Like Saint Augustine's fire, they were what they were; fire burned, or it warmed and comforted, and could not be said to belong solely to God or devil on that account. A little mischief, after all, distanced the two from the watery Christian myths mothers told.

That was what Pierrette intended: for their acts to erase the flawed Christian postulates that caused them to weaken. Besides, she thought gleefully, it was satisfying to watch the smug, staid *gens* walk about on tiptoe, for once aware that magical entities wandered about, whom they could not kill with their clubs and their torches. . . .

Pierrette still wore her boy's clothing, and had come no closer to making the change. Each day she promised her-self this was the day—but each afternoon she came home without having done anything about it. Each day she prom-ised herself to discuss it with Gilles, then decided to wait until he had eaten, then after he had a glass of wine beneath his belt. It was always too late. Either he got drunk, or he left for the tavern, and her chance was lost.

P'er Otho knew what she was, and would advise her. Yet that was easy to postpone, and not until one morning in early spring did she set out to do it.

✧   ✧   ✧

She found him writing to his bishop. He told of just such events as gave Pierrette great joy—yet his interpretation terrified her. "Satan?" she exclaimed. "Why do you say that such things are the devil's work?"

"God does not perform like a wandering singer for loaves of bread or cups of milk," Otho said. "Who else can be responsible?"

"You told me that it didn't matter how I prayed, because whether I prayed to a saint or a tree, my prayer would be heard by God. Is a loaf of bread on the doorstep so different from a candle on the altar? Is a lively yeast the devil's brew?"

Otho was used to her mysterious erudition, but that surprised him. "You mustn't hold me to that," he said. "I was speaking to a child. My words were meant only to comfort. The bishop wouldn't understand."

"Would you be in trouble?" Let Otho feel a threat in her question, and he would not send the letter.

She departed, having accomplished a postponement of that day when her experimental subjects would have to face the power of the Church—but without saying anything about her personal dilemma.

Pierrette found time to visit Anselm occasionally. He complained about her long absences—one more proof that neither he nor she understood the nature of fluid time, which could neither be dammed like a stream of water nor caught in a wooden bowl, and which could not be observed from any stable shore, but only from within the stream.

Time was not treating her master well. His white hair, once lush, looked sparse, and through the hazy mass atop his head she saw pink skin. His beard and mustaches bore yellow stains as if he neglected his treatments with warm oil. Wine stains blotched his once-white garment.

The old fortress itself seemed smaller, and bore signs that time did not entirely pass it by. The causeway had crumbled further, and was so narrow that one had to tiptoe, teetering anxiously, breathing a great sigh of relief when the safety of the portico was reached.

No black or vermilion paint remained on the pillars, so weather-worn that Pierrette could not have determined if they had indeed once been bold Minoan columns or plain stone cylinders.

The broken floor tiles and stained ceilings depressed her. Soon, she promised, she would have the proof to convince Anselm to save himself. But not yet. Another week, on the outside, would make no difference here—or would it?

A day or so later, she visited the priest, hoping that word had arrived from the nunnery. "The abbess won't write unless Marie's condition improves—or worsens. We must assume that nothing has changed."

She remarked the black scar on his writing table. "Ah," he said, perhaps too diffidently, "I fell asleep, and my candle burned down. The flame caught my parchment afire. Now I'll have to rewrite it."

Yet even weeks afterward, he had not replaced the charred tabletop, and there was no evidence that he had touched his inkpot or quills. If he had, he would have noticed that one feather was smaller than the rest, and too soft to make a good pen. That one had not belonged to a goose.

Anselm's capitulation, when it came, was sudden, and Pierrette did not have to call Yan Oors or Guihen for proof that her experiment indeed worked. One calm morning, a grinding roar was heard by the denizens of Citharista. They rushed outside, but saw nothing amiss. "The sound came from the sea," one claimed, and faces turned anxiously south. "No, it was a landslide in the hills," said another.

A week later, a fisherman brought news. "The Eagle has lost half its beak!" he cried, as he tied up his boat. "The old fort has lost a wall and lies open from top to bottom. The old magus must have fallen with it."

"How can you tell?" Pierrette demanded. "Did you climb up to see?"

The fisherman had not. "I'll go up myself," Pierrette said. Several women made the horned sign with their fingers. Pierrette ignored them, and departed immediately.

Anselm was not dead, but he almost wished he were, as he showed Pierrette the devastation. "The wall is gone," he wailed, "and the parapet where I sunned myself."

"This is only the beginning," she remarked coldly. "Minho's geas has trapped you in this pocket of unreality, and the machinations of Christians and scholars like ibn Saul nibble away at it."

"I'm doomed!" he wailed. "There's nothing I can do."

"That's not true!" she snapped, "Haven't you listened at all? Are you dead already?"

"I might as well be."

"The library and storerooms are intact," she observed, "and though my bedroom now has a grand view, your chambers are unaffected. When you decide you want to keep them that way, I'll help. Until then . . ."

"I have decided," he said. "Bring the women from the town. I'll see what can be done for them."

"And for yourself," Pierrette thought, though not aloud. It was enough that he had agreed to try her plan.

The next evening five people climbed in the shadow of the great rocks. Three were women, the others boys.

"I can't cross that chasm!" one woman protested, eyeing the narrow path to the gate.

"Your son is dying," Pierrette hissed. "You must cross." She went first, to show how easy it was—though indeed, the recent collapse had narrowed it so severely that at one place she had almost to leap across. Eventually all stood shakily in the entryway.

A flickering lamp halfway up the stairs revealed the whiteness of Anselm's now-clean garment, but left his face in shadow. "Enter, who seeks a boon," he intoned theatrically, then turned and ascended. The seekers followed.

His voice sounded resonant, not a querulous old man's. Had he begun to recover, though he had done nothing yet to warrant the women's faith in him? When they emerged into the sunlit court, they covered their eyes and cried out fearfully at such magic. Outside, it had been dusk.

There was no sign of devastation. All seemed as it had before the landslide. She burned with curiosity, but could not ask Anselm in the women's presence.

The mage gestured for the first woman to bring her son forward. She threw herself down, weeping. "Arise!" he commanded sharply. "I am no god, no king. Worshiping me would be a sin, and abasing yourself is foolish. I require your ears, not your soul."

Chastised, she stood, and described the wasting disease that consumed the boy. "Leave him with me," Anselm said.

"Wait on the crest of the Eagle's Beak. Kneel and pray if you wish—it can't do harm." Pierrette put a hand to her shoulder, and led her away.

When she returned, Anselm commanded her to take the boy, and to prepare a potion of herbs for him. Thus she was not present when he spoke with the second woman.

Pierrette had expected to give the boy a rich broth or a fortifying drink, not a black brew of seaweed and dung, laced with weeds that made sheep and cattle go mad. Yet the boy was weak and biddable, and he drank the strong purgative.

Later, she did not want to remember. She raged at her master for not warning her. After drinking the brew, the boy vomited what he had consumed—and more. His bowels became loose, and he voided on the bedclothes. He spewed not the ordinary contents of stomach and bowel, but white threads that writhed with hideous life all their own.

Pierrette bundled the bedclothes and threw them from the window, not caring where they fell, or that they were fine blue cotton from Nemausus. As soon as she spread fresh cloths, the boy fouled those, and again she tossed them away.

Thankfully, the potion had stupefied him. He was already dulled by starvation, because for months the worms had consumed everything he ingested.

Pierrette heated water to bathe her patient. The wood burned with loud, angry crackles that mirrored her mood, and the water boiled in minutes, though she uttered no spell.

After that first rejection of the demons that had tormented the child, his spasms diminished. At last he slept. The air cleared. She listening to his strong, regular breathing. Then she returned to the courtyard, where the third woman now stood before her master.

"Ah, boy! What kept you? I have heard these women's complaints. The one knows what she must do, and the other requires a powder of red fungi and crushed insects." He rattled off instructions—which red mushrooms and how many, and instructions for measuring several kinds of bugs from the storeroom's jars. Fuming, her lips compressed, Pierrette again departed.

When she returned, Anselm dismissed the women. The first woman's boy, he said, would be along shortly.

Pierrette informed him what a thoughtless curmudgeon

he had been. He listened without protest, and when she ran out of breath, his head hung low. "I'm sorry," he said. "I was having so much fun pretending . . ."

"Pretending? Is that what you think? The boy had worms, and your magic drove them out."

"It was hardly magic. It will seem so to ignorant folk, of course—especially when the boy is returned rested and fed, when for them only minutes have passed."

"Don't spurn their ignorance, Master. Nothing else stands between you and dissolution. If the boy retains drugged memories of demons being driven from him, it will strengthen you. Now tell me what transpired while I was gone."

The second woman, Anselm said, had become with child soon after the birth of her last babe. If she conceived soon after birthing the one she carried, she would die.

" 'Poor women don't suffer so.' I told her," said Anselm. "She would have given all her riches to be freed of her fear of untimely death—but I didn't require that." He laughed. " 'When this child is born,' I told her, 'send away the wet-nurse your husband brings, and suckle the child yourself—for a full year.' "

Pierrette nodded. "As long as she suckles, she won't likely conceive. But did you set her another penance as well?"

Anselm chuckled. "Her husband is a mason. I suggested he repair my crumbling causeway—so if his wife again required something of me, her path might be less treacherous than now."

"Thus building her conviction—and your reputation—into the stones leading to your keep. That was good, Master. You're catching the spirit of my experiment. Now tell me of the third woman."

"Bah! She could have asked any masc. Her cow is dry, and won't allow itself to be mounted. Without a calf, it will not give milk, yet it still eats grain, and requires care and shelter. I suggested she learn to enjoy beef, which is well-regarded in some countries."

Pierrette smiled. "I suspect she didn't take that well."

"She promised me a tithe of all the cheeses she'd make. That inspired me to propose a . . . a medicinal solution. The poor cow will have such an itch from those powdered bugs! She'll break fences to reach the bull. And the mushrooms will make a billy goat look good to her."

"You're being silly, Master. A cow can't conceive by a goat."

"Do you know that? Do your reasoned postulates forbid it? It once was not so. How else could there have been a man with the head and feet of a deer?"

Pierrette looked for a wine jar, then decided the mage was drunk on success and high hopes—a change from his previous state that she hoped would continue for a long time.

In the months that followed, Pierrette gauged the success of her experiment by subtle changes. There was tension in the air. Not bleak fear, as when fishermen reported the shark-fin sails of Saracen war-vessels cruising the coast, nor the dull anxiety of waiting, when the leaves fell from the plane trees but the winter rains did not come.

Folk walked hesitantly, as if rounding a corner might bring them face to face with an apparition out of some primeval past. As if the pool at the foot of the aqueduct might produce not a reflection but a chimera. As if angels might appear in a meeting of dust and sunbeam.

When shepherds returned from the hills, men bought them cups of wine in the hope that they might be the first to hear of a shadow-man with an iron staff, a sprite with clothes of willow leaves, with tinkling bells shaped like tiny lilies that grew in moist places.

Anselm's rebirth into the awareness of the *gentes* contributed to the zest and apprehension. Sometimes Pierrette was not alone on the path—and where she had hitherto been forced to clamber over rocks, she walked past cairns heaped by passersby. Where she had once teetered on the narrow causeway, she strode on a new, arched span.

People eyed her differently, too, for though Anselm bade supplicants keep silent about what they saw within his walls, people spoke in other ways than words. They had seen the boy Piers there. When one person raised an eyebrow as she walked past, another knew what that signified, without having to speak of it.

It would have been a good time to reveal that she was a girl; everyone was already whispering about her relationship with the sorcerer. Suddenly "becoming" a girl could not have increased the intensity of their surreptitious stares.

Yet she had not spoken with P'er Otho again, nor raised

the topic with Gilles. Her single concession was her hair: she had not cut it since her resolution, on the way home from Massalia. Now, it was longer than the other boys'. It was as black as crow's feathers. She often fondled luxuriant handsful, tugging as if that would make it grow faster.

Alone in the house, she brushed her hair. It became soft and glossy, and did not clump as boys' hair did. Perhaps if she said nothing, but continued to allow it to grow, Granna would remark it. Anything Granna found out was soon common knowledge; she would be saved the trouble of explaining, and could just arrive in the marketplace one day wearing a skirt.

Meanwhile, until her telltale hair forced her revelation, she would continue as she was. . . .

"Now Master," Pierrette said, one morning in the spring of her fifteenth year, "explain how the fallen wall of your keep was restored."

The mage—who appeared younger than Gilles, though his hair was still white—looked momentarily troubled. "I don't know," he said. "At first, I created an illusion, when you brought those first three women. Now . . ." He rapped the solid stone with his knuckles. "It appears genuine."

Pierrette did not question him further, but was not easy about the keep's restoration. A few days earlier, when fish proved elusive, she prevailed upon Gilles to head west of his usual fishing grounds, where she could see the steep, overhanging side of the Eagle's Beak.

Pressing Gilles to stray even that far from his "cautious" sea-routes had been easier than expected. Ordinarily, "west" was not even in Gilles's lexicon, and he never strayed farther than an invisible line drawn between the Eagle's Beak and the green island beyond it.

That short venture westward was a first, tentative step away from Gilles's despised "caution." He did not know how many such steps might be required, or if there was enough time in his waning years for him to take them, but he was determined to try—to be the kind of man who would not have abandoned his wife to Citharista's wolves, or his daughter to a castellan's lust.

The silhouette of the scarp was as the fisherman had described it before, and the west wall—perhaps even the west half—of the old fortress was indeed gone. Anselm's recuperating magic had progressed far enough that the keep appeared whole—but only from within.

There was clearly room for improvement. Though she realized what she saw from outside was false—as such things went—she had to restrain herself from urging Gilles to let her ashore so she could rush to the heights and satisfy herself that the desolate ruin was not the entire reality— and that her mentor still lived.

They had, however, sailed too far not to make an attempt with the net and—as it turned out—they pulled in a good catch, which Gilles sold at the wharf, saving a meaty red- fish for himself and Pierrette. She prepared it with crushed rosemary and first-pressed oil and sprinkled it lightly with red-brown sea salt.

Chapter 18 ∾ An Impressive Debut

When Pierrette left for Anselm's keep the next day, she carried a wrapped bundle—a white dress that had belonged to her mother.

She bid the mage a quick "good morning." A glance at the west wall verified that—seen from within—it was still standing. She had no idea how that could be—how it could look one way from without and different from within—but she had no time to ponder it. She hurried to her room. She was, at last, going to be a girl.

The dress seemed plainer than at home. It needed something. . . . She scampered from the room. "Master Anselm?" she said breathlessly. "I need to borrow some things. Those chests in the storeroom . . ."

"Ah! Snooping? You want jewels? Go ahead and take some. Try on the crown. It was made for a Caesar's swelled head, but with judicious padding . . . And the great ruby of the eastern khans . . ."

"Master, I don't covet your treasure. I thought perhaps a sash, and a pair of red leather shoes . . ."

"Of course—and a matching sword belt with a bronze scabbard . . ."

"A simple cincture, Master. Have I permission to look?"

"I said so, boy. I have no need of such things. I don't even remember where most of them came from."

"Thank you, Master." Pierrette dashed toward the storeroom.

When she found what she wanted, she slipped past the stairway leading to the entry gate, where several seekers of the mage's wisdom waited. There would be no need of her services right away, though Anselm liked to have her near to fetch, carry, and prepare nostrums. Though he almost never seemed to fade, even in strong sunlight, he still refused to apply what he called "real" magic to the problems the townsfolk brought, and confined his recommendations to "practical" solutions.

"Just because there's a material explanation doesn't make it less magical," Pierrette reminded him often. "You must stop denigrating yourself. You are a great sorcerer."

"Apprentice!" Anselm was calling. "Where are you?" No slight boy answered the mage's call.

"Your apprentice is not about, Master. May I serve you instead?"

Anselm stared, speechless, his jaw hanging. His visitors— an elderly sheepherder and one of the Burgundian soldiers— did not observe his reaction, because they too had eyes only for Pierrette.

Her hair was piled high atop her head with a loose braid of pearls and gold beads that enhanced its midnight darkness. Gold earrings dangled; where gold met flesh were tiny drops of blood from the recent piercing. The earrings' intricate Celtic design matched the flared gold torque that rested on her slim shoulders, over Elen's high-collared dress. A cape of crimson silk was held with a chain of twisted links and two blue enameled fibulae. Their tightly wound springs formed the eyes of cicadas, wings folded to cover the cleverly-wrought pins. Of her crimson leather shoes, only the curling tips could be seen. The belt was indeed a treasure—stranded gold beads and pearls that met beneath her breasts in a medallion enameled sky blue.

The visitors'—and Anselm's—speechlessness was all the confirmation she desired. Not one saw scruffy Piers in his baggy tunic, hand-me-down trousers, and dusty sandaled feet. They saw instead—a queen? A royal lady of some Merovingian house? She needed no mirror to tell her how well her transformation had succeeded.

"How may I serve you, Master?" she said. Even her voice seemed changed. As Piers, she had deliberately pitched it low; now her words had the timbre of bells, overtones of wooden flutes.

"Ah . . . a brazier, I think. Yes, the bronze one—and a handful of dry, sweet grass." She bowed slightly, spun on one heel—almost tripping over unaccustomed lengths of cloth that swirled about her ankles. She set the brazier of dry gray-green grass before the mage. "Come forward!" he commanded the shepherd. "Kneel, and . . . and my apprentice will perform the spell to clear your eyes and banish the pains in your head." He glared at Pierrette, as if he wanted to punish her for the shock she had given him.

"Of course, Master." She uttered soft words. Small flames danced on her fingertips. She lowered her hand to the bronze vessel, then stood back as white smoke rose. "Breathe deeply," she said. The shepherd obeyed—and began coughing. "Don't stop! Breathe!"

She then led him aside, giving him a fat pouch of the sweet herb. "Use it, when your vision dims or your head hurts."

The soldier's complaint was personal. He was reluctant to speak of it in front of a woman. "Speak you must," Pierrette said. "That's essential to your cure. Leave out one small detail, and your condition will remain unchanged." Stumbling and hesitating, he described his difficulty, which prevented him from satisfying himself atop his wife.

Pierrette, having no personal experience with such things, drew Anselm aside for a whispered consultation. "Considering his self-centered attitude, his wife might be content with the *status quo ante*, but I know too little of men and women. I've watched sheep and goats, but that isn't the same."

"For this fellow, I suspect it is too much the same," her mentor stated, "though I too am devoid of genuine experience."

"Then we must send him to someone who will understand," she concluded, satisfied. "I will perform a trick to impress him, and will then command him to make pilgrimage, with his wife, to . . . to Ma." Anselm eyed her as if she were clever indeed; let Ma work the cure, and the cult of the pool would acquire a new member—the wife—for the goddess would not encourage thoughtless ploughing of her sacred soil.

Pierrette uttered a small spell adapted to the conditions of the time, and to her understanding of the magical nature of

Citharista's valley. It would hopefully cause the soldier to see his wife not fat and blowsy, with missing teeth, but as when he first met her, when he burned with the heat of youthful desire—before his humping had become no more memorable than using the chamberpot.

Later, Anselm complimented her. "Your spell persists even now," he said.

Pierrette was confused until she realized he was referring not to the minor enchantment of the soldier, but to her femininity. "It's no spell, Master," she replied, smiling happily, spinning around so her white skirt billowed. "You see me as I am—without benefit of sorcery or incantation."

"Don't be so sure it's not magic," he said, "though I'm sure it's a most natural kind."

There was no word from the abbess, which meant Marie remained unchanged. Her absence was an ache, a void Pierrette became aware of at odd moments when her sister's voice might otherwise have been heard, or when she returned home brimming with things to say, and no one but Gilles to speak with. She felt useless, because she could do nothing to help. "If ever I have a chance," Pierrette vowed, "I will, no matter what the cost to myself."

As spring wore into summer, Pierrette was content with her ongoing experiment. Anselm's confidence grew, and his tentative dabblings with genuine sorcery caused no perceptible drain on his vitality. He worked only those spells Pierrette had studied—and in some cases modified, fitting their ancient assumptions to the way she perceived the world to work today.

The activities of Ligurian sprite and dark Celtic ghost multiplied in effect as folk attributed even the most natural of coincidences to them. Those attributions strengthened them, as she observed firsthand when she met with them in the high forest south of the dragon's bones. . . .

The campsite was unoccupied. She made fire—with a grand flourish that caused branches thick as her thumb to burst into flame without tinder. The leaves of a feral olive close to the hearth rustled with the gust of the sudden fire. But no gust had moved her long, loose hair.

She stepped back, eyeing the bush. The long, silvery leaves drooped, as if the fire's heat had wilted them. Two olives, green-gold, hung at the level of her eyes, about that distance apart.

"Guihen?" she whispered—now afraid that what she saw was not the sprite, but something else, something with eyes that took their pale shine not from firelight, but from some less benign source. She backed away—and was rewarded with a jolly laugh.

"Ha! I did it!" Guihen exclaimed, dancing on one foot then the other. "I fooled you! Now tell me you did not see an olive tree."

"I did," Pierrette admitted, smiling at his joy in his successful illusion, and from relief that he was, indeed, Guihen, and not some more sinister presence.

The sprite stroked the fat white hen cradled in the crook of his arm. "Now what do you see?" he cried, his words suddenly echoing as if from within a *dolium*, a grain vessel tall as a man.

Pierrette saw . . . nothing. Rather, she saw a background of bushes and trees that faded into night's darkness—which was what Guihen desired her to see. Then, as suddenly as he had disappeared, he was back. "I was invisible, wasn't I?" he crowed. "Truly invisible."

"Indeed. I saw right through where you stood, as if you had faded entirely away."

"Don't say that! It had nothing to do with fading away. The principle is wholly different."

"I'm sorry." This confident Guihen needed to be reminded that his new success was one small skirmish in a greater battle. Still, she chided herself for letting her fearful mood swing into momentary cruelty. "I'm feeling guilty, I suppose, because in your joy I saw myself. I've been thinking more of my successes than of the evil in this world, which concentrates itself while I play."

Guihen settled by the fire. "I suppose we must speak of such things."

"Let's wait until our dark accomplice arrives. Unless he is already here . . ."

"I would know!" Guihen shuddered.

"Don't you like Yan Oors?"

"Like? It has nothing to do with that. It's his staff!

That great pole of twisted iron. My bowels flux at the memory."

"Is that old wive's tale true? Does iron really repel you?"

"If you had been there when I was a boy, when Celt horsemen came in their four-wheeled war carts, you wouldn't ask. Iron cuts bronze . . . and they cut us, who knew nothing of *nsi*, the black metal."

Was that the origin of wood-folks' aversion to iron? Had the Celts' conquest of the Ligures—who worked only bronze and copper—become an aversion that grew until iron itself, not its bearers, was the enemy? More to the point, had that become not just an observation but a postulate—thus fixing the deadly nature of *nsi* into a reality more than historical? She must study certain old, faded spells with that in mind.

"John of the Bears comes," Guihen said, tilting his head.

Pierrette discerned a muffled, regular sound. "His staff," Guihen said, again shivering. "He swings it as he walks, so it strikes the ground every pace, every other step, just after his right foot lands."

Pierrette eyed shadowy woods. Yan Oors. She did not need to look right and left for the glow of green eyes to identify it: no faded ghost stepped forth, but a man.

He wore a black leather shirt and a kilt cut in strips over his thighs like Roman *pteruges*, and over the shirt a vest of linked mail. His gauntness engendered the epithet "Starved John," but he was not starved. Muscles flexed beneath the curly hair on his arms. His sandals, laced Greek-fashion, exposed the tops of great, dirty feet. His thick fingers were as knobby as his toes. His face held Pierrette's gaze. A ferocious face, a terrifying face—but she was not afraid.

Yan Oors smiled. Deep crevices fissured the corners of his mouth like slash wounds from nostril to chin. Crinkles formed at the corners of his eyes, in skin the texture and shade of old leather. Big white teeth glittered with red firelight, matching the whiteness around brown, warm eyes. His hair and bushy, pointed eyebrows were the same brown. His nose dominated everything—a great, crooked beak, asymmetrical from some old break. Wide, hairy nostrils flared when he breathed.

"Welcome, John of the Iron Staff," Pierrette said in old Gallic. "Please share our fire."

He pointedly rested his staff against the bole of an oak tree, nodded toward Guihen, and came forward.

"Thank you, pretty lady," he said in the same language. His voice was as deep and hollow as the surf that boomed in sea-caves. His words disconcerted Pierrette, who was dressed as a boy.

"Has my guise worn so thin?"

"I see a white dress, and gold, and a cape of crimson. The rest is but a spell you cast about yourself."

A spell? Anselm had said that too. Had she, without knowing it, augmented the simple deception of clothing and mannerisms? It would explain why her father and Anselm, who knew she was not male, could "forget." But could magic be done without conscious effort? Or had her mother cast the spell when she was small, and was it only now fading?

Yan Oors's mobile face shifted between melancholy frown and dry, prankish grin as he recounted his adventures . . . An unfaithful wife, out to meet her lover, was driven into a cave by a tusked boar, who ravished her as no human lover could, then left her alone with shuddering, erotic memories that might have been a dream.

"That was cruel," Pierrette said.

"Was it? She enjoyed my tusky kisses, and I her plump whiteness. It had been a long time since I sowed such a fair field."

"She's with child?"

"It was a good deed, little mother. What else did she seek, that her husband's bed could not provide?"

"And what will a boar's child be?" she asked. "And why not a bear, instead?"

Yan Oors allowed himself a ludicrous pout. "I'm not entirely cruel. The child will have a bit of a snout . . . but having seen her husband, there'll be no complaints." He shrugged. "As for bears . . . when I was a god, men called me 'Lord of the Animals,' and I wore whatever pelt I chose."

"Are you again becoming a god?" Pierrette asked uneasily.

"Don't worry, daughter of Ma. I am no more a god than you are a goddess."

That might have satisfied Pierrette, except that she saw

a trace of a grin at the corners of his mouth. She shrugged that off; this was not the cape, ensorcelled against the passage of hours. Too soon, it would be dawn. She pressed both of them for further tales of mischief and deeds well done, and told them her own, dwelling with delight on those occasions when she had appeared as . . . herself, a woman. As a sorceress of growing power, mistress of ancient words upon which she had put her own inflections.

When all was said, she guided their talk from the past to the future—to her still-nebulous plans. They all had to be ready when—and if—the moment arose.

"We'll know when to act," Guihen assured her.

"Never fear, little mistress," growled John of the Bears. "We'll keep an eye on you, and on those important to your schemes."

She shook her head doubtfully. "Some necessary events may not occur for months, or years. How will you know?"

Guihen's laugh was a tinkling like little bells. "When you see sunlight on the silvery backside of a windblown leaf . . . When a gamin begs a copper . . . will it be me?"

"And when a shadow falls across your path," said Yan, "or a gray ember brightens without a puff of air to feed it—can you be sure I'm not watching?"

Morning came too soon, and she bade regretful good-byes. Without sleep, the trek to Citharista stretched endlessly before her, and she considered going to the Eagle's Beak instead, for a good night's sleep, but there was much to do.

Tasks left undone fester like slivers beneath the skin. Pierrette had not spoken with P'er Otho in some time, having decided first to find out how effective her campaign was. Despite the priest's uneasiness about the town's backsliding into pagan beliefs, he had not written to his bishop. But he would not put it off forever. She had no idea how she would handle it when the bishop did visit Citharista. If she could put it off . . . Calming P'er Otho's fears was as good a way as any.

A horse was drop-reined beside his house. A soldier's horse, with those "stirrups" becoming popular with men who fought from horseback. She approached cautiously—and heard voices within.

"Why haven't you written? Are you afraid the bishop will

have you removed? If you don't, I'll see to it." Father Otho's softer reply was muffled.

"It's not just the woods demons," the voice continued. "The old mage has a new apprentice, a demon herself—though a lovely one, I'm told."

"What harm have any of them done?" Otho asked, "if in fact, such 'woodland spirits' actually exist outside the superstitious minds of my parishioners?"

"They exist. You should be glad, for if they did not, and you still lost control of your faithful, your superiors would . . . As things stand, you need only plead the demons' strength." The loud voice was . . . Jerome. The nature of his arguments had at first caused her to reject that identification. Why would he—a worshipper of the horned god—wish the bishop to intervene? And why would not Cernunnos—or the one who had consumed him—simply consume Guihen and John, instead of pressing for a bishop to drive them off? Was there something she did not understand—a faulty assumption? Jerome was a worshipper of Cernunnos—or was he? She was not absolutely sure that her confrontation with the Eater of Gods had taken place in the "real" world, or that Jerome was himself aware of it. Was he just an occasional tool of the one she feared most, and his words today entirely his own? That would explain everything.

Should she wait until the knight departed? She dreaded and hated him. She would wait, and speak only with the priest.

Her relief, when she decided that, made her suspect it was too easy. The knight's arguments threatened not only her, but Anselm, Guihen, and Yan Oors. And calling her a "demon" . . . She would show him!

The door swung open on creaking pintles. Pierrette and both men were momentarily disadvantaged by the contrasts of changed light. To Pierrette, the interior was dark, the men mere shadows, their faces white moons. From the table where they sat, she was a dark, wavering figure illumined from behind.

"Ah—Piers," said Father Otho, first to recover. "How timely. Perhaps you can explain the tales from the Eagle's Beak. Several folk reported seeing you there."

"He's the old wizard's helper," growled Jerome. Pierrette

saw that the knight sat not upon the hard wooden bench, but on a thick cushion. The boils still troubled him.

"Is that so?" asked Otho.

"The magus calls him 'apprentice,' " Jerome insisted.

Otho's gaze became suspicious.

Pierrette shrugged. "The old man orders me about. If he chooses to call me his 'apprentice,' what am I to do? If he called me 'goat,' would I grow horns?"

"You might," said the knight, "if the sorcerer wished it." He turned to Otho. "Write to the bishop. Put an end to this before the boy indeed wears demon's horns."

Had Pierrette not known what she did about Jerome, his words might have seemed sincere. Otho, knowing only that Jerome dabbled in the cult of the horned god, might believe that in the face of genuinely supernatural events he had repented. What scheme was the Burgundian promoting?

"I'll write the letter," Otho said. "But now, Piers—why are you here?"

She had intended to speak up for Yan and Guihen, but under the circumstances . . . Reaching for an alternative that was never far from mind, she said, "An old matter troubles me—a matter of which you already know. But it can wait for another time."

"Perhaps. But will that time come—or will you continue to put it off though it no longer serves any purpose?" Otho understood. Was he urging her to break with her false past here and now, in the presence of her sister's defiler? Otho, a priest, was a man. Did he consider maidenhood a prize to be won, and of no consequence thereafter? But the knight was the secular head of the town. Otho must think it reasonable that he be first to know. He would find out anyway. Did it really matter? Her burden was onerous. Why not rid herself of it?

She sighed, and reached behind her neck where her long hair was tucked under her tunic. She consciously willed the subtle spell that veiled people's eyes to fall away. She shook her head, and her tresses swirled about her shoulders.

Jerome grinned. His expression gave her second thoughts. What was he contemplating?

"Amazing!" he said. "Had I known your father had two daughters, how differently I might have done." He laughed dryly. "But that was clever Gilles's intent, wasn't it? With no son to inherit his grove, he would have been forced to sell it to me." He looked suddenly puzzled. "Have you no further concern for your toothless sire?"

"I'm no longer a child, *Miles* Jerome. I can't live for my father or an olive grove. When he's gone, what use will I have for trees? If you press him to sell the grove, and he accepts your coin, it would be money thrown away. When he dies, I won't contest your claim to the grove."

"You say that with the priest as witness?"

"If Marie does not recover, and marry, so that the grove falls to her spouse, I'll sell it to you for a single silver penny."

"Your husband won't thank you," he observed. "An olive grove is no small possession."

Pierrette wondered if she had erred. Ownership of land was all that distinguished *servus* from *miles*, serf from free. But she remembered an older Pierrette, seated on a throne, with lightning at her fingertips and thunderheads at her command . . . "I won't find a husband soon," she said dryly, "and when I do, I doubt he'll rue the sale of a few olive trees." She reflected upon the long, green slopes of The Fortunate Isles, and only with effort pulled her attention back to the tawdry present.

Jerome slapped his hand on the table. "Done, then!" he said heartily—then winced as he inadvertently shifted his raddled buttocks upon the padded bench. "Father Otho—you have witnessed our words."

"I have." Otho peered toward Pierrette, no longer Piers. "Are you sure? You haven't sworn yet. Let me repeat what I understand the bargain to be: for one silver *denarius* or Frankish mark, you'll sell the olive grove to Jerome, within a week of Gilles's last rites. No persons or other conditions will attach to the sale. If Marie recovers and marries before Gilles passes, the agreement is null, as the grove would thenceforth be inherited within Marie's husband's family.

"I so swear," Pierrette said, impatient to be done with the matter—and to begin her new life, free of pretense, free of threat to the grove her poor, drunken father held dear. She turned to leave.

Jerome rose hastily. "I'll accompany you. We can discuss how best your transformation can be revealed."

Pierrette immediately started for home. "Wait!" the knight called, picking up his horse's reins. "Why hurry so?"

"We have a bargain. As for the other matter, do as you will. When I reach my father's house, I'll exchange these clothes for a long dress, and soon all will know. There's nothing to discuss."

"I think differently," said Jerome, hurrying to catch up. "You are as one just born—reborn, if you will. You may think yourself a woman, but you're as innocent as a new-born. Perhaps I can begin your education . . ."

His unctuous tone repelled and frightened Pierrette. Had she made some terrible mistake? Why did he gloat so?

"I know what you could teach. P'er Otho would do better to eject you from the Church. He should spew you out, and make an honest pagan of you."

His reaction was not what she expected; she was prepared for his sneering laugh, but there was no humor in his eye, no scorn or coarse amusement—she saw pain, wistfulness, and terrible loss.

Then, like a mask over his heavy features, his smile became mean. Putting one foot in the stirrup, he swung awkwardly into the saddle, which was padded with a woolen blanket. "Pagan or flawed Christian I may be, but you have only begun to learn what I have to teach. And teach you I will. Count on that!" He neck-reined his mount and dug in a single-pointed spur. His horse's hoofs rattled on cobble-stones, the sound quickly diminishing.

Should she return to P'er Otho, and ask what mistake she had made—or what mistake the Burgundian believed she had? But what could he do? Nothing. But still, her concern erased the pleasure she had anticipated, when she at last became a woman.

Chapter 19 ∾ The First Blow Falls

Morning broke clear and cool, with a promise of wind. Pierrette considered Marie's limited wardrobe, and chose a brown homespun dress. She shouldered a jar of oil and a basket of full clay bottles. She wished to be firmly established in her spot at the market before anyone else arrived—anyone but Granna, always first to arrive and last to leave.

Hurrying through the narrow streets, she encountered no one at close range. Granna was already arranging her wares. "I wondered how long it'd take."

"How . . . how long have you known?"

"Maybe a year? I was worried when your voice didn't change, so I kept an eye on you. When you let your hair grow . . ."

"Does everyone know?" The old woman was known to gossip.

Granna chuckled. "The women do. It's like those patterns Moors carve—first you see one thing, like an upside-down stairway. Then your eye fiddles with it, and turns it right-side up. After that, you wonder how you ever saw it the other way."

Then there would be no great to-do, no laughter. "Why didn't anyone say anything?" Pierrette asked.

"You had to have a reason." Her eyebrows rose in a question.

Pierrette explained about her father and the olive grove. Granna was familiar with the problem. In the old Roman days, inheritance had been fixed by laws. Migrations and invasions had brought new customs. Now, depending on whether one considered herself Roman, Celt, Visigoth or Frank, different rules applied, and because everyone inter-married, there was no clear precedent. It was like having no laws at all.

"Besides," Granna continued, "more than one woman would be glad to be a man. It's easier. 'Fetch this, give me that,' or 'Where's my dinner?' No sneaking the occasional penny or saving spoonsful of salt to trade for a few yards of cloth, or needles to sew it. Sitting home when a hus-band goes to the inn for wine." She shook her head. "You used to go there with Gilles. You won't be welcome there any more."

Pierrette had not considered that.

"For all you know about being a girl—or a woman—you might have been born yesterday," Granna mused.

Pierrette felt cold, despite the sunlight. Jerome had said that too. Had she, a "boy" all her life, taken too much for granted? Of course the men would not welcome a woman, who might tell their wives how much they drank and spent, and of drunken revelations that would get them in trouble at home. Women wielded sharp-honed tongues. Would she be reduced to that?

Yet her situation was unique. She had always exercised a degree of control over Gilles. Why would that change?

Pierrette's metamorphosis caused little stir. Summer wore into fall, and she settled into her new role. There was gossip—but what was there, really, to be said? She had done nothing scandalous, had not harmed anyone.

As a girl, Pierrette maintained a brown, mousy appear-ance. She did not wish to be exceptional, only accepted—but that eluded her. Women treated her no differently than before. She did not become an intimate member of the clusters of girls who huddled together at noontime, eating, laughing, and gossiping. Girls her age had long since formed their friendships. They had known—and mostly ignored—the boy Piers, and they continued to do so. They did not know the girl Pierrette, and were not interested, except as an object of curiosity. No one rushed up to ask, "What was it like, being a boy?" They only looked—and those looks kept her apart.

She only felt like a woman with Anselm. After his initial

surprise, the mage's behavior shifted in some subtle male fashion.

The supplicants who came had weighty things on their minds, and paid little attention to her, as a person. Of course her position as Anselm's apprentice caused talk, but few Christians wished their visits to the sorcerer known. What was said was always attributed at second- or third-hand: "So-and-so told me she heard . . ."

No one seemed to notice that her arrivals and departures were almost simultaneous. To an observer, she would have appeared to enter through the gate, then to have come right back out again—though for her, hours, even days, elapsed inside.

She tried to reason out that paradox. If she arrived, ate a meal, read a book or scroll, and only then answered the bell's ringing when visitors came, how could she eat again after they left—their requests heard, their ills healed—at the same moment she had arrived? No matter how she struggled to force time to do her bidding—to become understandable— she never gained more than a headache.

She could not ask visitors about their perceptions of time's passage. Those who passed her in street or marketplace pointedly avoided her. Consorting with sorcerers, or their apprentices, was not openly acceptable.

Pierrette heard the crash of breaking pottery as she neared the house. "It's not here!" cried her father. Leaving her jars, she opened the door upon a shambles. Broken pots were strewn across the floor. The room reeked of spilled wine and spices. Bedding, clothing, and utensils lay in heaps, and furniture was overturned.

Gilles glared with sick anger. "What have you done with my silver?"

"Papa! You're drunk! Your money is where you hid it." She went to the hearth, and wiggled the loose stone free. "It's right here . . . It . . . Father! Did you move it again?" The niche was empty.

Twice before, brooding on the security of his money, Gilles had hidden it, then forgotten where. Pierrette checked the window ledge. "I'll look in the cellar," she said.

"It's not there!" Gilles wept.

"I'll look anyway."

The small opening was a tighter fit than when she had been a child. There was a snake. The same one she had entertained with her experiments, long ago? It was lodged against the foundation where she wished to reach. Despite her decision to find out if snakes, like light, were affected by people's assumptions, now was hardly the time. Nevertheless, she reached past the snake's fat coils, groping. Gilles's bag was not there.

"Someday, " she murmured, "we'll discuss magic—and the nature of your kind—but I must go." Getting out was no easier than getting in. By the time she ascended the stairs, she was bruised and scraped.

"My money!" Gilles wailed.

"Father! Hush! Do you want neighbors to hear there's a lost treasure? You'll remember where you hid it. Now help me clean up. We can't find anything in this confusion." She directed Gilles in the heavy tasks of righting table and bed, and heaped soaked clothing and bedding by the door.

"You'll have to sleep on straw tonight," she said. "It's too late to wash your things."

"My money!" he cried softly.

"We'll find it. Now I must find something for us to eat. You ruined everything here." She went out, leaving him with his head in his hands. It would not be long, she reflected sadly, before the knight got his way with the olive grove. Some of Gilles's befuddlement was wine, but not all. His mind was crumbling. When that happened, the body did not maintain itself long. He could no longer climb a ladder, or wield a pruning saw. A year, she thought. Two at most.

Anselm had been little help. "Only magic—or a miracle—could cure him. Would you dare wield such a spell?" He pointed to a shelf of ancient scrolls. "Would you trust yourself to determine what postulates have changed, and in what manner, in the thousand years since those were last tested?" Pierrette was proud of her success with small spells, but had no illusions about great ones, written when the world was new and vastly different.

Now, climbing the stairs with a loaf of bread and a salted redfish, she considered one of those "safe" spells, one she had successfully tested not a week before. . . .

✧   ✧   ✧

"*Wedh' arhentom*" she incanted, for the fifth time, laying down the tiny coin. "*Yemos trof' yemo* . . . Oh, it's no use, *pater*. The silver is not here, or the spell is wrong . . . I don't know."

"I'm poor again," Gilles said dully. "I have no pennies for wine, no . . ."

"Is that all you can think of? I'll buy wine, tomorrow. There is the oil money. But now you must sleep." Relenting her earlier statement, she said, "You may use my bed. My bones will suffer less from the hard floor."

When Gilles's snores became loud, Pierrette stood, holding the bit of silver in her tight fist. She had lied; the spell worked . . . and was working still. "Silver, find your way home," she had said in her mother's tongue. "Like to like, twin finding twin." Even now, the coin pulled—but not toward any hiding place within the house.

Pierrette worked her way eastward through narrow, moon-shadowed streets, her arm extended, held up less by her will than pulled by the coin, which was eager to be reunited with its kin.

Her direction hinted at a destination, but dread forced her to keep an open mind. Then she emerged on the soldiers' practice field by Jerome's house. The silver was beyond her reach.

Jerome had stolen it—or had one of his men do so. But why? She whispered quiet words, and the coin ceased tugging. The knight had not repossessed the money for its own sake.

Whose motives? she asked herself. Jerome the Burgundian's? The Celt god Cernunnos'? Or the unfathomable wishes of the dark one who consumed gods and drew power from their spirits? If the horned one had desire, it was not for silver, but for some condition the silver's loss would cause. But what?

Darkness, when the moon lowered itself behind the rooftops, thickened. As surely as the coin had pulled her hence, her feet now set her on the way to the cape and to Anselm.

"This much is clear," the old mage stated—though he no longer looked old. Black strands threaded his white hair. "The first blow has fallen. It's safe to assume that your father's impoverishment is incidental, and that you are the blow's target."

He sighed, sipped wine, and shrugged. "One such blow is a surprise, from which little can be learned. To discern a direction, a plan, we must wait for the next blow to fall. Two points define a line, after all. How many blows must be endured—how many points located—before we see the shape of things?"

Pierrette considered that with no great joy. The next blow, if she were not prepared, could be fatal. "It's possible," she mused, "that this is the second blow."

"What do you mean?"

Pierrette explained what had transpired at the priest's house. "My willingness to part with the olive grove was an unintentional parry on my part. The deflected blow was Otho's letter to the bishop. Jerome intended to strike at me through Guihen and Starved John—and through you."

"Then there will be another attack. We must be ready for it." Those were optimistic words, but though Pierrette and her mentor hashed them over through many hours of endless noon, they could only guess at the direction from which that attack would come.

Chapter 20 ∾ Time's Wheel Broken

The dappled trunks of plane trees stood bare, and the last lost leaves huddled soddenly in out-of-the-way places. Winter had brought only light rains, but it was chill.

Pierrette's first hint of new trouble was in the eyes of women. Actually, in those she did not see . . . There were averted glances, whispered comments. What were they saying?

Granna alone did not change. "They think you are a masc, like your mother. They're afraid your gaze will dry their breasts—and they remember the pox that still troubles the knight. He walks as if his trousers are full of twigs."

"My mother never did evil things."

"Your mother was not a succubus who changed sex as easily as those women change dresses."

"Neither am I!" Pierrette snapped. "What else are they saying?"

Granna sighed. "Will you snarl and gnash your teeth if I tell you? Remember, it's not me who's saying things."

"I'm sorry, Granna. Tell me."

"They say the magus seduced you, and that together you perform obscene rites with boars, bears, and even birds."

"Birds?" Pierrette snorted. "That shows how stupid they are."

"Did Leda consider it silly, when a god's seed swelled in her?"

"That's an old myth. Where do they get such stupid ideas?" How had she and Anselm been linked with John and with Guihen? As soon as she asked herself, she knew—

207

this was the knight's next assault, to alienate her from the townsfolk, as her mother had been. Coldness grew in the pit of her stomach. Had Elen felt like this? Shunned and scorned, had she too suffered this loneliness and . . . had her misery come from the same source? Had the knight, not the gullible *gens*, been her mother's true murderer?

The days became increasingly difficult, with no one but Gilles for company. There was no money for wine, because no one bought oil from Pierrette, and her father was forced to remain sober for the first time in years. There was wood, prunings from the grove, burned sparingly to make it last.

Pierrette had not told Gilles her suspicions, but in his new, clear state of mind he had reached a conclusion much like hers.

"Where are you going, Father?" She worried when he went out, because his lucidity alternated with episodes of confusion.

"I must speak with the castellan," he said. "I want to get to the bottom of this."

"He won't tell you anything." She did not try to stop him.

She had been too long without Anselm's counsel. If she walked with Gilles, no one would suspect she was going to the Eagle's Beak. Considering the *gens*' suspicions, she dared not go openly. When they reached the sloping field, she would slip through a breach in the town wall, then through a dense stand of pines.

"Are you sure you want to do this, Father?" she asked him as they drew near the Burgundian's residence.

"I hear what they're saying," he responded. "I heard such things before—when your mother was alive. If the knight is behind the rumors, I must find out what he wants. He is not one to thrash about without purpose."

Indeed, he was not. When she and her father parted, Pierrette pondered that again. Something she had read bore on the knight's motivations—but no matter how she tried, she could not remember it. She only remembered P'er Otho pouring oil back and forth between two jars: good and evil, back and forth . . . tides ebbing and flowing in the calanques, much as the influences of gods and churches did across the ancient many-peopled land . . . good and evil. . . . She was close to understanding, but could not quite get there.

Voices drew her back to the here and now, at the juncture of her trail with the one that led up through the cleft in the red rocks. Peering from behind a feathery tamarisk, she recognized the people ahead. One was Claudia, carrying a basket of bread. They were going to the cape.

Recent experience made her cautious. Trailing just out of sight, she heard the harsh voice that challenged them. "Turn around, you women!" It was the soldier whose horse she had ridden. "Go back before I get a good look at you, or I'll have to tell my master who came to visit the sorcerer. You don't want that."

"We're just gathering herbs," said Claudia—but she kept her shawl pulled across her face. "Why are you stopping us?"

"The castellan has had enough of warlocks seducing his folk from God. When the hermit weakens from hunger, we'll break down his gate and take him for judging. Now go, before I change my mind." The three erstwhile pilgrims fled.

She followed them back to town, because there was no other way to the crest: Anselm was isolated from the *gens* whose attention and expectations had given him new life and substance. Was that the knight's intent?

Slipping through darkening streets, the old stone walls seemed to lean in, great and ancient weights that would crush her if they shifted the width of one finger. She hurried home; that scant refuge seemed all the more important, her father's company all the more welcome.

She found him at the table. The old rusty spatha lay before him, the Roman sword he claimed showed his descent from a soldier of Rome. Pierrette had heard, even before she saw the sword, the scrape, scrape of the black stone Gilles used to sharpen his axe. "Father! What are you doing with that?"

"It is time," he said from between clenched teeth, "for a free Roman to stand up against the Hun."

"Father! Put it down, and tell me what's wrong." Was he drunk? There was no cup, no sickly scent on his breath. Gilles's eyes were unmuddled.

"I lost one daughter to the barbarian," Gilles said. "I won't give him another."

"Father, tell me! What did Jerome say?" This was yet another blow aimed at her, at her friends and family.

Gilles did not stop honing the pitted blade—but he told her of his visit to Jerome.

Two points, she reflected, determine a line, and she now had enough to know the shape of the knight's plan, if not its ultimate intent. The women's accusations—that she was a masc, a sorceress—had been only a beginning. She was (or so Jerome had told her father) not only a masc, but the consort of the old magus, a participant in ancient rites of a sexual nature. "It is necessary," Gilles said in a fair imitation of the Burgundian's accent, "for Pierrette to be married as soon as possible, to save her from further corruption—to save her soul."

"To bind me to a husband who'll guard me as a cock guards its hens. With children at my breast, I won't go to the cape."

"Tell me it's not so!" Gilles pleaded. "Tell me you haven't fornicated with that old devil."

"He is not a devil, Father. He is a kind man—and I am as pure as when I was born. I intend to remain so. I will not make the mistake that . . ." She had been about to say, "that my mother made."

Gilles stood, sword in hand, held clumsily, as if it were a pruning saw. "You are all the family I have left. I will defend you."

"No, Father! Put that down." She grasped his wrist—and forced the sword to the table. "I'm touched that you would give your life for me—but you must not. You can't defeat the 'Hun' and his soldiers like that. We must find another way."

Indeed, she was touched, but bitter as well, for it was far too late for his brave stand. That should have come when first Jerome importuned him, when Marie was still an excited virgin contemplating her wedding night, when . . .

Now a different path needed to be taken, not to Jerome's, not to the cape, blocked by the soldiers. There was only one way they could go. "We must ask Ma," she stated with confidence she hardly felt—but the walk might give Gilles's anger time to cool, for sense to prevail.

Always before, Pierrette had approached Ma as a child. This time, she knew what she wanted: a clear vision of what was to be, not in some faraway future time, but in the next days and weeks. The lines of battle were drawn.

As they neared the grove, the hot wind off the dry hills cooled, which was magic, of a sort—a spell whose words were the shape of the hills, the directions of seasonal winds, and entrapped moisture in the shadowed confines of the narrow valley.

"What will you do?" asked Gilles as they approached the pool.

"What did Mother do?" parried Pierrette.

Gilles hung his head. "I don't know. When we were young, we . . . we made love here. Then I slept. Perhaps my young wife did not—I can't remember."

"Perhaps it wasn't meant for you to know," his daughter said. "Perhaps you will again sleep, if the goddess commands."

"I don't want to sleep," Gilles replied. "I want to know what I must do."

"And you will, Father. Awake or asleep, the Lady will give you what is needed."

They stood before the small beech tree that was her special comfort. In a quiet tone, she intoned the first words of the spell her mother had taught her. Somewhere, in the leaves and branches high overhead, a magpie chattered, and she knew that all was well.

This time, she resisted the urge to lie down in fallen leaves and moss. Always before, she had let the spell take her where it willed, but then she had been a child. She was no longer innocent. The words she chanted were not rhythmic noises but a language, carefully constructed postulates that shaped her thoughts—and through them, her reality.

When first she had used the spell, she had not understood: she had wanted to peer ahead, but the spell's makers had not conceived of time as she did, and she had been thrust, as a magpie, into that dark future at the very end of time. Had time been a serpent biting its tail, she might have gone beyond that future to the past instead. This time . . .

Gilles's eyes were wide. What did he see, as the slender beech tree wavered and the woman of the pool stepped out from it? Did he too see Ma as a woman of middle years, ebony of hair and russet of clothing?

The figure shimmered, as if heated air rose in front of Pierrette's eyes, doubling itself, as if she were not focusing properly. One image stepped left, while the other remained still. The first took Gilles's hand. Pierrette let her fingers slip from Gilles's. The woman—whose face seemed subtly younger than her counterpart who remained still—led Gilles away. Pierrette did not turn her head to see where they went.

Ma-who-remained shook her head. "You don't understand the Parting of the Veil, daughter," she said softly. "Sit, and we shall explore it together."

Pierrette lowered herself to the leafy ground, as did her companion—whose skirts seemed without a hem, blending with the detritus of the forest floor.

"When time was a wheel, complete and round," said Ma, "the direction it turned did not matter." She looked expectantly at Pierrette as if she had given meaningful insight. "You must see it yourself, child. Rote learning suffices for a masc or a priest, but a sorceress must understand what she does."

When time was a wheel . . . The spell had come from the East with her ancestors' ancestors. Those unnamed folk had sown seeds in lands whose edges Alexander of Macedon had touched—Hindu folk who spoke of time as a wheel, and of events repeating endlessly. It did not matter which way the wheel turned. The furthest "future" might be reached by going "back," through the past. But time, Pierrette told herself, is a broken wheel with a missing felloe between past and future. . . .

"The spell doesn't reach to the future!" she exclaimed. "It reaches back! And because it postulates an unbroken wheel, it stops at the most remote place in . . . in the past?" The foundation of her universe trembled.

The past? Then was the Black Time not what would be, but what had been? Had the ruins of a greater Citharista existed before the busy Roman seaport of centuries ago, or the sleepy town of the present? It could not be. Yet it would explain much, if the spell sought the future through the past . . .

She covered her face with her hands. "It makes no more sense than the gate to Anselm's fort. It's not rational."

"Why is that, child?"

Pierrette explained about the black time.

"That must not trouble you," said the goddess. "Consider that the wheel is broken, now. You have seen the world buried in ashes. But when did the destruction occur?"

Pierrette's head spun as she fought to encompass new concepts. If she laid a rope on the ground, in a circle with both ends together, she could walk from any point on it to any other, whichever way she went. Yet if she stretched the rope straight, and stood at its midpoint, she could only tread half its length going one way, and half the other. One way was "past," the other "future." She was only allowed to go in a single direction. . . .

"The devastation occurred," she murmured, "before the break in the wheel. It 'occurred' in what is now . . . the future, and what I saw, as a magpie, was only its aftermath, on the other side of the break in time's wheel . . . in the past." She shook her head sadly. "I can't look into the days ahead, can I? The spell only allows me to look back."

"That is mostly so," said Ma, "for you can only see what remains after the destruction. What transpires in the days or weeks ahead is a vanishingly small part of the whole, and has left few traces."

"What is beyond the Black Time?" Pierrette wondered aloud. "Whether past or future, does time simply end at the broken place on the wheel?"

"I can't say. We can't go forward, but must become immortal and live through the destruction into the Black Time . . . or . . ." She raised one eyebrow—an expression that Pierrette, had she owned a mirror, might have recognized as her own.

"We can't go back, beyond the relic of the Black Time that we can see . . ."

"We need not go so far—but we will go back," said Ma. She reached with both hands for Pierrette's. "Here in Provence, the past is rich loam beneath our feet, and the present is only dust atop it. The Veil of Years is thin. Let's pierce it together."

Ma reached into a fold of her garment, and opened her hand to show Pierrette: a brilliant green-and-black feather, and a tiny mushroom, round and small as a button. "Shall we fly?" she asked, a happy twinkle in her eye.

For the second time, Pierrette felt the tremor of moving air on wings—air firm and uplifting, as cool and real as water. She soared with the ease of a swimming fish, a fish of the lightest fluid—a bird of the air.

She soared and swooped, savoring the solid feel of air beneath wings, flowing over long tail-feathers. She flapped, reveling in the action of tiny, hot muscles that knew just what to do: pull in and raise folded wings effortlessly, spread them and push. Feel the burning effort in muscles bound tightly to the great keel of her breastbone. She rose, laughing magpie laughs.

Ma rose more easily, an indulgent mother enjoying her child's delight in a sun-warmed pool. But the child tires of aimless splashing—and Pierrette tired of merely being a bird. She wanted to go somewhere—and as soon as she decided, Ma knew.

They flew neither north nor south, up nor down. Pierrette was a swift, iridescent shadow in Ma's turbulent wake. They flew . . . back. They also flew westward, and the Citharista below them was a busy place with many carts in the streets, galleys, fat merchant ships, and a Roman bireme in the harbor.

They flew over cresting hills. In that past time the dragon's bones lay amid oak trees that covered slopes barren when she had traversed them in Gustave's cart. The shape of the land itself changed as they flew. In the brief "now" the magpies inhabited, the sea was lower; bays Pierrette had seen before were dry valleys, miles from the mother sea.

They overflew the headland where Pierrette had flung a challenge of blue light at the stars, where she had heard voices raised in ancient song. There was the calanque, as she had seen it before as through a mist, but now clear, and her chattering magpie cries caused her companion to circle back.

"This must be the place," said Ma, though not in words. "Shall we descend?"

Pierrette tipped her wing, trading altitude for speed— instinctive for a magpie, a wondrous equation for the girl within. But she would ponder that later. . . .

The sea was low, and seals moved over the rocks at its edge. A tiny white beach was dotted with now-cool hearths. Folk lived there in caves whose mouths dotted the steep eastern slope of the bay—the folk who had called to her. Even now, from the depth of memory, she heard them singing. "Come to us, come back to when this land is new."

New—as it was now, in this moment. No cities had been

built. No ships sailed the shrunken sea. The elephants on the grassy flatlands were subtly different from the beasts Hannibal had led through Provence on his long trek toward the Alps. The deer in the woodlands were larger than those the *gens* of Citharista hunted. The people were also unlike the *gens* she knew.

Coming from their cave homes into the cooling light of afternoon, they did not notice the magpies that landed in the branches of a parasol pine. A man with hair like polished brass squinted into the lowering sunlight. "Tonight we'll make a fire on the beach," he decided, without speaking— yet the magpies heard his thought. They heard also his imagery of what would transpire at the edge of the fire, when all were full of rich meat from a fresh-caught seal, sated with crisp fat whose drippings fueled embers into fresh flame.

Pierrette heard those warm thoughts, and for a moment felt herself to be a blond-haired, full-breasted woman who lowered herself onto the man, smiling as she parted the strange, yellow hair of her womanhood to accept him . . .

Magpies could not blush, nor could their hard-billed faces feel heat at such delicious and unbidden revelations. Pierrette's discomfiture was not visible. Yet magpies could laugh, as Ma did then. The man, hearing magpie-chatter, looked up and smiled. He waved, and the two birds leaped into the air with a rattle of feathers.

The Golden Man, Pierrette marveled. The Golden Man of my daydreams. But we never did *that* in my reveries.

Later—aloft and westward—Pierrette turned her head toward her companion. The rush of air across her beak caused her to veer closer. "Is that what you wanted me to know?" she asked, remembering the man's hard heat and the woman's delight in the enveloping power of her wet loins, the quickening joy as her womb accepted his seed and made it hers.

"It wouldn't be fair to ask you to forego such delights if you didn't know what you might miss."

"Must I remain virgin forever?" Pierrette knew for the first time a small part of what her mother Elen had not been willing to do without.

" 'Forever' has no meaning for one who parts the Veil of Years," Ma replied ambiguously. "Yet if you part that lesser veil, your maidenhood, you will never again part the other as we do today. And if lesser is parted within greater, you may never return whence you came." That made little sense, but Ma did not elaborate.

They were high over land only vaguely familiar. "What is that?" Pierrette exclaimed, seeing a city; they had travelled more than mere miles since leaving the cave-folks' realm.

"That is Massalia," said Ma.

"But where is the abbey?" asked Pierrette. "There isn't even a road south of the calanque."

"They have only just paved the *Via Tiberia* from Arelate to Roma. The abbey will not be built for a century or two."

"Shall we land there?" asked Pierrette. "Shall we sit on a branch and peer down at Lazarus at his devotions—or has he not yet come to Massalia? What year is it, down there?"

"We are flying from the far edge of the wheel forward," Ma said. "Lazarus has not yet come—but you may see him, when we reach our destination."

They flew north, then westward, with low mountains on their left and a wide lake on the right, then over an arm of the sea onto a flat, featureless plain.

There Pierrette experienced a strange tremor within, and she hesitated, losing altitude, descending for a closer look. Something beckoned, much as the cave people had, long before.

Yet there had been a momentary sensation of dread, as if she had passed near a place of terrible unhappiness, then left it behind. "What is that place?" she asked. She knew it was not what Ma had brought her to see, or the other magpie would have slowed before Pierrette did.

"The flat land is the Crau—the Plain of Stones, where Herakles fought your Ligure ancestors, as he returned home with the red cattle of Geryon."

"Who lives there now—in this time, whenever it may be?" It was not easy to shape that thought in any language Pierrette knew. No verb tense defined a present within the past.

"Horses roam there, and men capture them for breeding. They are sacred to Poseidon, but the old god's protection wanes."

They flew on. A broad thread of water broke into many

channels—the mouths of River Rhodanus. They defined a sea of grass as splayed fingers define the space between them—the Camargue, where the old magics worked as they had been intended. Her excitement mounted, then faded—could a magpie's beak and lumpy tongue shape a spell? No, she would have to be there as herself, to perform her experiments.

Beyond a tangle of lagoons were low, sandy islands held together by the trees that grew upon them. Ma shifted her course. Straight ahead, Pierrette saw smoke, and discerned roofs thatched with long salt-grasses.

"That's where we're going," Ma said. "A fishing town that will someday be called 'the Holy Marys of the Sea.'"

Two magpies atop a dead cypress went unnoticed. Though out of their usual range, on beaches populated by gulls and stilt-legged birds, magpies were not the only foreign visitors to that remote shore, then or thereafter.

Then? Pierrette had seen Massalia when Romans manned its walls. She had seen the bay at Sormiou millennia earlier. If those houses were where the saints from the Christian holy land had arrived after the transfiguration of Jesus, then what Pierrette was seeing was "long ago."

The Abbess Sophia Maria, suggesting that Marie might benefit from a visit to her namesake's shrine, had described a bustling town where the Archbishop of Arles sponsored a fortified church on the site of the saints' graves. But Pierrette saw no church.

"'When' is this?" she asked her companion, twisting a Latin tense in an uncomfortable manner.

"It is forty-four years since the boy Jesus was born in Nazareth," said Ma. "Mad Gaius, called Caligula, is dead, and Claudius reigns."

People emerged from a thatched house. A skinny man waved and called to someone working in a boat on the beach. "Lazare! Come see us away." A husky fellow emerged from the vessel and swung gracefully over the rail onto the sand.

Pierrette intensified her gaze, as if to burn every detail of the scene into her mind. She was seeing an event of more than religious import. Those people would shape history with their words and deeds. Even in her time Provence—of all

Europe—echoed their influence. The borders of nations, the reigns of monarchs, would be decided by what they said and did.

Two white-haired women wore clothing like Grecian robes, but with a foreign drape to them, much stained and mended. Their faces and hands were dry and crinkled from a sun no less intense than that of Provence. A dark-skinned woman with a beaky nose and kohl dark eyes hovered close, a nurse or doting servant.

The fellow who had called out was perhaps fifty, dressed in undyed tunic and kilt, fisherman's clothes. Another, whose black hair was streaked with gray, wore a tannin-brown robe. His face held scholarly introspection, like Anselm's or P'er Otho's when deep in thought.

Beside him stood a younger woman who stood out because her hair was not black or gray, but honey brown. Gold highlights danced at her temples where wisps sprang free.

"Remember her," said Ma in a soundless whisper, "for you will meet her someday."

Another woman stood apart, facing the sea. Her dress was bright blue, faded and bleached from seawater. The man from the boat flung an arm about her in brotherly fashion—he was indeed her brother, and brother to the light-haired woman as well. A strong family resemblance showed in their faces, and in the lightness of their hair.

"Remember the two oldest women," said Ma, "for you will meet them—and not long after we return to your own place and time."

"I wouldn't know what to say to them," Pierrette replied. "Those are the saints—the two Marys who lie buried—who will lie so?—in a crypt beneath the shrine."

"You've had no trouble speaking with old women before," said Ma with an ironic overtone. "There is Granna . . . and me."

"That man who came from the wrecked ship is Lazarus, whom they say was raised from the dead. She whom you say I'll meet someday is Marie Madaleine—Magdalene—whose bones will lie in the valley of the Holy Balm, below the cave that is her shrine."

"Indeed. And do you know the others?"

"The skinny one is Cedonius—born blind, it's said, but now healed; the other must be Maximinus. Lazarus embraced

Martha, whom P'er Otho says Jesus chastised for her busyness. The one who cares for the old women, then, is Sarah the Egyptian, patroness of Gypsies." Pierrette sighed. Of course, a magpie cannot really sigh, but Ma heard a sigh when Pierrette intended one.

Seven people saying good-bye. Magdalene would wander Provence, preaching in Lugdunum and in villages, and would at last retire to her cave a few valleys north of Citharista. Sarah would remain with the eldest Marys, and would minister to the pagan Gitanes, the Gypsies—and thus to all the world "Romish" folk wandered. Maximinus would build his abbey, and would bury Magdalene there.

Lazarus would become the first bishop of Massalia, and would at last lie beneath the stones of Saint Victor's. His sister Martha would subdue a dragon—the Tarasque. Was it kin to the dragon whose bones lay atop the hills east of Citharista? And Cedonius, living testament to what Pierrette considered the magical power of Jesus? Perhaps he remained on the coast with the three women.

The group divided. Four remained, and four departed. The road led north until it met the stone of the *Via Tiberia*. Those four would walk together on the cart track until they reached the Roman road at Arelate.

"Come child," said Ma. "We must return, or the fine thread that joins you to your mortal self may part, and leave you forever a bird."

Pierrette, having been told nothing of that, became suddenly willing to depart. The remaining women had gone beneath the thatched roof, and Cedonius sat alone outside, peering at the sun-sparkling sea—as if he could not, in the years remaining to him, ever see enough of what that sun illuminated.

On the flight homeward, Pierrette was not tempted to dawdle over even the most impressive sights.

Over the Camargue's sea-wet grasses a flock of flamants arose. Black, white, gray, and rose feathers flashed in the evening light.

An old man emerged from his reed-thatched cabane, and fed sweet grasses to the lithe doe who crept from the thicket. Pierrette's bird-shadow flickered across his upturned face, but her magpie eyes were looking far ahead, to the beech trees where her true body lay, a silent husk without spirit to motivate it.

With great relief the eager magpie spiralled down among leafy branches to the pale form asleep on a bed of leaves.

With equal relief, Pierrette lifted sleep-tingling hands before her face, reassuring herself that she had indeed returned, and was a bird no longer.

Gilles was rubbing his face, as if his body also had been untenanted, and himself far away.

"Where did you go, Father?" she asked as they walked westward down the broadening valley. "Whom did you see?"

"Go? I didn't go anywhere. I remained beside the pool the whole time you slept. I . . ." His face reddened, like a blushing child's.

"Tell me!" she pressed mischievously, already suspecting what had—or what he thought had—transpired.

"I . . . I was with . . . your mother," he said, not meeting her eye.

"I'm no child, Father," she protested, giggling. "Did you speak together, as well as . . ."

"We spoke!" Gilles said quickly. "My beloved gave me good news."

"Tell me. I need good news."

"I've been afraid, child. You've seen my hands tremble, and . . . and I haven't been right in my mind. Now I know I'm not doomed to suffer the madness and foolishness of old age. I'll live a while, with all my faculties, and then I'll die. That's a promise."

"I'm glad, Father," Pierrette said softly. "I feared for you." She had no doubt that it would be as he said. Whether he died in a month or a decade, there would be no degrading descent into childishness or second infancy—and that was promise enough.

As for her own voyage—or vision, if such it was—she was less satisfied. What did she know that she had not known before? What had she learned that was of use? Flying across so many miles, years, and centuries, she had been too busy to ask what she had wanted to know.

Now it was too late. Her problems had not lessened, for having flown so far from them. Her only reassurance that she would prevail against the castellan Jerome—and whoever hid behind his coarse Burgundian face—was that Ma's intentions for her seemed to stretch long ahead, and she would have to survive the next days and weeks to fulfill them.

The door of their house was ajar. They had not left it so.

"Gilles," said the horse-soldier whose bowed legs stretched across the hearth. A heartily uneconomical fire blazed. A month's firewood was being consumed to warm one soldier's damp toes. "And Piers—no longer a boy, I'm delighted to discover. We, too, have much to say to each other."

Gilles stood there, angry over this violation of house and hearth. Pierrette was lost. What was there to speak of? "You gave me a ride on your horse, once—but I don't even know your name."

"I am Lucius," he said. " 'Luc,' like the gospel writer." He chuckled self-indulgently. "I'm a bit of a physician myself, having patched a few sword slashes in my time."

"What do you want with us?"

"Why, to discuss our future—yours and mine—with your father. I'm a northerner, but customs can't be all that different between us. Dowries . . ."

"Marriage? You want to marry me?" She could not decide to laugh or to scream—so she did neither. "Where did you get the idea that I'll marry you—or anyone?"

His eyes were glittery hard. "You've heard what they're saying about you? Marriage is the best you can hope for. You won't find a better man than me—nor another willing to have you." His words dripped scorn, but his expression was unperturbed, as if he spoke only of common facts.

Pierrette, raised as a boy, had no practice in the womanly art of getting one's way without confrontation. Her perspectives were not a girl's, either. She saw the gnarly soldier as the boys had, when she had been one of them. His wiry toughness, the strength in his bare, tanned forearms, even the fine tracery of scars from enthusiastic workouts and actual battles did not repulse her, but added glamour to an otherwise ordinary middle-aged man.

That attitude saved her from a tactical mistake. When she replied, she was neither arch nor mocking, haughty, nor flirtatious. "I'm sure I would find no better man," she said evenly. "You were kind when you thought me a boy, and

I suspect you would be no less so to a wife . . . but what are people saying? No one has threatened me."

The soldier reacted well. He told her she was accused of licentious acts and pagan rites—mostly with the old magus, but with husbands from the town too. "If you remain unwed, the jealous wives will come for you, some night." He glanced at Gilles. "Just any husband may not be protection enough—but no man in Citharista will willingly face me. They'll keep their wives at home." He smiled, patted his thigh. "Come here, and we'll seal our bargain with a kiss."

"I've never been kissed," she said truthfully. "I'm not going to begin today. And I am a maiden," she said with a certain heat, "despite what the women in the market may say."

He peered closely at her, with a curious expression. "Protestations are unnecessary. I'm not too proud to march in the dust of the van. At any rate, you wouldn't be a virgin by the time you came to my bed. The castellan would see to that."

The obviousness of that had escaped her. Of course—that was Jerome's intention. Yet Pierrette felt only sickened and sad, thinking of poor Marie, not herself. The Horned One would not drive her mad. It was not going to happen.

"I'm not lying. I am a virgin—and I intend to remain so. It has nothing to do with you, or your offer. There are other considerations."

"I'm not offended," said Luc, rising to his feet. "Should we marry, we would have a fine time—but I'm content as I am." At the door he turned. "If you want to save your own skin, you'd better be able to prove you're virgin still. If you reconsider . . ."

"I won't," Pierrette said firmly. "Tell your master that one of my father's daughters is enough. He shall not have—nor destroy—the other."

The soldier nodded, and set off eastward, his leather soles making little noise on the dirt-covered cobbles. Gilles nodded his approval of his daughter's handling of the affair. "It isn't yet time for me to stand up for you," he said sheepishly. "You did well by yourself. Don't be angry."

"Angry, father? You know what you must do—and what not."

"Still, I wish . . ."

"Hush, Father." She placed a finger on his lips.

When Pierrette went to shut the door, she saw Father Otho, bearing a scrap of parchment. He waved the page at the soldier, then read from it. Luc shook his head. Pierrette was curious. But when Otho arrived at the door, other concerns intervened, and she did not ask.

"I came as soon as I heard," he said. "He did no harm?"

"He's not evil like his master Jerome," said Pierrette. "We parted without anger, but without settling anything between us—or between me and his Burgundian lord." She sighed. "This can't go on," she said. "I must leave Citharista."

"Leave?" asked Otho. "Where would you go—a lone young woman?" He glanced at the parchment, now tucked beneath his cincture.

"I can be a lone boy, if I need to." She brightened—suddenly understanding the meaning of her recent magpie's voyage. "I have a destination in mind." She mentally traced the route the two birds had taken.

"Jerome won't allow you to leave," Otho said. "If you anger him, he'll turn the *gens*—and his soldiers—toward the Eagle's Beak, and the old mage."

"No! Anselm has harmed no one! Jerome has no quarrel with him."

"He'll use him to have his way with you. The old fort's walls wouldn't hold against a platoon, nor the mage's magic against swords and axes."

"Don't tell me I must marry Luc, the soldier, and spend my wedding night with that . . . that goat."

"You must leave Citharista despite Jerome," Otho reflected. "I was about to show you this. It's from the abbess." He handed the parchment to Pierrette, who struggled to read the crabbed hand:

Marie has taken a turn for the worse. She rallied briefly, and began taking walks with sister Claude, though she refused to join us in prayer. Now she sits alone in darkness. We dare not leave her a candle, because she set her clothing on fire once, and didn't even cry out for help.

Send the boy Piers, to take her to the shrine of the Marys, by the sea. We have done all we can, and it is not enough.

"I must go!" Pierrette cried. At last there was a difference she could make, however slight, and however poor the chance of a happy outcome.

Otho shook his head. "I showed the letter to Jerome, and just now to Luc. The one will not allow you to depart, and the other will not turn his head and let you slip past—even if you swear to marry him when you return."

"I don't think he cares about marriage—but he's a good soldier, and does what he's ordered to." She shook her head hopelessly. "Is there no way?"

"Perhaps there is," Otho said. "Tell me the truth, child—are you indeed a maiden still?"

"Is my maidenhood the talk of the town? Yes. I am untouched. Now tell me what must be done."

"The castellan has made much of the pagan rites he claims you have practiced. He calls you a *maenad*—one who cavorts with Dionysos."

"I know what a *maenad* is. Does he claim that I—with other madwomen—run through the woods tearing apart woodcutters and hunters?"

"I don't think Jerome knows of that part of the rite," Otho said.

"His master does," Pierrette grumbled angrily.

"His master? The Frankish king?"

"His master who wears horns. His master, whom you call . . . Satan."

"Those are harsh words, child. Jerome pays tribute to Cernunnos—but Satan? If so, you are at terrible risk. If not . . . such an accusation puts your soul in danger. 'Do not speak his name, lest he hear you.'"

"You said there was a way to defeat him."

"A way for you to get away, to make him seem a fool for his contentions, so no one will pursue you—or slay old Anselm. Now you must trust me."

He would say no more. "Your reactions—everyone's—must be natural and unrehearsed. Friday we'll meet outside the chapel, where I hope your difficulties will be resolved." He chuckled. "If all goes well, a problem of mine may well evaporate too." He would not explain what he meant.

Pierrette felt as bleak as the weather. Cold rain splattered the steps and pavement, for winter had come. There had been little sunshine in her life, and the future looked no brighter. If P'er Otho's "plan" failed, Anselm, alone on his bleak cape, would weaken, or would be overwhelmed by soldiers.

Her thoughts strayed to the Camargue, seen through a magpie's eyes. If she could escape Citharista, perhaps there in the vast unruly sea of grass, where old magics were said to endure, she could utter an ancient calling-spell, and cry out to Minho of the Fortunate Isles to allow long-lost Anselm to return home. . . . Then she could continue with Marie to the saints' shrine.

Would Gilles have to sell the grove for a crust or two of bread? How could she abandon him? He was too proud still to accept charity from the small-minded *gens*. Ma's prophesy did not promise long life—only that he would not sink into the madness of age. But would Marie languish and die if Pierrette stayed here?

In the climate of fear and distrust Jerome fostered, Yan Oors and Guihen would suffer as well. Even if the Evil One did not consume them as he had Cernunnos, no loaves of bread would be left on doorsteps, no bowls of milk.

When Otho left the house, neither Gilles nor his daughter spoke. They went silently to their beds without supper—for there was no food in the house.

Chapter 21 ∾ The Trial

"How can anything be discussed out here?" Pierrette protested to Otho, in the bleak light of a stormy dawn. "What unpleasant weather."

"It's lovely weather—for my purpose," said Otho. "I asked the castellan to bring only those people who are to witness against you, but I know him—everyone will come to see you humiliated."

"What's good about that?"

"It's good that the weather is nasty, because when I offer the involved parties the shelter of my chapel, Jerome will have no good reason to refuse. We'll shut the doors on the mob the knight hopes to incite against you."

Pierrette looked at Otho with new eyes—the humble, fumbling priest had not impressed her as especially wise. "And I'll be safe from them, in your sanctuary," she said.

"There is that," Otho said with a smile.

Indeed, the Burgundian was angry—but had no reason to insist on another venue, or to postpone the confrontation until the weather cleared. The parties to Pierrette's persecution—and some whom Otho seemed to consider her defenders—entered the chapel, where three candles burned in a single sconce. The altar and crucifix at the far end were obscured by gloom.

On one side stood Otho, Gilles, and Pierrette, and opposite them were Jerome and the soldier Luc. Also present were others of whose alignment Pierrette was unsure. Granna will not speak against me, Pierrette thought. But she was not sure. What would Granna's self-interest dictate? Claudia the baker had always been kindly, but who could tell? The tavernkeeper Germain and his wife Julia were there, and Parvinus, a stockkeeper and cheesemaker—and a terrible gossip. Whatever transpired would soon be known by all the town.

Of the rest, there was little doubt. The soldier for whom Anselm had recommended a cure for impotence was there, with his broken-toothed wife. Pierrette did not think they were present out of gratitude to the mage's apprentice. There was the shepherd whose headaches Anselm's herbs had relieved. What would he have to say?

Gilles stared at the knight, his fists clenched. "It's not yet my time," he muttered under his breath. "It is not my time."

Pierrette felt reassured when Otho began speaking as confidently as if this were a mass. "Much has been said of this child's sins," he said, "but we are not here for marketplace gossip. Are there real charges?"

"Indeed there are!" Jerome said loudly. "Bruno, tell these people what you told me." The once-impotent soldier was unused to speaking in front of groups, and was embarrassed to air his private disability. He blushed apple red, and stammered meaningless phrases.

"Get to the point!" Jerome urged. "You couldn't turn your rope into a spear, so you went to the sorcerer." Bruno nodded. "Then what happened?"

"The old man said words over me, and sent me and my wife up the valley, to a spring beyond the Roman fountain. There we . . . we did it, and I was cured."

"What? Is that all?"

"Well . . . no."

"Tell us!"

"It wasn't her!" Bruno blurted. "I mean, it wasn't my wife. It was her!" He pointed to Pierrette.

At Jerome's curt urging, Bruno's tale emerged. When he made love with his wife beside Ma's pool, she metamorphosed into . . . Pierrette. From a huge old tree sprang Anselm, who cavorted while they coupled in the leaves. As if that accusation—adultery as well as sorcery—was not enough, the soldier declared that it had been the same ever since: the woman who came to him every night was Pierrette also.

"There you have it," said Jerome. "Bruno, you may go."

"Not so quickly!" Otho said. "I have a question or two."

The priest turned to Bruno's wife. "Didn't you mind? Did you stand aside with the mage Anselm, to watch your husband and his lover?"

"There wasn't no lover!" she bellowed. "There wasn't nobody! Just him and me!" She glared at her husband. "Thinking about young girls when you're swiving me, will you?"

"We've heard enough," Otho said, waving Bruno and his expostulating wife away. Pierrette had no doubt they would have a long discussion, one that would arise anew whenever poor Bruno felt male urges and approached his wife. Pierrette giggled, and earned disapproving looks from Jerome and Otho alike.

"Are there others you wish to call?" Otho asked the knight.

"Ah . . . perhaps it can wait. I'll question my witnesses further, to make sure there are no other misguided fools like Bruno. We can reconvene another time, when the weather . . ."

"Oh, no! Let's weed out the fools and be done with it." A murmur of assent from others sealed Otho's decision.

Unhappily, Jerome bade the shepherd tell his tale.

"I saw her in the woods," he said, and described how Pierrette removed her skirt and bleated like a goat, until someone—something—responded to her noises. "I saw his goat's legs, and his great tool. They did it again and again."

"She submitted to a demon, half-man and half-beast?" Jerome prodded him.

"She didn't even lie down! He leaned her up against a tree, and . . ." The shepherd enthusiastically described Pierrette's debaucheries with the pagan god, now granted demonhood.

"I see," Otho observed, pointedly staring at the shepherd's crotch, where the fabric bulged noticeably, "that you aren't revolted by what you're telling us, Claudio. Did you enjoy watching them? But no—let me remind you that though you are in my chapel, and I am your priest, this is not confession. You don't have to answer . . . now."

Claudio was well aware that he was not in the tavern among friends, but was facing his confessor—and the memory of all his past confessions. Herding sheep was lonely, and masturbation was not the worst that the priest had heard of from shepherds. It was good, Otho thought, that ewes were not quickened by human seed, or there would be children in Citharista with legs like Pan's. "Claudio, tell me what you really saw."

Hanging his head, Claudio related—with significantly less enthusiasm—how he had heard a bleating goat. Berenice's buck had gotten his collar caught, and Berenice was trying to free him.

"Berenice, not Pierrette?" Otho interjected. "You're sure?" There was a distant resemblance between Berenice and Pierrette—both were female and had black hair. But Berenice was twenty-five and had borne six children.

"It was Berenice," Claudio admitted. When Otho pressed him, he told how the woman's skirt became caught in the thorns. She removed it, thinking herself alone. When the goat was freed, she untangled her garment and again covered her white buttocks and heavy, dimpled thighs.

"Is that all?" Otho asked. "A woman removed her skirt, freed her trapped goat, redonned the skirt, and departed? No unnatural acts were performed?"

"Well . . ." said Claudio.

"No woman performed an unnatural act, I mean."

"No. I mean yes . . . She didn't do anything."

"I'll expect you at Sunday mass, Claudio—come early." For confession, of course. The only sexual act performed in the woods that day had been Claudio's, involving no goats, pagan gods, or women. Otho was sure it would be a long time before Claudio regaled tavernmates with his fantasies.

"There is a lesson in what we've heard today," Otho said in his sermon-voice. "Men and women make scapegoats of the innocent, rather than admitting their own sin, weakness, or foolishness.

"Have we weeded the fools from our midst?" he asked Jerome. "Are we done with fanciful tales?" Several people nodded. "Then the charges of sorcery are laid to rest."

"Not quite!" Jerome blurted. "There is the matter of her changing from a boy to a woman. She was no woman before! I, and a dozen others, can swear to that."

"You might swear that you did not know she was a girl," Otho corrected him, "but others knew.

"Granna—when Pierrette began coming to market, how long before you knew she was a girl?"

"Hmm . . . last year—or before that. When she caught young Marius behind her market stall with . . . with Claudia's daughter Marcella . . ." Granna glanced toward Claudia, and raised her hands palms up, as it to say, "What can I say but the truth?" Claudia shrugged. After all, Marcella was safely married—though not to Marius.

"Pierrette saw them futtering," Granna continued. "I found her weeping—which was odd, for a boy. My curiosity was aroused, and I watched her more closely. The signs had been there all along—the way she walked arm in arm with Marie, when a boy wouldn't walk the same side of the street as his big sister."

"Why didn't you say anything to me? Wasn't it my concern, as shepherd of Citharista's flock?"

"You already knew, Father," Granna stated. "You had to know the reason, too. If you weren't doing anything about it, why should I?"

"Indeed I knew," Otho said. "I knew Gilles's fear for his olive grove, if he had no son. Of course I thought the deception would be done with when Gilles remarried and begot a male heir, but that didn't happen. Still, the child didn't seem burdened by the masquerade, so . . ." He turned to Jerome.

"She consorts with the sorcerer!" Jerome grated angrily, his scheme eroding away.

"As do others," Otho countered evenly, "others who do not stand accused today." He turned to Claudia. "You bring bread to old Anselm," he said. "Couldn't a sorcerer make bread from stones, and wine from seawater?"

"Not like my bread," Claudia said.

"You go there often. What have you seen?"

"A hungry old man," said Claudia.

"Your bread condemns you!" Jerome spat. "He gave you a magical yeast."

"I use the yeast my mother gave me!" she protested. "You're jealous your cook bakes only bricks."

"You leave loaves on your doorstep each night," Jerome said. "Sacrifices for the old man's demon minions."

"Demons? Don't be silly. You're a foreigner, and can't be expected to understand. We leave bread and milk for the

Shy People—the fairy folk. They herd no cattle and sow no wheat. Would you rather they worked mischief on us?

"Father?" she asked, turning to Otho. "Is it a sin to leave bread for them?"

"You leave a loaf on your doorstep, and in the morning, it's gone. Who's to say what hungry soul picks it up? Do you pray to false gods? Do you ask favors for your bread?" Claudia shook her head.

"Then I see no harm," Otho concluded.

"We have strayed from the subject," he then said, "which is Pierrette. All that's left to discuss is what to do about her." He held up the letter from the abbess. "She must take her sister to the shrine of the Holy Marys," he said, "but our castellan has bid her remain here and wed the soldier Lucian. What is the reasonable course?"

"The sister will die one way or another!" snarled Jerome. "She's completely mad anyway. The girl is of marriageable age, and has no other suitors. A husband and a baby or two will keep her out of mischief."

"She claims to be a virgin, still," Otho said. "If it's her wish to remain unwed, and her father's . . ."

"It is!" interjected Pierrette.

"She's no virgin!" cried Jerome.

"Then the last dispute has been clearly expressed," said Otho. "If she is not virgin, Jerome's contention is supported— though not proved. If she is virgin, her own assertions are clearly proven, and Jerome's are invalidated. The solution is simple—and we have just the person here to provide it." He turned to Germain's wife. "Julia—you've attended most births in Citharista?"

"I lost count after the hundredth, twenty years ago."

"And women come to you for advice about . . . womanly ailments?" Julia agreed they did.

"Can you determine if a woman is a virgin—or not?" Of course everyone knew the answer, but Otho wanted everything laid out so no future dispute could nullify what was decided.

"I can tell if some women are virginal," Julia stated, "but I can't say for sure that any particular woman is not—unless she has borne children."

"Let me make this clear," Otho said. "If Pierrette is untouched, you may determine that beyond doubt. If not, it still doesn't disprove her contention. Is that so?" Julia agreed. It was possible to prove Pierrette's assertions, and impossible to prove the castellan's.

"Then let us put an end to this. Pierrette, go with Julia—and Granna and Claudia; three witnesses will suffice. We'll wait here."

Pierrette was more enraged and humiliated than another girl might have been. Had her mother lived, she might be enured to intimate examination by women. Had she been raised as a girl among women, it might have been less traumatic to lie with her legs apart while each woman held a candle close and peered at her. Only Julia—after murmuring a quiet incantation and washing her hands in a bowl of wine—actually touched her.

Despite her awkward pose, Pierrette could not resist asking . . . "What spell is that?"

"Spell?" replied Julia. "I asked Mary, mother of God, to guide me."

"And the wine?"

Julia was nonplused. "Why . . . My mother and my mother's mother always washed with wine. There's no spell—I'm no *paganus*."

Paganus. How words changed. It meant simply a rural dweller. Why had it changed, to mean a believer in old gods? Because Christianity had always been a city faith? Contrary to the old, earthy religions, it had nothing to say about farrowing hogs, the culture of olive trees, or the illnesses of sheep or goats. *Paganus*. Pagan. Of course.

The four women pushed through the chapel door. Claudia and Granna looked smug. Pierrette's visage showed bitter confidence. Only Julia's face showed nothing at all.

"She's been with no man," Julia stated. "There's no question about it."

Jerome's face was neutral. It was no surprise. Had he had his way, though, it would never have been revealed.

"Let's be done," Otho said. "The girl is untouched, and the tales about her are vicious rumors. Pierrette, is it your intention to remain unmarried—and virginal—at this time?" Pierrette nodded. "Speak up, that we may all witness it." She did so, between clenched teeth. The humiliation would not fade soon.

"Will you take your sister to the Marys' shrine?"

She nodded again.

Otho turned to Jerome. "Are you satisfied with the women's finding? Is she free to depart?" The Burgundian nodded.

Of course he was not satisfied, Pierrette reflected. He must be enraged. Yet the question that plagued her was: Why? Obviously, he had lost his opportunity to deflower her, but that was not his real obsession. Was Cernunnos angry that he had lost a perquisite of his fading godhood? She could not forget the consuming fire she had seen in the haunted eyes of the horned god: Jerome's anger at being thwarted was explainable; she could speculate about Cernunnos's motives. But behind the horned one was greater Evil, the Eater of Gods. What was its aim? What was so important about her?

"You're wiser than I thought," Pierrette admitted when she and Otho were alone. "You hand-picked each person, didn't you?"

Otho smiled. "My 'education' in Massalia took two years," he said. "My real education began when I returned here as a priest. I exercised what choices I could. Not Jerome or Lucian, of course, and not Bruno or Claudio either, but I knew Jerome would choose men with lurid tales to tell, tales that would only hold up outside, where the shouts of his mob would muffle me."

"I know why you chose Claudia and Granna," Pierrette said. "They're respected. But Parvinus? Germain? Neither man said a word."

"Look beyond your motives and mine, to theirs."

Otho wanted her to figure it out for herself. Parvinus was easiest—he was a gossip. Now the gossip he traded would not be rooted in Bruno's self-justification or Claudio's fantasies, but in their foolishness—and Jerome's. The knight's star would fall as her own rose—and therein lay her continued safety. Not soon would the *gens* of Citharista rise to destroy one of their own over baseless rumors and malicious lies.

And Germain? Would Julia's husband entertain suggestions that impugned his wife's skills? He would defend her—and his "forum" was the largest in Citharista: the wine shop, where every man went when he had a coin to spare. No one would imply that his wife was a fool or a liar.

"And your motive, P'er Otho?"

"Mine? Consider, child. A herd of cows can have only one bull, and horses one stallion. Of course I am neither—though priesthood has not unmanned me—but a town can have only one spiritual authority, and one temporal. Jerome crossed the boundary between our domains. Now he'll no longer threaten to have me replaced by a more docile priest."

"Will he keep a guard on the trail to the cape? Will poor Anselm remain without a soul to visit and cheer him?"

"He'll have his bread and wine," said Otho. The priest did not know the whole of it, Pierrette reminded herself. He did not know that those visitors who brought no bread and no wine, only requests for his aid, were the greater sustenance the mage required. "Even if Jerome doesn't withdraw his soldiers at once, Lucian and his men won't watch closely."

Pierrette was not ready to depart the next day, or the one after. "Wait," Granna advised. "Let the *gentes* guilt work for you, as their small minds once worked against you." Pierrette did not know what she meant, until the third morning.

Gustave the carter was the *gens'* messenger. "This is for you," he said, handing Pierrette a small, heavy sack. "Open it!" A dozen coins poured into her hand. "They took up a collection. Is that enough?" Pierrette suspected it was—though not too much. Gilles would have to live on what he was able to make selling oil. Neither she nor P'er Otho had devised a way to get Jerome to return the coins he had stolen—or to admit that he had stolen them.

"I'll manage," Gilles assured her. "Nothing will happen to me because . . . it is not yet my time."

Pierrette did not think Gilles would be lonely. She had seen the looks that passed between him and Granna. It was almost as if he could not wait for Pierrette to depart, so he would have the widow to himself. Of course Granna was too old to give Gilles the heir he had wanted, but there was more to life than babies.

Before Gustave departed, Pierrette made her first use of the new coins. She dickered with the carter for his donkey. His heart did not seem to be in his bargaining, and

they reached agreement at a price far below what she would
have paid. She thanked Gustave—but remembering how the
beast had always eyed her with suspicion and resentment,
she wondered how good a bargain she had driven.

With regret that she must again pose as a boy, Pierrette
folded a dress, chemise, and shawl and stowed them in the
bottom of a wicker pannier. She would be walking over rocky
ground and through thorny brush. She didn't expect to meet
many people on the high track, but still, a boy might be
less tempting than a young woman, should she encounter
anyone with malicious intent.

In a less practical sense, she felt less vulnerable. She took
on a brasher attitude with her clothing, an ability to joke,
bluff, even posture threateningly. She had learned the "rules"
of male social intercourse while avoiding physical confrontations. She had learned how to back off short of violent
conflict, but to hold her own, right up to that. Other girls
didn't learn that, not in the same way.

Perhaps there was good in her skewed "education." She
had bemoaned what she was missing; now she realized she
had gained something in compensation: confidence, if not
actual competence, in dealing with the world of men.

Several well-wishers accompanied her from the town, then
one by one dropped away. Otho was the last. "You'll stop
and check on Anselm?" she asked. He assured her he
would—though his parishioners would gossip. "Wear your
shiny pectoral cross, and chant in Church Latin. They won't
suspect it's a social call."

"Will it be?"

Otho had never met her mentor. What would the two men,
so different, yet in some ways the same, think of each other?
"I can't imagine you not getting along."

"I suppose I'll find out," he replied. She had to be satisfied with that.

"This will be a long journey," she sighed. "When it's over,
I wonder how ready I'll be to settle down?"

Otho chuckled. "I have a feeling that this trip is only the
beginning of your journeyings. . . ."

What god or prophet, Pierrette would ask herself in the
years that followed, had spoken in the priest's ear?

✧   ✧   ✧

Otho's quill snapped in his hand. He spat an unpriestly word when he saw the spattery blotch on his parchment. What had the girl said, that day when she made pact with the knight about the olive grove? Something about making an honest pagan of him?

Otho was not sure, but it was something she had said. Something about jars of oil? About Good and Evil, and . . . about pouring all the oil but a single drop into one jar. Yes! That was what she had said. And what else? That Christians had created Satan, and should pour half the oil back. . . .

Otho's thoughts raced. Pour it back? An honest pagan? He groaned as the stiffness in his limbs made him aware how long he had sat. "Ah, well, I'll work the kinks out on the way to the knight's house."

Indeed, he felt fine and feisty when he arrived. When the elderly gatekeeper attempted to stop him, he fired off phrases in his best Latin, of which the poor man understood only that, as God is everywhere, he could not deny entrance to a priest, unless God was also absent from the house. Otho encountered no one else on his way to the knight's bedchamber.

Jerome was abed, but his painful condition made sound sleep impossible. He awakened before the priest at the foot of his bed finished three sentences of his unconventional chant. Jerome sat up, confused, but not yet afraid. Otho continued his singsong, his hand raised as if in benediction.

". . . and forgive you, and release you from your Christian pledges as if you had never heard the word of God, as if you were indeed an innocent, a child of nature not yet schooled. Jerome, protector of Citharista, you are freed. Jerome, priest of Lugh, in the name of the Father, the Son, and the Holy Spirit, I release you and give you back your name, Reikhard. I withdraw your baptismal name, Jerome."

"Reikhard," the knight murmured. "I haven't heard that name in twenty years. The last priest of the old gods gave it to me. He died before I had memorized the sacred texts. . . . I was still a boy when your priest-blessed waters washed that name away. But what have you done?"

The impact of the twisted rite had not struck him yet. There was no recognized ceremony for freeing a man from the Church. Excommunication barred a man from the sacraments; it did not wash away baptism or erase professions of faith. There was exorcism—but he did not intend to drive out a demon. He intended only to make its dwelling unhabitable. . . .

"Indeed, what have I done?" Otho replied. He had likely damned his own immortal soul. "I have freed you. I have poured half the oil back. You are no longer Christian."

"Are you mad? You can't do that!" Jerome swung his bare legs from his bed. Otho backed away fearfully, for the voice was not the knight's.

"Depart, fallen one!" Otho's voice was not quite a shriek. "This pagan is not your meat. You have no place here. Depart, I command you!"

Jerome—now Reikhard—gagged as if vomiting. His heavy frame heaved, and his legs stiffened, forcing him to his feet, arms outstretched and fingers curled as he tried to grasp the priest's neck. Otho stepped backwards. The knight's throat welled with wet words no living man knew, and a fetid stench rolled out upon them.

He opened his mouth, as if to scream. Black smoke belched forth and gathered like a storm among square-hewn beams, seeking exit between the planks of the ceiling. The shapeless darkness squealed as if a crowd walked on the floor above.

The knight sank back to the bed, and with one final eructation expelled a last wisp of blackness that chittered like a mouse underfoot as it fluttered upward to join its whole.

"Depart!" Otho screamed, ducking low beneath the roiling mass. "Begone!" From the noisome cloud issued sounds of scurrying rats, hissing of vipers, wet rending of living flesh. It moved, blown by an unfelt breeze, toward the tall window. It billowed, and then was gone.

The Burgundian's retching did not deter Otho from rushing to the window, in time to see something dark coalesce in the branches of the plane tree in the courtyard, to hear the hoarse croak of the great raven that took wing. The priest stared wide-eyed as black wings momentarily obscured the moon. The creature flapped away westward, and was soon lost in the night.

Part Four ❧ *Exercitator* (Magician)

The folk of the land are layers of an onion, whose thin skin is the distant overlordship of the Franks. Beneath it are "Romans" of Latin, Celt, and Ligure blood. At the core of the onion are small, dark people, elusive forest-dwellers, fairies, and Gypsies, who still sip at the breast of Ma. Thus are the people.

The land is sunny. Broad rivers run deep in one season and trickle in others. Mountains stand white and ocher above fertile plain and desolate heath. Vineyards huddle on southern slopes. Elsewhere ancient olive groves shade the rocky ground. For a few months, cold winds from the Alps contend with wet ones from the Mediterranean, and chill rains fall. Then the *Mistral*, the divine wind, drives men mad.

The land is uncrowded, for there has been much slaughter. The Moors swept through. Charles the Hammer defeated them at Poitiers, and ironically, Christian Charles's hammer fell harder upon the land than did Saracen swords. Roving Magyars and Norsemen contributed to the devastation.

Thus are the land and its peoples, so ancient that every cut of spade or plow upturns shards, coins, inscribed stones, and bones of peoples gone before, who live in the blood of all who followed. This is the land, the people, and the tale of a girl, now a woman, born of both.

Otho, Bishop of Nemausus
The Sorceress's Tale

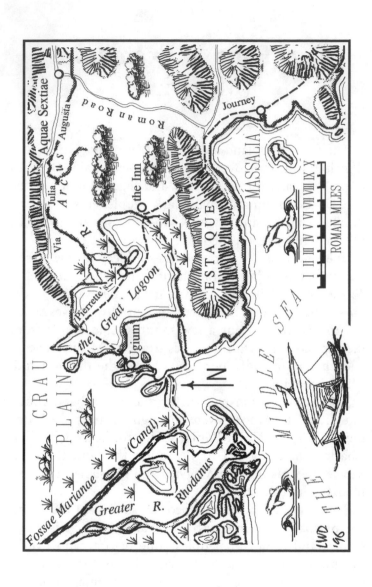

Chapter 22 ∾ Dangerous Magic

Pierrette's Journal

Otho was right. Reikhard's Christian demon could not live within an honest pagan. Bereft of the conflict that had divided the knight, the demon had nothing to feed on.

I departed before Otho performed his unconventional exorcism. Had I known of it, I might have been more prepared, for the raven had gone westward—as had I. Yet even with the demon gone, the knight was no different, except that his lust for women, land, and power was now wholly his own. At least I was free of him. . . .

"Tell me again," said Reikhard, after rinsing his mouth and throat with wine and spitting it on the stone-flagged floor.

"You tell me. How do you feel?"

"Like a boy, my Christian years gone. Am I truly free of them?"

"Of your years?" Otho was, having matched the Burgundian gulp for gulp. "You look no younger, but indeed you are free of your Christianity."

"Can you really do that?" wondered Reikhard pensively. "Still, the foul thing that oppressed me is gone, see?" He raised his stained nightshirt. There were pocks, scabs, and round scars, but no suppurating sores. "What I mean is, does . . . your Church . . . allow you to do what you did?"

"I don't think so. But it worked. No Christian demon can inhabit your pagan flesh."

Pierrette walked lightly, the morning sun at her back, warm against the chilly air of late winter. Though the route west was one long rise from sea level, the ground seemed as flat as a plain. The ass—whom she called "Gustave," after its former owner—carried food, water, and blankets.

The miles passed swiftly. By evening, the dragon's bones and the windy cliffs were behind. She ate cheese and bread drizzled with olive oil, with a pinch of dried thyme. Then she rolled herself in her blankets.

She had forgotten to weight the lids of the donkey's panniers with heavy stones. The beast had already nuzzled one lid off. She threw a loose stone. It struck Gustave's nose, and he backed away, snorting.

"If you eat my food, as well as your own, what use are you? I can carry my blankets myself. Without bread or cheese, I'll have to eat donkey meat." She was half-convinced that the ass understood.

She awoke before dawn colored the hills, and loaded Gustave, who had not further disturbed the panniers. She did not follow the track down to the village at the head of the calanque, but kept to the high ground where no brush impeded her.

The second night, having crossed the first divide, she realized that she had missed the chance to experiment with the changing nature of magic. She murmured the words of the fire-and-light incantation. A faint, blue glow, a cool halo, hovered by her fingertips.

At least the changes were consistent. She would try "Guihen's Charm," which conferred invisibility—her mother's spell, learned as a nursery-song:

> "I cannot see my soul;
>   When I die, it will depart on the wind;
>   My soul is air.
>   My soul rises, and looks down on the rest of me;
>   What does it see?
>   My flesh is Water, running down the many ways;
>   My flesh is Earth, dust gathered by Air,

Moistened by dew.
The willow leaf and the wild olive tree
Are dust and water
Gathered by the wind,
And when my soul rises,
It will see my leaves and my branches."

She felt a brief flutter as if something wanted to change, to reflect the moonlight like silvery leaves, but Gustave's near eye was fixed upon her. He still saw her—the spell had not worked.

She pondered the words. What was different here? Ah! There were no willows or olives; the land was bleak and stony, scarred and dried by winds off the sea.

She changed the spell slightly. ". . . My flesh is Earth, dust gathered by Air, moistened by dew. *The stunted oak and the fragrant bush* are dust and water . . ." This time, the shimmery feeling was stronger. When it passed, she felt stiff, and strange. Why would an illusion make her feel so? Why couldn't she see anything?

She reached to brush an imperceptible veil from her eyes . . . but her arm would not move. Panic arose. She was as stiff and wooden as . . . as a stunted tree, and blind as wood. Sickened, she realized what had happened. She realized where she was: the high country, the wild land of Breb's primitive folk. "And," she said silently—because she could no longer speak, "seeing is believing!"

"*My soul rises, and looks down on the rest of me; what does it see?*" Belief was Anselm's sustenance, Yan Oors and Guihen's support. "What you see is what you get," Breb had repeated. And here she was, in this land where the essential postulate was "What you see, you must believe, and what you believe must be . . . real."

In Citharista, the spell made its utterer appear as willow or olive. Here the postulate equated perception with solid reality. The spell's user *became* a tree—a stunted, twisted oak with prickly leaves the size of a thumbnail, with a trunk no bigger around than a woman's arm. An immobile, speechless, helpless . . . tree!

Dawn rose over the humped hills. Pierrette was well and truly trapped. She could not speak, to utter a negating spell. Her roots went deep in fissured rock. She felt the sun quicken her sluggish sap, but could not see it, because she had no eyes.

Yet she could sense things. A disturbance in the breeze told her Gustave was edging close to the wicker pannier. Could a tree sense that? Of course it could. Perhaps the trees in Citharista's valley were insensate, but here trees—and rocks, even donkeys—had souls, because Breb's people believed they did. And she was caught in the web of their conviction. She wanted to weep, scream, tear out her hair—but she could not move a single twig.

The shadow of great wings flickered across rocks bleached white as bone, briefly blending with dark crevices and the pooled shade beneath stunted trees. Sensing a rich savor of despair, headier than carrion, the raven circled, its craving festering within.

There! But such agony of the soul could not spring from a mute donkey. What creature filled his nostrils with delicious hopelessness? With a rattle of rough, black feathers, it alit in the topmost branches of a straggling oak. Awareness surged upward through his feet—the tree was the source of the wonderful suffering.

The bird's guttural croak of joy did not go unnoticed. The ass edged closer, its wide, heavy-lidded eyes doubting, threatening. Why did the beast menace him?

Gustave brayed, teeth bared. With a raucous croak, the raven flung itself into the air. The donkey snorted as if it had scented something foul. Wide, brown donkey eyes followed the bird's flapping ascent, and its straight-winged course westward, daring it to return.

The sun rose higher. Pierrette wailed soundlessly. She struggled to move her wooden limbs, but her leaves trembled only with the breeze. Ever cautious, Gustave nosed closer to the panniers.

A strange sensation moved slowly as sap from Pierrette's roots upward, at last reaching the seat of her consciousness: among her roots she felt cool, smooth motion. A snake. She reached out with thoughts, not hands, to the dry, sinuous body she could not see. The serpent lay quiescent beneath her caressing thoughts, and Pierrette's panic faded, like heat absorbed by ophidian coolness—

as if Ma herself had spoken calming words to a frightened little girl.

As smoothly as the snake had come, it departed. She felt the scrape of scales on rooty bark. "Thank you," she said—she would have said, had she a voice. Was the poor beast's soul now burdened with her departed terror?

Did a snake have a soul? Mother Sophia Maria would say not—mankind alone was in God's image, and had souls. But this was not Massalia; here other realities obtained. And if snakes had souls . . . then donkeys did too.

Gustave, though hungry, still hesitated, not convinced that his mistress, who had turned into an inedible oak, would not again reappear as a woman with a hefty stone in her hand.

Pierrette grasped that thought. Breb had not used a mule, because if he believed in mules, he would have needed one. His inhuman strength was inconsistent with donkeys and their kin. Beasts of burden were not part of his people's world. They were, however, of Pierrette's . . . and Gustave did not truly believe Pierrette was a tree. She collected her scattered thoughts, and remembered . . .

Ma had uttered no words, when she and Pierrette had become magpies. There had been only an inward twisting, then her soul flying free. Pierrette remembered how it felt. She wriggled inwardly, not disturbing her tiny, leathery leaves.

She rose, weightless, and drifted toward the unsuspecting—but always suspicious—burro.

Donkey-head. Donkey-brain . . . not very smart, but determined. Donkey . . . soul? The small, shapeless entity shrank from her. There was no room in Gustave for two souls.

The ass brayed and kicked up its heels. It backed away from the pannier of bread, cheese, oil, and dried, salted fish, eying it suspiciously. Pierrette, shaken, was cast off, to hover unattached.

"I knew it was too good to be true," the beast seemed to say, eying Pierrette indignantly. "I never believed she was a tree."

Pierrette felt the thread that linked her to . . . to a tree? No! To her body, standing upright, her toes curled to grasp stones under her feet, her arms outstretched, fingers spread to catch the noonday sun.

With a silent, joyous cry, she plunged down that thread, and into . . . herself. Her cry burst out aloud, from her own throat. Tears sprung to her eyes and blurred her vision. She let aching arms fall to her sides. She sighed, and felt the rush of breath from supple, moist lungs.

Gustave eyed her skeptically, more willing to believe her a young woman than a tree. When the crying, laughing girl flung her arms around his neck, and kissed his bruised nose, making him snort, he was not sure—if donkeys could indeed entertain such complex thoughts—if he could believe it. "This," he might have said, if donkeys could speak, "is entirely too good to be true."

It was too good to be true when Pierrette fed him choice morsels of yellow cheese. When she broke bread, she gave him the fine, chewy end of the loaf.

When she loaded him, she refrained from putting her foot on his ribs to pull the girth-strap tight, but merely waited until he could no longer hold his breath, then gave a quick tug when he exhaled.

When they walked, she left slack in his lead.

Stopped for a meal, she gave him oats, and let him drink a whole pan of water—though not enough for the oats to swell and bloat him.

She rubbed him down with rosemary before arranging her blankets for the night.

Yet his jaundiced view remained unchanged: he watched as she carefully weighted the panniers' lids with heavy stones. For her to do otherwise would indeed have been . . . too good to be true.

Magic was dangerous. Shortsightness made it more so. A spell like "Guihen's Charm" was not a simple geometric proof, but the hard center of an olive, surrounded by the ripe fruit of worldly belief. Postulates that shaped spells were not always expressly stated; sometimes they were only implied by the fabric of belief that enfolded and empowered them. That was the lesson she should have learned from the snake in Mother Sophia's herb garden.

She promised herself she would design an "escape hatch" from the next spell she uttered. She was lucky that Gustave had been there, and was skeptical. When Pierrette hugged his neck again, he remained skeptical. She felt it in his stiff, locked knees, saw it in the roll of his brown eyes, and she loved him for it.

Yet Gustave alone had not saved her. She herself had participated. . . . Had there been other influences? The shadow of black wings, darkened her thoughts—but her tree-memories held only the vaguest impression, and the thought slipped away. Had there truly been a snake amid her roots, a snake who reminded her that even the lowest creature possessed a metaphysical essence?

Occasional carters had levered obstructive rocks out of the way. Still, the "pavement" alternated between gravelly low spots and expanses of cracked bedrock. Afoot with Gustave, she took more direct routes than carts could follow.

She experimented cautiously, now understanding that crossing a divide was to become like a baby, with no understanding of the realm of beliefs and magics it was born into. Careless utterance of spells was suicide, unless one wanted to live as a tree, a stone, or a fading ocean wave.

Her spells were small. She changed the color of a flower, or shaped blue light into faces of people she knew. She really wanted—needed—to try one particular spell in this place she had named "Realm of Blue Light." It was *Mondradd in mon*: Parting the Veil of Years.

"Time will not change from one realm to the next," she told Gustave. "That would not be . . . elegant." She had read of the principle of elegance in an ancient scroll: the best spells were the simplest incantations that encompassed the desired effect, and that did not contradict others whose utility had been demonstrated.

Time was elemental, imbedded in the fabric of thought and magic; a spell that contradicted it would rend the universe itself. She suspected even Anselm's time-binding merely rearranged events without changing them. Was that what the Black Time was? Had some ancient mage constructed a spell so all-inclusive that he broke the wheel of time and stopped its turning? Was the darkness that divided Beginning and End the site of his experimentation? Gustave made no reply.

She did not think time's nature would be changed by so small a thing as a watershed, subject to time's passage; it eroded and wore down; the course of rivers changed as a function of time.

Time and Earth. Time acted upon Earth, and . . . and was constrained by it? Was the material universe a vessel that contained fluid Time? The land was like an onion, many-layered, some thick, some thin. Were events the substance of time?

Pierrette stretched her finite mind: time had been a wheel—one point defined its axle, one its rim. Now only the points remained, and time was a line, not a circle. Onions, wheels, and linear spokes tumbled in her head, almost making sense, never quite coalescing into a coherent image.

It stood to reason that where much had happened, where events were heaped thickest, one might find a flaw in the layering, a place where one time was close to another, and there part the veil of years between one era and another, from the Provence of Greeks, Romans, Phoenicians, Franks and Muslims to a simpler, less weighty time . . .

Yet might it not be easier to part that veil where nothing much had happened, where "now" was so little different from "then" that she might step through the barrier without even noticing it? Could both be true?

She stopped. Gustave, brought up short by the rope around his nose, balked and brayed. "Oh, be quiet," Pierrette said. "We've gone entirely far enough in this direction. I will not avoid the issue by engaging in fuzzy speculation."

Indeed, she had been avoiding a decision. Ahead, the trail wound on toward Massalia; to her left, another led southward to a broad calanque with a small beach at its head, a beach blackened by hearth-fires . . .

Wrangling with the nature of time, she had avoided facing this moment, where two paths branched. She could only take one path at a time. But what was time?

For all her thoughts about onions and wheels, certain truths remained: magic was dangerous; spells were complicated, and it was impossible to consider all the implications of place and belief. She had wanted to look like a scrub oak, but had become one. The Veil was a more complicated spell. Did she dare use it here?

She turned first one way, then the other. This way or that? Here or there? Then or now?

Stepping back in time was no different than stepping through Anselm's portal into the ever-noon of his keep . . . was it? Coming back from the calanque and the deep past, she would trace the same path and step forth into the moment when she had turned aside from the Massalia trail. With a sigh indistinguishable from a moan, she turned toward the sea.

"Bah!" the old man expostulated. "Are there no small stones on this bleak path?" Grunting, he pushed a flat limestone chunk atop his new cairn, a half mile beyond the last. He brushed sweaty locks from his face, noticing that his hair was quite dirty. Had he looked closer, he would have seen that his hair was not gray with dirt, but had black strands among the white. But there were still many white hairs.

The raven floated over the city, sensing something among the cut stones, wood, and red-brown tile roofs. Somewhere amid thousands of delectable, vulnerable souls, was one whose internal battle between Christian virtue and lust, between Christian lust and virtue, had once pleased him. Now she was an emptiness waiting to be filled. His circles became smaller, centering on the south shore of the harbor, on Saint Victor's abbey, a radiant source of strengths and weaknesses . . . and then on a smaller place nearby. With a croak of ravenlike glee, he pulled in his wings and plunged earthward like a great, clumsy hawk.

Marie sat up suddenly. What was she doing in this strange bed, this cold room? Her mind seemed filled with dark thoughts, like the rasp of stiff, black feathers. Gradually, memories filled the yawning chasm between her vows with Bertrand and her awakening here.

Memories: Jerome cavorted like a goat, deer's horns on his head, his great, crimson member distended. Herself in his bed, and her cries as he took her—cries at first of pain, and then . . . Her pallid skin flushed with arousal, and her breath came in short, shallow gasps. Jerome's low growls vibrated in her ear.

"Jesus help me!" she cried. In the corner of her eye the pale Christian wraith shook his head

"God help me!" she moaned. But the only god present

was the Horned One, whose pleasuring she could neither deny nor live with.

Darkness had followed: Jerome had left her. She heard the glug, glug, of wine, and the knight's sigh. Then the other Marie, the pitiful, guilt-ridden Christian girl, had awakened, and had crawled out the window. She had fled through dark streets, naked but for her torn wedding dress, and had crawled up the stairs to her father's house.

"Fool!" grunted Marie, remembering the heat and the pleasure, not the shame. Fool to have run away. Fool, to have fouled her body and starved herself. For what? A tiny film of torn flesh? A god who let pious children be raped? Jesus, who stood by unmoved? Jesus? Perhaps it had been Otho, instead, or even a trick of moonlight.

"Priests!" Marie spat. Priests and nuns. She now remembered taciturn Agathe and motherly Clara, who had almost gotten her to smile.

Marie looked around the room. The door was heavy oak; she could not leave that way. She crossed to the unshuttered window. There was hardly any drop to the ground. . . .

Chapter 23 ✎ Parting the Veil of Years

Sea breezes pushed up the eroded ravine in gusts and surges, like the ebb and flow of surf on the tiny beach below. Farther along, beneath the calanque's present waters, was another beach, that existed *then*, but not *now*.

Pierrette removed Gustave's halter rope and retied it around his front legs. "Don't try to chew through this hobble. Be good, and I'll feed you half the remaining oats tonight." She stopped, patted his snout on the side opposite his bruise, and turned away.

After an hour's walk, the sun seemed no further west. It was hard to tell; the path down took her deep within great eroded cracks in the creamy limestone. The sky was a narrow swath of blue. The azure and viridian of the inlet seemed no nearer. She had murmured the spell in rhythm with her footsteps, a long time ago. Was this timelessness a sign that the spell was working? Did every shimmery step part one small veil like dew-laden spiderwebs?

The endlessness of the descent reassured her. If the spell was not working, it would have been shorter, as in her time. And among familiar bushes were others that only grew in cool, wet places. She cast back in memory, to see this place through a magpie's eyes. Had the skin-clad hunters' world been cooler and more moist?

A rattle of stones startled her. She slipped behind a projection of rock. Someone was angry, and in pain. She

251

crept forward and looked down on a head of shiny red-gold hair.

The girl, no older than she, wore a skirt of softened hide—and nothing else. Her speech seemed familiar, though Pierrette could make no sense of it. But then, when someone was holding her foot and trying to suck on a bloody toe, that was expectable.

"Let me help," Pierrette said quietly, in her mother's language and Ma's. Only afterward did she understand that the girl's words had triggered it. Both tongues had the same lilt and inflections; only time separated them.

Pierrette knelt, and uncorked her water bottle. Holding the girl's foot, she washed away bright, fresh blood.

"*Edh merr*," the red-haired girl murmured, sighing. Then: "*Kwi h'es?*" That sounded, to Pierrette, like "Feels good," and "Who are you?"

"I am Pierrette." She reached for the cloth that bound her hair, and wrapped the girl's toe with it.

Bright blue-green eyes, like white sand in the depths of a still pool, darted from the dark waves of Pierrette's hair to her own hurt toe, now wrapped in strange, unfamiliar stuff. She said something that sounded like "That is strange (something). What kind of (something) is it?" Strange skin? Or was it "What kind of beast?"

"It's made from flax," Pierrette replied. "It's not . . . not *pwel*?" How strange, Pierrette thought. We seem to be speaking the same tongue, but some words are different.

"Phlax . . . ?" The girl looked at her wrapped toe. "It does not look like a (something)." A leaf?

"*Phlaxa?*" said Pierrette, pulling a leaf from an unfamiliar, scrubby growth.

The girl giggled. "*Fou-leya*," she said.

"Well," Pierrette thought, "whatever 'flax' means, it isn't 'leaf'—or 'linen fiber.'"

The girl's name was Rheudhi, which meant "red" to both of them. Fiery hair must be unusual, worthy of a distinctive name.

"Come," Rheudhi said, testing her injured foot. "We go down to people." She turned away from the trail to the beach "Quicker way through (something—*kwah?*)." Pierrette followed. "Something" was a shelf of looming rock overhanging a dark hole.

Rheudhi scrabbled in fallen detritus. "My fire," she explained, holding up a soapstone dish with holes in the top. She heaped crumbled twigs, set a bundle of dried weeds next to it, then shook a coal from the dish. She blew. Oily, fat-soaked weeds ignited. She stepped into the cave.

Pierrette could see only a few paces, once the blue-white light of day faded behind. Rheudhi knew where to turn, where to warn her of obstructions. Sometimes her voice sounded stifled, as in a small room, and at others it echoed, bouncing off faraway walls and columns. Had the torch gone out, or had Rheudhi left her, she would have starved before finding her way back. It seemed an eternity before she realized the glow ahead was daylight at last.

Rheudhi called out, her words too swift for Pierrette, and the women's and children's voices that answered tumbled word after word in untranslatable noise.

Pierrette stepped outside the cave. Above, cliffs and white pinnacles supported tufts of brush and twisted, feathery pines. Ahead, blue-green salt water gleamed.

"*Aure Mamh'es*," said Rheudhi, taking the arm of a light-haired woman. "This is Mother Dawn." Mother-Gold? Ah—Rheudhi's mother, Aure. Like Rheudhi, she wore only a scraped hide. Unlike Rheudhi, her breasts rested upon a swollen belly. Pierrette did not have to be a midwife to know she was near term.

"My brother is inside," Rheudhi said, stroking Aure's belly. How did she know it was a male child? It could be a sister, couldn't it?

"Come. The men return at dusk," Aure said. Actually, Pierrette heard, "Men, darkness, they come," but it was clear enough. "We gather (things) to eat with them."

Curious children fingered Pierrette's cloth tunic and trousers. A small hand brushed Pierrette's breast. "She's a girl!"

"Come," Aure said.

Pierrette found herself wading with ten women in a tidal pool, sifting sand with her toes, reaching down to grasp a mussel or clam when she felt hard sharpness, then tossing it ashore.

Her clothing lay on a rock, neatly folded. She had protested removing her garments. Rheudhi had laughed, and darted off, returning with lightly furred skins. She tugged until Pierrette unlaced her tunic and pulled it over her head.

When the trousers and sandals followed it, Rheudhi tied the skins around Pierrette, one in front, one behind.

Self-consciously feeling every breeze that ruffled dark hair beneath the fur apron, Pierrette waded into the water, reminding herself that she was as well dressed as anyone. Besides, all were women, except for a few truly naked little boys and girls who splashed everyone.

"Did I come here to dig mussels with bare-breasted women?" she asked herself. "I should be fetching Marie." She had established that the spell Parting the Veil worked properly, and that was what she had set out to do.

Yet she was content, with her feet in cool water and her back exposed to warm late-afternoon sun, hearing a murmur of voices she could almost understand. Children's laughter was less than language, and more, needing no translation.

When she heard a resonant male voice, she wanted to squat in the water to hide her nakedness. She had wandered far from her clothes. But the pool was only ankle-deep, and the others were happily greeting the men.

"This is my father Bhirge," Rheudhi said, bringing Pierrette face to face with a blond, bearded man. "This is P'erit," Rheudhi told him.

Bhirge looker her up and down, his eyes thankfully spending no more time upon her breasts than her face or knees. She suspected that to this man she would be as easily recognized by the tilt of her upstanding nipples as by the shape of her nose. "Pebble," said Bhirge. "That's a funny name."

Pierrette caught a glint of red-gold on the shore. She looked up—and she saw him. She gasped. It was the man from her magpie flight, from her daydreams. He stood in a beam of sunlight, smiling as if expecting her, and glad she had at last arrived. "That's nonsense!" she told herself. But why was her heart thumping so? Why did her knees feel loose, and the breeze like feathers tickling her inner thighs?

"Pebble!" he said. He dipped a hand in the water, then splashed her lightly, laughing. "I wanted to see if you became even prettier when you were shiny and wet." Pierrette felt hot, and blushed all over.

Abruptly, the man raised his voice to speak to everyone. "The *phokw* have left us," he said. She was grateful for the respite.

She heard scattered moans, and a soft wail What was *phokw*? Obviously not happy news.

"We'll eat mussels," said Aure. "And we'll move on. It is the way."

Phokw? Like Latin *phoca*, seal? The seals were gone?

Women and men alike gathered mussels, lifting apronlike garments to hold them, unshyly exposing their most private parts. Only she and the man from her dreams did not lift their furs to collect shellfish. Rheudhi's thin tuft, she observed in a sidelong manner, was the same fiery shade as her head, while Aure's was dark, as if sunlight and salt-sea air accounted for her hair's coloration. Bhirge and the other men remained unstudied; Pierrette's eyes rapidly skipped away, unfocused, when her gaze accidentally brushed them.

"Help me prepare a fire," the man said. She willingly followed. Despite evidence of previous fires, there was plenty of driftwood. The waters of her time, that inundated this beach, these caves, had already begun their rise, washing trees loose, to gather in brittle heaps in sheltered bayheads.

Soon they had a crackling blaze. By the time the last of the mussels had been heaped beside it, the wood was settling, becoming embers with flickering tendrils of brilliant blues, greens, and yellows from salts and minerals left by seawater.

They draped mats of flaccid seaweed over the coals, then spread mussels on them. They built several layers, then mounded more seaweed and pebbly sand on the impromptu oven. Only vagrant wisps of steam escaped, but Pierrette knew the heap was hot and moist within.

She shied from that imagery, very aware that the man stood close by, and she had never felt like this, even in her dreams. What was wrong with her? She remembered the magpie dream—the woman, strong and lustful, who had . . .

"You're bright and pretty even when you're not wet," the man said, with soft humor. "Are all your folk so pale? Does your mother's skin talk so much too?"

"My people's skin," she murmured, not looking up at him, "is usually covered up, and cannot be . . . 'heard.'"

"I'm glad yours isn't," he replied. "I like 'listening' to you." Had her grasp of this dialect so suddenly improved, or had he spoken in Ma's tongue, not his own? She had understood not only his words, but . . . but what underlay them.

Her thoughts strayed to her one encounter with male desire. Jerome. Cernunnos. The Eater of Gods. But this was not the same. This was a man, not . . . something else . . . in man's guise. She felt like the woman in the magpie vision, and she had no idea how to deal with that.

"Why must you move away?" she asked him, to cover her discomfort. "Won't the seals come back?"

"Only when we have gone. The seals tell us we have lingered too long. We'll sicken." She asked him to explain.

He considered himself a predator like a fox or a wolf. Lingering too long, it had to take healthy prey, instead of culling the weak and sick, which it had already eaten. That was not good for predator or future generations of prey.

He told how foxes moved their young from nest to nest, leaving fleas and parasites behind.

"We'll need meat for the journey toward morning," he reflected. The journey toward . . . dawn? Eastward—toward the place Citharista would someday stand. "Tomorrow, I'll climb up to the high land, and will find a deer."

Pierrette envisioned his route—and conceived an opportunity to test the spell again. If she retraced her steps without invoking magic, she would see clearly what she had once seen in vision—the landscape of this time, laid out before her. Could she find the spot where she had left Gustave as well, or would it be too different?

"I'll go with you," she announced.

"I hunt best alone."

"I learn quickly."

He considered it carefully, and did not prate about hunting being man's work. "I'll teach you," he decided. "Tonight we'll go to the Place of Being Prey. If you are a deer, you'll know it."

The odd phrases reminded her she did not understand his speech well. She decided to wait and see what he meant.

"Rheudhi!" he called. "I think the mussels are cooked." They pulled the seaweed heap apart and tossed hot shellfish to those who stood around, laughing as people juggled their dinners to keep from burning their hands, then collected mussels in their skin aprons.

Women brought wild berries, crunchy roots, and nuts. Pierrette did not hesitate to lift her apron to hold her share.

She was no longer surprised that no one's eyes lingered overlong in passing. She settled beside Rheudhi.

"Aam likes you," the redhead commented. "Will you (something) with him?" Pierrette repeated the unfamiliar word, as a question. Rheudhi made a poking gesture, and Pierrette's skin "spoke" loudly.

She opened her mouth to assert that she would die before . . . She did not say it. It was not so.

In her childhood fantasies, she had only envisioned kissing in a restrained way. Later, such imaginary embraces had become more intimate, her body pressed against his, feeling his warmth, his smooth skin, and the muscles beneath it.

Only after the magpie flight with Ma had her mental imagery grown up. Only then had she trembled with the desire and enveloping power her dream-Aure had felt. She had rejected those feelings with muted cries of despair— even as she would reject the man himself. She had to—or she would never leave this place, this time near the beginning of time.

"Why do you call him Aam?" That meant simply "man." Didn't he have a name?

Rheudhi giggled with girlish condescension. "What's wrong with 'Aam?'" she asked. "I am Rheudhi, and see?" She lifted handsful of fiery hair. "He is Aam, and . . ." She lifted her skin apron, and feigned surprise at what she saw beneath it. ". . . he is a man." Again, Pierrette's skin "spoke" brightly.

When all had eaten, some departed for the caves. Others— couples—remained. Pierrette eyed what they were doing, and was glad that it was dark, and that the moon had not yet risen.

Aam came for her. "Let's see if you are a deer," he said. At least that was how she interpreted it. He led her toward the cave she had emerged from, the womb from which she had been thrust into the light of this strange world. He took her hand. His calloused palm satisfied a craving she had not known she had.

Inside the cave, they scrambled upward by torchlight, retracing her path and Rheudhi's. "There is where you entered the earth," he said, pointing toward a faint, distant glow, less red than a torch's light. "Tomorrow, we go that way, but now . . ." He guided her through a narrow cleft in smooth, water-shaped rock.

She could hear the echo of their soft footfalls; the space ahead was large. Aam's torch made a whooshing sound as he swung it in circles, fanning its blaze, illuminating the cave. She gasped. Where torchlight fell, the walls were covered with pictures. On her left danced running horses—gray-white mares and stallions, and dark, small colts. On the ceiling, black and white birds congregated, some upright, like herons, others sliding on plump, feathery breasts. Great, dark beasts humped sullenly across a plain of oxide-stained rock. In an alcove were hundreds of stencilled human hands.

"Go ahead," Aam murmured. "The deer are beyond. I'll light a fresh torch." His broad hand guided her. On a lumpy, irregular column, shaped as if by a potter working wet clay, a beast with a single long horn on its nose trembled in flickering light. Overhead, a tuft-eared cat crept forward on bent legs, his penile brush dragging on undrawn, unseen ground.

"*Phokw,*" Aam said softly—slim, almost legless creatures with pointed noses and long whiskers. Seals.

They bore left, around a stone veil like a carved curtain, past a composite beast with horns, fangs, and broad clawed feet. A chimaera? A griffin? Had such things once stalked among the eroded rocks overhead?

"*Ker'ph,*" said Aam, stopping. "Deer." The creature on the wall was no elusive woodland creature. It stood taller at the shoulder than the top of her head, and branching antlers stretched wider than her arms could reach. Pierrette's eyes were drawn within the beast. If she stared enough, she could see its beating heart, the rumbling progress of leaves and moss through its gut.

Once amazement faded, she saw that the effect had been created by many paintings, one atop another, seeming transparency with no real hint of internal organs.

"It's so big!" she marvelled. She had not seen spears or arrows in the cave-folk's camp. How would Aam take such a beast?

"Yes," he said. "It is big—I am big. But you are not. Come. I will show you yourself." *It is big. I am big.* He had inflected the words as if he considered himself not a man, but a stag. And the reflexive pronoun "yourself." As if Pierrette were also portrayed on these buried walls.

Again Aam whirled the torch into new life. The next deer

was antlerless, with donkeylike ears. Her thoughts strayed: where was Gustave? Had he chewed through his hobble, and raided his feed? But enough! This deer . . . this doe . . . was special. Again, Pierrette felt as though she could see within the painting, as if she were falling into . . .

She pranced, sharp hooves soundless on the forest litter. Aromas swirled. She sniffed drifting scents—pine needles and moldy oak leaves, mice and chattery, furry things seeking the faint odor of . . . of him.

There! She raised her fine-furred muzzle, feeling the breeze on one side, edging sometimes in the stag's direction, sometimes not. She was in no hurry, and stopped to nibble succulent branches. When the time was right, he would find her.

Her nostrils trembled with the faint scent of his arousal. She moved on, foraging. He stalked, not stopping. Rut was upon him; he would not eat. Her droppings fell here and there, but he left his in heaps, mute warnings to other males of his strength, his confidence, his single-minded purpose.

Her hoofprints were clear and sharp, two horny toes together, dewclaws held off the ground. Heavy with his spread of antlers, his toes splayed, and dewclaws marked the earth. She followed a trail where others had gone. He strode as if all the forest was his, his hoofprints straight and purposeful. She ambled and nibbled, waiting . . .

"You are a deer," Aam murmured ever so softly.

"Yes," she replied, no louder. "I am a doe."

"When we hunt, will you know where they are?"

The paintings were not icons; people did not prostrate themselves before horse- or deer-god, or pray to the images for a successful hunt. One did not hunt deer—one hunted . . . oneself. "I don't know," she replied. "They are in a forest, but where?"

"Find out where you are, then in the morning we'll go there."

Again she peered into the transparent layers on the wall, and again fell like a stone into the mind of the doe, herself.

✧   ✧   ✧

Elsewhere, fifteen thousand years away, shadowy antlers danced on another wall. Below pranced not a deer, but a two-legged figure that leaped around a blazing bonfire. When the horned man stopped dancing, he said, "It is enough. The green season will come, in the god's good time."

How good it felt to be himself again, not slave to . . . to that other god. How sweet to dance on Cernunnos's deer's feet, to pray as his grandfather, the old shaman, had taught him.

Reikhard set the horned headdress atop its folded sack. Spring would come—brought perhaps in some small measure by his prayers. He kicked loose soil over embers and his fellow worshippers rose to depart. The warm, brown of his deer's eyes grew pale. Illumined by moonlight alone, they were the blue of the horizon at sea on a hot day.

"I have the Christian Otho to thank for my rebirth," he said, for his own ears alone. "I will have to thank him someday."

The stag followed her lingering scent and, because her track wandered and his did not, he gained on her. She quivered in anticipation and fear.

When she saw him, he edged sideways as if her presence was incidental. He circled the clearing, marking it with pungent urine, sealing it from encroachment. He approached, and she skittered aside, her tail half-raised, unsure. He nosed beneath it, and drew in her identity.

Shyly, she circled away, but he followed, carrying his weight on his rear hooves despite the heaviness of his antlers. His forelegs floated off the ground. She jittered away. He followed, rising, bumping against her flank. They danced in a circle that became a shrinking spiral. Nose to tail one moment, the next his hooves brushed her flanks, his antlers rising high above her, the weight of him bearing down on her hindquarters . . .

"No!" Pierrette cried out, trying to roll away. Aam's chest pressed her breasts flat, his thighs inside hers. "No!" she moaned. "I must not!"

Aam's eyes widened. He lifted himself by the strength of his arms, and felt damp cave air rush in where he had lain upon her. It cooled her reddened breasts and belly, and dampened his raging heat.

His eyes asked, "Why?" but he did not speak. He watched panic fade from her eyes. He wanted this small, dark-haired woman, so unlike those he knew; he craved the difference, the fresh forest glade where no man had walked before.

He forced a smile. He was Aam, Man, not a boy whose member ruled him. He was Man, a hunter, and did not, in boyish excitement, throw his spear when his prey was too far away.

If he allowed rut to overpower him, she would not resist— but he would destroy something precious, something he had not felt with any other.

Sighing, he rolled to one side, and lay with an elbow beneath himself, a hand supporting his head. He felt the chill of the cave in earnest. She was shivering. "Come," he murmured, offering her a place close by himself.

He could almost feel her eyes' questioning touch. She smiled ever so slightly, and nestled against him, sharing her warmth and his. Both looked to the painting on the wall . . .

The stag lowered himself to all fours, and the doe skittered aside, kicking at air. Sometimes it was like that. Some does would not carry fawns their first season, but were the stronger for it the following year. He snorted, and sniffed the air. There were other does. Even now, the slow breeze that weaved among the dark-boled trees brought scents. Proudly, not looking back, he walked away. His trail in the forest mould was a straight line as before, purposeful tracks that did not wander.

Marie awoke from a dream of stags and does. Beside her snored a bearded Iberian sailor. His speech had been incomprehensible— as if that mattered. His loving had not mattered either; she had felt not the least flutter inside, though the man had pumped on and on, thinking himself a stag indeed.

She scowled. At first she had reveled in sensuality. She had eyed men's members speculatively—but only a god's great tool could sate her. How many men? She had lost count.

She nudged the sailor awake. She could not earn money while he occupied her bed. When he departed, she pried up a loose tile and gazed upon things that did matter: warm gold coins among cool silver ones, an emerald necklace that glittered enticingly in the strong light of afternoon.

Aam had no sense of time beyond the passage of days and nights, the march of sun, moon, and familiar stars, changing seasons, and migrations of seals and men.

"Another day," he said.

"When I go, I won't come back," she replied. The trail led not only through rocky declivities, but through years, centuries, and millennia. Going back to Gustave, would she pass herself coming down? Once returned, how could she come again? Could two of her exist here? Even without reasoning, she knew it could not be.

She wept silently, her back toward him, her buttocks snuggled against his warmth.

"Morning comes soon," he said softly. "Sleep, and later we'll find you again in the forest."

"Will we kill . . . me?" she asked, without the dismay she thought she should have felt.

"Of course. There's no foal in you. It is best—only one killed for one eaten."

That made cruel sense. It would be wrong to slay the stag in the peak of his years and his strength, to slay the strong young fawns he carried in his hefty sack, wasteful to slay a doe who carried a fawn.

As she drifted toward slumber, she thought she heard Aam speak again. "Don't worry, Pebble," he said. "You only think you know everything. We'll meet on another path, and finish what began on this one. We'll meet again and again, until at last it is done."

That was a dream, of course. Those were not Aam's words, just wishful thinking. Tomorrow, after the hunt, she would depart, and never return. Even in sleep, tears flowed, and when she awakened, her face was sticky with them.

The cave's chill awakened her. Where was Aam? Was he angry? But no—there was a flickering glow. A torch.

"My spear," he said, proudly turning a smooth shaft in the torchlight. Red highlights danced on smoothly flaked chalcedony fixed to the wood with fiber and pitch. "Your spear," he said, displaying another. She hefted it. How light. Thrown, it would not penetrate a deer's hide.

"This will help," Aam said, handing her a carved stag's antler as long as her arm from elbow to fingertip, with a crook at one end. A polished stone disc fitted just beyond the crook.

"A long-arm," Aam explained, showing her how the spear's butt fit in the crook. She hefted spear and long-arm together, and saw how it worked, like a lever to magnify the force of her throw. She would still have to be close.

"You can't run from yourself," he replied. "You'll be close enough."

She knew the way, despite the years that had not yet worn down the rocks, despite all the goats and sheep that had not yet grazed the high ground to barren rock, and all the men who would not begin cutting the timber, for yet fifteen thousands of years.

With a kind of double vision, she saw where Gustave the donkey would someday wait, a tall man's height below ground not yet eroded away.

With second sight of a different kind, she was aware of Aam beside her as they emerged on flatter ground high above the calanque, and was aware of her four-footed self somewhere ahead, grazing on leathery leaves.

She had practiced with the spear-thrower, and no longer feared she would throw it instead of the spear, or send both spinning away. She was cool, light-headed, and eager. She wanted to throw the spear.

Uneasy, she stopped nibbling to sniff the air, yet no threatening scents came. No moving shadows loomed among the further trees. There was only . . . herself.

"When you walk," said Aam, "put all your weight on one foot slowly, before you lift the other. Feel for twigs with your toes, and move between them." She slipped from one tree to the next. At each, she stood half-exposed, her human silhouette broken, like a burl on the trunk, yet not behind the tree, where she could have seen nothing.

"There's no hurry," Aam said. "She won't go far unless something frightens her." Then he lagged back, thinking stag-thoughts.

At first, she saw only a leg. "Look for part of a deer," Aam had said. "For something that isn't a tree trunk or a leafy branch. You may not see all of her until you are upon her." It was a foreleg. Pierrette studied the brushy cover. The foreleg blended into its surroundings. She did not see the deer's muzzle or long ears until it moved its head in search of forage. Movement stood out amid stillness. Had it been windy, she would have seen nothing.

Could she get closer? Had Aam circled, and stationed himself in the doe's path of flight?

When the deer moved its head, it could not sense external motion. Pierrette waited until it had stripped the branch, and it shifted to another. She slipped forward one step, two, masking her outline with low-hanging boughs.

She settled the long-arm, and snugged the spear's butt against it, balancing both atop her arm, keeping them in place with a curled finger. The fur of the doe's flank looked like dappled leaves.

Pierrette tensed, then flung her arm forward, a long motion, an exercise in geometry, not strength. The spear leaped ahead without effort.

It buried itself in the doe's side. A fiery pain shot through her. She grasped herself below her ribs: the spear twisted in her flesh, tearing her insides. She felt flint break against bone. She leaped away. The spear shaft thumped against a tree, tearing her more before it fell free.

She ran. She bounded ahead, fleeing the pain . . . and she ran behind, clutching her side with one hand.

"The first throw need not kill," she remembered Aam saying. "It is the running and bleeding that kills." He was ahead, somewhere, waiting.

She stumbled. Everything was blurred and faint. Her hooves felt far away, unconnected. She caught herself before she fell, and staggered on. Something was in the trail ahead. The wind was behind her, so she could not smell it. From behind came a scent, unfamiliar but . . . but not. She stopped, confused. Her flanks heaved. Blood dribbled down her belly. The pain was unendurable.

"Kill me," said the doe as its forelegs folded.

"Kill me," Pierrette said. "I hurt. Make it stop."

Aam shook his head, and handed her his long flint knife, a single blade flaked from a favorite core, unused and sharp. She grasped its leather wrapping and put an arm around the doe's neck. She pulled its head back, and sawed at its neck. A great artery slid sideways against the edge, and she pressed harder, feeling the icy slash against her own furless throat.

Blood gushed in short, regular pulses, and day turned to night. She lay still. Then there was only one of her, standing over the motionless doe, weeping, no longer in pain.

"Why didn't you tell me?" she asked Aam. "You should have warned me about the pain."

He looked surprised. "Haven't you ever hurt yourself before?" he asked. "Of course there's pain. How could you not feel it?"

Of course. How could she not? She had raised her tail to the stag, and had wettened between her human legs. She had browsed, and tasted sweet leaves. How could she not have suffered when she felt the spear point wrench at her insides?

"Show me what to do," she said. Aam did so. With quick, inexpert motions she made slits between tendon and bone above the doe's rear hooves, and together she and Aam hoisted the body by a thong. It hung with only its forehooves touching the ground. Following Aam's guiding fingers, she removed pebble-sized nodules from the insides of its thighs, then cut around all four legs, and up toward its belly. Her blade followed his finger, slitting skin without cutting muscle or rupturing the whitish sack around its organs.

The heavy skin pulled free. Aam held her wrist while she cut the peritoneum. Wet, pale organs fell free in heavy coils, and an odor of incredible foulness hung in the too-still air, making Pierrette gag.

Aam chuckled. How much the girl doesn't know, he thought. That took her by surprise. What a strange place she must come from. He did not think he would like living there.

When they left the site of the kill, little was left behind. Because they were far from the camp, they ate morsels of liver. Leaving the most perishable parts for scavengers, they wrapped the rest in the hide, which Pierrette carried. Aam shouldered the carcass.

It made cruel sense. If there were magic in "becoming" a deer, it was tacit magic without incanted spells. She had not tried her own lore since coming here. Her spells would do nothing. Here predator and prey were one and the same. There was no clear good or obvious evil, only an undefined sense that one was much as the other, seen from a different perspective. That was an important thought to remember. . . .

"Kill me," she had said, as much to free her terrified doeself from pain as to relieve her human-self from it. The world would have to change greatly before men hunted deer with no thought for the pain they caused, because they did not feel it themselves. Was that evil? Did predator and prey feel less pain here and now, because it was shared?

She envisioned Father Otho pouring oil from one jar to the other. "Is there less evil now?" he asked. "Is there more good?" Did good and evil even exist here, where no distinctions were made between them, where gods and devils alike were unknown?

Pierrette heard a woman's drawn-out screams long before she and Aam could see the light of day, beyond their torch's red light.

"It's Aure," he said, and tightened his grip on her hand. "It's the birthing-time." Yet he did not hurry. Aam loved Aure. She had felt it in her magpie-mind. Why didn't he hurry?

When they emerged there were no more screams. "Aure is dead," said an old woman. Blood specked her arms up to the elbows. "The infant lives."

"Show me," Aam commanded.

She brought a small, fur-wrapped bundle. "Aure nursed him, but her bleeding didn't stop. Now Aure is getting cold."

Aam pulled back the skin covering the infant. "This might have been my son," he said, flicking its tiny penis with his finger.

Aure lay at one side of her cave. Aam held Pierrette's hand as he knelt to look at her. Tears streamed down his face, but he did not make a sound.

He stood. "Prepare her," he said. "Give me the infant." The baby slept. Pierrette watched as Aam took a fold of its wrapping and pressed it over the tiny face, holding it firmly. What was he doing? The child could not breathe. She reached to pull his hand away. His wrist and forearm were like stone. She could not move a single one of his fingers.

Aam looked her in the eye. "Was it so terrible to die?"

he asked. "Does this motherless child deserve less kindness than you gave yourself?" Pierrette's vision blurred with angry tears . . . but her hand fell away. For long moments, nothing happened. Then tiny arms stretched out. They jerked slightly. One final convulsion . . . then the little body lay absolutely still.

Aam placed it in its mother's arms. "Cover them with stones," he commanded harshly. "We won't use this cave next time." Tears rolled down his face.

"Why?" Pierrette asked, looking up at him. The baby wasn't suffering."

"None of the women have milk, and we must march. Better it die now."

Better it be with its mother, she thought. Pierrette gazed at Aure, shrunken, without the vivacity that had swelled her in life. "Where have they gone?" she wondered aloud. These folk had not spoken of heaven, or an afterlife.

"Where has the doe gone?" Aam asked.

Where indeed? Pierrette looked within. Was the soul of the deer within her now? She did not think so. When she had felt its life depart, it had just faded. She turned away, her vision blurred.

"Come," said Aam. "Rheudhi will prepare the deer. We can watch the sun go down."

From the rocky spit where the calanque opened into the sea, they could indeed see the sun. Pierrette's sense of direction felt subtly skewed. Unless it was summer, shouldn't it be further south?

"Does it ever snow?" she asked Aam, suspecting that the word *nhiegh* would be as unknown to him as were so many others.

"*Nheedge?*" he asked, making fluttering motions with his fingers. "Of course—in winter. Not now."

"Oh," she replied, nodding. This chill season was spring, or fall, and her sense of direction was not faulty. There was no reason to have assumed that she arrived here in winter just because she had departed from it, and would—hopefully—return to it again. This was a colder world than hers, in more ways than one.

Yet Aam was not cold. He grieved for Aure, and for the child he had stifled. His grief was no less for his pragmatism, and he did not even have the consolation of an afterlife to ease it. Pierrette asked his feelings. "I'm sad," he said, surprised that she did not know. "I'll never see her smile, or lie with her."

"Aren't you angry?" Angry at a god or universe that had taken her away . . .

"It wasn't her fault!" said Aam, misunderstanding. "She didn't mean to die."

And there it was. No god had taken Aure. Her death was neither good nor evil . . . only sad. Was that so terrible? What good to rail against fate, to blame the heavens for a loved one's death? Did people suffer less for having divided suffering and joy, calling one evil and the other good? She did not think so. Yet she pitied Aam, because he had no god to blame.

She took his hand. For a long while, nothing more was said. Her thoughts were a tumult of relief and regret. Her rejection of Aam, and his restraint when she was helpless to stop him . . . Regret that they had not made love was mixed with profound relief that she was still free to leave this place. After Aure's death and the child's, she could not stay.

What if she had given in . . . not to Aam, but herself? She had not known then how different these folk were. She could think of a hundred things to try, to save the child. Yet herbs and potions could not replace milk. There were no goats to milk, likely no honey to sweeten it with. There was only quick, quiet death.

Yet beside her was Aam, the first man she had desired. Was he also sad that no more had come of it? Was he relieved that this strange, unpredictable woman, with her ignorance of ordinary things, would be on her way?

She awakened when Rheudhi stirred. They had slept, huddled against the night's chill, beneath ill-tanned and smelly furs. She did not know where Aam slept—if at all.

Today, all the folk would crowd into the cave, and would become seals. Had the seals all gone to one place, or had they split up? Had others, from other migrating groups, joined them? Where would the folk go? By evening they would decide.

She would go to the cave with them, and would continue

on through. Had Gustave broken free of his thongs? There was much she did not know about Parting the Veil of Years. That magnified her ignorance of other magics: if she had to learn everything from the details first, she would never be wiser than now. There had to be a better way. Already, her ranging thoughts prepared her to return to that more complex world.

She could not say good-bye to Aam. He was convinced they would meet again, and they would not. But Rheudhi? When she shook out her woven garments, and laid her fur aprons neatly on the cave floor, Rheudhi knew. "I wish I could go with you," she said, but did not really mean it. Even the girl's hesitancy to hug her, to touch her strange cloth garments, showed that.

"I've never had a friend like you," Pierrette said. Besides Marie, she had not had friends at all. That, too, was sad— that a few brief days was the extent of her friendship with young women.

When they stepped from the sleeping-cave, the beach was deserted, the folk gone into the deep cave. Even without Rheudhi, Pierrette could have found her way by the low, droning hum of male voices, the soaring notes of female ones calling out—but not, this time, to her. They called to the seals—to themselves. Even that first time she had heard the steady "hunh, hunh" of the song, had it really been for her, or had she only overheard it, across those thousands of years?

They came to the painted chambers. Rheudhi's eyes darted from Pierrette to the others. "I can find my way from here. Go. Find yourself among the seals."

Rheudhi planted a kiss on Pierrette's cheek, and fled. Her red-gold hair was like another torch.

Aam was there. She could not distinguish his voice among the others. She murmured quiet words, and from her fingertips sprang clear bluish light. She would need no torch. She allowed herself one last sad glance. Aam saw her face bathed in elfin light, and he smiled.

She did not remember picking her way through the cave, but there, ahead, was sunlight. She quenched her own light, and began speaking the Parting of the Veil of Years.

Burying sadness beneath scholarly detachment, she observed

how things changed as she ascended. At first were bushes she had no names for, then a tiny cypress, a sprig with a single whorl of branches. A dozen steps on, pushing up from a soil-filled depression, were two parasol pines.

She smelled thyme. She was home. Home? No—but whence she had come. Gustave heard her footfalls before she came into view. When she checked his hobble, the hide thongs were hardly damp with saliva.

The sun had moved no further across the sky than it should have, had she taken a short hike. In Gustave's world, an hour had passed, but she felt years older, her youthful face and body a disguise. She had known passion, and had denied it. She had come upon the throes of birth, and had seen death. She had witnessed . . . murder, and she loved the murderer, who was not an evil man.

Yet all that was long ago. Bright Rheudhi had loved, birthed children, and died. Aam too was gone. Aure's bones, and her child's, lay crushed beneath rocks, washed by the waters that now filled the low caves. Had she really been there? Had she voyaged into the depths of the past in body, or only in mind? She could not say; she had brought nothing back—not a chipped flint or a clamshell.

What if she had? If she had carved an initial into a soft seaside cliff, would it be there still? If she had made a handprint among those painted on the cave walls, would it be there now? There was no way to say. She had looked back after leaving the cave. The great brow of rock that overhung it had fallen, and the place where Rheudhi had kindled the torch was buried.

There were no answers. Still, she could not help but wonder. What if she used the spell *Mondradd in Mon* to journey to some more recognizable past? What if she visited the Eagle's Beak, at that moment Marie and her own younger self discovered her mother's sash on the trail, and moved the sash back? What if she had hurried the children (who would not recognize her adult self) along the trail and safely away? Would the whole course of events be different now?

Such thoughts occupied her, but those questions, fraught with paradox, could not be answered. She eventually put them aside, and turned her speculations in more immediately relevant directions. . . .

Chapter 24 ∽ The Demon

Pierrette's Journal

The Law of the Conservation of Good and Evil

There is Good and there is Evil, just as there are
warmth and cold, light and darkness. The shepherd on
his far hill knows this, though he forget speech and
bleat and grumble like his sheep. He needs no priest
or scholar to weigh the long brilliance of summer against
the darkness of winter: as he sweats, so shall he shiver.

Were the sun to linger all night, or the days to remain
long in winter, his sheep would graze until they bloated,
and no greening autumn rains would tell him it was
time to return to the world of men. The shepherd knows
that summer is not good and winter evil, but priests
and theologians have forgotten.

Aam's folk were simpler than the shepherd; they had
no word for good, none for evil. They rejoiced without thanks, grieved without blame, having no gods or
devils to attribute joy and sorrow to. Just so, they did
not call roasted meat good, and the pain of dying evil.

Aam's language had no subjunctive mood, no *if* and
then, no *should* or *might*, to divide cause and effect.
Their paintings did not *cause* prey to come, but aided
them in becoming what they sought. When they killed,
they suffered, as did I, the agonies of death.

We stand between Aam's age and the dark time.
Logical men draw lines between Good and Evil, dividing

271

the universe between God and his counterpart. Scholars who explain how evil can exist in a world created by a good God are pouring oil from one jar into another; naming one "Good" and the other "Evil," they are making them so. Yet the sum remains the same. As they define ever smaller aches, pains, and transgressions as Evil, does Good diminish? Is that the meaning of the Dark Time—when everything good has been written away, and uncaring wraiths drift through dead cities, beneath a sunless sky?

Pierrette laid her half-reasoned ideas out as if Gustave could understand. "Mani's heresy created Satan," she told him, "explaining Evil with a second creator to create it. Augustine refuted Mani, but his logic was so dense that few really understood."

Gustave snorted.

"You're right," Pierrette said. "That's why 'heresies' keep arising, because evil doesn't exist by itself. When P'er Otho's bishop declares old Pan Satan in disguise, and people believe it, they abandon the poor old god to be eaten, like Cernunnos."

Men renamed old gods as devils or saints. They named Ma's lovers serpents, trod on them, and drove them from the garden. They cut down sacred groves and built chapels of their wood. Virgin Diana became Virgin Mary. The logical religions, goodness all gathered and evil thrust outside, drive the world not toward salvation, but toward that dark moment at the end of time.

Their logic shaped old magics into one overweening spell, one vast chant that reshaped nymphs, harvest gods, and quiet spirits into saints and demons, all dancing to one tune.

"But what can I do?" she asked the donkey. "The world can never go back to Aam's simpler time. What's to stop learned men from refining goodness until it's so pure that all the rest of creation is in evil's jar?"

Gustave plodded on, contemplating the oats in the sack, wondering if Pierrette remembered her promise to feed him.

There was still hope, Pierrette told herself as she crossed the final divide, where the blue glow of illogic was the final transition from Citharista's pagan flame to abbess Sophia's pure Christian light. There were still high mountain ranges, and vast oceans, and beyond them lands where no priests had gone, where no wandering ibn Sauls had observed and written and destroyed the magics.

Was Father Otho right? Was this voyage one of many? What far lands, strange magics, and unimaginable gods still flourished over the next range of hills, the mountains beyond?

She shrugged. Below were the roofs of Massalia. Soon she would see Saint Victor's, and the towering ruins across the long harbor. Soon, she would be arranging transport east to the little town she had seen through a magpie's eyes.

Shortly after dark, Sister Agathe responded to the gateside bell. As if Mother Sophia had never rescinded the order commanding her to silence, she held up a finger for Pierrette to wait while she struggled with a heavy oaken bar.

"She lives," Agathe said. "Mother will tell you." Her lip curled as if with great distaste. What was wrong? Marie, in her weak condition, could have done nothing to offend the taciturn nun.

By the light of a smoky candle, Agathe led her to a windowless room with a straw pallet on the floor, a crucifix on the far wall. "Mother prays," she said. "Rest now."

"Sister? May I have a light? There's no window." Agathe set the candle on the floor, then fumbled down the dark stone stairs toward the moonlit courtyard.

The pallet was less uncomfortable than the stones of the high country. The drafts were less chilly than night winds. She slept. The candle guttered out. She awakened in darkness total and stifling. Where was the door? She whispered old, magical words terribly out of place in that Christian warren, and held her fingers up, as if to catch the light . . . but there was no light.

Darkness pressed like wet crow feathers. She groped for the door, but her hands met rough, unpolished stone. Moving sideways, she found a corner, then edged along from it, muttering the useless spell.

Her hand struck something. Light flooded the room. She was facing away from the door: the object she had encountered was the crucifix. The light was more than the glow of understanding—real, perceptible light emanated not from the remains of the candle, or from her fingertips, but from the tiny statue.

The cross was two splits of firewood pegged with trunnels. The hanged man slumped with arms outstretched, rudely carved, his face a caricature—splintery nose, eye holes bored with a red-hot awl, a slash of a mouth, whittled arms thrust into holes. His hands were flattened paddles. Char ringed the pegs that pierced them.

Pierrette drew back from the glowing apparition. Her near panic, awakening in featureless darkness, transmuted into anger.

The spell was hers! This effigy, hacked by some unskilled hand, had been relegated to the dark cell because it was too ugly to hang in a public place. How had it usurped her spell, and drawn the light to itself?

Pierrette wrinkled her nose at dribbles of gaudy red paint on tiny feet, and the crimson streak on the left side.

When she heard the clatter of sandaled feet in the hallway outside, she began to understand the magic of this place. The first time she had called for light had been at the holy woman's request, its purpose not at odds with Christian charity—to diagnose Marie's ailment. The second time, also at Mother Sophia's bidding, had been in the sun-flooded shrine of the Virgin.

"Ah, thank you, child," said the abbess. "My sleeve brushed my lamp, and put it out. Until I saw the glow of yours . . ." The abbess abruptly realized that no candle lit the room, and she gazed with awe upon the crucifix.

"Thank *Him*, Mother," Pierrette said acidly, nodding toward the effigy. The spell did not work properly, because its axioms had changed. Here, light did not emanate from the sourceless substance of the world, like the nighttime warmth of a rock heated by the day's sun. Here it sprang from a Christian artifact, focused, not diffuse. It was only one small spell, but what would she have to learn, to command it? Would she ever learn enough to dare a greater spell, in this Christian land?

She would never utter the Parting of the Veil of Years here. What did these people understand of time? Would she trap herself without a skeptical donkey to pull her back? What vast libraries of Christian thought weighted the scale against her? How many books would she have to read to define the postulates of a spell like the Veil?

She was not here to learn Christian sorcery, but to take Marie to the two Marys, her namesakes, who wielded it. Must the beggar know how to make bread rise, how to bake it, to gnaw his dry crust?

She sighed. "Thank *Him*, for in this place even a poor effigy commands the light."

Sophia Maria smiled. "It's a poor likeness, but a treasure— made by an imprisoned saint, to comfort himself in the days before his martyrdom by Wambo, the Wisigoth king." Pierrette nodded. Here nothing could be assumed. Here her eyes and her experience were useless.

"Come," the abbess said, laying a hand on Pierrette's arm. "Let's visit your sister."

"Is something wrong, Mother?" Pierrette asked. "Sister Agathe would not say, but . . ."

"But you sensed her disapproval? Come. Marie has been moved to a . . . a safer place."

Had Marie contracted some foul disease? Pierrette remembered the pox her spell had given Jerome.

"How sick is she, Mother?" Pierrette asked. "Will she be able to travel?"

"Oh, child!" said the old woman. "She has no fleshly illness." She squeezed Pierrette's arm, and Pierrette felt her hand tremble. "You must see . . . She is greatly changed."

The abbess stood in front of a door with iron straps and clenched nails. The oak bar was no less massive than the one on the front gate. "She escaped, a month ago. We only just found her."

"Did she try to go home?"

The abbess shook her head sadly. "We found her in . . . a house of women. She didn't want to leave."

Wasn't this a house of women?

"A whorehouse," the old woman said harshly. "Where women are paid to lie with men."

"Had she . . . been there long?" Pierrette's heart sank.

"Almost a week. She's been angry with us, since we brought her back."

Pierrette was stunned. Her Marie, in a whorehouse? Pierrette would have thought such a place her worst nightmare. Was she truly mad?

"Be careful," the old one said. "She knocked Sister Martha down last night."

At first, Pierrette's attention was drawn to the barred windows. She realized how seriously the nuns took her sister's condition. Marie was sitting on a bed, the only furniture. There was not even a crucifix.

"Hello, sister," Marie said from behind tousled strands of dirty hair. "Have you come to take me home to Jerome?" She was unclothed beneath the white linen sheet.

"I'll wait outside," said the abbess.

"Don't forget to bar the door, 'Mother,' " said Marie, investing the title with bitter irony.

"Oh, Marie, what's happened to you?" Pierrette cried, flinging herself to her knees beside the bed.

"Happened? I'm a prisoner. Ask them what they did with my jewels and clothes."

"You don't own jewels."

"I did! Emeralds and tourmalines. A ruby ring! Gold coins too—gifts from my lovers, hidden beneath a tile. Will you get them for me, sister? Please?" Marie's tone was sickeningly sweet.

"I don't know. I'll ask. Oh, Marie . . ."

" 'Oh, Marie! Oh, Marie!' " Is that all you can say? Does Jerome miss me?" Marie's eyes glowed with hard light.

Didn't she want to know how Father was? Why Jerome? Does she, in her madness, think she married the Burgundian? "The knight is ill," Pierrette said. "Father Otho says he—"

"Otho! That mewling snit! That gelded ninny! Don't speak of him!"

"Then shall I tell you about Father? You haven't asked . . ."

"Has the old fool swallowed his last tooth? I hope he choked on it. Tell me he did."

Tears blurred Pierrette's vision. "We missed you. We prayed for you. At least Father did . . ."

"Prayers soil me. Get out of here. Tell Jerome I want him."

"I . . . I can't do that. It's not you saying that. It is . . ."

Marie threw off the sheet. "Tell him you saw this!" she spat, spreading her legs. She cradled her ample breasts in her palms. "He'll come."

Pierrette stumbled to the door. "Mother! Let me out!"

"Pierrette!" That sounded like the "real" Marie. "I'm sorry! Don't go. I don't know what came over me."

Pierrette hesitated. She heard the bolt being lifted. "I . . . I'll come back." She slipped out.

"Tell the hag to give me my hairbrush!" Marie squalled, her familiar self gone. Mother Sophia Maria lowered the bolt in place.

"Can she have the brush?" Pierrette asked. "Her hair . . ."

"I'm sorry, child," the abbess said. "She only wants the handle, to . . . to . . . She calls it 'Jerome.'" She put both arms around Pierrette, and held her until she could weep no more.

∾

Pierrette's Journal

Augustine called them "demons of the air." In Christian lands they occupy the void between heaven and earth.

Marie said that a raven brought her memories back. Raven or demon? Before our horrible reunion, I did not believe in demons—only gods, some kinder than others. Demons are the most frightening entities in Christian lands. Were they once gods of the *paganorum*, weakened like poor John and Guihen, then consumed? In a way, I hoped so, for then there was still hope for Marie. Hope—but not in that Christian place. The Camargue beckoned; there she could be freed—if it was possible at all.

∾

Lovi led Pierrette to his master's courtyard, where the scholar awaited. Even seated, Muhammad abd' Ullah ibn Saul's eyes met hers on a level plane.

"Master scholar," she greeted him. "The magus Anselm sends his regrets that he is not able to be here himself."

Ibn Saul smiled broadly. His long, narrow face creased into deep grooves beside his beaky nose, prominent even by the standards of Provence. "He regrets that he can't drink my wine."

Pierrette sprang to Anselm's defense. "He has more on his mind than wine. He cannot—yet—come this far from his keep, and . . ."

"Easy, boy. Anselm and I are old friends. I was teasing you as I would him." His black, bright eyes were framed with crinkly lines of laughter that belied sinister, shrouded eyelids. "Tell me why you're here."

Pierrette did so, leaving out nothing. Her listener remained still, hands folded atop jutting, bony knees. Her tale consumed an hour. Ibn Saul rang for a servant to bring fruit and wine, instructing him in a harsh, staccato tongue. "That's the speech of the high steppes, beyond the Oxus," he said.

"Is it your native language, Master ibn Saul?"

He laughed indulgently. "I puzzle you, do I?"

"Yes Master Muhammad, worshipper of Allah, yet of the house of Saul—a Jew? Your name contradicts itself."

Again, he chuckled. "Such confusion aids my travels. Few hinder me, not knowing what ruler—or god—they might offend. I, believing in no gods, am welcome in mosque and synagogue, ashram and cathedral . . . though not always in the same towns. I'm known differently in different places."

"I read of a lizard that changes color as it crawls across dark rock or bright sand. . . ."

"A chameleon? Exactly so. I am all things to all men— yet kin to none. But it's your need we must address." Again, he rang his tiny handbell, and commanded his servant.

"I have sent for two people who know the route you must take," he told Pierrette. "Now let's give proper attention to these lovely pears. . . ."

For the half of an hour, they enjoyed crisp, succulent fruit in silence. Then two short people were ushered in.

"This is Cullain, a salt merchant," said the scholar, introducing a dark man with teeth worse than Gilles's and—as Pierrette was to discover—breath that would befuddle an ox. "Cullain knows every dry path through the Camargue, and Mother Ars"—he nodded to an even smaller woman— "knows every old story. She also knows medicines, and the means of making them. She may remember a spell or two, passed down from a grandmother." He departed the courtyard.

The woman, Ars, remained silent while Pierrette and Cullain drew maps on the cobbles with fingers wetted in the fountain, maps that evaporated soon after they were drawn. He recommended the route by boat across the lagoon to half-ruined Ugium.

"Follow the salt," he recommended. "Salt is life. From the *salin* by Ugium, sail to the mouth of the Fossa, Marius's canal. Leave the boat short of Arelate, where first you see the River Rhodanus on your left." He named boatmen and fishermen, praising or criticizing their knowledge of the waters and the conditions of their vessels. If Pierrette could remember all he had told her, she would have no trouble reaching remote Saints Maries.

She turned her attention to Ars, and spoke quiet phrases in her mother's ancient tongue. Ars grinned. "Few folk know Ma's speech," she said. "How did you know I did?"

"When you greeted me, I heard familiar intonations."

"Then I have no fear of speaking truth with you. Well-wishes in the old speech are a magical spell—as are all words."

From Ars, Pierrette learned of the saltwater tamarisk, the three kinds of reeds, and the tiny telltale flowers that marked solid places in the deceptive sea of tall grass, the Camargue. She learned also of what she most wanted to hear. . . .

"Old incantations still have power there," Ars said. "*Fadrad meh sor . . .*" she began.

"*Penan mo ser,*" Pierrette continued, then stopped. "Is it the same? Does it repel flies and mites?"

"Anything that stings," Ars replied. "You can tell when you're near a *salin*, when you get bitten."

"A salt-drying pond? Why?" Pierrette asked. "Are bugs attracted to salt?"

"I don't know. But I can tell a *salin* is nearby before I smell it."

Pierrette had only to speak the first words of a spell for Ars to chime in with those that followed. She was delighted; the magical country was all that she hoped. Those spells had done nothing in Citharista, yet Ars had used them to good effect.

"Master ibn Saul said you know old stories," Pierrette remarked.

"Stories! That's what he calls them. I enjoy his hospitality. I would not speak ill of him, but . . ."

"But?"

"He's a pragmatist. That's to say, he's blinded by what he believes, and what he does not. He doesn't believe anything that defies explanation, so he won't bother writing

my 'stories' in his books." That, thought Pierrette, was all
to the good. He had "explained" the Wendish rite, and
look what happened.

"Will you tell me a story?" asked Pierrette.

"What do you want to hear? There are many."

Pierrette explained how tales heard from Christian tellers were subtly changed from older versions. "I want a story
that Christians tell one way, but that you know differently."

"Tell me one you know, and I'll let you know what's
wrong with it," said Ars.

"Very well," Pierrette replied. "A hundred years ago, a man
named Giles was touched by God. He gave away all he owned,
and departed his native Greece on a raft and, like the three
Marys, was borne to Camargue's shore. He was dying of thirst,
but a hind showed him a hidden spring of sweet water . . ."

Ars was agitated. "What is it?" Pierrette asked.

"No, you go on. I'll have my say when you've finished.
It's all wrong, the way you tell it."

Pierrette continued. "A noble hunter shot an arrow at the
hind, and Giles snatched it from the air. The hunter was
so impressed with Giles's feat—and his holiness—that he
commissioned a shrine of stone over the hidden pool.

"Another tale of Giles," Pierrette said, "recounts how he
was given two carved doors by the Holy Father in Rome.
He threw them in the Tiber River, and they floated all the
way to Camargue, and washed up near his chapel. I think
that story has been confused with the one about the raft,
and with the boat without sails that conveyed the *apostoli*.
Only one may be a proper account. I don't know which."

"Bah!" said Ars. "The tale of the hind is also told about
Saint Godfric, in the North, and the one about the doors is
elsewhere attributed to other saints. Neither is Giles's true
tale."

"Then tell me what is true," Pierrette urged . . .

When the Wisigoths conquered Arelate, said Ars, Giles,
the bishop, would have nothing to do with the Arian heretics. He walked westward on the Roman road, then into
the trackless Camargue, and dwelt in a hovel of leaves and
branches. He lived on wild berries and drank sweet water
from a hidden spring. The thickets were home to tusked
sangliers—wild boars—and roe deer.

One evening, as the birds became silent, he heard rustling in the underbrush, and saw two great yellow eyes. Terrified, he hid, sure he had seen a full-grown boar, not a young pig. Ha! The animal that emerged to drink was a shy doe with white stockings. "I've gone mad from solitude!" he cried, "to take a graceful *biche* for a *sanglier*."

He had spoken aloud. The frightened doe ran away. "Don't go!" he called after, suddenly aware of how lonely he had been—but she was gone. Only the calls of wood owls and the hoots of great round-eyed *hiboux* filled the night.

In the days that followed, Giles got little joy from his solitude. He tried to remember what the deer had looked like. Brown or beige? Skinny or plump? Every night at dusk he waited quietly behind a tree, hoping to see her.

A month passed, and at last he heard the rustle of brush. The doe! He crept hesitantly toward her as she bent to drink. Ah! She was so beautiful. Her tapered legs were white from knee to shiny hoof, and her curved neck bent with the grace of a windblown vine. Her eyes were so warm Giles could crawl right in them.

The hermit remained still until she had finished drinking, his silence broken only by the beating of his lonely heart. At last, the doe departed. Would she come back?

Giles cut tender, fragrant leaves, and left them by the still pool, on the rock where the doe had placed her forefeet while she drank. She soon came to drink and feed almost every evening, as the birds' last songs faded. One night Giles did not lay the fragrant herbs on the stone. When the sweet creature had drunk, he held out the delicacies, and slowly approached her. "Don't fear, little one," he murmured, a man addressing a shy lover. The doe stretched out her neck, and took his offering. . . .

"From then on," said Ars, "the doe and the old *fou* had an understanding. He fed her, and spoke to her as to a friend. She listened, and the regard of her soft, brown eyes was more welcome than words."

Man and doe lived thus, he feeding her, she easing his loneliness, and both were content. Neither pondered the doings of men in the lands beyond—but that did not mean nothing was happening. Wambo, the Wisigoth, and his chiefs and sons, were not content to lounge about the fountains of Arelate, with fawning servants to bring them wine and fruit. They were forest men who loved to hunt with their great, rangy hounds.

One morning, the ground beneath Giles's hut trembled with the impact of hooves. The silence was shredded by howls of the pack and cries of hunters. The hermit's beloved companion fled. The forest resonated with tramping feet, stamping iron-shod hooves, and shouted orders. Giles covered his ears and shut his eyes.

When he opened them, he saw the doe at the edge of the clearing. She staggered toward the spring, her neck wet with fresh blood. She fell. Giles dragged her to the pool, and washed her terrible wound.

"The *biche* is ours!" shouted a young chief, pushing through the brush.

The old hermit stood his ground. "She is neither mine nor yours, but merely honors us with her presence."

Several Wisigoths laughed. "You old fool! Get out of the way and let us finish her off." One horseman struck him a blow that sent him reeling into the thicket. "Call the dogs! Set the hounds on both of them."

When the dogs burst from the woods, they ceased howling, and came as one to a sudden stop. As if terrified, they stared at Giles, who had regained his place by the doe. She lay licking her wounds. Bellies against the ground, the dogs crept forward. They surrounded man and doe, then turned outward, and allowed no warrior to approach.

Astounded, the Wisigoths sheathed their weapons. "Sorcery!" one said. "We must tell the king." In a thunder of hooves, they rode away. The hounds followed.

Near dawn, Giles and the doe were awakened by hooves and cries. Wambo had come in person to see the madman— or sorcerer—and the doe. He peered into the hut, and stood looking for a long time. Then he turned his mount and rode off, followed by his horde.

"And that," said Ars, "is the story of Giles, as the folk of the villages tell it. There is an addition to the tale, in which Wambo was baptized in the spring. When Giles died, the king commissioned a shrine and a tomb. Thousands of pilgrims visit there." The old woman's features crinkled like a dried olive. "There's no carved sarcophagus for the doe, in that shrine."

Pierrette's disappointment showed. "What's wrong?" Ars asked.

"It's a splendid tale, but the one recounting doesn't greatly differ from the other. Nobleman or Wisigoth, it's the same story."

"Ah," sighed Ars. "You're wise. How did you know there was yet another tale?"

"Because hidden within the one you told me is a love story," Pierrette replied, thinking of a stag and a doe in another forest, of love that remained unconsummated, and ended in tragedy—the tragedy she had made of it, with the spear. Yes, Ars's second tale was indeed a romance, but an impossible one, the way she had told it.

"Then tell it properly," said Ars, "and I'll listen."

When the Emperor Constantine issued his edict that all Rome was to worship the Christian God, old spirits trembled, that he had dared utter such a terrible spell. But the empire was large, and Constantine a lesser sorcerer than . . . than Minho of Thera . . . and folk did not everywhere take him seriously. The poor older gods lingered.

Gaul, once the heart of the empire, was far from the new center in Byzantium. Old gods and new coexisted, but when the Wisigoths came, people blamed pagans and heretics for the invasion, wrongly believing their sympathies lay with the conquerors.

He who wore stag's horns departed into the Camargue and made his home beside a spring sacred to Ma. There he dwelt for many years, but he was lonely, having no worshippers and no companion to celebrate the rites.

From where came the *biche* who sipped at his spring? Was she a virgin child of Arelate, or the daughter of a farmer who kept the old ways? Perhaps she was sired by a stag and nursed by a doe, and only took human form when she drank from the sacred pool. He whom we call Giles was content—for a while.

When Wambo's sons hunted *sangliers*, they did not disdain to take what other prey was driven before them, to wound deer, aurochs, or even wild horses and track them until they weakened and made their hopeless stand—flanks heaving, froth-mouthed, bled until they had no strength to run or fight.

When the hounds tracked Giles's companion to his pool, they found not a doe, but a wounded girl, wild-haired and naked. Did she wear antlers upon her head? I don't know what the hounds saw, or what Wambo did when he came to see. I do know that Wisigoth, Gaul, and Celt all spoke the ancient tongue before they divided into tribes, and worshipped the same gods. Wambo knew Cernunnos and his mate, and left them in peace. No doubt he sent gifts, and Goths made pilgrimage to the sacred spring. Some clever bishop put a stone shrine and sarcophagus there, but Cernunnos is not in it, nor a saint. And that, my new friend, is the story heretofore untold.

Old Ars emerged from the spell Pierrette's story had cast. Tears streaked her cheeks. "The Christians renamed the god 'Saint Giles.'" She sighed breathily. "The monks built the shrine not to honor the real Giles, but to keep him out."

"They built it to fix their story in stone," Pierrette replied. "They claimed the magic of the spring for their own, and they wrote their Christian tale so no men would believe otherwise."

There was no more to be said—or rather, there were too many stories, and no time to tell them. The old woman was tired, and dusk had fallen.

The nuns would be anxious if Pierrette did not return soon. Besides, with all she had learned from Ars and Cullain, she found herself eager to be gone from the city. The Camargue beckoned, and she was eager to put her new knowledge to the test. . . .

A silent servant with eyes like shelled almonds accompanied the ancient woman to the door. Ibn Saul bade Pierrette stay.

"Assuming that your premise is valid," he said, "you may free your sister of her affliction. But if she catches word of your plot before it is too late for her . . ."

Pierrette thought of a long-ago hunt, of silent stalking with a care for the direction of the wind and the brittleness of twigs underfoot. "Once we have crossed the final divide," she said, "Marie can only run deeper into the trap of my choosing."

Ibn Saul wished her good fortune. "If you succeed—or

even if not—perhaps you'd consider joining me. Though my present apprentice is competent enough . . ."

"My sister's fate isn't the last of my challenges," Pierrette replied, thinking of Anselm's precarious existence, and more generally the fate of magic in the world. "Perhaps when other issues have been addressed . . ."

"Or perhaps in the course of addressing them?" he rejoined. "I sense that the thread of our common interests does not end here." Pierrette too felt that she was not seeing the scholar for the last time—or perhaps it was only wishful thinking. But now was not the time.

Again, Pierrette heard the heavy bolt drop into place behind her. Marie lay draped in white linen, as if with the red silk of a whore. "I missed you, sister," she said, in a little girl's petulant voice. "I thought you had gone away."

"I considered it," Pierrette lied. "Before I return to Citharista, there is another place I must go, and I'm not sure I can trust you to come with me, without your running away."

"I've seen nothing of the world. I'll go with you, wherever it is."

"It's by the sea, east of here. I'm afraid, because I must pass through a pagan swamp where old gods reign unfettered by Christian goodness." Pierrette kept her voice neutral. She wanted her sister's tormentor to come willingly, thinking that it was Pierrette herself who was deceived.

Did Marie's eyes brighten? "I won't complain," she said. "And I won't run away. After all, you're my sister. I have no one else."

"We'll leave tomorrow," Pierrette said, her cheerfulness unfeigned, though the one who looked out from Marie's eyes would have been dismayed at its source. The trap was set. Marie circled the bait, sniffing. Soon the jaws would close.

But plans had a habit of going awry, and things magical were unpredictable. If only remnants lingered in the Camargue, and the Christian demon had consumed the rest, then nothing could prevail against it.

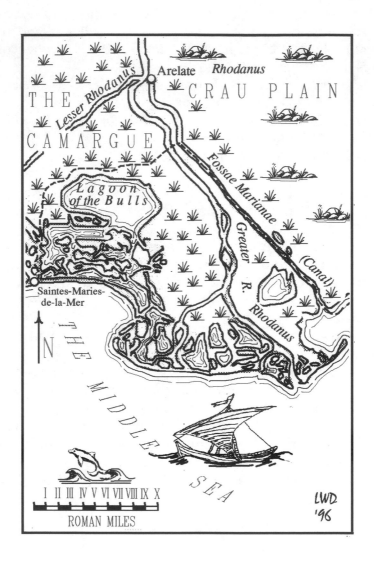

THE CAMARGUE

Lesser Rhodanus

Arelate Rhodanus

CRAU PLAIN

Lagoon of the Bulls

Fossae Marianae

Greater R. Rhodanus

(Canal)

Saintes-Maries-de-la-Mer

N

THE MIDDLE SEA

I II III IV V VI VII VIII IX X

ROMAN MILES

LWD '96

Chapter 25 ∾ A Hideous Light

Taciturn Agathe accompanied Marie and Pierrette when they left the nunnery. She hoped to stay in Saintes-Maries, perhaps hovering in silence over the Marys' graves. Sister Clara's boy Jules, who had found a cart for Gustave, had begged to go, but his mother would not hear of it. "There's nothing to see but rocks and dark forest, until the lagoon—and then nothing but water and swamp." Agathe was not daunted.

Mother Sophia Maria drew Pierrette aside. "I took the liberty to reveal your secret to Agathe. You need a sympathetic companion who knows your secret." Pierrette was not so sure—but it was done.

Beyond Massalia, their road—a real road, paved with stones—led through fields not yet greened with new growth, through clumps of trees larger than those of the forests Pierrette had traversed before, the more somber for their majesty. Still, in flashes of sunlight that penetrated the canopy, she glimpsed an occasional low-lying bush of a comforting, silvery hue, and felt reassured.

At nightfall, they camped near the foot of the last mountains they would see, according to Cullain. There, when firelight glanced from brush and trees, she caught glimpses of another glow, as if unseen eyes watched, and she felt comforted, not afraid.

Marie, as she had promised, was obedient, even subdued. Though she did not help prepare beds or cook, she rubbed Gustave down with pine needles—an unaccustomed luxury he accepted without biting her.

Pierrette and Sister Agathe sat late by the fire. Marie had fallen into exhausted sleep. "Don't relax your guard," the nun advised. "I've seen her like this before. As soon as you think she's become reasonable—whish! Off she'll be."

The ascent and descent of the rocky range consumed the daylight hours. The winding trail was so steep that Gustave had difficulty pulling the cart even when Marie got out and walked.

With others present, Pierrette had not dared essay a spell to test her conviction that watersheds were magical divides. The abbess had accepted her mutated fire-spell in its "Christian" form, but Agathe would not be so tolerant. Still, she sensed a change in the air as they ascended, and a corresponding shift in the nature of things as they descended toward the broad expanse of blue water to the north.

They took a room at an inn by a shoreside wharf, a mean place kept in business only by undemanding salt merchants like Cullain, who had recommended it. "The smallest copper will be enough for the two of you," he had said. Two coins got them supper and breakfast, and oats for Gustave. The odd, round grains were not what Pierrette called "oats," but the donkey was not displeased.

"Whose boats are in?" Pierrette asked the innkeeper. Cullain had given her several names.

"My own boat will carry the three of you handily."

"Your boat hasn't been hauled in three years," Pierrette said. "My donkey would kick through its planks, and then where would we be?"

"Ah! I had thought you'd trade the beast for passage. Of course mine isn't large enough for him. The big red boat belongs to Caius. The blue one is Flavio's. Either will suit."

"I wouldn't trust Flavio to raise sail on your watering trough," she replied, depending on Cullain's assessment to make her seem informed—and thus not to be cheated. "Speak to Caius. I'll pay two pennies to be set ashore at Ugium."

Caius was a large man with red-brown hair, boarlike, though without a *sanglier*'s tusks. He glanced toward the three travellers, made count upon thick fingers, and held up four—just as Cullain had said he might. He winked.

"Three," Pierrette rejoined, smiling broadly. Caius looked as if he wished to join them at their table. "Tell him I'll speak with him when I've eaten," Pierrette commanded the innkeeper. She could speak softly in a manly tone, but as her volume increased, so did her pitch. Her masquerade would have ended right then.

Being three, they had a room by themselves, with reed pallets that smelled fresh. Had they not, Pierrette would have hesitated to use their own blankets, for fear of carrying biting things with them. While Sister Agathe and Marie settled in, she returned to the common room, and spoke with the boatman, and gave him one coin. She showed him two more, but kept them for now.

Pierrette awakened in the middle of the night. Something was not right. She heard only air whistling within Sister Agathe's large nose. What she did *not* hear had awakened her: from Marie's pallet came no breathing. Marie was not there.

Pierrette willed herself to be calm. Where could she have gone? Back to Massalia? Marie was not that mad. The beach to the west degenerated into reedy morass. East and north were salt pans and the River Arcus's delta, impossible to cross.

Pierrette thought back across the evening. They had eaten, Pierrette had spoken to the innkeeper, and later with Caius . . . Wait. Caius had smiled across the room, and . . . had winked. Had he winked at her, or at Marie, sitting next to her? She knew where her wanton sister had gone—or at least who Marie had gone to find.

She quietly pulled on her clothing. When she found Caius, she would find Marie.

In the common room, she heard snores—rattling old men's breathing. She crept past long tables, benches overturned atop them, guiding herself with a trailing hand. The inn sprawled along the stone wharf, and could not contain more than a hallway and a row of rooms facing the sea.

The hearth fire was banked, and she did not dare crawl over sleeping men to ignite a candle. Did she dare a spell? She was afraid that she was not far enough from Massalia, that the range of hills were not high enough, and that she could not evoke light without some clearly Christian purpose. Still, she had sensed change as she crossed the divide, and this place had no Christian feel.

She uttered old words . . . and recoiled, gasping in shock and dismay.

Light. An oily red glow, rank as burning, rancid fat, emanated not from her fingertips, but from every object in the room. There was no smoke, but the ugly light made the air seem thick. The corridor at the far side of the room yawned most brightly, and she knew where she had to go—down a glowing tunnel lined with the embers of an undying fire.

Pierrette's breath caught in her throat. A trick of perspective made the hallway seem too narrow, the ceiling too low. The floor seemed to rise, so that she would have to crawl to reach the door at the end of it. Her bare feet were lumps of wax that adhered to the tiles. She forced herself toward the rectangular opening, hunching as if its black wood frame was a farrier's hot iron. The corridor seemed to stretch, the dark door at the end to recede.

At last she stood before it. A latchstring dangled. The wrought-iron strap inside had not settled into its slot. Hesitating as if the string were hot wire that a smith might cut into nails, she tugged the door open.

A single candle warred with the crimson light of her spell, casting sharp highlights on the moving shape in the floor's center. Low moans made her ears tingle. Slowly, her eyes untangled the twined bodies: a broad male back and white buttocks, and slender raised legs with small feet whose heels drummed irregularly between jutting shoulder blades.

She heard Caius's quick, panting breaths and Marie's small cries, and she stopped in mid-step, caught up in the scene, horrifyingly aware that she was admiring the breadth of the boatman's shoulders, the play of muscles . . .

Marie had not run away, nor was she going to, that night. As Pierrette backed out of the room, she pushed the door firmly shut.

Pierrette heard Marie slip beneath her covers. At least she had not stayed past dawn, and Sister Agathe did not know she had been gone. "Psst! Pierrette! I know you're not sleeping."

"I'm awake."

"You were spying on me. I saw you in the doorway."

"I wasn't spying. I didn't stay, once I knew you hadn't run away."

Marie giggled. "Perhaps you should have. You're as stuffy as a nun."

Was she? Pierrette had not been disgusted, just angry. Marie could do whatever came into her head, yet Pierrette had forced herself to deny Aam. She remembered the dream of herself, weeping for the fate of her own daughter—the unchild of her selfishness, who would have had to suffer in her stead, with even less chance of succeeding. She remembered Elen, who had made the easy choice.

"I'm not a prude, Marie," she said, as if the shadow on the pallet next to hers were no more and no less than her sister. "I envy you your . . . freedom." But only in the most limited way was Marie free.

"You don't have to envy me, sister. I didn't use Caius up. Go to him. Yes—go." Her voice conveyed feral eagerness.

"I'm tired, Marie, and tomorrow may be a long day." She rolled over and pulled her thin blanket over her head. It did not muffle Marie's scornful chuckle.

The most important industry on the lagoon was salt. *Salins*, shallow salt pans walled with rock and earth, were flooded. Sunlight drove off moisture, leaving a crust of red-brown salt. Caius made his living transporting that raw salt to the mills. There, it was crushed, redissolved, and refined in pools.

Pierrette shuddered, remembering last night's oily, evil light. What was the nature of this place, that her spell had changed so? The very air, though clean and clear, seemed to carry an invisible taint.

Caius's boat was larger than Gilles's fishing craft, designed for hauling cargo. Uneasy with her thoughts, Pierrette kept to herself by the boat's stem, where she could watch Caius at the tiller, or rushing about to trim the heavy lateen sail.

Gustave was tethered nearby. He had stepped willingly across a plank between boat and wharf, and settled, hooves widespread on the sole planks for stability. Had the beast sensed the malaise of the place, and welcomed the chance to win free of it?

Pierrette glanced at Sister Agathe, dozing in the sail's shadow, and watched Marie play the coquette for her lover, as if she had never seen better seamanship. That offended

Pierrette, who had sailed with her father in rougher water, in a frailer craft.

When Sister Agathe awakened, and saw Marie's fingers snake lightly up the inside of Caius's inner thigh, Pierrette laid a restraining hand on her shoulder. "Now isn't the time, or this the place. Here neither of us have the strength to best her demon."

"Saint Paul said we must confront the error of our fellow," the nun replied.

"Only wait. What couldn't be done in the sanctity of Mother Sophia's chapel can't be accomplished here, on this pagan lake. Consider the damage long since done, and forebear."

"What demon peers from behind your eyes, child?" asked the nun—though with the slightest of smiles. "Or what wise old woman? You make me feel like an impetuous child."

"Sometimes I feel old, sister," Pierrette replied cautiously. "Some say experiences age us more than years."

That night they pulled ashore near the extremity of the Arcus's delta. The next day they sailed for Ugium on two long tacks that took them first to the northern shore of the lagoon, then southward as close to the wind as the clumsy craft could sail.

Caius, deciding he could sell his salt for a higher price in Arelate, volunteered to take Pierrette and her companions further than originally agreed. Pierrette suspected his desire to keep Marie close accounted for his generosity.

"Ugium is there," said Caius, nodding toward a deeply rutted dirt track. "Tomorrow we'll be towed through the marsh to the Fossa, the Roman canal."

The moment Pierrette's foot touched soil, she knew something was terribly wrong. It was as if she had stepped in crusted dung, but the reek did not assail her nostrils alone: it seemed to penetrate her very soul, and a curtain of darkness dropped between her and the bright Mediterranean sun. She gasped.

"What's wrong?" asked the nun.

"Yes, sister, what troubles you?" echoed Marie, though without genuine concern.

Pierrette could not explain. In that brief moment she had sensed corruption, a hideous taint worse than the carmine light of her spell. Were she even to think words of magic here, she might be consumed by the spell's evil heat.

"A sudden nausea is all. The last tack enured me to the boat's motion, and now . . ."

Marie laughed. "You were like that as a child. You'd wobble ashore from father's boat, and demand everyone's attention. Stay aboard. We'll tell you about the town when we return."

Sister Agathe looked from Caius to Marie to Pierrette. "I'll stay also. I've seen towns before."

"Not like this one, sister," said Caius, chuckling. "Ugium is special."

"I don't doubt it. That's why I'll remain." The couple laughed, and strolled off arm in arm.

"You're pale as a fish," Agathe told Pierrette.

"I felt evil in that soil, evil so profound that I should sink in it and never again see the sun."

"I don't think Ugium is for the likes of us," Agathe said thoughtfully. She squeezed Pierrette's hand. "Never mind. I saved bread and cheese from our last meal."

They ate before sundown, and Agathe made up her bed. "I'll stay here a while," said Pierrette, eyeing the bloody red sky over the unseen town. A vast malaise oozed from the russet clouds like the stench of things long dead, and the rattle of twigs in the evening's last breeze was the rattle of old, dry bones.

In her mind's eye she saw Ugium not as it was, but in its glory days, when Greek engineers had built its thick walls, when it rivalled Massalia as the queen of the Salyen ports. It had been called Heraclea then.

In her hesitant vision, she threaded narrow stone-paved streets that changed and became more ancient even as she walked, putting whole centuries behind her with every turn and twist, as if she had accidentally parted the veil of time. Stiff sandals with crisscrossing thongs chafed her feet; a soft wool dress brushed her ankles, and a veil of lighter stuff puffed out from her face with every breath. Her hair felt tight and heavy, bound atop her head in a coif that reeked of strong-scented oil.

A low, stone building presented a lintelled doorway to the street . . .

Pierrette shuddered, and the vision shattered—but not

before she had seen dark decorations adorning the portal: niches, each holding the shrivelled, blackened remains of a man's head with an iron pin driven through it.

Heraclea's honored dead. Flesh mummified by sun and hilltop winds drew back from teeth in joyless grins—yet despite death and decay, from those dead eyes emanated fierce protectiveness. Their warlike spirits watched over portal and town, joining seamlessly with the thoughts of living warriors atop the protecting walls.

Yet there were others, angry spirits not Heraclea's own. She peered at the wizened face of a Greek merchant soldier. He raged within his spiked head, forced to lend the power of his death to his enemies. He yearned for a ransom that would not be paid—his head's weight in gold— and for a funeral pyre that would free his captive spirit.

Shudder after shudder racked Pierrette's slender body. What, exactly, had she seen? Gauls had kept spirits, ghosts or *fantômes* of their dead heroes, in such sancta. They were the strength of the tribe, wisdom and succor in war and trouble. They were not themselves evil. But surely, in this present day, the niches in the pillars of the sanctum were empty? Her vision had been of a time long past. It did not explain the noisome evil she had felt earlier.

What postulates had changed, that her spell evoked crimson light and a soul-polluting stink? Had the ancient Gaulish rite been perverted through time and misunderstanding? Thinking of the nunnery garden, and its snakes, she hesitated even to imagine what serpents dwelled in this land.

There were no more mountains between here and the Camargue. Were there boundaries of another sort? If not, then as she journeyed toward that watery plain, would the stench of evil only thicken? But if the blended magics of land, river, and sea nullified this curse—would the old magics be revived, as she hoped?

What then of Mother Sophia's hopes for Marie? She shook her head. The Christian saints' intervention was a last resort, for to depend upon them was to surrender—to save Marie at the cost of giving up all hope of averting the black time at the beginning and end.

Pierrette sensed she would find no answers now. She

sought her blanket, but instead of lying down, leaned against the boat's rail, and wrapped herself against the night's chill.

Caius and Marie returned at first light with teamsters and four horses, who towed the boat through a narrow, reed-choked channel. Perhaps because their placid progress bored her, Marie became talkative. "Where does the pagan land begin? When will we be there?"

"I'm not sure," Pierrette admitted. "We must cross the gulf to the Fossa, once we're free of these reeds, and then make our way up the River Rhodanus. Perhaps it begins on the far shore of the river."

"Isn't there a quicker way?" Marie chafed with impatience. Just who was so eager—Marie or that other entity within her? Which stood to gain? Pierrette had dangled the temptation of a land free of Christian strictures, hoping to ensnare the demon with false hopes of unlimited license, but Marie's eagerness had no evil edge. Was it indeed Marie herself who questioned her?

Pierrette was afraid that the demon might sense the trap. "If we were rich, and had hired a fast galley, we would have sailed right past it by now. But the open sea belongs to Allah—or so I'm told. Men like Caius know channels among the sandbars, where Saracen vessels can't go."

"I'll be glad when we get there," said Marie, in a little-girl voice Pierrette could not but believe was her own. "This land frightens me."

"And me," Pierrette admitted—though not sure they spoke of the same fears.

The channel opened onto a lagoon whose waters were blood-red with salt-loving algae. Caius's heavy craft floated inches higher than before. "I think it's magic," he said.

Pierrette did not; she remembered Aristotle—how the tonnage of boats could be measured by the weight of water they displaced. If this water was heavier than the sea because it was saltier, the boat would displace less, and would ride higher. She giggled.

"What's funny?" Caius demanded. "It's true."

"I don't doubt it," Pierrette responded. "I was laughing at myself, not you."

She now understood ibn Saul, and the seductiveness of "natural" explanations. Perhaps the death of magic everywhere was prefaced by just such realizations—that most phenomena could be explained without it. It was not a comfortable thought for someone who aspired to become a sorceress.

They tossed the tow rope ashore, and raised sail. Southward toward the gulf, trees gave way to reeds, sand, and tamarisk, and daylight surrendered to dusk. Caius guided them through shallow backdune waters. Pierrette slept, and thus had no way of knowing when they passed beyond the influence of the red-lit blight. When she awakened with sunlight on her face, she could feel the difference, as one felt the absence of a toothache.

"Let me walk on shore," she pleaded with Caius.

"Ahead, a mile or two, the banks are firm gravel. Wait another hour."

The land on the left was dense, grassy marsh—the beginnings of the Camargue—yet on the right, beyond a margin of reeds, she saw a flat plain that supported only sparse grasses. It was littered with rounded boulders. "Is that the Crau Plain?" she asked Caius.

"Indeed," the boatman replied. "It's said to be made of stones thrown down by a god upon Herakles's enemies."

"I don't wish to hear it!" exclaimed pious Agathe, covering her ears.

Marius's canal was a ditch with stone walls. The towpath blocked the view across the Crau Plain, but to the left was the river, behind tall, old trees. Light flickered oddly there, stray sunbeams where no sunlight should fall, and shadows darker than they should be. Both observations made her feel less helpless and alone.

There was just enough wind for Caius to nurse his boat northward. Alone in the bow, Pierrette risked whispering the words of her small spell . . . But nothing happened. It was as if she had uttered the incantation upon a mountaintop— no spark, no fire, no blue or white light . . . and no oily, emberous glow.

Pierrette smiled. "Q. E. D." Rivers—and even this broad canal—were like mountains, barriers against magical forces. Whatever lay on the other side of the waterway would not be the evil light of some festering underworld. What would it be?

They landed on the right bank. Pierrette stepped ashore on the cobbled verge. A cool breeze stirred hairs at her temples, so cool and refreshing it felt misty, but there was little moisture. "The Crau!" she exclaimed. "The breeze is off the plain of stones."

The others stared as if she, not Marie, were possessed, but Pierrette did not care: with the breeze had come a sensation, a yearning to step across the sun-warmed stones and stiff grass of the plain, as if Aam himself awaited her there, tall and bronzed, his sun-colored hair blown by the breeze. Out there, in that bleak desolation, something called, something cool and sweet, hot and exciting, giddy and sad. "Not now," whispered a voice borne on the soft air, "but soon . . . But soon."

She shook her head to clear it of silly notions. Aam was miles east and south, and indeterminable years away. Across the Crau Plain lay Ugium's Greek walls, the long-gone streets she had trod in ill-fitting sandals, her face half-hidden behind a veil. Yet the air that caressed her sunburnt features held no trace of corruption, as if the flat, treeless plain had purified it.

Caius pointed. "The teamsters! Soon we'll be moving again." He strode to meet them and their beasts; short, scruffy oxen, this time. Soon the party was back aboard, and Pierrette's strange yearning faded. She stared across the plain when the towpath dipped low, and over the reeds that passed slowly rearward. "Gustave," she said, "couldn't you pull us faster?" The donkey eyed her, as if he were not so stupid as to be trapped into any such admission.

Nonetheless, miles passed beneath the boat's keel, and by sunset the canal and the River Rhodanus were only paces apart. Tomorrow morning was going to be difficult. According to Cullain there was a boatman to ferry them across the river, where the Camargue began. Them: Pierrette, Agathe, and Marie. Not Caius. Would Marie willingly leave her lover? Would Caius resist her leaving? Pierrette decided to say nothing until morning, lest she awaken to find Marie gone, or herself left behind.

At first Pierrette thought the noise was the anchor chain, as the boat rocked—but Caius's anchors were secured on deck. The boat was moored to the wharf. *Clink-pat, pat. Clink-pat, pat.* What was it? Where had she heard that sound?

Then she smiled. She had not been wrong when she had seen the green glow of animal eyes in the gloom beyond a fire's light, and shadows darker than dark. A friend was near—and it was time to spring her trap.

She heard Marie stir. Had she heard it too? Her eyes were wide. "What is that?" she whispered breathily.

"Wake the nun," Pierrette commanded tensely. "We must slip ashore." Could she use Marie's fear? Marie's—or what lurked inside her?

"I'll wake Caius."

"No. That's Yan Oors. Caius can't stand against the Starved One. Hurry—wake Agathe. Do you want to mate with a bear?"

Marie scuttled away. Pierrette wondered if indeed the demon were afraid of the ghostly starved man. Who ruled here? They were not in the Camargue, but neither were they in a Christian land. What influence did the horned one have?

Marie returned with the nun. "She heard it too! What must we do?"

"There's a boatman. The creature won't follow over open water. Come! Once adrift, we'll be safe." She did not want either Marie or the nun to have time to think. She had not planned this, but she intended to use it.

"Come!" she repeated, slipping over the rail. She heard the faint *clank* twice—the *pat* of footsteps was lost in the sounds of their own movement. "This way." She quickly untied the donkey Gustave, then led him and the others between the trees that separated canal from river. "The boatman can't be far." They drifted like shadows along the river's cobbled bank, beside mirrorlike water unbroken by a ripple—or by the shape of a boat drawn up on shore.

"Stop!" said Marie. "This can't be the way. We can cut Caius's boat loose, and push away from shore. The canal is water, too."

Pierrette had hoped Marie would not think of that. If she got back to the boat, it would be impossible to force her across the river. Pierrette paused, listening, hoping . . .

"Oh no!" her sister gasped. The dark apparition was between them and Caius. Pierrette gestured upstream, where the gleam of the river was cleft by a dark shape. A boat. Marie saw it too. Its owner was awake, waving what appeared to be a rusty sword. "Keep back!" he said in a high voice. "I'll defend my boat!"

"We don't want your miserable boat, you old fool!" snapped Marie. "That is, we don't want to steal it."

"We'll pay for passage," Pierrette added.

The boatman caught sight of Agathe's tightly coiffed hair. "A Christian sister?" he exclaimed. "Very well. Get aboard— but show me your coin first."

Pierrette waved a Massalian drachme. "This, for all of us— and no argument." The boatman reached for the coin. "When we're in midstream!" Pierrette snapped, pulling it out of reach. Would the boat hold all of them? "Now help me get this intractable beast aboard." For all his stubbornness, Gustave got himself aboard with almost no persuading. He, too, must have sensed something . . .

She turned to grasp Marie's arm, but her sister had backed away. "What's wrong? Come on!"

"His ears!" wailed Marie, her eyes flashing like a cornered, wounded deer's. "You tricked me! Caius! Caius! Help!"

Pierrette lunged, but Marie eluded her. Ears? What had she seen?

The elder girl turned to run back the way they had come— and grunted as she came up against a tall, dark, shadow. Yan Oors's great arms enfolded her. The boatman threw off his night-cloak, dropped his sword-shaped root, and darted forward to help. Guihen's ears were now obvious to all.

Agathe, in the narrow boat, stared wide-eyed at the apparitions who held the struggling Marie. Too frightened to flee, she shrank low on the sternmost thwart. Her weight caused the boat's bow to lift clear of the bank.

Guihen and John of the Bears tossed Marie into the boat. Pierrette leaped after. "Hold her, Sister Agathe!" she gasped, grabbing handsful of Marie's dress. Guihen pulled free the oars and seated them between the forwardmost pins. The boat slid into open water. The sprite, with a neat thrust and tug on the oars, turned the overburdened craft around. John stayed ashore, and was indiscernible among the shadows of overhanging willows.

Agathe's knuckles were white with fear—and the effort of holding the thrashing Marie.

"Bitch! Whore! Sow's leavings!" spat Marie.

Pierrette was not sure whom she addressed, but suspected her sister's—the demon's—anger was directed at her. It was not Marie, but her enemy, whom they struggled to hold.

"Let go of me, woods-witch!" snarled Marie.

Sister Agathe snorted. "Just who is she talking to?"

"It's the demon saying those things, not Marie."

"Of course, child. I know that." She glanced behind Pierrette, looking at . . . Guihen.

"Don't be afraid of him, sister. Guihen won't harm you."

Marie mouthed foul expletives at the forest-sprite, and Agathe, having enough, stuffed her mouth with a handful of her dress, and held it there. "That's better," she said, smiling.

They reached the middle of the stream. "Guihen?" inquired Pierrette, "can you keep us here while I decide what to do next?"

"The current is slow. A few strokes will keep us in line with the landing on the far side. As for what to do—you've done well enough, so far. Why should it be different now?"

"I don't know what magical postulates are in force. I don't know what Marie . . . what Marie's parasite . . . will be capable of, in the Camargue."

Guihen chuckled. "I'm not worried," he said. "I only wonder what *you* will be capable of."

"So do I," Pierrette admitted. "So do I."

Chapter 26 ∿ A King's Conscience

"Can you keep Marie aboard?" Pierrette asked Agathe and Guihen. "I need to walk about, and get a feel for this new land." Her footsteps felt light, as if she were floating whole inches above the ground, and the air smelled sweet and salty, yet not at all like the sea.

Guihen nodded. "Take all the time you wish. If Marie is wise, she won't want to go ashore at all—not that we'll give her a choice."

Pierrette strolled away from the boat. There were still cobbles embedded in the brown soil, but this was no longer the Crau Plain; it was the Camargue, where all magics worked. Did she dare essay a spell? A little one? The light spell, the fire spell, was her measure of things magical. An essential principle of inquiry was to maintain consistency in all things except one, so that when she wished to see the result of a change, she introduced no deceptive unknown elements.

She whispered the incantation, as if the softness of her words might mute the effect she sought to bring forth. She pointed to a straggling tamarisk as she uttered the last syllables—and leaped back as the entire bush burst into flame. She smelled burnt hair and eyebrows. Dry tamarisk crackled and popped merrily, spraying sparks afar.

Amazed and elated, Pierrette stared into flames made transparent by morning sunlight. Fiery tendrils formed elusive shapes like figures dancing upon the charred, crumbling branches. She kicked dirt at the blackening bush, but only dirtied her feet. Flames resumed their happy celebration a few inches away. Even when the embers were entirely smothered, tiny dancers flickered atop the heaped dirt.

Pierrette had no spell to put out fires. When the spell gave light, it always faded by itself. Candles burned down. She remembered being trapped as a scrubby tree. Her magic might be stronger here, but that did not solve problems; it only made the solutions more dangerous.

Agathe led Marie ashore. Marie's face was a mask of girlish puzzlement, as if she did not remember who she was, or why she was in this place.

"Has the demon fled?" Agathe asked.

Guihen answered her. "In this land the fiend's influence is limited. The spirits don't accept its claims. But it hasn't departed."

"Spirits?" Agathe glanced around as if the reeds and low bushes might conceal things worse than beasts.

"You need not fear," the sprite said. "The one you call 'Mary' knows you."

"Don't say that. The Mother of the Lord isn't a pagan spirit."

Guihen shrugged. "She is mother of all. How could she not be the mother of one—or One?" He said that softly. Pierrette did not think Agathe heard. She believed Guihen; here the Christian grip on the old spirits was weak. Besides, they were not deities at all, in the sense that Agathe thought of such.

"I don't think it matters what you—or Guihen—call them, sister," said Pierrette. "Pray to whom you choose. The spirits of this place won't fault you for it." Her conviction reassured her that Ma indeed had heard, and did not disagree.

Pierrette wandered off by herself. She had perceived the spirit of the sacred pool first as someone much like herself, but older, and then more clearly as her dead mother. Later, there had been "Ma-who-was-not," a crone, the spirit of a far future time, haggard and worn; at other times again, Ma was merely kindly and middle-aged, resembling Pierrette in a tribal way. How could she, who was all women, not be Agathe's Mother of Christ? Yet the reasoning seemed convoluted. Though built upon axioms as small and basic as "two points determine a line," or "God is," theology was a vast, confusing edifice.

Pierrette's hypothesis would be unacceptable to Sister Agathe—but Ma had existed from ancient times. Where had Mary been? Though Agathe feared and loathed "false gods," the converse was not true. They hated her no more than she, Pierrette, would hate Mary.

❧

Pierrette's Journal

There may come a time, on the way to the ashy blackness of the Beginning or the End, when all the wise old women, the mascs and crones and witches, are forced apart from Ma by Christian believers. Unable to reach the gods, banned from that Mary locked in a pretty church, where will they turn? I am glad I do not live in that time. I fear that with all the chapel doors closed and Ma locked inside, I would find myself in the arms of that dark spirit who owned Marie.

Sometimes, I despaired. Were my plot and plan doomed by the weight of time past and yet to be? I was only one girl, despite my years of study, and had not made much impression on the village of Citharista. But the great religions spread wider every year. What hope that I could force the uncaptured spirits of this vast, watery land out into the world, in defiance of the writers of rules and builders of churches?

True, I caused the tamarisk to burn with a "small" spell magnified by the nature of this land; true, Marie's possessor seemed stunned, and she herself had no memory of events since her wedding; but could I call upon Minho of the Isles, and prevail upon him to transport poor Anselm home? Could I—with the help of the spirits of this place—drive out Marie's demon? Or would I have to take her to the Christian shrine at the edge of the sea?

❧

Dancing sprites lurked in the light of the cooking fire, though no one remarked them. Pierrette squirmed as if a sharp stone prodded her buttocks, though the silty delta soil had no rocks, and the ground was clear of twigs.

Agathe noticed, but said nothing. Marie was hardly aware at all—her condition had worsened; in the afternoon, she fouled herself; her chin glistened with drool. Had her possessor been all that had animated her? Was this frail husk all that was left of Pierrette's sister?

But no—Pierrette had caught flashes of the old Marie all along; her laughter had been her own. Even her lust was no more and no less than what the two sisters had imagined in the safety of their bed, before there were demons, voyages, or great, fearful magics in their lives.

Marie was not gone. Just as the demon had given her strength when it had been strong, now it sapped her in its weakness. It had to be driven out, but was Pierrette strong enough? Her spells were stronger here, but she did not have one to drive out evil spirits.

In the afternoon, plagued by stinging insects, she uttered the ancient bane she and Mother Ars had shared in ibn Saul's house, and the voracious creatures vanished. Yes, spells would function properly—but was she ready? An exorcism was a battle of strengths, wits, and weapons, and though she felt strong, she had only plodded one spell at a time, and doubted she would be quick enough.

She felt like an ignorant farmer given sword, shield, and dagger. How would she know which one to use, and when? How would a body used to a scythe's rhythmic motion adapt to a sword, or plowman's eyes to the dagger's thrust and slash? There was no way she could practice to become proficient.

If she drove the demon out, what would become of it? It had been made in the drawing of distinctions between good and evil, from the offal priests rejected when they butchered the land and its spirits, taking only the sweet morsels and calling them good. It would not be enough to exorcise the demon, and leave it to prey on another, but it could not be destroyed, because it had not been separately created, only assembled from the pagan leavings of the Church's feast.

What was the use? If she scattered its parts, how would she prevent them from reassembling? She could not. Not by herself.

Guihen brought her back from the brink of despair. "Come, girl," he commanded. "A walk will do you good. The flowers are blooming by moonlight." Pierrette rose, but did not think a walk would ease her.

She would never have found dry ground between the reedy hummocks, but Guihen leaped like a hare over soft, wet places. Stepping in his footprints, she kept her sandals dry.

It looked no different than any pool, at first glance. "Wait," Guihen said. A cloud drifted past the moon's full face, and then she saw . . . stars, in the water. A thousand thousand white blooms scattered over the pool twinkled like starlight.

Like a gold ring around the moon, yellow irises emerged from clumps of dark, swordlike leaves at the margin of the pond.

"They're beautiful," Pierrette exclaimed. Breeze-driven ripples caused every white bloom to bob and flicker, every iris to nod. A different ripple caught her attention—a green snake, bright as spring's growth, disappeared among the reeds.

"These flowers bloom in a pool in . . . the Fortunate Isles," he said. "They took root long ago, when the Isles were here."

Pierrette's delight disappeared. She knew why Guihen had brought her here. "I'm not ready," she protested.

"You never will be," he countered. "But you need to trust your magic. Haven't simpler conjurations obeyed your commands here? You're as ready as you can be."

She sank to her knees amid dry reeds. He was right. The only way she would gain confidence was to stretch herself . . . to dare. "Will you stay?"

"I won't be far away," he replied, "but it's not my spell— and the sorcerer-king Minho is a stranger to me."

"And to me," Pierrette said.

"I'm not convinced of that," he replied. "Didn't you meet him once—and didn't he know you?"

"That was a dream!"

Guihen chuckled. "And what is not?"

What is the difference between calling forth a storm cloud, a sea mist, or a confusion upon one's enemies? Is the sun a fire or a plate of polished gold? Those are concepts. If the sun is fire and gold, can a gold coin burn a hole in one's pouch? Can a mist be not vapor, but confoundation, or confoundation veritable fog?

A spell is an equation; is an equation a spell? Just as one phrase, one side of an equation, can be substituted for what lies on the other side, so can a spell be altered by the insertion of equivalent terms. Just as a mage might seek to define the universe in one grand equation containing all the rules for everything, so might a sorcerer strive, but with spells and concepts.

Guihen pondered things beyond the competence of a wood-sprite. He watched from a tamarisk bush as Pierrette prepared a new kind of spell.

A man may curse his neighbor's strayed sheep or the neighbor, but that does not make him a magician, only angry. A masc may know a few spells, and herbs that bring fever or allay it, but a spell or two do not make a masc a sorceress.

Feathers, smoke, and powders focus the thoughts of witch and bewitched. But Pierrette gathered ideas, concepts, and similitudes from one language or another, from nations a hundred leagues or a thousand years apart.

In the frown lines of her forehead, the plump bitterness of her lower lip, Guihen read her effort—not just to remember a spell, but . . . to create one. No existing spell would do, for who would have written one to call out to a mad king who had placed walls of unreality between his kingdom and the world—a king who ruled a land that did not exist in time or place, and where no evil, none at all, was allowed to exist?

At last she beckoned to Guihen. "What's that for?" he asked, touching the furrow between her dark eyebrows.

"I hope to pay a call upon a man who asked me to be his bride. Are these boy's clothes right for such an occasion?"

"Get rid of them. You'd look fine in nothing but sunbeams."

She blushed. "How about moonbeams? Ibn Saul says everything that we see is light bouncing off what it touches." She reached skyward, curling her fingers as if teasing a wisp of wool from a dense fleece. "Light is what we see, and what we see is only . . . light." She teased a moonbeam from a fleece of cloud, and spun around, wrapping herself in silvery light.

"The stars are twinkling jewels," she said softly, creating a necklace—stellar brilliants on a shiny wire drawn from the bud of an iris—a yellow iris men called golden.

"The moon's path," she murmured, "is a goddess's silvery footprints," and she pulled on pointed shoes woven of water and silver.

Her dress coalesced into shimmery silk, and she bound her waist with a tamarisk branch, emerald and gold of early spring. "There!" she exclaimed, pirouetting for his approval. "How do I look now?"

"You're lovely," he said, amazed. Then his ears twitched. "But you'll look a foreigner to Minho, who is of Cretan birth."

"Oh!" She blushed again as the shimmering gown shifted and bared small pink-tipped breasts in the Cretan fashion of Minho's day. "No!" she said firmly, covering her chest with a handful of tiny flowers plucked from the pond. Her bodice became delicate lace.

"You did that on purpose!"

"I wanted a look at your pretty bosom," he said. "But be warned. Just as I put a thought in your head that changed what you wore . . . Don't let others suggest things. Don't let them change . . . what you are."

"This isn't all play, is it? Thank you for reminding me." Seeing how far the moon had ridden across the sky, she said, "I must do it now." She turned away and began to chant . . .

All her years of study went into the careful phrases. Guihen understood only a passage here, a word there, for she spoke in tongues of sorcerers past. It was not a language. *Here* was a phrase of succinct Latin, subtle meanings compressed into a few inflected syllables. *There* was a fulsome word in rolling Etruscan, followed by a sentence in the harsh Greek of Odysseus's time, a clause in a Galatian Celtic dialect long extinct, and an exclamation barked in the Salyen tongue.

There was, Guihen reflected, no one spell, and no one tongue to express the subtleties of time, distance, and unreality Pierrette wished to bridge. A single phrase, translated into a language less flexible, or more, might change meaning and effect, so Pierrette spoke each one in the original words that expressed exactly what she wanted.

That was why no ordinary man understood great spells. That was the barrier so few could cross—between mere magic and genuine mastery. Guihen gazed with awe at the girl who uttered the words, and considered with cold trembling the power she drew into herself.

He watched mist coalesce upon the pool and gather at her feet, a carpet thick as moss by a holy spring. He watched her step delicately onto it. It rose, and bore her upward and away.

This, Pierrette marvelled, was no magpie's flight. Mist was vapor was cloud—and clouds scudded across the sky, wind-driven. Clouds were white pillows, and she reclined at her ease, her moonlight dress shimmering, her dark hair one with the blackness between the stars.

She flew on unseasonal wind, north over Arelate, glimpsing Nemausus's roofs on her right, and then over bare highlands cut by immense gorges. Beyond the high country the land was green with the first leaves of spring, then turned russet and brown over lands still locked in winter's grasp.

Her course shifted westward over dark forests of the Frankish domain. She drew a wooly cape of cloud about her shoulders, against the moist chill, without a word aloud to make it so.

Still far, but visible from her great height, was the moonlit glitter of the western ocean, her goal. At last the steely water was beneath her. Ahead only groping fingers of black rock reached into that emptiness that few ships dared sail. The tide rushed like a river in full spate between a rocky point and a low, offshore island. The tide was the ship-breaker that swelled the cold population of Sena, Isle of the Dead. Her conveyance of moonlit cloud began a long, gentle descent.

Beyond that island was a wet hell, home to unimaginable beasts, and souls in lonely torment.

Yet looming up from the sea where no land should be, surrounded by a veil of mist (or merely confusion) were black scarps in concentric circles—islands and harbors, houses, wharves, and green, green fields abloom with the colors of summer and sunshine. The Fortunate Isles were aptly named.

She drifted toward a small central island. A pillared temple

with fat black and vermilion columns reminded her of the
portico of Anselm's keep. There in a courtyard with tiles
painted to match the cloudless sky, she alit. Her misty
conveyance drifted away. Where were the priests and aco-
lytes Anselm had described?

"I sent them away," said a warm, resonant voice, "when
I was sure you were coming." Minho. The king. The sorcerer. "Welcome, Daughter of the Moon."

". . . Of the moon? Oh, no—I only borrowed a few threads
of moonlight for this dress."

"Don't be offended if I doubt your modesty," he said,
smiling. "But come—I have mixed water and wine, for the
end of your journey." He was as handsome as she remembered him from her childhood vision, and though his hair
and clothing reminded her of the young Anselm—the kilt
longer in back than in front, black hair in oiled ringlets—
he was not the same. There was strength and confidence
about him, calm assurance that stemmed from aeons of
unquestioned rule.

His smile was easy and unaffected. "I missed you," he
said. "It's been so many centuries. Have you come to stay?"

How could she answer? She had never been here, except
in a dream. As if expecting no answer, Minho led her into
a cool chamber. A table was laid with platters of summer
fruit. He spoke as if they were old friends—immortal friends.
Missed her? Who did he think she was?

"It hasn't been that long," she said, fishing for informa-
tion, selecting a slice of crisp apple from a wooden plat-
ter inlaid with gold. How long was it? Six years? Seven?
She could not remember exactly.

He offered her a graceful folding chair in the Egyptian
style of a thousand years before. "Not long? I've yearned
for you while nations rose and fell."

Pierrette was amused by his hyperbole. Few nations rose
and fell in the span of a girl's childhood. Still, his intensity flattered her; she was hardly more than a child, and
he was as handsome as Aam—though his curls were dark
and his skin had an olive cast, whereas Aam's had been
golden.

"I came for your help," she said tentatively.

"And if I help you?" He grinned. "Then will you stay?
Will you claim the throne that has awaited you all the

hundreds of years, since last we loved on the Plain of Stones?"

He knows I won't stay. He's teasing me. And where is the Plain of Stones? It sounds like the Crau, but I only glimpsed that from afar. She thrust curiosity aside. "My sister is terribly ill, and unless I return, she'll die. And there are poor Guihen, and Anselm, and Yan Oors . . . Yes—Anselm, whom you sent out as a boy, and who now cannot return."

"Anselm? Who is that?"

"*Ansulim?*" she essayed. "The boy you sent to subvert the Apostle Paul. He pines away in Provence, and longs to come home."

A shadow crossed Minho's ageless countenance. "Ansulim," he said softly. "A fine boy. I sent out only the finest. But he failed. Paul's Church flourishes, and the opportunity to nip it in the bud is gone. The distance between my kingdom and the world grows." He shook his head. "Ansulim couldn't return now even if I allowed it. You are the first visitor to my shores in half a century, and his magecraft is less than yours."

Pierrette put a hand on his forearm. His skin was smooth and warm, his muscles distractingly hard. "If I succeed in my own task," she said, "then perhaps your islands' eloignment can be reversed."

Though infatuated, Minho was nevertheless a king. "How?" he asked, his eyes hard.

She explained her hope to undermine the terrible conformity of the great religions not from within, but from without; not through the encouragement of schisms and subversion of apostles, but by strengthening small gods and goddesses, magics of special places, and the nymphs, sprites, gnomes, and faery creatures that inhabited them.

She laid out her vision of the Dark Time coming, that had once been. She told him of the broken wheel, and the Eater of Gods.

Minho paled. "What hope can you offer, in the face of doom? Why shouldn't I simply wait until the distance between my Isles and the world is infinite? Then I and mine will be exempt from the universal degradation you foresee." He sighed. "If I can't have you, why not simply allow things to finish their natural courses?"

"You flatter me," she replied shyly, lashes masking her

eyes. "But wouldn't you want the opportunity to remain, even if unfulfilled for the present?"

"Go on," he said at length. "Tell me more of your hypotheses."

She explained that she would not try to counter priests or churches, with which she had no quarrel, but would confront the Dark one whom their worship fed. She told him what she hoped to accomplish. If Anselm—Ansulim— were free to move about at will, he would help her, and thus himself and Minho also.

"I won't leave these isles to aid him," said the king.

"Will you allow him to be his own man?"

The king smiled. "I can. Will you stay?" He put his hand on hers.

"Only long enough to write a letter," she said. "If, that is, you will deliver it for me."

"How can I? I've said I can't leave these isles."

"You said you will not—but there's a way, isn't there?"

He nodded reluctantly. "I'll deliver it—if only because while you write it, you'll remain here a little while."

He led her to a tall room with shiny tables and walls lined with shelved scrolls, a hauntingly familiar room—the original after which Anselm's library had been patterned. Minho did not have to show her fresh vellums, or where was a cabinet of inkpots and quills. Even the furniture was identical to her own master's.

She wrote, explaining what had to be done to drive the demon from Marie, and to keep it from the world.

Minho put hands on her shoulders and smiled down at her. "I wish you would reconsider."

She enjoyed the warmth of his touch, and would have been glad for more of it—but shook her head. "Would you give up your kingdom and come with me into the much-changed world beyond?"

"You know I can't."

"You will not. You could. As I could linger here."

"I'll wait for you to finish your task. Come back, when you can—and will."

"And Ansulim?" she asked.

"I'll see what can be done. Now go, before I weaken and create a spell to hold you here—a spell to make you want to stay."

She stood on tiptoe to kiss his cheek, a mere brush of her lips—but he turned his head and held her for a protracted kiss. His lips were feverish. Long moments elapsed before she even thought of pulling away.

"Good-bye," she said, her cheeks flushed, her legs shaky. She did not recreate her misty conveyance. Instead, a magpie fluttered upward with a great commotion of feathers and cries.

A magpie on silent wings alit beside the sleeping Guihen. "You're back!" he exclaimed, immediately wide awake. Then he glared. "You said you would *speak* with the king. You didn't tell me you were going to . . ."

"Oh, hush. I tried to send a voice on the wind, but my whispers echoed from the rocks of the coast, and only sea birds heard them. You can't imagine how difficult it was. I combined seven spells to carry me, and seven more, ones never before spoken, to slip past the confoundations that lie like mist around the Isles."

"Was Minho surprised that you defeated his defenses?"

"Guihen, it was so odd. As if he knew me; not just in Ma's dream, when I was a child. He asked me to wed him. And I don't believe that his spells alone isolate him—the working of events in this world wall him away, though he won't admit it, and he said he'll try to help Anselm, and . . ."

"Ah, child, take a moment to breathe. Even my ears can't take in so much, so quickly. Now tell me—one thing at a time."

"We must return to camp," Guihen said, rising. "Time hasn't been stilled while we talked, and the others will be concerned."

"Oh. Should I have . . ."

"No—no more spells. You've amazed and frightened me enough."

Pierrette had not thought her effort frightening. The magic had been complex, but here where all magics adhered precisely to their original postulates, precision was enough. There had been no need to dodge shifting, changing premises, constantly on watch for the slightest unpredictable result.

"I fear your blindness," he added, "not the inconstant nature of spells."

"Blindness? What do you mean?"

"You call what you have done 'magic,' as if any masc could do it, but you did what few could—making new spells on the wing, and shaping reality to your requirements. That's not magic, and you're more than a mage. You are a sorceress."

Was it true? Was that the difference—shaping new concepts and connections instead of reusing old? If so, she had realized her childhood goal . . . but she felt no different. There had been no clear crossing from one state to another. She had grown. So had her abilities, and the scope of the challenges she took on, but there had been no qualitative change, only a continuum of learning, study, and practice, of making connections between widely separated parts of a greater whole. Everything had begun when she first opened her eyes and made a simple association between her mother's face and the sweet milk from her breast.

If there were no clear divides between child, masc, *maga*, and sorceress, how far could one strive? Could even death limit her, or could she continue to grow, reaching mental fingers into every nook and cranny of the universe, encompassing all that was, that had been . . . that could be?

She shuddered, envisioning herself a fat, black spider with legs uncountable, each one touching a person, an idea, a single grain of sand, until the entire universe was in her grasp and gods twitched with her touches—and she created that Dark Time she most feared.

She was terribly cold. Guihen saw that she understood his warning, though he had not seen what she envisioned.

"Fear for me," she said. "Fear that I might learn so much that I cannot grow old and die."

"Your own fear will keep you safe," he replied softly, "and I trust you to remain as frightened as needs be."

"Minho is ageless," she mused, "yet he is no eater of gods. Why is that?"

Guihen, not privy to her revelation, shrugged helplessly.

"I think he has limited himself by his fear," she mused. "When he pulled his islands and people from the cataclysm, he was for one moment as a god—and he dared no more. Now he is trapped in the consequence of his withdrawal, and will let it destroy him rather than become . . . something . . . he cannot control."

"But that's good, isn't it? After all, his islands are already long gone, destroyed in a burst of earth's fire—in this world."

"I'm not so sure. I can't believe his role will end with him simply fading away."

"Is that a prophecy?" he asked.

"Only a suspicion," she replied, thinking how sure the king had been that all was not over between them. She shrugged. She could not see how it could be so, and there was much to do. Above all, there was Marie—and sorceress or not, she did not think she would ever be completely prepared for the confrontation that awaited her.

Part Five ∾ *Maga* (Sorceress)

This is Provence, a Christian Land. Christendom is comprised of many folk, and the Faith that binds them in One's name is not the same in every heart; priests and bishops are comfortable with Faith, and treat doubt with grave suspicion, denying unbelievers our miraculous feast. Still and all, were I to choose one person, from all those I have known, to share my own bread and wine, it would not be a priest, but . . . a sorceress.

Otho, Bishop of Nemausus
The Sorceress's Tale

Chapter 27 ∾ Unlikely Companions

Back at camp, the others were astir. A visitor had arrived early, awakening them. "Yan Oors!" Pierrette crowed happily. "But . . . you're different." He was bare from the waist up despite the morning chill, and clad only in the skimpiest of leather kilts. His hair was tangled with twigs and burrs. "What have you been up to?"

"Ah, little lady. I've been playing with the wild Camargue horses."

"Playing?" Guihen grinned—lewdly, Pierrette thought. Yan Oors skin darkened—a blush?

"Have you brought horses for us to ride?" asked Guihen.

"Indeed," Yan replied. "When I told them you wished their aid, I could have had all the herd. I don't know why they like you, elf; you're nothing special, as far as I can see."

"Perhaps it's the succulence of my leaves," Guihen muttered acerbically. "Where are they?"

"I'll call them." Yan Oors whinnied like a stallion. Pierrette's eyes swept the brush and the shadows, but heard no pounding hooves.

"Whoof!"

She squealed, and jerked away from the sudden gust of breath on her neck. Turning, she saw a great, white head with lovely brown eyes that laughed at her. "Where did you come from?"

The horse pushed aside tall reeds screening the shallow water beyond. Several more heads pushed through, all white,

317

with long, silky manes and tails that—unlike Yan's hair—looked freshly brushed.

"You're beautiful." The horse was unlike the scrawny, undersized cart-pullers she was used to, or the tall, ungainly beasts soldiers prized. They were broad, legs and bodies covered in short white hair. "Epona," she quietly named the lovely mare. Epona, a goddess, and a white horse.

"And who do you belong to?" she asked a spindly colt anxiously looking around itself. It was dark, as if a different breed entirely. The mare whuffed again, and with a happy whinny, the colt reached up between her flank and her haunch, and nursed noisily.

"They are born black or gray," said Yan. "Only in their fifth year do they become white." He stroked the mare's soft nose.

"Is there a stallion?" she asked. "I see only mares."

"Didn't you hear me call them? I am their stallion."

Despite herself, Pierrette's eyes strayed to his short garment, unable to imagine a man performing that service for mares. "Then indeed there is magic in this place," she said, embarrassed.

"As long as a single mare runs free, and a stallion to serve her, magic will endure," he replied softly. Pierrette suspected that he had indeed told her something of great significance—not merely a hope or an observation, but an essential postulate of Camargue.

The colt let go of its mother's teat with a loud, wet *pop* and, glancing sideways at Yan, approached Pierrette, short muzzle level with her chest. He nuzzled her abruptly with an upward jerk of his head.

"I'm not your mother!" She covered her breasts with an arm, and stroked his soft mane. Thinking how the colt had looked at Yan, she whispered, "Is he your father? You're as dark—but surely, he's more than five years old."

The gaunt man chuckled. "I won't test your credulity by claiming to have sired him."

"If you did, I would believe you." It was true. Could she—who remembered flying as a green and glittering magpie, deny that this man might remember running with horses? If so, would those memories be . . . real?

Could she say with conviction that her own cloud voyage and magpie flights had not been? She could, with little mental effort, feel the high air flowing over her freshly preened feathers; could Yan with no more difficulty feel himself a stallion, with broad hooves and a great prong?

The moment passed. "We have to go," he said loudly, addressing the others, "if you wish to sleep dry tonight."

Getting Sister Agathe mounted even on the smallest mare was no easy task; she had never ridden. Yet once astraddle, clinging white-knuckled to its mane, Pierrette thought it would take as much work to pull her loose.

Yan and Guihen lifted listless Marie to a mare's back. With no more skill than Sister Agathe, and without the will to hold on, would she fall beneath the horse's hooves? It did not prove so; Marie slumped low, as if part of her mount— an ungainly but well-attached hump. That was well, because Pierrette had become daily more worried about her deterioration. She had lost weight, and her cheekbones were sharp as knives, her eyes unnaturally bright and sunken.

Yan had not attempted to direct the horses, who had presented themselves to their riders of their own accords. No mention was made of reins or halters. Pierrette was pleased that the nursing mare had chosen to carry her.

She was surprised to see Guihen vault over a stocky mare's hindquarters with a shrill whoop, like a barbarian warrior. What other surprises were in store?

Much could be observed while riding above the tops of even the tallest reeds. Wending westward, the last remnants of forest were soon left behind except along low dunes, where stone pines' roots held the loose, dry soil.

Kestrels hovered over dry expanses as if suspended from invisible threads, alert for mice to bring home to their young. Pierrette allowed herself to savor a small raptor's singular concentration, its excitement when it spotted a vole exposed on clear ground. She shared its accelerating plunge earthward and aloft again, limp prey in its claws. She landed on the abandoned magpie nest where her hatchlings waited, and watched the clumsy, white-downed infants rend their meal. Their wide-eyed, reptilian stares never changed while they ate.

It was springtime, a time of change in a land of changes. The kestrel had only recently arrived to breed. Rough-crested Egyptian vultures high overhead, harriers, ospreys flying low over the water— all came north from Africa to breed and savor the rich meals the delta provided lavishly.

In the fall they would depart, and golden eagles would fly in from the Alps, white-tailed ones from unknown arctic lands.

Mallards and red-crested ducks, with trains of fluffy, flightless offspring, scurried into willows, reeds, and tamarisk as the mounted party passed.

Constant transitions kept the land alive. As ducks, hawks, brilliant-winged flamants, songbirds, terns, swans, and storks arrived from the north in the fall, summer fliers departed for lands now greened by seasonal rains.

The Camargue's invisible influence spread widely, to the ice where summer knew no night and winter no day, to unknown deserts, jungles, and bleak, rocky islands no man would tread until the Black Time was upon the world. It was a heartland from which all life, all magic, sprung, a single pulsing organ upon which all depended.

Creeks and channels trended southward, mere traces among clumped reeds, carrying fresh waters from the mountains, becoming ever saltier as they neared the sea. Salt governed all, and life adapted to it. Purslane grew on rises of ground where rains washed away salt, and sea lavender in lower places, exuding droplets of concentrated brine from the undersides of its leaves.

The channels were home to eels which, when grown, departed to Ocean, to breed within the vast tangle of Sargasso seaweed that marked the edge of the world. Gray mullets entered Camargue, but did not linger in fresh water. Sweet-fleshed bass and trout pressed seaward from clear streams and lakes, but shunned the saltiest marshes. Carp coveted brackish waters. The pulse of life's heartbeat began here.

The first night they camped near a trickle of almost-fresh water. The horses drank with gusto, even though Pierrette thought it warm and salty as blood.

Agathe was distant and silent. Marie remained dazed. Her face and arms broke into red rashes from the moist heat.

No one slept well. If Guihen slept, it was elsewhere, in a place of his choosing. Yan disappeared into the reeds with his mares. Pierrette could not help imagining him prancing and snorting among them, a stallion in form as well as thought.

Near the end of the second day, the glitter of sunlight hinted at a large body of water on their left. "The lagoon of the bulls," said Yan.

"Bulls?" asked Pierrette. "And cows also?"

"Of course. But not milk cows that suffer man to pull their teats or decide who mounts them. Such cows are lucky to be undesirable, because they remain free. The bulls . . . that's a different story, for men desire them." He shrugged. "But many bulls are born, and only one is needed to quicken a herd."

Pierrette pressed him to explain.

"Herakles passed through Camargue, driving Geryon's red cattle. He allowed his cows to breed with fierce black Camargue bulls. The fame of Camargue bloodlines spread." Romans sought bulls for their arenas, for though small, they were quick and intelligent, and many a lion and man were skewered on their lyre-shaped horns, even in Rome itself.

"I hope we'll see them," said Pierrette.

Elsewhere, over the high, forested country of the central massif, a great bird flew southward on black-and-white wings. Reaching the confluence of the Rhodanus and the Druentia it turned eastward. Such a course, had anyone noted it, would have seemed unusual, for storks migrated south in September, not May. They mated and nested in the Camargue. Why would a stork fly toward Massalia? And why would it carry in its long bill a vellum scroll tied with a red silk ribbon?

Its route took it over the long, white scarp where Marius defeated the Teutons, then over the valley of the Holy Balm, Magdalen's resting place, and at last came in view of the red scarps of the Eagle's Beak.

Had Minho of the Isles not possessed a stork's bill instead of lips, he would have smiled: Ansulim had been homesick indeed; his home's portico was not unlike the colonnade of Minho's palace, or his brother's, in Crete—that long-abandoned edifice called the Labyrinth.

He circled on broad, outstretched wings, and landed atop a parapet, amused that while it had been sunset a few moments before, now—here—it was high noon. The boy had learned a trick or two, he reflected. He himself could scarcely bind time more effectively than his student had done—though the Fortunate Isles were of greater extent than this small keep.

The king sent tendrils of thought seeking his erstwhile pupil. He was surprised to spot him miles to the west.

As soon as Minho found him, Anselm knew. He abandoned his half-built cairn, and hurried homeward. Minho waited patiently—if a bit sadly, for lost youth was nothing if not sad—and at last heard the clatter of the aged boy's sandals upon the steep stone stairs.

"Master!" Anselm cried. Then: "Master?" The tall shape was still a stork. While an unseasonal stork was unusual, the presence of the King of the Isles within the flowing river of time, was . . . impossible. There was no saying what havoc it might have wrought with the world.

"Master, is it truly you?"

Minho did not like reunions with boys no longer young. He did not enjoy the guilt. He could only free poor Ansulim from the geas that had held him—but then there was the fresh guilt of commanding him to one final task. As a stork, he could not speak aloud, but Anselm heard him . . .

"You must not fail this time," said the king, when he had given his instructions.

Anselm looked up from his perusal of the scroll. When he had first unrolled it, he had found another rolled inside. "That one is not for you," said the king. "You must give it to the scholar ibn Saul." Anselm stuck the scrolls in his sash.

"This is a formidable task, Master," he said, wrinkling his forehead, "but at least it's not—like the last one you gave me—absolutely foredoomed. This requires only the active cooperation of an ignorant fisherman, a Christian priest, and an atheistic scholar . . ."

Ah! The poor aged boy. Guilt lay leaden in his stork's gut. How could he fly without ridding himself of it? He sighed (silently, of course, for storks did not express themselves so) and said *"Ahribad ne poharta, merati haralmer akkarimad."*

Anselm looked confused. What tongue was that? It sounded only vaguely Minoan.

"It's a spell from my remote ancestor," said the king. "Once our people lived in bands like seals. They could no more build cities than can wolves. Selfishness, diverse interests, and conflicting behaviors prevented them from sharing tasks like building walls and bastions, or digging canals to irrigate fields. This spell freed men to join in cooperative effort."

"It's an ancient spell, Master," reflected Anselm. "If my apprentice Pierrette is correct, the beliefs that supported old spells have changed, and the incantation may have unforeseen results."

Minho puffed up his long, stiff feathers. "Look around, boy," he said, raising a wing. "Are there walls, cities, bastions, palaces? Are there aqueducts? Of course there are. Thus this spell functions. *Quod . . .*"

". . . *Erat demonstrandum*," Anselm finished the sentence. "I believe it will work, then, for surely the men who created such things were no more cooperative than the ones I must deal with—a priest, a cowardly fisherman, an atheist . . . and myself, a crazy old sorcerer," he added, "whom none have reason to trust."

"The task, boy! The task makes the spell work. The common goal allows enemies to smile while they pull at a common oar, or stand side by side at a capstan bar. It is the vision of what lies ahead—and you must give them that."

Minho sleeked his feathers with his great bill. "Now hear the rest of the spell. You must not misplace a single syllable."

Anselm listened. He did not wish to see aqueducts and city walls crumble for want of the cooperation to have built them in the first place.

When the king was satisfied with the mage's mastery of the spell, he did not bother to say farewell. His weight of guilt was gone. He leaped from the parapet into the air, and was soon winging northward and out of sight.

Anselm accepted the task. Though Minho might profit, it was not for the king that the old mage undertook it, nor for Marie. It was for Pierrette. He strode across the causeway that separated him from the world. . . .

His step was light. The youngster who lived within every man had assumed control of his skinny legs. He wanted to do things he had never done, to experience everything he had missed in studious youth and isolated manhood.

He felt no libidinous arousal, and accepted that he would likely refrain from chasing tavern girls . . . but taverns? Ah yes! To drink wine shoulder to shoulder with shepherds, masons, soldiers . . . to laugh and make jokes, and sing maudlin songs . . . but that must wait. He had an important meeting.

The mage had last trod the streets of Citharista when it was a thriving Roman seaport, in the time of his nemesis, Saul of Tarsus. He was saddened to see it shrunken and crumbled, and was unimpressed with Otho's chapel, plainer than the humblest Roman shrine.

"*Ahribad ne poharto . . .*" He murmured the unfamiliar words of the spell. Though the chapel door was ajar, he knocked, as if it were not a public place. To him it was indeed a stranger's house.

Otho knew immediately who he was, sensed his discomfort, and led him to his little house. He lit a lamp, because dusk was falling and there were no windows.

Over a cup of wine at Otho's scarred table, the mage recounted what Pierrette's letter required.

"Saintes Maries? To exorcise a demon from Marie? Of course I'll go with you—but how can we get there in a fortnight?"

Anselm had no answer. Weren't there boats? Were not the Via Tiberia's bridges intact? Otho was not sure.

Of one thing he was sure—one thing that disconcerted Anselm no end: the castellan Jerome (whom Otho now called Reikhard) must accompany them.

"Pierrette asked for her father," Anselm protested. "She said nothing about the castellan."

"I told you how I freed him from the demon. He should have a part in releasing Marie—he's not without guilt. The demon could not have invested him had he truly resisted it." He sighed. "In any case, it feels right—and this letter requires that you heed me. Listen: 'My father and P'er Otho will know what they must do,' she says."

"I've heard nothing good about this Reikhard," the mage mused. "How will Gilles feel about voyaging with his daughter's defiler?"

"Gilles conscience is far from clean," Otho replied. "The knight could have done nothing to Marie without his consent—bought with a bag of coins. If forced to admit which is most despicable, Gilles would name not Reikhard, but himself."

"I hope he'll do some good," the mage mumbled dubiously. "I can't imagine what it could be." He hoped Minho's spell was powerful. A surly German knight would test the limits of magic.

"Don't concern yourself," the priest said. "Pierrette says this will work." He shrugged. "I don't know what good I can do, for that matter. I'm not an archbishop or a theologian, and I've never seen an exorcism, let alone participated in one. . . ." That was not strictly true. There was Reikhard. But the point stood: a village priest might get by being empathetic, knowing his parishioners' strengths and foibles, and with a bit of jargon or gibberish . . . but what Pierrette wanted . . .

Anselm smiled. "Perhaps you can read up on things, before we go."

"Read what? Do you see shelves packed with scholarly books?"

"Come." The mage took the priest's arm. "We have a little time." Otho reached to snuff the lamp. "Leave it," said Anselm. "We'll be back before the oil is half gone."

How long had it been? Otho wondered much later. Surely a fortnight had passed while he sat at Anselm's library table, or slept in the bed that had belonged to Pierrette. That memory caused him guilty chills. The scent of that bed reminded him of Elen, so long gone, except from his poignant memories.

Surely, he reflected, a month had elapsed while he read the Gospels, the Old Testament, and whole scrolls of apocrypha that Anselm insisted should have been included in that collection called the Bible. Surely a year had gone by while he read Justin, Augustine, and a dozen other saintly scholars.

He could not guess how long he was in the mage's keep, because the sun on the terrace was always at high noon. "Shouldn't we be going? What about Pierrette and Marie?"

"Time is the least of our concerns," Anselm assured him. "When you have learned what you must, we'll depart in a most unseemly hurry." Drugged by his understanding of all that there was to know—and all that he did not—Otho returned to his table, his books, and his scrolls.

✧   ✧   ✧

When the two men at last crossed the causeway and returned to Citharista, the moon was rising, and the last roseate wisps of day glimmered atop the ridge. Those disappeared as the men descended behind it.

"Who's there?" Otho called out as they approached his house. He could see warm light inside. No one answered. The lamp burned unattended, just where he had set it long ago . . . and the oil was only half gone.

"And now," said Anselm, when Otho had packed a few things, "we must hurry—we have only a fortnight until we must be in Saintes-Maries-by-the-Sea."

Otho's head felt stuffed with wet cloths. A fortnight? Then had he fallen asleep at his table, and only dreamed the months and years of study? Was everything he thought he had learned only nonsense created by his sleeping mind? But the knowledge was coherent, and made sense.

Between his new learning and the strangeness of finding his lamp still lit, with no time having passed, it was perhaps forgivable that the priest choose to accept the sense and to avoid thinking about the logic of it.

The castellan's dwelling was nearer than Gilles's house. The soldier at the door stared goggle-eyed. He saw the priest every Sabbath. The old magician he had seen only once, when he had been cured of a piercing whine in his ears that had almost driven him to suicide.

"*Ahribad ne poharta,*" muttered Anselm as they waited for the Burgundian.

Reikhard was not yet abed. When Anselm put his request to him, the knight accepted immediately. "But there are no ships in the harbor," Jerome stated. "Shall I call my men? Without them we won't dare travel overland by road."

Anselm shook his head. "Gilles may know a way."

The knight bade them wait. When he reappeared, they were amazed. Jerome was clad from shoulder to thigh in fine old mail whose like had not been seen since Roman fought Teuton and Gaul. He carried a long sword over his shoulder.

How strange, the knight reflected as he trudged through Citharista's streets. His horned god was not one to listen to crying virgins, old women, or a crucified weakling who begged an end to his suffering. Otho had freed the knight of the demon, but not of the memory of his captivity. No longer a slave, he was not free of the stink of slavery. Only that evening he had knelt at the foot of his bed and begged his god to free him of guilt he could not shed.

Who had heard that prayer? Had Cernunnos sent these men with the means of his expiation, or had the god only passed his plea along to the mage's unknown deity or even P'er Otho's Christ? But who was he, unlettered as he was, to speculate about where a prayer went, once it was uttered?

"Marie sickens more every day," Pierrette told Sister Agathe. "I fear there is no time to get her to the shrine; the demon consumes her. It won't give her up until she is dead, and of no further use. I have to drive it out."

The sister shook her head. "You aren't a priest, child."

"Here, a priest might be less advantaged than I am. If you disapprove . . ."

"Not enough to leave you, girl," Agathe grated. "Marie needs me. I've come this far, and I won't walk away now."

"Thank you," Pierrette said softly, putting her hand over the nun's. "Your faith and prayers will be a comfort to Marie—the Marie I knew—and to me also." If that admission surprised the sister, she did not let it show. For Pierrette, it was true, as far as it went: after all, it was still a Christian demon. Had it been a pagan spirit, she might have been able to reason with it.

They found Gilles at the wharf. He eyed his unlikely visitors—the armed knight, the priest, and the white-bearded elderly mage (who was mumbling words that sounded Arabic). They, in turn, had eyes only for the battered fishing boat, hardly a craft to evoke confidence.

Gilles was pale, as if seasick—unlikely for a man who divided his time between land and sea. The cause of his discomfort was soon evident.

"Well, get in," he said. Gilles, though very much afraid, would not be "cautious." He would take them in his boat. "You didn't come looking for a better boat, because any fool could see there are none." Gilles, despite his greenish hue, did not act the least afraid . . . the least "cautious."

This was not the Gilles Jerome had persecuted, the man Otho had confessed. This was not cautious Gilles, who

refused to sail to Massalia with a fresh catch. True to Otho's
prediction, Gilles made no objection about Reikhard.

"We must catch the morning's wind, or the three of you
will have to row." The thought of rattling knight, clumsy
priest, or frail old man rowing—and the tangle of oars that
would result—made Gilles feel superior.

He was immediately ashamed; he was hardly better than
the worst of them. That was the old Gilles. He was no longer
"cautious," but neither was he superior to anyone. He was
free of such things, because he no longer cared if he lived
or died. He would be surprised to survive this journey. What
mattered was that the others did, the ones who could help
Marie and Pierrette. He did not understand the terrible trouble
his daughters were in, but it was important that they have
succor.

All three settled in the boat, and Gilles pushed off. Rounding the rocks that defined the harbor, the sail snapped full
of a following breeze, and Gilles pointed the unpainted stem
just enough offshore that the looming mass of the Beak
would not steal wind from the patched sail. It was not a
cautious course. There was a risk of being driven against
the rocks at the foot of the wave-washed cliffs.

"It wasn't your fault," said Sister Agathe, throwing an arm
around Pierrette. "The demon's claws are wrapped around
her heart. Wait until we reach the shrine. We'll find help
there. Marie won't die before we get her there." It sounded
like wishful thinking. Pierrette's mood was too black for
words, and her voice worn out from incantations.

"I had to try," Pierrette cried. "I had to know if I could
do it."

"I know you did," the nun replied.

It had seemed to make sense. Marie had been empty after
her wedding night. Her soul fled to some inner recess where
it felt safe, but not so far that her body, untenanted, began
to die. The fiendish spirit had come later, discovering the
empty rooms of Marie's being, and inhabiting them. One
night Marie had been docile and uncaring, and then she
had run away, to return from the house of women much
changed.

Pierrette had been sure that when they crossed the
Rhodanus and entered the Camargue, the Christian demon

would have weakened. She had been right. Marie's parasite's reaction, when it realized it had been tricked, supported the hypothesis. Only John and Guihen's quick action, stuffing Marie into the ferryboat, had prevented her escape.

So she had tried. She called the fiend forth, tempting it with her soul and body for Marie's. It had blackened the air, shed feathers, fur, and scales, and squalled with the voices of crows, ill winds, and banshees—rejected creatures turned loose when the Church had made saints or demons of old gods.

She called it forth—but she could not destroy it, because it was of the earth and the universe, and could not be dissolved. The hideous thing screamed when she suffused it with baleful fire. It gobbled and thrashed in desperation when dark, ephemeral waters rose up around it. It coughed as the smoke of herbs and powders suffocated it—but only Marie's poor body burned, became sodden, and coughed wracking coughs. Agathe had been right to stop her, for Marie might have died. The demon was unharmed.

There were no burnt crusts or weeping sores where Marie had been burned, and the dampness of her shift was only sweat, and the magical waters of Ma's source, carried all the way from the beech grove in a green glass bottle. Her breath was soft and easy, as if no harsh smoke had entered her lungs.

The damage was not physical, and left no trace—but Marie had suffered, and within her the fiend still gloated, unharmed and undiscouraged. Pierrette wanted to save Marie on her own, but she had failed. There was no choice but to continue to the shrine—and to place her in Christian hands again.

Pierrette's concern went beyond her sister's welfare. A Christian exorcism would not stay the Black Time's coming. World-spanning faiths destroyed the variety, the sparkling unpredictability, of the world. A victory of pagan magic over Christian would have set back that final, unvarying, predictable doom. She would have been happy if it had been delayed by a year, a week, even a minute. But now, the opportunity was lost. She had failed, and the Black Time awaited. . . .

Pierrette awakened after sunrise, to the hooves of horses,

the creak of harness, and the sounds of unfamiliar voices. "The Gitanes have come," said Yan, shaking her shoulder.

The camp was encircled by four-wheeled wagons. Their spoked wheels were red and vermilion sunbursts, yellow daisies and blue tare flowers. Folk rushed about clearing hearths. Breakfast fires were fanned into bright, smokeless blazes. The clatter of iron pots, staccato laughter, and the rattle of an unknown tongue drove off the last vestiges of sleepiness.

"The Gypsy queen wishes to speak with you," said Yan Oors.

"With me? Why? Why are they here?"

"They're on their way to the shrine where their ancestor lies buried. They do this every May. All the bands come, if they can, or send a few if all cannot. And the matriarch would hardly deal with me—a man."

Pierrette shook off the last vestiges of exhausted, disconsolate sleep. She observed wagons loaded with crates, bundles, and rolls of bright cloth. One was stacked with dried reeds and hung with finished baskets.

Since the queen of the Gitanes expected a woman, should she take the time to unpack a dress? She laughed quietly and uttered old words, creating a small glamour that made her feel quite feminine, and brushed her hair, bunching it at one side and tying it in a casual but un-boyish way.

Guihen sat cross-legged at the nomads' fire; evidently, sprites were exempt from male or female roles. Sister Agathe sat at the queen's left. Guihen motioned Pierrette to sit. The matriarch was fat, and glittered with gold—ear-spools with tiny bells, chains, bracelets around her wrists, and rings on each plump finger. Pierrette felt plain.

"I am Marah." The Latinesque patois was not her native speech. Her dark skin was naturally the color of old leaves.

"I'm called Pierrette," the girl replied, suddenly aware that her name, "little stone" or "pebble," sounded trivial—though she was unsure why that should matter.

"It's good to be humble," the Gitane queen observed, "but I felt the rumble of great stones beneath my feet, and I knew to come here."

"I felt nothing." Pierrette thought of the landslide that had devastated Anselm's wall, and the roar heard even in town. But there were no rocky cliffs here.

"Does the horse feel pain when he kicks the smith who is shoeing him?" Marah said, with the ghost of a smile. "I felt your magics from afar. It was no 'pebble' rolling about."

"Then . . . you know magics also?" Pierrette was eager to learn anything, from anyone. Only knowledge routed the fear that she was inadequate to her tasks. She was like a boy gathering sling stones to protect his sheep against wolves: the small stones could only sting, but the more he had, the more secure he felt.

"Yours is strong magic. Ours is a fortune told, a flock hexed or unhexed, a pot or two healed . . ."

"Fortunes? The future, you mean?" Could this Gypsy look forward on the broken wheel?

"One man's—or one woman's—future, Mistress," she replied. "I doubt that such a trick would impress you."

"Knowledge impresses me. Magics and 'tricks' stem from one source. I've learned much from folk less wise than you." She was thinking of ibn Saul and the Wendish woman-magic.

"Will you ride with me?" the queen asked. "Talk makes long roads short."

"Are we going the same way? I was told you would visit an ancestor's tomb."

"Not an ancestor, my dear. *The* ancestor—Sara, who pulled the Christian saints from the sea."

"Saint Sarah?" Agathe gasped. "Your ancestress? How can that be?"

The Gitane smiled wryly. "It wasn't me called her a saint. Perhaps in all the centuries, memories have become confused. At any rate, I won't argue religion. Such talk has spoiled many a journey." Her round face lost all expression, and she stared straight ahead, as if no one but she herself sat by the fire.

"The road," as Queen Marah called it, was a rutted track through the morass. Pierrette sat on comfortable pillows. A young Gitane drove the wagon's stout brown mares. Yan and Guihen rode well behind, because the Camargue horses— or perhaps Yan himself—seemed to upset the gypsies' horses. Agathe rode in the wagon ahead, trailed by the sullenly plodding Gustave.

"You know the Christians' tale of the three Maries, don't you?" Marah asked. Pierrette affirmed that she did. "We tell

it differently. That's why I shut up like that, when Sister
Agathe was around. Do you want to know the true tale?
You have to promise not to tell it to any Christians."

"Aren't you Christians? Agathe said you were going to
worship in the church at Saints Maries—to pay homage to
Saint Sarah, the servant who was buried with the two
Marys."

"There are Christians . . . and then there are Christians,"
said Marah, "and one woman's saint is another's ancestor."

"Tell me!" Pierrette urged.

The Tsiganes were a fierce tribe, Marah told Pierrette
throughout the long, sunny afternoon. Their chief, who
decided where the nomads would travel, where camp, and
when depart, was called Sara. She was loved and respected,
for she had always led her people well. She knew stars and
seasons, wild horses and black bulls, migrations of flamants,
hawks, and songbirds, and where sweet water was to be
found.

One night in a dream, Sara saw a ship adrift off the
farthest sandbar of the Camargue, bereft of mast, sails, and
oars. She saw men and women whose faces were suffused
with a kind of interior beauty, though worn by suffering
and starvation.

"It was only a dream," said her councilors, seated around
the dying fire. "No ships come near the beaches, or they
become stuck on the offshore bars. Go back to sleep."

Despite those words, Sara did not sleep, and first light
found her peering out through spray and spindrift. The
terrible sea battered the wrecked ship, threatening to break
it apart. Murmuring ancient words passed from chief to chief,
she flung her wool nightcloak over the waves, where it
became a raft to carry the unfortunates to the safe shore.

They were Mary Salomé, half-sister to the Virgin, and Mary
Jacoba, mother of James and John, Mary Madeleine, Martha,
Lazarus, Cedonius, and Maximinus.

"I suppose," said Queen Marah, "that the Tsiganes mis-
trusted them because they spoke a foreign tongue—Greek,
perhaps, or Latin. Chiefs learn such tongues, to negotiate
and trade." She continued her tale. Sara calmed her folk:
the strangers were not herdsmen come to drive them from

the land or farmers to cut and slash it. "Can't you see what I see?" Sara demanded, thinking of the internal light that seemed to emanate from certain of the strangers. The Tsiganes did not.

But pressed by their chief, they offered the refugees food and drink, and listened to the tale of their long and arduous voyage from the Holy Land to bring word of death, resurrection, and a new message of hope to Gaul.

The younger saints chafed to be about their missions, but the two elderly Marys could not go on.

"Leave them here," Sara commanded the holy ones.

"We can't abandon them!" protested Magdalene.

"I'll stay with them, as long as they and I live," Sara said. Magdalene was reassured. After tearful embraces, she and the others went on their way.

The tribe packed their wagons. They came to Sara to ask her where they would be going, for it was her task to choose route and destination.

"We are staying here," she said, astounding her councilors. Never before had any Tsigane chief said that. Always Tsiganes moved on. Always, when the grass was trodden and brown, it was time to depart, as if an invisible sign drew them toward the far horizon, an unheard song called them to new, unexplored trails. . . . But no one protested. They remade the camp, and there they remained.

"Years passed," recounted Marah. "The old women and Sara died within three days of each other. The Tsiganes took them to the far dune where the holy ones had landed, and buried them in the sand. They marked the spot with an ancient altar stone.

"Some Tsiganes stayed to watch over Sara's tomb, and built houses near an ancient well. As time passed, a town grew up. The Tsiganes returned from time to time to visit Sara's grave, and to make offerings upon the altar stone.

"And that," Marah said, "is the true tale of the founding of Saintes-Maries-by-the-Sea."

Pierrette nodded, thinking deeply, remembering. She reviewed her magpie-flight and her vision of the Christian saints' parting. Had "Saint Sarah" in her vision looked like these Gypsies? The woman she remembered had been aquiline, and shaded her eyes with kohl. She remembered a village and fixed dwellings, not a nomad encampment. But such details did not invalidate Marah's tale—or Pierrette's vision.

"Several things puzzle me," she mused. "Does the nature of your magic change as you travel from place to place?"

Marah glanced sidelong at her. "Change? How could it? Magic is magic. As I said, ours is simple—it's hard to make mistakes. Does yours change?"

Pierrette explained what she had deduced about regions of magic, beliefs, and the boundary natures of rivers and watersheds.

Marah laughed. "I know what the difference is. 'Place' doesn't mean the same thing to Gypsies. All places are home, when our tents and wagons are there. Since it's our magic and nobody else's, it goes with us. It doesn't hang around here, or there."

"How about mountains?" Pierrette pressed.

"I don't know that any of us ever climbed one," Marah said thoughtfully. "We stay on the tracks our wagons can manage. I never paid attention to watersheds."

Was Gitane magic free of restraints, restrictions, and changing postulates? That did not seem right. If the universe were a rational place, rules must apply universally.

Pierrette sighed. "Have you gone anywhere where people never heard of you—of Gitane magic—and did not believe it?"

"Ha! If they don't believe our magics, it doesn't take much to convince them. The trick is to convince them to be afraid enough to leave us alone—and not so afraid that they stay away entirely, and their money with them."

The answer was not entirely satisfactory, but Pierrette had explanation enough: where people believed in such magic, Gitane "tricks" worked. And because nomad bands travelled widely, belief in their skills was widespread. Should they enter a land where folk were not convinced, deceptions and sleights of hand created a climate of conviction. They kept expectations small—minor hexes and cures. Fortunes told were vague enough that the tellers would not be caught out by events.

"Are you Christians or not?" Pierrette asked, not expecting a straight answer.

"We are, I suppose," said Marah. "Sara accepted what the

holy women taught her. But the priests' religion is not the
same as theirs was. They didn't care for chants and ceremony, only for the words and deeds of the Son of God."
She laughed—half a chuckle, half a scornful snort. "See?
Priests call him that. The old women called him 'My sister's
son, the carpenter.' The rest came later.

"So, are we Christians? We pay homage to Sara at the
old pagan altar stone, and we honor the old saints she loved,
but what the priests say goes in one ear and out the other."

Pierrette felt a sudden chill—and an accompanying excitement. So: the monolithic Church was not immune to the
effects of scribblers and codifiers. The same forces that eroded
old gods and spirits, that had—almost—turned Yan Oors into
a shadow and Guihen into a Christian boy, had turned a
Jewish carpenter and rabbi into—the Son of God? The forces
of belief and conviction, of scholarly parsing and reasoning, had molded infant Christianity, a Babel of beliefs, magics,
miracles, and speculations, into a monolithic army, marching
across the face of the earth . . .

*I believe in God the Father, Creator of Heaven and
Earth . . . in Jesus Christ . . . he descended into Hell . . . on
the third day he rose . . .* A spell. A tremendous, powerful,
all-encompassing, incontrovertible, rigid . . . spell. The first
time those words had been uttered, the world changed—
and that unity of belief and purpose would bring the terrible sameness, the end of all.

But . . . there were cracks in the monolith: heresies,
schisms, new ideas at odds with old. There were secret rites
hidden in outward ones: Gitane rites buried in Christian
worship; Sara the Tsigane ancestress, hidden within Sarah
the Egyptian Christian saint; ancient pagan altar stones now
part of the church building itself.

Had those Christian Marys viewed the pomp and rituals
with jaundiced eyes like Marah's, holding to their own
simpler faith, unsure, exactly, of what the Nazarene carpenter-
turned-prophet was, or had been? Was the Church that Saul
of Tarsus had built foreign to those old women—or had they
bowed to the pressure of belief and written creeds, and
become what the priests expected of them?

"Don't ever forget!" Pierrette blurted, grasping Marah's
wrist. "Never let Sara become entirely a Christian saint, or
you'll lose everything that makes you special."

"We won't forget," the Gitane queen replied softly. "At the end of time itself, there'll be a Tsigane of Sara's lineage, looking for the road out."

Would there be a road out? "Help me," Pierrette asked. "Don't let me stray from that road." Marah squeezed her arm.

∾

Pierrette's Journal

After a week of freedom from Camargue's voracious insects, they returned to teach me a lesson about the nature of the Black Time. I call it "The Law of Locks," because those mechanisms illustrate the principle—but had I named it then, I might have called it "The Law of Salt Mills." Old Ars thought stinging bugs were attracted to salt mills. The truth is more significant.

The mill was not much to look at: wooden hoppers above and below a pair of rough-hewn millstones. Slabs of raw salt were broken with a maul, then tossed in the upper hopper. Ground salt was taken out below, and pressed into molds. Oxen harnessed to long poles drove the upper stone.

Stinging mosquitoes descended in clouds, as if determined to take all at once the volume of blood my spell had heretofore denied them. Gitanes lit smudges—pottery jars stuffed with oily rags and fragrant herbs. Marah held one for me to ignite, but nothing happened—no spark, no burst of flame, no wan glow. For all the spell's effect, we might have been atop the highest mountain or in the middle of the broadest river. Our driver scurried to the next wagon and brought our pot back lit, which helped keep the bugs at bay.

Having been severely bitten, I collected drops of blood on a finger, and marked a spot on the wagon wheel's rim . . .

"What are you doing?" asked Guihen, when we stopped for the night, beyond the mill's influence.

"I'm measuring the circumference of this wheel." I had counted the wheel's turns, aided by the spot of blood, and was about to calculate the radius of the mill's dampening effect upon things magical. It was about a half mile.

Locks, I determined much later, had a more limited radius of effect. I know two ways to protect a room or a box from intrusion—a warding spell, and a lock. A spell protects hasp, hinges, and leaf or lid against anyone who does not possess the counterspell, the metaphysical and metaphorical "key."

But a box under lock and key cannot be warded with magic, and no magic can open a locked box. In fact, a lock brought close to a warded box is itself a counterspell, as a salt mill is.

Lock and mill are machines, devices with parts that move, built to a purpose—and machines, I determined, nullified magic. There are exceptions: wheeled wagons do not affect spells, nor do hinges or clasps. A grinding quern has no effect, nor do deadeye rigging blocks on boats. Sheaves do, though their effect is limited. A sheave on a boat's mast will not neutralize a spell cast from the deck, but a pulley in my pocket will . . .

~

Pierrette's memory, though disciplined by years of timeless study, was not perfect. As the caravan rode away from the mill, as the swarms of mosquitos dissipated, she had made another connection between spells and machines. It began with a vision remembered: Citharista, seen through a magpie's eyes, ashen and overgrown by huge buildings.

The port's spidery towers were machines: hoists with cables thick as trees, pulleys like ponderous wagon wheels, huge enough to lift whole ships from the water. Their baleful effects surely spread for miles. Was there, in that bleak beginning or end, a single valley or spring-fed pool free of the influence of such machines?

That night, deep in a gloom she did not want to explain even to Guihen, Pierrette pondered her realization that there was more working against her, and toward that future, than she could bear to imagine.

✧   ✧   ✧

"That's it!" Gilles explained happily, pointing at the gray headland. There had been little cause for happiness on the sea voyage. Rough seas and freakish winds had almost driven them against the rocks. They had been forced to stand well out at sea, where land was only a rough line on the horizon. They had sighted a triangular sail once, and had hidden for a whole day in the lee of an island, baking in sunlight and bright reflections off the glassy sea.

Gilles had not thought to ship extra water, because Massalia was only a day's sail. After three days and two nights, it was long gone. The bread was hard, the cheese slimy, and chewing dry, salted fish was unthinkable.

They were far from compatible shipmates. Gilles wondered how the four of them had kept from each other's throats, even when not hot, damp, tired, or thirsty.

Why had they come at all? He knew what motivated him: Marie and Pierrette were his daughters. Wouldn't any father worthy of the name go to his children's aid? He would take risks to repay the debt he had incurred by risking nothing, before. It would never be enough, of course. Elen's murder, Marie's rape, could not be undone. He eyed Reikhard with scarcely concealed loathing.

The Burgundian saw that look. He did not blame Gilles, considering what he—and the demon, of course—had done. That, however, did not make him admire the snivelling fellow. Gilles had conspired in his daughter's degradation, taken money for turning his back, and did not even have a demon to blame . . . Did he? The Burgundian looked more closely at the haunted glitter in Gilles's eyes.

"Well?" demanded Reikhard harshly, to break the tension between them. "What do you see out there? Another dolphin?"

"I see the glitter of water where the hills slope together. The land to the left is an island."

"I've seen islands before," the knight grumbled, rubbing his mail shirt with a rag from which all the oil was long gone. The mail was orange with rust.

"There's only one island that close to the coast. When we round it, Massalia will be six miles away—we'll eat dinner in port."

"I'll drink my dinner," said Anselm. The others vocally agreed.

"I know just the place," Gilles said. "It's only a few steps from ibn Saul's."

"Good!" exclaimed the mage. "I'll take on a jar or two of wine before my visit. Though an old friend, he's reputed to be stingy with his cellar—though he does not mouth Allah's proscription against drink, when he himself is thirsty."

"Good!" said Reikhard.

"What is?" the mage queried.

"That his place is only a few steps from Gilles's tavern. You won't have time to fall down, and have to crawl there." He grinned.

"I'll go with Anselm," Otho stated. "I wish to speak with the scholar also—and to hear what is written on that mysterious scroll you carry."

"Yes!" Reikhard said. "Me too. Read it to us, old man."

"I can't," Anselm demurred. "It's for ibn Saul. You'll have to wait." The mage was not blind to the tension between his shipmates. The spell must be working, he mused. If he heard them aright, they had all agreed to go to a tavern and drink together. No common goal could explain that. It had to be the spell.

True to Gilles's estimation, the sun had not yet set when they drifted up against a stone wharf on the north side of Massalia's harbor. Thirsty as they were, none had given thought to a place to sleep. If worse came to worst, Gilles thought, there was the inn, and there was room on his boat.

Chapter 28 ∽ Ancient Saints

Eager as Otho was for a drink, he had not failed to notice that when the four of them sat at a table in the tavern, Gilles and Reikhard hesitated until the others slid onto the middle of a bench, and then took places as far as possible from each other. That was no surprise. But now—unless the wine's fumes had made him fall asleep, and he was dreaming—the two men sat, arms around each other's shoulders.

And what was that gleam on the Burgundian's cheek? It was not sweat. Both men were weeping. It was a sight to behold. Otho was glad that Gilles, at least, was a Christian; should he feel need to confess, Otho would hear part of the story. For now, he simply thanked God for whatever He had brought about.

Anselm, true to his word, polished off two flagons of wine, but when he rose to cross the street to ibn Saul's, he was still steady on his feet. Drunk—but not on wine alone. For more centuries than he liked to remember, he had been cooped up in one place; his youth had departed, and the prime of his manhood. But now he had hiked the streets of Citharista and Massalia, had taken a sea voyage, and made three friends. He had complained with them about salt, waves, and glaring sun, drunk with them in a tavern, and now he was going to see his old friend ibn Saul. It was so very fine that he hardly thought about why Minho had visited him. . . .

"Anselm? Is it really you?"
"I'm not a Wendish virgin."

341

"It is you! Come in! I must hear how this has come to pass." He looked over the old man's shoulder, and saw Otho.

"He's a friend—a Christian and a priest to boot. But he has promised not to pray loudly, or to pee on your carpets."

Ibn Saul realized then how drunk the mage was. "Loud prayers are the least of my worries," he said, smiling broadly. "Still, I think I'll seat both of you on a tile floor."

"You," Reikhard announced to his sole drinking companion, "are a coward and a whoremaster."

Only another drunkard could have understood the Burgundian's slurred speech—and Gilles was just that. "I should die for my sins," he agreed, tears trickling down his cheeks. "I am that, and more. I'm as despicable as you."

Reikhard bristled momentarily, before realizing that he entirely agreed with Gilles. "Perhaps we can die together, shoulder to shoulder, in battle with the demon."

"Indeed so," agreed Gilles. "It is the least we can do for Marie."

"For Marie," the knight repeated, raising his cup. "We'll fight the demon for Marie."

Anselm, had he heard, would have marvelled at the power of the ancient spell. Otho would have thanked God. Reikhard and Gilles, with wisdom found in the bottom of a wine-cup, knew that the magic was in the goal they shared, the expiation they craved. No supernatural intervention was necessary.

Otho sucked pulp from a pomegranate seed. Having drunk much, he was content to nibble at fruits and nuts, and to pretend that the unsteady rolling floor was the boat's deck, and no cause for him to become ill.

"So," ibn Saul said, when Anselm had told him everything. "What about the letter? I find it curious that the legendary king of the Fortunate Isles should have heard of me. . . ." What he found most fascinating was the implied existence of the Fortunate Isles. He had always considered Anselm's claim of origin charlatan's mumbo jumbo. Had Anselm written the letter?

Had Pierrette been there, and read the doubt in his face, she might have observed that ibn Saul was as cynical as

the donkey Gustave. She might further have observed that
such suspicion could be useful.

"This isn't from King Minho," ibn Saul told them, peering over the top of the document. "It's from your apprentice, Pierrette."

"Let me see it!" Anselm demanded, reaching. "What does
she say?" Ibn Saul raised a hand to forestall him. His eyes
tracked down the page.

Ibn Saul rolled the scrolled letter up. "I can't tell you. I
can't tell anyone."

Otho, a new guest in the scholar's house, did not react
obviously, though disappointment and curiosity alike crossed
his features.

Anselm felt no such restraint. "She's my apprentice, not
yours. She has no secrets from me. Let me see the letter."

"It is . . . an experiment, if you will. If I were to reveal
it to you, you would not react without expectations and
preconceptions, and the . . . the test would be ruined."

"Test? Experiment? Now I'm convinced the letter is from
the unruly scamp. Geometry, postulates, hypotheses . . . It
makes my head spin."

"Your head is spinning for other reasons entirely," said
ibn Saul. "Lovi! Show my old friend to his bed."

The apprentice appeared so quickly that ibn Saul knew
he had been listening. He guided the old man from the room.

Ibn Saul sent Otho to fetch his companions from the
tavern.

"Well?" Gilles asked, with the precise speech a drunkard
affects when speaking to the (presumably) sober. "What does
it say?"

"Yes!" urged the no less inebriated Reikhard. "Tell us!"

"The second letter was also from Pierrette," Otho told
Gilles. "I'll explain when you're sober. If you two can find
three good legs between you, I'll show you to a nice soft
bed . . ." And somehow, without a fall, without more than
loud eructations, he got them as far as ibn Saul's door, where
he turned them over to the scholar's apprentice. He himself felt quite sober.

"I will," he announced to ibn Saul shortly thereafter, "have
to test further this hypothesis I have formed." He saw
nothing ironic in that turn of phrase, but ibn Saul, recognizing Pierrette's influence, smiled slightly.

"What hypothesis is that?"

"That pomegranate seeds are a cure for drunkenness," Otho explained. "I am entirely sober, now."

"That is an interesting notion," the scholar reflected quietly, smiling ever so slightly. Because the fellow was an entertaining talker when drunk, and because ibn Saul had never seen him sober, he sent Lovi to the cellar for a jar of cool wine to maintain Otho in his pleasant state. The conversation, turning to other things, continued for another hour.

"I'm going on ahead," Pierrette announced. "Riding alone, I can be in Saintes Maries tonight." She sought out the free-roaming Camargue horses and, walking among them, spoke to them as if they were people, explaining that she wished to ride to the town. A gray mare—three or four years old, and not yet white—sidled up as if she had understood.

Pierrette flopped belly down across the mare's back, and then swung a leg over its rump. The mare chose an easy gait. Pierrette had to trust the horse to choose the best route southward.

They crossed a low sansouire—exposed soil white with salt from winter's flooding—carpeted with leafless glasswort. Where sea purslane pushed up, her mare stopped to munch. Pierrette, a passenger by courtesy alone, made no attempt to urge her on.

Crossing two miles of sansouire, where Pierrette herself was the highest feature of the terrain, their pace slowed as the mare's hooves sank in loose-blown crystalline sand. Ahead lay a haze of stone pines, the roofs of the town, and the open sea. One gray shape, higher than the rest, was surely the church, ruined years before in a Saracen raid.

Had she waited too long to begin? Quietly, she murmured the ancient words: *"Mondradd in Mon,"* she whispered. *"Borabd orá perdó."* A quiet breeze cooled her face, but beyond that she sensed nothing new, nothing . . . changing. *"Merdrabd or vern,"* she continued. *"Arfaht ará camdó."* Only the sun's shimmer on the sandy track, and her mount's plodding step, gave motion to the stillness. The trees and low roofs ahead wavered as heat rose off the sun-baked sand, and gulls flashed whitely. A lone harrier or osprey, too high for her to be sure, rode rising hot air, hardly moving, its wings imbedded in clear amber touched with blue.

Approaching the reed-thatched town, she looked for the church wall, the landmark seen from afar, but could not find it; the roofs looked further away than a moment before. Then she knew: no church had yet been built among the twisted pines; the houses she had seen from afar would not yet be constructed, in this time; the sharp-grassed dunes were barren, the town still a quarter mile away.

She slipped from the mare's back. "Thank you," she said. "You should return to your herd—to your stallion." She thought not of a white horse, but of Yan. The mare brushed its velvety nose across her cheek, and then turned northward, its hooves making only the softest rustling in the stiff, silica-rich grass.

Pierrette sighed, and began the long trudge to the sea.

Ibn Saul still refused to reveal the mysterious scroll, now hidden among thousands that filled the cubbyholes and shelves of his library.

"Well then?" queried the scholar impatiently. "Are you too sick to walk down to the quay?"

"Are you that eager to be rid of us?" Anselm grumbled—softly, because his head felt large as a melon. Even the dribble of the fountain was painful. "I did not piss your carpets or your fine bed. What have I done to offend you?"

"Offend me? Why, nothing. But the sun is high, and we must be off."

"We?" asked Reikhard.

"I'm going with you," the scholar announced. "I can't perform my—Pierrette's—experiment, unless I'm on the spot. Gilles—is your boat large enough for five?"

"It will suffice."

"Very well. Lovi!" ibn Saul called out. The ailing men winced. "Bring as many jars of wine as you can carry."

On the way, the scholar recounted what Pierrette's letter said about Marie. He was unwilling to discuss why it was necessary for them to be in Saintes-Maries-by-the-Sea, but Gilles sensed his urgency, and added it to his own.

The boat was crowded, but stood high enough that there was little danger of swamping. Ibn Saul assured Gilles that the coast was sandy past the Estaque range and the gulf of the Fossa. They could run ashore if rough weather threatened.

"How far is it?" asked Otho.

"About fifty miles."

"Fifty?" Reikhard growled. Then he remembered his swollen brain, and muted his voice. "That's twice as far as we've already come."

"They should be easy miles," Gilles responded. "The wind is off the sea, and we're south of our destination. With luck, we'll be able to maintain a reaching course. The Rhodanus's currents may push us out, and give us even more sailing room."

Gilles amazed himself. Already, he had sailed as far as he had ever done, even before he became "cautious." Now he contemplated a further voyage, with no more knowledge of their course and destination than a few words with a merchant captain at the wharf.

Life is better now, he mused. Was that a selfish thought? The new Gilles was concerned about such things. Life was better, because he was no longer concerned about himself, but about others—his daughters, and even these four men whose lives he held in the hands that now clutched tiller and sheet. If it were selfish to enjoy his new freedom, surely it was not wholly terrible. . . .

The sea, when it was calm and the wind was right, fostered contemplation. Each passenger indulged in his own quiet thoughts.

Reikhard did not know what to expect when they arrived, but he had much to atone for. A priest of the horned one, he had taken Marie as a prize of battle, not a burden of blood that a man strong in the god's presence must bear. The Citharistans were his tribe by adoption, and one of them was lost, by his doing. He begrudged the vast, sparkling sea between him and his unfulfilled obligation. His eyes hurt from staring into the glare of the lowering sun.

Otho was curious and concerned, but he had been that way so long it felt almost comfortable, like a callus on his finger from clutching his quill. He was not convinced that the king of the legendary Fortunate Isles had actually appeared to the mage, guised as a stork, and bearing letters. He was less doubtful that Pierrette and Marie would be in the seaside town.

Anselm had an inkling of what Pierrette was up against, but his apprentice's tribulations could not make a dent in the ecstasy he enjoyed—he was free on the blue-green ocean. He was not young, but was sprightly as a youth, and was neither dying nor fading away. Though his companions were not ones he might have chosen—with the exception of ibn Saul, of course—they improved after a cup or two of wine. The jugs now stored under the boat's thwarts promised to last until they reached shore. If only Gilles did not notice every time anyone else reached down for a sip, and demand one for himself . . .

Everyone believed Muhammad abd' Ullah ibn Saul knew more about the situation than they did, but that was not so. Desperate urgency hid between the lines of Pierrette's neatly scribed words, but she had only told him what he was to do. It was nothing difficult, and was quite in character for him—but what did she *really* intend?

The breeze off lagoons north and east was hot and cool at once—or perhaps Pierrette's chill was internal. The village had continued to recede as she approached. There were only scattered houses, as when she had viewed it through magpie eyes. Most had faded with the evaporation of the years. When she looked away from one, then looked back, there was only sand and sea grass where it had been. When she looked down at her feet, the sandy path was a cobbled street a few paces on, but the next time she looked, having walked several paces, the cobbles were still a step ahead, then gone entirely. The settlement was as she had seen it long before, but rife with a wealth of detail her small magpie brain had not absorbed. Fish nets were draped to dry in the sun, a chime made of potsherds tinkled, and a trickle of smoke beyond the hump of a thatched roof carried a hint of roasting lamb that made her mouth water.

On the beach lay an abandoned boat—the one Lazarus had emerged from. Ahead was the house the old women had retired to. . . .

"Where did you come from, child?" Pierrette spun around, and faced an ancient woman with a shawl on her head. "Are you a girl or a boy—forgive these old eyes. . . ."

"I'm a girl, mistress," Pierrette said meekly. Was this one of the women in her magpie dream? She could not tell. How many years had passed since then? How would such a woman have aged?

"Come, let's sit in the shade. There's water from the well. I must let down my hair and brush it." Her gaze was warm. "I am Maria. Who are you?"

"I'm called Pierrette," she replied. The woman's accent was not unlike ibn Saul's. "Would you prefer we speak another tongue?" she asked in the Aramaic of the Talmudic scholars.

"Heavens, child!" the woman said, her coarse skin breaking into a grin of deep crevasses. "I haven't heard such speech since I left home. You put music into those plain words—can you sing, too?"

Pierrette hesitated. Sing? When had she last sung anything? The only songs she knew were the baby songs her mother had taught her, but those . . . were magic. "I don't sing much."

"Never mind. I'm a bit silly with age. There's music in your accent alone."

They sat beneath a twisted old pine. She was Maria . . . but which one? Did it matter which Mary this was? Pierrette did not know much about either of them.

The water was deliciously cool. The old one untied the heavy knot of her hair. She smoothed and straightened her lead-gray locks with a stiff, boar's-bristle brush.

"Are you alone, lady?" Pierrette asked. "Is there someone to care for you?"

"Sarah is nearby—Sarah the Egyptian. You'll know who she is when you see her, because she's very dark."

So much for Marah's tale, Pierrette thought. Sarah is an Egyptian, not a Tsigane chief. But the old woman had not mentioned anyone else . . .

"Will you stay a day or so?" old Mary asked. "For the burial?"

"Burial, lady?"

"Maria's burial. My sister Maria." Again, the face-crackling smile. "I won't be long, myself," she said. "Nor will Sarah, I suspect. If the Tsiganes be wise, they should dig one large hole in the sand for all three of us. . . . But forgive my rambling. Tell me—why are you here?"

Pierrette had hoped the wise and holy old women would take pity on their namesake, Marie, and exert what ancient Christian magic they knew on her behalf. But . . . was this Mary befuddled by age? Pierrette sighed. It could not be helped. She would do what she had come here to do.

Old Maria was a good listener, though perhaps only caring for the "music" of Pierrette's accent. Pierrette told her of Ma and the pool among the beeches, of Marie and Gilles, of Cernunnos's rape of Marie. She spoke of Anselm and everlasting noon, of skeptical Gustave and cynical ibn Saul . . .

Another woman brought two earthenware plates, one with fine-cut morsels of food, the other well covered with tender spring lamb, long beans, and crusty bread. "I am Sarah," she said. Seeing Pierrette's hesitation, she shrugged. "I'm not hungry. A nibble or two is enough for one my age. It makes no sense to be buried with a full stomach."

Buried? She was not dead. Then Pierrette remembered: " . . . and at last the old women and Sara died," Marah had told her, "within three days of each other." Sarah and Mary spoke as if the time of their deaths was no secret, but a comfort. Would they indeed be buried in a common grave—tomorrow, or the day after?

"Go on, girl," Maria urged. "You've hardly begun your tale." So Pierrette told of her quest for the logic behind the illogic of magic, and of her fear of the Black Time. The sun's last rays slanted through soft pine needles.

"Poor Anselm," Marie said. "That Saul—Paul, he calls himself, now—would be a thorn in anyone's side." Pierrette, thinking her senile, was surprised that she remembered the brief retelling of Ansulim's tale. "The king of those lost islands was right. Paul did change the nature of things." Maria's voice held aged petulance. "Our nephew would never have founded a new Church. The Church was old in David's time. Paul didn't need a new one. That wasn't the point. . . ."

"He did it, though," Sarah commented. "We've gotten letters, over the years . . ."

"Oh, yes," Maria cut in. "From Peter, and copies of Paul's. Our nephew would never recognize what they have created. He'd not recognize himself, from what they say about him." Sarah handed her a cup of water to smooth her cracked voice.

"I think you're right, child," she continued. "Things change with the telling, as what people believe changes. Isn't that right, Sara?" She purposefully cut the other woman's name short, emphasizing the Gitane pronunciation.

The dark woman nodded. "I am not Egyptian," she said, "but sometimes I forget I used to be a . . . a Tsigane. She gestured toward the distant huts, the boats drawn ashore in front of them. "Those folk call me 'Egyptian,' all year long. Only in spring and fall, when my people visit, do I feel like Sara the Tsigane.

"It's late," she said abruptly. "Come, Maria. It grows chill."

"Wait," Maria commanded her. "Do you have a place to sleep, child?"

"Over there." She gesturing toward the faintly defined road. "It's not far."

Sarah nodded, ready to hustle Maria inside, but the old woman paused. "We'll help you, child," she said. "When the time comes, we'll be there." She held out her hand, and Pierrette grasped it. She felt something soft and springy against her palm, but did not look to see what it was.

The dark Gitane nodded agreement. "You have only to call us." Old Maria then allowed herself to be led inside.

Pierrette trudged wearily back the way she had come. In her half-open palm lay Maria's parting gift—a clump of gray hair pulled from the bristles of the hairbrush. "What must I do with this?" she wondered.

She was hardly surprised to see Gitane wagons pulled up along the road, to see the glimmer of campfires, to smell smoke and suppers cooking. Neither was she surprised, when she looked back, to see the stone wall of the church limned by the sun's last rays, its yellow limestone blocks turned to fire.

Chapter 29 ∾ An Unhallowed Mass

Ibn Saul was first to notice that Gilles had changed course. When he fell asleep they had been sailing due west on a close reach. Now the yard was around, and the sun's glow was on the port side.

Anselm also knew celestial paths. "Is the sun rising in the south—or are we sailing toward Africa?"

"Africa?" growled Reikhard. "Are we lost?"

"The wind," Gilles explained, "is out of the west, and I can't sail into it. We must zigzag south, then north, to keep the wind from backing the sail."

"How long will that take?" asked Reikhard. "We're almost out of wine."

"There's water." Gilles no longer kowtowed to the knight. When fear is behind, he reflected, vast freedom lies ahead.

Fear still limited Anselm. He could have called a favorable wind, but would it be breeze or tempest? He hunkered down next to Gilles, and eyed the fog that obscured the coast astern.

The new church, the monkish engineer explained, was a fortress. What Pierrette had thought were ruined walls were newly constructed ones. There were no windows on the ground floor, and only slits above, for bowmen. The stout oak main door faced west, sally ports north and south. The old stones were weathered to a rich ocher, the new were blindingly white.

"Saracens burned the houses," the monk told Pierrette, indicating the open square, "and we won't allow anyone to

351

build there again—for a clear field of fire. And the well is within the church, now. None who take refuge there will thirst."

"Pier . . . Piers!" Agathe called to her from the shade of a nearby doorway. "Come here now!" Pierrette recognized that authoritative tone. "P'er Alfredus wishes to speak with you," the nun said. Pierrette remarked the odd shift in her voice, as if the sharp-tongued teacher had suddenly become the least of her own pupils. Sister Agathe hustled her inside.

Father Alfredus was a large, brown man with bushy eyebrows and hazel eyes like a Burgundian. She thought he would have been more comfortable clutching a war axe than the quill he fiddled with.

"Your sister," he announced portentously, "suffers from a feminine complaint." Considering Marie's difficulties, Pierrette was inclined to agree with him, but his authoritative tone made her uncomfortable. "Without a mother to advise her, she went to the wedding bed unprepared."

"She was raped!" Pierrette said, almost forgetting to keep her voice low. "The demon came later—in Massalia."

"Oh, come, boy—in the nunnery? Surrounded by holy women? There's no demon, and I'll waste no effort on exorcism. She is listless. Perhaps that is swamp fever—has she had chills? Yellow skin and eyes? No?" He shrugged, and turned to his papers.

"Thank you, Father," Agathe said, grasping Pierrette's arm tightly and ushering her out of the priest's house.

"He's wrong!" Pierrette snarled, when the door had shut. "He's a pompous fool."

"Pierrette! He's a priest!"

As if that were an excuse. "He hides ignorance behind an air of authority. What do we do now? We can't take Marie back to Massalia, and there's nothing for us here. Why didn't you stand up to him?"

"He's a priest!"

"He's an ass. You are wise and kind. He should listen to you."

Agathe sighed. "I'm happy you think well of me, but even Mother Sophia must obey the newest-ordained boy, fresh from school."

In the nunnery, the women were free, within the limits

of their rule, to express their thoughts. P'er Otho, Pierrette's only other exposure to Christian structure, was perhaps atypically mild.

" 'My nephew's church was for women and slaves,' " Pierrette quoted, " 'but the new Church I foresee is of men and kings.' "

"Who said that?" Agathe asked her.

"Mary," Pierrette said idly, without thinking. "I never found out which one she was, but her name was Mary." Agathe stared, afraid to understand.

The Gitanes remained camped north of the town, waiting for other bands to join them. When all were gathered, the chiefs would occupy the church.

"The holy fathers will be in a dither," Marah told Pierrette across the fire. "They don't know why we come, but they can't stop us. There are enough of us to storm the fortress church, if we wanted to."

Pierrette nodded. She was braiding a cord out of undyed fibers, to keep her hands busy. She was thinking about Marie, and worrying that Gilles and the others would not arrive in time. What if she had to confront the demon alone again? What if the old Mary forgot, or had not been real?

Marah's eyes grew reflective. "Once everyone followed the wild horses, fished in lakes and rivers, and gathered the land's bounty. There were no towns, and no man owned anything. Everyone was a nomad then, though some folk stayed closer to home than others, if the land provided well. . . . Only we Gypsies have kept the old ways."

Only nomads refrained from cutting the Mother's flesh and trampling it beneath hooves of captive herds, or burrowing like maggots for wealth. They loved gold because other wealth was forbidden; they did not own land, and gold was free in Mother's streams.

"We have only one fixed place," Marah said. "Our ancestress's grave." That grave was now within the church of the Marys. Twice each year gypsies came, in May for the feast of Mary Jacoba, the mother of James, and in October for Mary Salomé's.

Carrying statues of the two Marys, surrounded by men on Camargue horses, Christian women from Arelate marched through the streets to the beach and the sea. At the same time, the Gypsies marched with Sara's statue—but their chiefs remained within the crypt, by Sara's sarcophagus, reclaimed for their people.

"They think we venerate Saint Sarah," Marah said, "but that's a ruse; we pay respect to an ancestor. We ask her advice, and her blessing when a new queen is chosen."

"Do all Gypsies know that?" Pierrette asked.

"When they're old enough to keep secrets."

"You must be careful," Pierrette said. "If you forget that Sara is Tsigane, not Egyptian, she'll be lost."

Marah peered closely, narrowing her eyes. "That's not an idle remark. Who told you?"

"A woman who . . . who used to live in a small house, over there, by the sea."

"Her name, girl? What was her name?"

Pierrette sighed. "Sara. She called herself Sara the Tsigane. She said that only on the feast days, when the Gypsies all come, does she remember she's not Sarah, the Christian saint. She's afraid that someday you will forget, and . . ."

"We do not forget!"

"There was an old woman called Mary. Another Mary had died, and was not yet buried. I think the others expected to die also, as your tale remembers it, within a few days. They said they would help when the time came."

"As will the Tsigane," Marah said, accepting her words without question or doubt.

"I'll need help. Father Alfredus won't aid me—he says there is no demon."

"Priests know nothing." She stirred the fire's embers. "Did you sneak into the church, to speak with . . . those old women?"

"There was no church," Pierrette said. "There were houses, and an ancient altar stone . . . I used a spell my mother taught me."

"What spell?" Marah demanded harshly, intensely. "What words?"

"*Mondradd in Mon,*" Pierrette said, with considerable hesitation. "That means . . ."

"To Part the Veil." Marah shuddered. "Dangerous words. Women have been trapped by them, and have never returned. After a while, their bodies just died."

"It would be easy to be caught," Pierrette reflected, thinking of Aam and Rheudhi, the painted cave, and the powerful stag who . . . "I won't utter those words again soon."

"Good. But you asked for help. What must we do?"

Pierrette told her.

"The festival begins tomorrow," Marah said. "Will you be ready?"

"I don't know. If my message got through . . ." If Minho of the Isles were not a figment of deranged imagination. She had stood on the edge of a swampy lagoon. That was all. From the Fortunate Isles she had brought back only memories that could be a dream.

If my father puts aside his fears. If Anselm does not fade. If P'er Otho will participate in un-Christian sorcery. If Muhammad abd' Ullah ibn Saul does not dismiss me as a madwoman.

There was no way they could arrive in time except by sea, but that afternoon great banks of fog had rolled in, and the wind died. No boat could put in at Saintes-Maries-by-the-Sea until the fog cleared.

"Go to bed, girl," Marah said. She raked ashes over the embers. "Always sleep when you can. That's an old rule of soldiers and wanderers."

Pierrette dreamed she was Sara the Tsigane, peering through the dense fog. Out there on the water, a boat beat back and forth seeking safe harborage; aboard the frail craft were not saints, but men . . . A bell was ringing, an eerie sound muffled by the wooly fog.

She sat up, the dream shattered. Anselm, Gilles, Otho, ibn Saul, and . . . was that big, light-haired man Jerome? The castellan? What was he doing in her dream? And what had been so different about him? Why were they all singing?

They were drunk. The dream was so preposterous she lay back down and tried to return to sleep, as Sara had done. But like Sara, before creeping dawn touched the church's fog-shrouded walls, she was at the sea's edge.

The fog was as in the dream—or was the dream's mist a recapitulation of the fog she had seen the night before? Something was not as it should be.

She heard the faint tones of a bell. But there was no bell, only the drip of dew from pine needles. That was not right. There should have been a bell to guide the boat to the unmarked strand where she waited, not far from the gray bones of the old ship.

A bell. She remembered the proud monk pointing. "The bell is up there, on wooden blocks. We have erected pillars and an arch to hang it from. . . ." Pierrette hurried back to the plaza. Fog's tendrils crept over cobbles imported at great cost from the hills north of Arelate. No one was about. She pushed and pulled at the church door. Was it barred from the inside, or was she simply not strong enough?

She rushed to Father Albertus's house, and pounded with a closed fist. A man stuck his head out a window. "Go away until morning."

"There's a boat out there. They can't find port because of the fog. Someone must ring the bell to guide them to shore."

"Let them sail down the coast, or wait until the fog lifts. The bell has not been hung, and can't be sounded."

"We must hang it, then. Call Father Albertus."

"You're mad. There's no boat. If you'd seen one, its captain would have seen you also, and would have no trouble finding port. Go away, before I call guards."

Pierrette turned away. Indeed, she must seem mad. She walked around the church and examined the small doors. Both were snug in their stops. She sat disconsolately on the front step, head in hands. There was a bell, but she could not ring it. Soon drunken Gilles would give up, and would sail down the coast, or back to Massalia.

A sound startled her. A sharp, metallic clank, not the melodious tone of a church bell. Again the off note sounded—and Pierrette's heart grew light. "Yan Oors," she whispered. "You kept your promise."

She felt a hand on her shoulder. "Yes," said John of the Bears. "I am here—and you must not be. You must return to the beach and await your father."

"I wanted to ring the bell, but . . ." She looked up speculatively. He was big, and strong. If he struck the unhung bell with his iron staff, it would be loud enough to be heard at sea. "Open this door for me. Strike the bell with your staff, to make it ring."

"That is a Christian shrine. I don't wish to shrivel into a Christian boy who hasn't discovered his prong."

"People's beliefs, not piles of stones, shape us. Hurry! Open the door."

Yan Oors put his shoulder to it. "It's barred from within."

"Let's try another." The southern sally port was locked, not barred. Had it been warded by spells instead, she would have whisked them aside. Yan prodded the keyhole with his knife, rotated it, and pushed the door open. "I don't want to go inside," he said.

Pierrette grasped his arm. "Come." She pulled him along the church wall.

"Look!" A wan, blue light sprang from her fingertips. They peered at the carved stone set into the wall. "What do you see?"

"A swineherd with a fishing pole," he said, "and two sows."

"Yan! Don't tease me. That is you, with your staff, and . . ."

"It cannot be. Not here."

"But it is. This far out on Rhodanus's delta, even cobbles must be carted in, so the masons reused old stones—and this was one of them. It was an altar. You aren't unwelcome here—you've been here all along. Now will you ring the bell?"

With a backward glance at his own worn image graven in the church wall, the big man edged toward the doorway. "I'll ring it. You must go."

She hugged him. There was nothing vague or unreal about that; he smelled of leather and sweat, of wool moistened with dew, and of damp iron. "Go now," he urged, pushing her away. "Bring them ashore."

The fog was thick. She almost took the wrong street; all were so narrow she could touch the walls of houses on either side. Once upon the proper alley, she hurried, stumbling. Before she felt sand under her feet, she heard the raucous clank of the bell. It was not sweet, because the bronze was dampened by the timbers it rested upon, and because the instrument that struck it was not a leather-wrapped clapper, but a great, iron staff.

Clank, the bell sounded. *Clank, clunk*. Pierrette hurried through a swale filled with sharp grass and scrub poplars, and out onto the strand.

Clang, clank, went the bell. She heard shouts; the priests and laborers were awake. How long could Yan Oors ring before they stopped him? She must hurry her father and his companions ashore.

There were the bare timbers of the old boat. Pierrette leaned on one to catch her breath. It snapped off below the sand. Others were equally frail. She heaped them against the boat's stem, and stretched forth her hand . . .

Flames sprung up as if kindled in pitch and splinters. Gold and orange sparks floated above the fog's gray blanket, a tower of blazing light.

She heard the sodden thunk of oars and the rumble of voices no longer lifted in song. Gilles's rang with a commanding tone. "Pull together now! Stroke, stroke, stroke! Sir knight, that's an oar, not a broadsword. It does no good waving in the air. That's it, now. Stroke! Stroke! There's no telling how long that fire will last. We're still a quarter mile offshore."

A quarter mile? The voices seemed to come from no distance at all. And how did her father dare command the Burgundian? Was this too a dream? Had she indeed crossed over into madness?

She glanced toward the towering fire. The wood seemed unburnt, as if the flames were a dream, and only the wood real. She shivered. Was she unable to separate magpies, beech trees, fires, and the blue glow of swamp wisps from her own imaginings? Was Marie's complaint also a derangement of the mind, passed from mother to daughter in their ancient blood?

Full of terrible doubt, Pierrette ran from the fire to the shore, and awaited whatever came. . . .

She saw the masthead poking through the gray moisture, then the familiar rigging—handmade sheaves her father had carved, frayed ropes she had hauled to raise the spar. The boat's battered stem pushed from the fog. The craft shuddered as it ran up the sandy shore. A rope uncoiled in the air and slapped down on wet sand at Pierrette's feet.

"You there!" Gilles barked. "Tie us off." Her father had not recognized her. He hardly glanced at the small figure walking the rope ashore. "All of you! Out! You too, Reikhard. A little more salt water won't worsen your rust. Help pull us ashore."

Even the big man, Reikhard, who looked like the knight Jerome, leaped to obey him. Pierrette did not know what amazed her most—that they were indeed here, or that Gilles was transformed, confident, and that the others accepted it.

Otho was first to recognize her. He gasped.

"Keep pulling," she said. Over the panting of straining men, the lap of waves, and the thudding of her heartbeat, Pierrette heard an angry roar from the town. She tied the rope to a slender poplar. "Save your questions for later." She led them the way she had come.

Her only question for Otho, jogging beside her, was the identity of the big German. His explanation was as complete as it could be, he being out of breath and hurrying to keep up.

Her tension drained. The knight had been as much a victim as Marie. Still, she was glad he was behind with Gilles, Anselm, and ibn Saul, so she did not have to deal with her entrained fear and revulsion.

"That explains what changed Marie," she stated. "This Reikhard's demon flew westward no further than the nunnery." Otho had been right to bring the castellan, for though the demon had been forced out of him, he had not forgotten it, and might know some weakness that would help destroy it—instead of merely driving it to another victim.

Dawn. Sun drove back fog. The square was full of angry people. The Gypsies had arrived, dressed in their best and brightest. The women's skirts were black, banded with ochre, orange, crimson, green, and a blue as intense as sunlit shallows. The men's shirts were rare silk, embroidered with herbs and vines. Gold glittered like fragments of sunshine. Gitanes stood six deep in front of the church door, brandishing staves quartered from upland oak, or crosstrees taken from their wagons, still jingling with bronze fittings.

Separated by the length of a Gitane club were dun-, brown-, and russet-clad churchmen, Bishop Albertus in their midst. It was not the first time the Gypsies had taken over the church, Pierrette remembered. Still, though the confrontation seemed to have elements of ritual, the angry faces were not mere convention: the Gypsy defiance was real; this was their time, their shrine, but the priests and monks who had spent years of effort rebuilding the edifice did not willingly cede it.

Pierrette pushed through, and her companions followed. The space between priests and Gypsies seemed wide as a

Roman road. The Gypsies parted, making an aisle to the church door. "Where is Marie?" Pierrette hissed anxiously.

"Here," said Marah. Guihen and Yan held a litter—two poles and a blanket. Marie was humping and writhing like a fish dying on the sole-boards of Gilles's boat. A dark-clad figure with a hoodlike shawl bent over the stretcher like a crow over carrion. Who was that?

Marie had soiled herself. Her arms were bound at the wrists, and her legs had been belted with a Gypsy cincture. The dark-robed stranger backed away.

Swallowing her risen gorge, Pierrette leaned close to Marie and looked into panic-widened eyes. "Everything will be all right," she said loudly and firmly, so she could be heard over the crowd's din and Marie's inarticulate mouthings. "Hold on, sister. We'll free you." She desperately wanted the real Marie to hear, to take comfort. She wanted to believe Marie understood—but it was the demon that struggled and heaved her body about in its desperation.

"Release her, uncreated one!" Pierrette shouted. "Depart before you are brought inside. You'll never leave the sanctuary whole." It was bravado, but the crowding, the battering noise, and her hammering heart filled her with excitement. Now everything would be decided; all the principals were here.

"Bring her inside," Pierrette commanded. She held a braided, knotted cord out of sight behind her back.

Marie flung herself sideways, almost wrenching the poles from the hands that held them, then vomited over the side, spattering Pierrette's feet and adding acrid foulness to the stench about her. "I'll kill her," grated Marie's tormentor through a throat roughened by screaming, acid, and bile. "She'll not survive my departure."

"She will, and you will not," Pierrette responded angrily. "You are worse than doomed." Holding up her hitherto hidden cord, Pierrette made a bight and dangled it in front of Marie's face. "I have bound you. *Chev't santú, chev't sanitú*," she murmured, watching Marie's eyes widen. "*Ligure e' ligamen; salix, Lex Salliorum*. I bind you with a virgin's hair and a saint's, with the old law remembered, and the law written."

She drew the bitter end over the bight, around, under, and up through. She tugged on both ends, leaving a loop just large enough to slide over one finger. "As I bound you, I will lead you." She walked around the litter, and went inside the church.

She could see little, but the first bay on her left held something large and brightly painted. A boat? In a church?

The litter bearers followed. Marie struggled feebly now. "Place her there," Pierrette said, nodding toward the second bay, by an ancient carved stone. Her eyes adjusted to the low light.

She looped the long free end of her cord around a pillar and, withdrawing her finger from the bight, pushed the end through it, pulled it tight, and knotted it. "Here you will remain," she said to the demon.

"Come, Marie," she said softly. "Leave him behind. You have friends here. They await you." Guihen and Yan bore the litter toward the altar.

Marie shrieked. She struggled to rise. The knotted cord tightened as she was moved away, as if it were tied to her— to something that hovered about her face, in her breath. The complex, asymmetrical knotting reached out to her, and the cord drew straight. The knot hovered, held by some invisible bond.

Marie's blanket smoldered, but there was no flame, only an oily puff. The cord thrummed like a tight-wound harpstring. "Pull!" Pierrette commanded. "Pull her away." Marie screamed—this time in pain, not a fiend's anger.

Pierrette looked along the cord to the pillar where it was fixed. The roiling smoke remained bound to the cord braided of gray hair and black, a saint's hair and a virgin's. Red-brown shreds of willow bark were braided in it, and a ribbon that had once bound Anselm's law tables of the Salian Franks. It was a binding of twisted words and changing meanings, deadly humorless puns—ligatures, or binding spells, and Ligures, Pierrette's ancient kin, salix, which was willow, and Salian lex, or law.

The smoke billowed and fought to be free. People pressed into the church. Pierrette did not dare to turn to see who stood behind her, but felt their warmth, and drew strength from it. She could not prevail alone; she was no more than a focus for the hatred all felt toward the evil bound by the fragile cord.

"Marie is free of you," she exulted, despite her fears.

Whether or not her sister's frail body survived the separation, she was free. Alive or dead, she was no longer bound by . . . The beastly essence was shaping itself to its lone existence. She did not recognize the form it was taking, or know what strengths it might call upon.

Tusks gleamed yellow in faint western reflections of the sun just risen in the east. The *sanglier* lowered its head to charge. It snapped at the frail, tight-drawn cord, and severed it. From the boar's bowels rumbled words: "You did not expect that to hold me, did you?"

"Only long enough," Pierrette murmured, shifting between Marie and the demon. "Marie is free of you. Your fate and hers are separated."

The boar lunged—and a leathery, black-clad arm pushed Pierrette aside. Tusks rang against forged iron.

"I am lord of animals," growled Yan Oors, holding the beast at bay with his staff. "I am master of he whose guise you wear."

The boar-shape hunched down upon its belly. The demon snarled, the boar wavered and shifted, becoming again formless smoke, its tusks the flicker of impending flames. "You can't elude me," Yan Oors said. "I'll have my part of you."

Flames consumed smoke, and Pierrette felt the red heat of Cernunnos's eyes. . . . She uttered soft words, and the lapping tongues dipped and danced to her cadence, trapped in her spell of bound fire, as any real flame would have been. Yet no magic could defeat the beast of many shapes. Only her friends could exhaust it. But there were many shapes, and so few friends.

"Become what you will," she said. "Shift and change, and someone will counter you as Yan Oors is doing. You will *be* whatever you seem, and one of us will defeat you." She hoped that was not a lie. She hoped the others had heard her words, and would heed them.

No longer bound, the demon's formless voice became the sound of the sea in a storm, and the air stank with the tang of lightning. A cold wind whipped her hair and she was transported to another place, where wind, water, and rock were entangled. She could not see or hear anything over their tumult. Still, she sensed something besides the clashing forces of earth, air, and sea. She heard someone shouting into the teeth of the wind. . . .

✧   ✧   ✧

Giles did not know what Heaven was, but Hell was no mystery. Hell was a coward's denial. Hell was his daughter's degradation, his wife's death, and his silent acquiescence. Hell was the seat of his fears.

Hell was the storm and the clash of waves over rocks. Heaven was beyond: the glow of promised day on a far, low horizon, unattainable except through the churning black gut of the tempest that lashed his small boat.

"The dead don't fear!" Gilles shouted at his adversary. "And I am like a dead man. I will win through you, *for now, at last, has my time come!*" He pulled the tiller against his skinny ribs, and slatted the sail fore-and-aft. His frail, punk-rotten craft plunged toward the black rocks on the tightest tack its clumsy rig could handle.

Ahead, massing on his left, was the Anvil, and offshore of it the smaller knob called the Hammer, obscured by spume and surf. The wind on his sail pushed him west of north, but his waterlogged hull made leeway. Only by heading directly at the Anvil's rocks could he squeeze between them and the Hammer; only by confronting his nightmare head on could he avoid it.

Bitter salt spray harsh in his eyes, Gilles held course for his doom, and trusted the providence of his long-ignored God to push him through the narrow passage. Wave after wave sprayed over his rail and sloshed about his toes, then his ankles . . . The deeper his hull rode, the less leeway it made. Hell ahead, Heaven beyond. No man's effort would determine whether he lodged on the rocks, or came about behind the islands and made safely for the open sea, the light sky beyond the storm.

Ebon rocks loomed off his bow, but he kept his course. To aim for the safety of the passage, toward the perception of a clear way through, was a fool's heading. Wind, and the drag of his half-sunken hull, dictated whether he would clear the Anvil and pass the Hammer. Only by sailing closest to doom could he hope to avoid it.

His hull rose and fell, shuddering with the backwash of waves from the rocks on his right. Spray from the left stung his face and eye. He shot beyond the promontory into the Anvil's lee.

He laughed. He had won through. Snatching his bailing

bucket, he began to empty his boat. Behind him, among the rocks, the wind screamed its thwarted hunger.

The demon screamed and thrashed amid the coastal rocks. Gilles, drifting now, had eluded him.

Gilles felt emptiness within, hunger like the wind's and the sea's. Gilles, the empty man, devoid of fear or hope, had set his course to the rocks. God himself, he decided, had provided leeway to carry him past them. God had saved him—but why? He was a sinner of the worst sort: lazy, weak sins of omission. He had grasped sin no more firmly than virtue. His self-disgust was a shapeless puddle of reeking seaside mud. Had there been genuine Evil in his sin—that thought shot into his brain with shafts of piercing sunlight as the clouds broke overhead—he might at least have been a manly sinner.

As his small vessel rolled and plunged outward from the shore and the wracking waves, he understood his emptiness. As he would put it years hence, "a bit of Evil is not a bad thing." He looked down at the bailing bucket half full of froth—the product of miscible wind and sea, the demon's substance. He now owned that small portion of Evil he had to have. . . . Then waves and sea faded, and Gilles was once more within the church.

Pierrette saw her father turn his back on formless blackness, and push through the shoulder-to-shoulder crowd, his head high. Swinging heavily from one hand was his bucket. Salt water within it sloshed with darkness. "This is my portion of you!" Gilles called out. "And I'll sip it with my evening wine until I have consumed it all."

Gilles had done what he needed to do, and Pierrette did not wish him to stay. She, too, had set her course, and could not change it without dooming herself.

As she looked around at friends, acquaintances, and strangers, she saw them nodding their heads, and knew they had understood what Gilles had done—and that it was the only way to rid the world of that demon. They saw, and she hoped each would be able to do what he had to, because she could not do it by herself.

The black shapelessness that had been rock and sea a moment ago loomed to engulf the slight girl, but someone large and rusty stepped between them.

"Traitor! Betrayer!" squalled the fiend, red eyes coalescing in the darkness, reflecting crimson from Cernunnos's
antler-tines, mounted on Reikhard's casque. The knight was
not the hideous, priapic god who had cavorted at the mass,
but the spirit of the forest, the deer god as generations before
had known him, with warm, brown eyes—yet also a man
wearing an antlered helm.

"You cannot shed a hundred generations of sacrifices,"
shrieked the demon. "You are mine still."

"A hundred generations of druids' sacrifices, not mine,"
growled the deer god, whose visage looked much like the
castellan Jerome's. "The last druids who remembered the
sacred texts are gone, and I'm not bound by their acts—
or by you." Christian priests had named the druids evil,
because of deaths done in their gods' names. "No lives have
been taken in my name," bellowed Jerome—or Reikhard,
or Cernunnos—in the voice of a rutting stag. "You have no
claim on me."

Pierrette's eyes betrayed her; deer, god, and armored man
appeared and disappeared between one blink and the next,
images fleeting as firelight shadows. The knight's opponent
lashed out with red claws, a shapeless, inchoate beast, yet
more fearsome for that. Cernunnos, again wholly stag,
lowered his spreading antlers, and the creature backed away.
It changed . . . Sooty blackness stretched out and coalesced
into a long warrior's sword. Darkness swelled and split,
forming legs and arms, solidifying. Circlets and eddies of
smoke shaped themselves into a sculpted bronze cuirass.

Fully armored in blackened bronze, the demonic warrior
raised his long sword and charged the stag. He met
Reikhard's iron blade, not soft horn: Cernunnos was illusory, the armed knight real. The two crashed together, plate
against rusty mail, bronze against iron.

"I am free of you," shouted the Burgundian, dancing back,
swinging his weapon.

The demon warrior met his arcing blade, and twisted it
aside. "I will have you again," he boomed, thrusting with
a dagger hitherto concealed in his other hand. The short
blade grated against mail . . . and it snapped. Reikhard
stepped back, catching his opponent off balance. He spun,
pivoting on one foot. His sword came around from an
unexpected quarter and struck his foe's unarmored neck.

The fiend's head teetered long enough for Reikhard to snatch its helmet.

"This is mine!" the Burgundian bellowed, backing away from the headless body, already dissolving into foul smoke. "This trophy will hang from my rooftree." Reikhard swaggered away with a rattle of linked iron rings and scabbard chains, his portion of Evil swinging against his thigh: the demonic warrior's grimacing head, already shrinking but still helmeted, like a melon thumping and rolling around in a pot. The watching Gypsies, villagers, priests and strangers parted to let him pass, carrying the head of the demon.

Old Anselm then stepped forward, spreading his arms like a hawk's wings, and came at the greasy apparition. Though diminished by a head and a bucket of sea water, the fiend still swelled to great bulk, and seemed unweakened. Like black, oily waters, it roiled and rippled, and above the waters an osprey circled on wings held at a high angle, watching the surface of the sea to see what swam below.

The grudging ocean danced with obscuring ripples, but the osprey plunged anyway, its eyes locked on a shadow shape seen a moment before. Down it shot in a flurry of black and white, into the sea, downward into the echoing silence of the deep. Talons stretched out two by two, backward and forward, and snatched its shiny, wriggling prize, a fat red mullet.

The fish hawk shot upward then, borne by air in its swollen lungs and trapped in its feathers, rising toward the shimmery hammered-tin ceiling of the foreign sea. It popped into the air. With great thrusts of its wet wings, the osprey lifted the plump mullet above gathering waves that came too late to foil it. Its wings folded and drew upward, then spread and beat down against the air, tips touching the water with each stroke. The bird turned its prey in its grasp until the hapless fish faced forward as if swimming willingly where the osprey took it.

Above, a gray-headed eagle, more thief than hunter, stooped to the attack.

"Mine!" the osprey squalled, warned by a stray reflection on the water. It leaned heavily left, skewing its course to take it toward dense pines at the foot of the promontory—and its nest.

"Give it to me," the eagle shrilled, threatening to strike the clumsy, prey-laden osprey between its laboring wings, to force it to drop the sluggishly waving mullet. Ordinarily, an eagle would not strike until an osprey had attained almost the altitude of its nest, so when it dropped its fish, the eagle had time to plunge down and catch it still tumbling in air. But this great gray-headed bird was no ordinary eagle, and was not motivated by hunger.

"Catch me, then!" the smaller bird called, and plunged back into the water, still holding its mullet. No eagle had ever seen an osprey do that. It turned sharply, dipping a wingtip into a wave, and returned to the spreading ripples . . . just as the osprey again shot from water into air, aiming itself toward shore and the safety of tangled pine branches no eagle could penetrate. The eagle was flying at great speed, and though it wheeled quickly, the fish hawk attained sanctuary with whole wing beats to spare.

Gray-head circled offshore, emitting loud cries. The hawk tore shreds of cool flesh from the fish, and the sounds that accompanied its feast were the strangest ever made by a bird—like laughter one moment, like a man gagging the next.

"Mine," it squalled happily, filling its throat with pale meat. "Ach!" it said then. "I hate raw fish!"

Soon nothing was left but scraps and sharp bones. The black-and-white osprey's feathers blurred and became a white garment and black, shiny oiled hair. Anselm the mage belched fishily, and grimaced at the flavor of his eructation. "Raw fish!" he grumbled, "but the spice of evil makes it tolerable."

The sea again coalesced into formless darkness, and if Anselm's breath, there in the church of the holy Marys, smelled of raw mullet, no one seemed to notice—not even Otho, who stood next to him. But Otho was already busy. Again, the fiend had changed . . .

"I know you," Otho said to the raven-winged angel. Eyes of crimson fire bathed him in their glare. "I know you, and I will have my piece too." He now understood what must be done. Reikhard had taken a head, Gilles water—demonic substance—and Anselm had consumed more, in the form of a fish. What would he, Otho, take from the abomination, to call his own?

He stood forward, fingers clawed as if both to grab at the demon and to fend it from him. He grasped its long, black hair. Huge wings beat at him, buffeting him, but he did not let go. He wrenched the hair, and came away with a bloody hank. The fiend screamed.

Otho staggered back, battered and bruised. He hurt as if the demon's wound was in his own scalp. The creature grinned, holding up a lock of Otho's hair. The priest raised the demon's torn forelock to his own wound. When he pulled it away, his scalp was no longer bloody. The devil's black hair had taken root, and grew as if it were Otho's own, giving him a strange, shadowed, lopsided look, right different from left. The shuddering demon still held Otho's skin and hair in its clawed hand.

"Keep a bit of me, if you want," Otho said. "It's only hair. I have my share of you, and more than enough; I'll give some away, as it grows."

In the struggle, demon and priest had gotten turned around, and the uncreated one stood between Otho and the door.

"*Hypage opiso mou,*" Otho said in Greek recently learned. "*Skandalon ei emou.*" He pushed the demon aside. Wearing his black lock of hair, he strode from the church.

Priests drew back, afraid of his terrible taint. "I will pluck hairs as they grow long," he told them, looking directly at Bishop Albertus, "and I will braid bracelets of black hair for each of you, to wear in remembrance of this day."

Albertus was astounded by the hard strength and conviction in the newly arrived priest. Was he a saint? An emissary from Roma? He had addressed the demon with Christ's words: "Get back, Satan. You are a stumbling block before me."

"You don't understand what you saw," said Otho, "but I will teach you."

Pierrette stared at the smoke. Was it fainter by the sum of a bucket of sea water, the flesh of a mullet, a lock of hair, and a warrior's severed head? Its implacable hatred was undiminished. If it reached her, she could not withstand it. But as it again approached, someone else leaped in its way.

✧   ✧   ✧

"Blight!" cried Guihen, and darted forward. He snatched at the smoky air. "Smut and ergot!" he exclaimed, making motions as if he were stuffing a pouch with demon-substance. "Hellebore and nightshade," he crowed, shredding wisps of vaporous substance with his long fingers. "Mold and mushrooms, poisons and potions. I claim them all." He leaped away with a tinkling of muguet-flower bells, leaving a silvery scent of the tiny lilies that ornamented his shoes and cuffs.

"I've always had evil enough," he announced, "so I will share these with everyone."

He grinned at Pierrette. "Good and evil," he said, making a motion as if pouring oil from one jar to another. "Medicine and poison. Which is which, and when? Ask Augustine of Hippo. He knows." The priests shrank back in terror as he ran laughing and leaping from the sanctuary.

"Did you hear?" Otho asked Bishop Albertus. "Do you remember what Augustine wrote? In the substance, not the usage, does evil lie." Albertus had not read the saint's works, or much else. Pierrette wondered when Otho had found time to do so. He had always portrayed himself as an uneducated village priest.

"Come," Otho commanded the churchmen, "now do as you have seen done." He led them forward. First Albertus, then each priest and monk in turn, stepped up to the pillared bay where the roiling darkness stood. Each one reached out a hand and took a portion—a wisp of smoke, a pinch of swirling soot. When they were done, the demon indeed seemed diminished. It twisted in upon itself, as if by becoming dense and solid it could prevent further attenuation.

Marah, queen of Gypsies, gathered her people behind herself. For a moment, Pierrette saw no fat woman in bright clothing, glittering with gold, but a figure in uncut cloth draped in an ancient manner: the *pneuma*, the soul and breath, of Sara, unchanged and undiminished by births, deaths, and generations.

She saw no demon of smoke, whirling dust, and stygian blackness, but a great loaf of coarse bread resting upon the pagan altar. Sara broke it across her knee.

Once she had taken a pinch of blackness and chewed it,

Pierrette again saw Marah, gold bracelets warm in the faint, indirect light. Each Gitane partook of the unconsecrated feast, then retired to the front of the church, where Pierrette heard water being drawn from the siege well. The well: the ancient source and soul of the community, one reason why folk had built houses on this undistinguished strand.

Marah and her folk left by the south portico. The church seemed empty. Pierrette, dark Yan Oors, and Marie remained. She heard a faint scratching, like a mouse gnawing a crust; the scholar ibn Saul sat cross-legged against a pillar, a filled parchment on his writing board.

Yan Oors approached the ancient stone. The shadows his bulk cast seemed out of proportion, as if independent of him and the light from the distant doorway. One shadow followed his movement, and two separate ones dogged his heels. He broke chunks of dark bread from the loaf, taking the greater portion of what remained on the stone, and fed one to each of his shadowy companions.

For a moment—just a brief span, hardly a heartbeat— Pierrette saw in those umbral shapes two great bears, male and female. Their small eyes gleamed balefully as the stars between the cleft to the Eagle's Beak. "My brother, my sister, and I will slip out by the north portal," Yan said quietly, his resonant voice echoing in the empty church. "No one will notice us. They are all outside, waiting for you."

"Will I see you again?" Pierrette asked plaintively.

"You'll see us—all of us—better than before." He chuckled. "So will all the folk of this country—and when you don't see us, you'll hear tales . . . for there are pranks to be played, mares and housewives with a lust for wildness . . ."

Pierrette giggled . . . and he was gone. No shadows stirred. Pierrette felt battered by strong winds, each having struck her from a different compass point. She felt fuzzy-minded and deafened. She glanced at the pagan altar stone, which held only crumbs and a single crust, and knelt beside Marie.

Her sister's face was serene and childlike. She looked too innocent to live in the harsh world.

"She's too frail indeed," said an old, cracked voice. "As she is now, she'll again be taken by darkness. She's an empty vessel with no lid to protect it, no contents a demon would have to displace."

Pierrette recognized old, gray-haired Maria, her shawl thrown back on her narrow shoulders—the dark figure with Marie when Pierrette had first arrived at the church. Or was she an apparition who looked much like Sister Agathe? Nothing was what it seemed. Was all this a mad nightmare?

Maria shook her head. "Wake her, child, and we'll help her to do what must still be done." Trustingly, Pierrette knelt and gently shook Marie's shoulder, feeling the warmth of her through the blanket and the palm of her hand.

Her sister's eyes opened. Pierrette helped her sit. "Is this a church?" Marie asked. "I've never been here before."

"It's the church of the Holy Marias by the Sea," Pierrette replied.

Old Maria—or Sister Agathe?—murmured something in Marie's ear. The girl shook her head vehemently. "No. I don't want to."

"You must, child, or all you have suffered will be for naught." She turned to Pierrette. "Help her stand and walk. She knows what she must do."

Pierrette also knew. "She's so innocent," she protested.

"She must," insisted the woman.

"Who is she?" Marie asked Pierrette.

"I'll explain later," Pierrette said. Had Marie forgotten everything that had transpired while the demon had resided within her, since her wedding night? If she had forgotten, it might be for the best. But there was something that had to be done. . . .

"Come," she said, and led Marie to the pagan altar stone, and picked up the crust. "Take this, and eat."

"I don't want it," Marie responded, grimacing. "I don't like black bread. I will not . . . Oh!" Marie gasped as the old woman grasped her arm, squeezing it painfully.

"Eat it," Maria commanded. "Eat it, or suffer again all those things you do not wish to remember."

"Is it blessed?" asked Marie, confused, thinking that as this was a church, and the bread had been taken from an altar . . .

"It is not," Maria grated. "It is dark as murder, sour as envy, coarse as a whore's laugh, and heavy as guilt. Yet eat it you must, for there is not one of us without sin, and that crust is your fair portion."

She guided Marie's hand to the crust. Marie took it, her whole body trembling as if with ague. She pressed it between slack, trembling lips and chattering teeth, and the sound of her chewing was loud in the silence, a silence broken only by a faint scratch, scritch, scratch, as of a mouse somewhere in the shadows. Marie choked the dry stuff down.

"Now come, and drink," Maria said. A wide-mouthed clay jar beside the well brimmed with water.

"Is it foul too?" asked Marie, her voice rough and choked with course bread.

"It is water, fresh drawn from the earth," said Maria.

Marie drank. She took a second sip, and a third, darkening the front of her thin garment with spilled water.

"Come," said Maria. "Friends await outside, in the bright sunlight of morning." She led Marie away. The robed figure whose arm encircled Marie's waist resembled Sister Agathe, from behind. Where had the nun been during the terrible confrontations, and how had she appeared so suddenly, as if from behind a pillar?

"Pierrette?" Marie called out, turning back.

"She'll come soon. She still has one task to perform here," Agathe said, soothing her. "Come." It was Agathe. . . . But then, where had Maria gone? Had she really been there at all? It was all too confusing.

Pierrette knelt by the stone altar, not in reverence, but like a housewife; she swept the remaining crumbs into her palm, took one pinch of them, and ate. The gritty substance was like sand on her tongue. The rest she carried to the well, and brushed it from her hand, for the earth itself was not without pain, nor its waters without sorrow, and all who walked upon the land and drank from its breast must accept their share of it.

She then sighed loudly, and walked toward the light. "Are you coming?" she asked ibn Saul, still making mouse scratchings.

"Soon," he said. "I've almost finished writing what I saw here."

"Good," she said. "Guard your scribery well, but let no one see it. The truth of what you have observed—and what you did not see—may be all that stands between us and terrible doom."

Ibn Saul did not understand. Of course, facts written by

an unbiased, rational observer were important, but what did she mean, "a terrible doom"? Nonetheless, impressed by the gravity of her statement, he tucked the sheets beneath his belt.

Chapter 30 ∾ The Voyage Home

From the crypt beneath the church, the Gypsies took Saint Sarah's statue, dressed it in bright clothing like their own, and adorned it with gold. From the bay next to the pagan altar they took the old wooden boat, and carried boat and statue through the streets, singing.

As every May, they reenacted that long-past meeting of the Tsigane queen Sara with the holy folk who had come in just such a boat.

The priests could not have helped but notice that the Gitane ritual did not tell the conventional story of Sarah's arrival with the saints. When the Gypsies carried the boat into the waves, they swam with it, then floated it back to the saint's effigy, which remained on the strand, awaiting its arrival. It was not Christian Sarah they celebrated, but Tsigane Sara, who had thrown her cloak upon the waters.

The priests did not protest, because when the Gitanes had feasted, made betrothals among members of their different tribes, and settled matters of law that required their queen's judgment, they would depart, and things would return to normal until fall.

Pierrette stood on the beach by black ashes already half-buried in sand. She knew that the boat the Gitanes carried was not the one the saints had arrived in, but that troubled her no more than it did the Gypsies, who may or may not have known the truth, but did not care.

When boat and saint were returned to their proper places within the church, the Gypsies feasted.

Otho sat long with Bishop Albertus and a cluster of priests

and monks, a teacher before his students. He spoke of what they had seen, and its meaning, reassuring them that what had transpired was no abomination, but the righting of balance, an evening of scales.

"Poor Marie wasn't a Judas goat," he told them, "to bear all our sins. As holy Augustine said, evil cannot be confined so, because it belongs to all of us. God didn't create it, nor did Satan, who creates nothing. Evil stems from the sins of men and women, and as we are men, we must bear our fair portion, or abandon all claim to free will."

Otho plucked black hairs from the right side of his head, and braided them into thin bracelets. He gave one to Albertus, and then, as often as he completed another, to each of his listeners. "Wear this," he told each man. "Remember: when you are tempted to say 'That is evil' of this small godlet or that, of one pagan relic or another, or of a woman who gathers herbs by moonlight. Remember that you are not pure, and draw no lines of distinction between a prayer to virgin Diana and a plea for Maria's intercession with her Son, for you cannot say for sure where the pagan's honest plea may be heard, or who hears it."

Pierrette, listening, may not have agreed with his interpretations, but just as she had not told the Gypsies their boat was not the original, she did not remonstrate with Otho. No human's understanding was complete, hers least of all.

If one priest among Otho's pupils departed while nursing grave doubts, Otho might yet be called to account before the archbishops in Lugdunum or even Roma, and be chastised. The part of the Wheel that Pierrette could look upon led backward, not forward, and she could not tell if her forebodings were true sight or merely the pessimism of a girl who had seen too much.

She did not see Guihen again. Her last memory of him was as he capered from the church. Yet she did not doubt that she would hear of him, as he scattered the bits and pieces he had carried from the church—the blains and poisons that caused suffering, even death, and those, like hellebore and nightshade, that could kill or cure. Such evils should not be separated from the world. Only the separation was Evil.

Neither did she see John of the Bears. He and the Camargue mares had faded into the reeds and morning mists unnoticed. If in future days she pined for him and Guihen, whom she had known almost from the beginning, she knew a place, on the way from Citharista to the dragon's bones, where she could light a campfire and call them for an evening's recounting of adventures.

Someday she would ask Yan Oors how it was to grow up among bears, and ask him how he slew the dragon whose bones lay on the heights—if indeed that were not just a folktale told to explain the strangely shaped white rocks; reality was shifting smoke, and no two pairs of eyes saw the same thing.

Marie had little recollection of anything that had transpired since her wedding night. She sometimes looked puzzled when she remembered Bertrand, as if wondering why she was not wed to him.

"The marriage was annulled," Otho told her. She accepted that without curiosity, regret, or relief.

Marie spent much time with Gilles, having taken an interest in her father and his boat. At her insistence he, with the aid of strong-backed fishermen, raised it on blocks for the first proper recaulking it had received in years.

"When it's repainted sky blue, with a red stern and gunwales, we'll sail into Massalia in style," Marie announced with girlish eagerness.

Pierrette had not considered how they would get home— or indeed if she would return to Citharista at all. But such a trip sounded wonderful—with her sister restored, her father strong and unafraid, in a shiny blue-and-scarlet craft that cut through the water with the grace of a porpoise. She would accompany them as far as Massalia—and then, who knew?

Jerome—Reikhard, as Pierrette learned to address him— planned to stop at every town along the Roman *viae*, to confer with castellans, magistrates, and fellow knights about policing them, making them safe for traders and pilgrims. He took his responsibilities more seriously than before, not from fear of his distant Frankish lord, but as a part of his newfound manhood.

That did not mean he was without fear. He had fought his demon, had won a skirmish and a head now steeping in cedar oil to preserve it, but would he ever truly believe the demon was gone, and relax from his self-imposed penance of good works? Pierrette did not think so.

"I may find some villager's lovely daughter along the way," he told Pierrette shortly before he departed, "a girl who would not object to my donning the god's antlers on our wedding night. . . ."

Pierrette did not think he would have much trouble finding a wife. His keep might be more pleasant with a woman in it. Still, she did not think she would be among Reikhard's visitors, despite his changed nature—the sight of him raised terrible memories. She doubted that even the longest lifetime would enure her to him.

At last, all was ready.

"Have no fear," Gilles told Marie as they clambered into his freshly outfitted boat. "We were five before, when this craft was low in the water and soggy with rotted planks. See how high it rides, even with six aboard?"

Gilles had learned that the open sea was not the worst he had to fear. He had partaken of the demon's substance, diminishing it, but could he truly believe it had been vanquished?

Anselm, Sister Agathe, and Muhammad ibn Saul made up the rest of the company. "I'll be along in good time," P'er Otho said. "There are things I have yet to convey to the fathers and brothers—but when that is finished, I plan to spend more time in your library, Magister Anselm." He said "magister," meaning "teacher." Having the same root as "magus," perhaps it reflected Christian Otho's compromise between his growing affection for the old man and his uneasy feeling about the arts Anselm practiced.

"My discussions with Bishop Alfredus have revealed vast imperfections in my understanding. You have the works of Augustine, and the writings of Irenaeus, bishop of Lugdunum. I must study those, and more, before I'll be able to argue what I have learned, perhaps even in Rome."

Pierrette thought Otho's ambition, far from being as simple as her own piecemeal dismemberment of one demon, was akin to marching straight to Hell to confront its master in person. Of course Rome was not Hell, but she thought Otho mad to consider flaunting his heresy so. She shrugged; it was no more foolish than what any of them had done, confronting their worst fears head on. She would not try to dissuade him.

✧   ✧   ✧

The voyage was swift and smooth, though not uneventful. The wind mostly paralleled the coast, and the lateen sail performed well on running or broadly reaching courses. When the wind died, Anselm tested his hypothesis that magics of the sea were little changed by scholars' piddlings upon the land. Two dolphins and several large seals came when he called to the sea god Poisedonos; the dolphins pressed alongside and the seals grasped the thrown painter in their teeth, and pulled the craft eastward for most of the night.

When the wind freshened toward morning, the creatures swam off, not waiting to hear the humans' shouts of appreciation. Was there some unexpressed *quid pro quo* at sea, and would Anselm—or any of them—be required to do service at some future time?

"I won't jump into the sea, then hold my breath waiting for the god to importune me," said Anselm. "In fact, if he's so ungracious as to resent me if I never again take ship, but only watch the waves from my high aerie, let him strike us now with a great wave, and get it over with!"

That did not set well with the others, who were unwilling to endure the wrath of a god because of Anselm's ebullient bravado. A demon had been quite enough. They understood that his speech had been figurative, and that the mage only meant that he did not intend to make a habit of sea voyages, but . . .

The great wave, when it came, did not crush their frail craft; it lifted them above the chop as if atop a hill from which they could see not only the headlands of the Estaque, but the massif south of Massalia, twenty miles further on. And because a full morning separated Anselm's improvident utterance and the great standing wave, there was no absolute causal connection between the two events.

When the wave subsided, ibn Saul held forth at length, explaining the entirely ordinary nature of such a "rogue wave," which was no more than the additive result of ripples driven from this direction and that by winds out of Africa, Iberia, and down Rhodanus's valley.

Everyone heard his rational explanation, but no one— possibly not even ibn Saul himself—believed a word of it. The scholar's blathering was snatched from his mouth by the sea breeze, and dissipated. If all the magics of the land were to die, and the Black Time drew near, the seas would be last to succumb. That thought cheered Pierrette greatly.

They reached Massalia before darkness, and sailed smoothly into the wharf-lined calanque. Ibn Saul directed them to the mooring closest to his house.

Sister Agathe returned to the nunnery with Marie. Agathe was full of tales, and wanted Marie there in the flesh to prove that she herself had not gone mad and imagined it all. Much of what she had witnessed was beyond her ability to understand. Was the demon truly gone? Was not one demon only a single source of evil in a world teeming with others? Had their efforts made any difference? She could only hope so.

All she could be sure of was that Marie was free of her demon, and that she, Agathe, intended to celebrate that with the sisters. She would never admit that her celebrations would have much the nature of whistling in a sepulcher, but of course that was so. Nun and girl set off directly from the wharf, around the long horn of the calanque.

Anselm expressed his intention to stop at the tavern, and only later to seek his bed across the street. Gilles echoed him, and ibn Saul did not try to dissuade them.

Despite his throbbing head, sure that a he-goat had grazed the night on his tongue, Gilles insisted they set off promptly in the morning. Ibn Saul sent Lovi to fetch Marie.

Gilles fretted. "What good is a fine boat if everyone in Citharista is sound asleep when I sail it up to the wharf?"

Pierrette hoped he had not ingested more than his share of the demon with his bucket of salt water. She need not have feared, for Gilles's new pride was the reasonable counterpart of his past self-humiliation, and there was only a little evil in it.

Lovi returned with Marie. "I'm not returning to Citharista," she told them. "If Mother Sophia deems me worthy, I'll say my vows."

Gilles drew breath to protest, but Pierrette stilled him. "Let me speak with her, Father—though I don't think I'll change her mind."

She did not, but Marie surprised her anyway. "Did you really think I had forgotten such a large chunk of my life, dear sister?" Everything I did—from my wedding night to the demon's investment of me and thereafter—happens all over again, every waking moment, and in my dreams."

"Oh Marie! I'm so sorry!" cried Pierrette.

"I don't need pity—only peace and prayer. I regret my abdication of self, after my wedding night, because I caused you and Father, and poor P'er Otho, so much worry. I'm sorry the emptiness I left behind—when my soul hid from me—was such an attractive home for the demon who tormented you."

Pierrette's head spun. Marie was not making sense. Had her soul hidden not from the terror of her night with Jerome, but from herself? And had the demon tormented not Marie, but Pierrette? What did she mean?

"I fled because I enjoyed Jerome's caresses, dear," Marie explained without self-condemnation. "I was as hot in his embrace as I had hoped to be with Bertrand—and that's why I fled. I thought I was corrupt, that I should have wailed and been shamed. I think Mother Sophia knew all along.

"When the demon overwhelmed me, I could have jumped from a roof, but I enjoyed the lust of men—until I became bored—and I loved the sparkle of emeralds, the gleam of gold."

She put her arms around Pierrette, who stood stunned by the depth of her own misunderstanding. "Rest easy, Pierrette dear," Marie murmured. "I'll do good to make up for the evil—the suffering I caused you and Sister Agathe, the work and trouble when I fouled myself. I'll say prayers and do penance for that—and for the crust of Evil still in me—as long as I live."

"But Marie! I hoped you would marry, and have children . . ."

"The ones you don't intend to have? There are many children, sister, and I'll serve by teaching them, and taking in those who have no one. Is our old blood so important that it must be passed on? Don't press me to be what you will not, and I won't question your decisions, either. Is that fair?"

"I only wanted you to have a full life," Pierrette replied.

Marie chuckled, and lifted Pierrette's chin. "I've known fleshly lust, little sister. I willingly relinquish it. I have love—yours and Father's and Sister Agathe's. I don't need more."

Feeling Pierrette soften in her arms, Marie knew she had surrendered. "Come on. I must say my good-byes."

"It's only a short sail from Citharista," her father told her. "I'll visit you whenever I have a catch to sell. And I'll bring Pierrette." Pierrette nodded. She would make sure of it.

She felt impatient to be at sea, to see the red rock of the Eagle's Beak lit by the slanting rays of the late-afternoon sun. She clambered into the boat and pushed off vigorously, and Gilles did not have to help her haul up the yard or set the sail.

The second leg of Pierrette's return went even faster than the first. Sailing out of the harbor, the sun was at their backs. Where the coast turned eastward toward Sormiou—where she had cavorted with Aam long ago, where his large cloven hooves and her dainty ones had stirred the leaves as they danced—the sun was high overhead, because it was only weeks to the solstice.

The solstice . . . there was magic to be done then, Pierrette knew, and she would have much reading and studying to do before she was ready for that. She gripped the boat's rail as if she could urge it ahead with bodily force. The whole of the seventeen-mile southeasterly run to Citharista seemed to go by in hours compressed to minutes, so perhaps her urgings helped in some small way. Perhaps Anselm too, eager to be home again, by choice this time, not coerced by Minho's geas, gave some small magical impetus to their vessel.

Perhaps, Pierrette thought, laughing quietly, he was eager to be out of the sea's grip before some resentful god called him on the carpet for his impudence.

Chapter 31 ～ Small Evils

Pierrette thereafter divided her time among the Eagle's Beak, Citharista, and the woods and trails of the high country that cupped the town like toy blocks in a giant child's hands.

Sometimes she was alone in the mage Anselm's keep, because the old man had developed a taste for the company of men, and spent the sunset hour in Germain's tavern.

"She's *doing things* again," the mage would grumble softly to Gilles. "Sometimes the whole scarp shakes with the force of her 'experiments.' If my poor residence tumbles into the sea, I don't want to be in it."

The men of the town became used to the old mage who, in his cups, exhibited no great air of mystery. Perhaps that was all to the good, because the town's drinkers could not deny that the wine was smoother in their throats when Anselm drank with them, and the mornings thereafter always the kind a man enjoyed getting up to. There was magic in that.

When Reikhard returned with a pretty young wife, he too found the tavern congenial, and Gilles and Anselm pleasant company. Pierrette thought them three frightened little boys. Together, they spoke bravely and ebulliently of their adventures. She wondered how different their thoughts were at night, when sleep would not come.

"What town is she from?" asked villagers about the slender, doe-eyed girl the castellan had married.

"I met her in the forest west of Arelate," Reikhard told anyone who asked. "She's not from any town."

"What were you doing there, off the Roman road or the beaten tracks?" people asked.

"Looking for her," the knight told them—and would say no more. Those who followed the pair of them into the hills when the good fires of autumn burned, and danced the flames around, did not have to be told how Reikhard had found his wife, or who her father was. There was magic in that, too. Though Pierrette knew what it was, she did not mention Saint Gilles and his doe to anyone, but when the young bride's eyes caught hers, it was as if they shared a secret, and there was magic in that.

Pierrette could not tell how the evil the knight had carried away from Saintes Maries now manifested itself. Unlike the others, he had not been seen to consume his portion of the demon. Was there, somewhere in his large house, a secret room smelling of sharp cedar oil, where a Celt warrior's sightless eyes stared down from the rafter? Pierrette did not want to know, or to speculate about what magic it held.

Otho returned to Citharista with the *Mistral* wind that shook the leaves from the platanes and the oliviers. He led the wise and cynical Gustave whose skepticism, the priest said, had been an excellent foil for his own gullible nature.

"I have met monks and priests who spoke much and said little," the priest volunteered over his wine-cup, "and a bishop who spoke all the time and said nothing at all. The donkey, who has never spoken a word, is wiser than any of them."

Perhaps Otho's reasoning left a thread or two untied, but having met Bishop Albertus, and having travelled with Gustave, Pierrette was not inclined to reject his conclusion. His sermons were well-attended, and no one slept through them even when Otho lost track of time and the sun's rays illuminated the oculus over the chapel's west-facing door. As any preacher would have been first to admit, there was surely magic in that.

Perhaps only Guihen and John of the Bears stalked the forests where men came to cut wood. Perhaps they alone haunted rocky places, and frightened lonely shepherds. Perhaps no other sprites lurked in rock piles beside fields of grain and under broad melon leaves, or threw lemons on the heads of passersby, or quickened barren housewives, but if that were so, the two of them were surely busier than even magic could account for. Besides, the apparitions men told of in their cups were more often female than male. Not all were combined of a glimpse of a village girl and a lonely man's wishful thinking, because not all men were fools and liars, even when drunk.

Everyone, drunk or sober, agreed that there was magic in the air's whispering, the murmur of brooks, and the grumbling voices under bridges. Every Sunday the little chapel was so crowded that a collection had to be taken to add a new bay, and to move the rood-beam twenty feet, to make room for everyone. If not magical, that was no less a blessing, as the archbishop admitted when he came to say mass at All Saints, and it rained. Everyone who had come fitted inside the church.

There was magic on the winds, said Gilles, who sailed often to Massalia to sell his catch, to visit the novice Marie, and to sip a few cups with Muhammad abd' Ullah ibn Saul. They drank in the tavern, because the scholar was too tight with his own wine to invite Gilles into his cool courtyard.

Though Gilles had not grown new teeth to replace those he had lost, his wife Granna did not mind. There was magic in that, and in her calm acceptance of the evil side of his nature, that manifested itself when he cursed the treacherous currents that tangled his nets, or the bad weather that diminished his olive crop. There was—and Gilles was first to admit it—something magical about Granna's love, because though he was no longer despicable in his own eyes, he did not consider himself a loveable man.

Pierrette sometimes sailed with him, and found it true that the winds were mostly fair. She had no magical hand in that.

At first unsure that Marie's decision was the right one, she was convinced when they shared a pallet in the nunnery, giggling like magpies until Marie rose to begin the hours of prayer that would occupy her until dawn.

Even sleepless, Marie maintained her serene good cheer all day, and through a second night of magpie-talk. Though Pierrette slept while her sister knelt in prayer in the morning, she was first to fall asleep at night, and often wondered what magic her sister had called upon.

"Are the ladder snakes in the herb garden still deadly?"

Pierrette asked between giggles. "Is Mother Sophia still afraid to stick her nose in the rosebushes?"

"No one's been bitten," Marie replied, "but I'm not about to test your hypothesis. I keep my feet up on the stone bench."

"Are you less good than you used to be?" asked Pierrette, wondering what had become of the black crust Marie had eaten.

Her sister giggled, and lifted her skirt to display grimy knees. "I allowed Sister Roxana, a novice, to become lost in the old theater precinct. I haven't finished my penance yet—I was lucky Mother Sophia let me see you, this trip." She chuckled, and Pierrette was reassured by the mischievous gleam in her eye. There was no risk that Marie would allow her portion of malice to escape—it was far too much fun, and no penance was too much to pay. There was magic in that.

After one trip to Massalia when Pierrette had stayed behind, Gilles came tramping up the path to the mage's keep with a bundle from ibn Saul. While Anselm entertained her father on the high terrace beneath the ever-warm midday sun, Pierrette read the lengthy document the scholar had written—the very scroll that she had commissioned of him in a letter that had been delivered to Anselm in the beak of a stork.

There is no need to repeat ibn Saul's dry words, for he went on at great length about what he had seen—which was not much, and was quite uninteresting. Suffice it that he did not see smoke arise from Marie's blankets, there in the Church of the Holy Marys, but only steam rising from a breathy crowd

He saw no black demon with eyes of fire, and did not see Yan Oors confront a *sanglier*, though he heard sounds of grunting, perhaps made by a man with a painful stomach cramp.

Ibn Saul did not see Gilles sail between rocks, trusting to his God's providence for his life. When Gilles pushed his way out of the church, the scholar saw no bailing bucket in his hand.

He saw only rusty Reikhard in his funny old helmet, not Cernunnos, and heard Reikhard's voice alone, not the dialogue others remembered. He heard no clashing blades, only the swoosh of Reikhard's sword through empty air.

Ibn Saul watched Anselm run around with his arms outstretched like a crazy bird, but he did not see an osprey or a gray-headed eagle, or a shiny mullet.

He admitted that he had not noticed the dark lock of hair on the right side of the priest's head before he entered the church, but he saw no devil at all.

"Ibn Saul overlooked Guihen," said Anselm later. "He saw only Marah, not Sara the Tsigane, not Maria, only Agathe, not even the loaf of black bread, only char on the old stone, from some ancient fire. What good is this? A blind scribe could have done better."

"Oh, no, Master," Pierrette said cheerily, "He did everything satisfactorily. He didn't believe anything, whether he saw it or not, and provides 'rational' explanations for everything that transpired. The dismembered demon whose evil we share is locked within the coils of his disbelief, within the words of this scroll. His skepticism is the most powerful spell of all, against which no magic—and no supernatural beings—can prevail."

She rerolled the document, tied it with a red silk string, and placed it among the others. "Now try to find it, Master," she challenged the mage.

He reached for the scroll, and opened it. "This is the wrong one," he exclaimed. He had not taken his eyes from it when Pierrette put it away. He tried again and again, but could not find ibn Saul's scroll. Neither could Pierrette. She was satisfied. It was a very old spell, not long, but powerful: from the beginning of time people had lost things, and refused to believe that no malicious spirit had hidden them.

Somewhere within the clutter of Anselm's keep, the small leather sack the child Pierrette had brought lay forgotten, bound by a similar spell. Anselm knew what was in it, once, but he had now forgotten that too. Perhaps someday, if it became important, he would remember what it was, and where.

Pierrette, reflecting upon her life, was content that she had lost nothing of importance, and had gained much. Even her mother was there to commune with her beside the sacred pool. That did not mean she had no further desires, or that she would be content to remain where she was. Her victory was substantial, and satisfying, but it was only one victory, in one small place within a world unimaginably vast. Sometimes, on gray days, she saw shadows of great iron towers against the backdrop of Citharista's leaden sky.

The Black Time. Perhaps the battle in Saintes-Maries had been truly won—one demon, created in the conflicts of human hearts and minds, had been vanquished. But there were many hearts and minds, many beings like Yan Oors and Guihen yet to be freed of the Christian, Muslim, or scholarly spells that held them. There were surely other demons, greater ones, to be negated by pouring the evil concentrated in them into other vessels, a little here, a little there. That would demand greater magics than she had mastered, sorceries built upon axioms yet undiscovered.

On the sunless days that generated such pondering, happily rare in sunny Provence, she yearned for a man's arms around her—Minho or Aam or someone not yet met—if only to comfort her. But she had just begun to learn her trade, and could not give it up now. There would be no man for a long time. In such melancholy moments, she returned to her books and scrolls, and there by magical light caught in a blue Roman glass bottle, pored over maps of all the places she had not yet been.

❧ Epilogue

The teller of tales is a worm in an onion. Finding a layer sweet and juicy, he may follow it, nibbling what pleases him and ignoring the rest. Much remains untold, of course.

The folk of Citharista are mere shadows in this tale, though the woman in the third house from the olive press still trembles with delighted recollection of a night in the woods, as she nurses her pig-faced baby. Young Marius regales his drinking-mates with episodes of life as a soldier under Reikhard, chasing thieves and highwaymen from the Roman road. The shepherd Claudio still excites himself with imaginary women, and has not married. In Massalia Lovi writes accounts of what he has seen every time he returns from a voyage with Muhammad abd' Ullah ibn Saul.

At crossroads Gitane nomads meet others of their tribes. Around their campfires they share what they have witnessed, and the stories spread. They are told around Illyrian and Iberian campfires, on the Silk Road to the Far East, and in the fields of Saxon England. Does this spreading plague, this insidious propaganda, have effects outside the minds of those who hear or tell the tales? Is the Evil One's calendar set back with each retelling? We do not know.

Sometimes our small worm, finding his layer gone papery and dry, will burrow deeper and taste perhaps the childhood of a boy who would become Yan Oors, witnessing the forging of his iron staff and his slaying of the dragon. Perhaps our burrower will glimpse Protis the Phoacean in bed with Gyptis, the Ligure princess, whose dowry was the hill upon which old Massalia stands. . . .

Perhaps the rootworm will find Pierrette dreaming of the Black Time, and she will again fill baskets with dried fish and cheese, and lead the dubious Gustave on another trail, for much remains untold. Of Magdalen, Ma promised Pierrette "Remember her well, for you will meet her again, some day," and that day has not yet come. Pierrette's sandals have never touched Ugium's cobbled pavements, nor has she discovered what sweet sorrow awaits her on the desolate Crau Plain. She has not solved the riddle of King Minho, or his conviction that she has teased and tormented him for at least a thousand years. She has never seen the wild black bulls of Camargue, and the Black Time still threatens, perhaps a bit further off than before.

Yet for now she abides, learning her craft from books, testing her mastery of spells. Winds blow the scents of rosemary and thyme from the heights, the odor of salt from the sea and the Camargue, and the fragrance of wet greenery from the head of the long valley where her mother has become a thick tree with roots deep in the earth.

If sometimes a stork lands with a rattle of feathers upon a parapet high on the Eagle's Beak, remembering a love that has not yet been, and is long past, and silently watches her at her study, that tale lies deeper within the onion of the land and the years, and remains yet untasted.

Otho, Bishop of Nemausus
The Sorceress's Tale

Historic and Other Notes

My study of myth has been influenced by French anthropologist Claude Levi-Strauss, especially his *Structural Anthropology*, the section entitled "The Structural Study of Myth." I have put my own spin on his work, seeing myths not only as mediators between conflicting social or religious concepts, but as analogous with genes. A body's genes (and a culture's myths) evolve by addition, subtraction, recombination, and mutation, and those that do not serve, or that debilitate, are lost when the body or the tribe that contains them dies. Those that enhance or maintain the tribal body's survival are passed on.

Myths evolve. They are kept and retold, or discarded and forgotten, as the needs and natures of societies change. Saint Augustine, an early revisionist, realized in the Fifth Century that it was not enough to eradicate pagan myths and the practices that sprang from them, so he suggested that every holy pagan tree should be made into planks for a Christian shrine, every sacrifice replaced with a Christian feast, and—by extension—every pagan myth with a very similar saint's tale. This dynamic, changing mythic fabric is the framework for *The Sacred Pool*, the first volume of *The Sorceress's Tale*.

Myth is not history, though some historic tales serve as normative myths; evaluating a myth for historic accuracy, or worse, debunking and rejecting it on historic grounds, is akin to rejecting gold coins because their pouch is frayed.

Because I am "cautious" (though arguably less despicable than Gilles), I have chosen to tell of old myths indeed and, like the Jewish scholars, have written a *midrash*, a tale intended to elucidate without dry and lengthy argument.

Such tales are dangerous. They flesh out austere principle and pristine reasoning with appealing, unfounded details that work themselves into common belief. When did angels, beings of fleshless light, grow feathers? When did Leviathan become a toothed sea mammal? At what age did God's salt-and-pepper beard turn white? In the interest of maintaining the boundary between myth and deliberate fiction, and of making excuses for myself as well, I have prepared the following notes.

Myth and Perception

The Sacred Pool contains two "mutating" myths. The Tsigane version of Sara and the saints is from Claude Clément's wonderful children's book *Contes Traditionelles de Provence*, and represents either the iconoclastic extreme or the earliest, least-changed myth. The more conventional version is recounted briefly in the Michelin Green Guide to Provence.

Saint Giles's story, the Visigoth version, is from Clément also. The variation Pierrette first recites is the "accepted" one. Pierrette's last, pre-Christian tale evolved from my own realization that its common elements are widespread in Celtic, Gothic, and Germanic tales, individually redacted as Saint Giles in Provence and Saint Godfric in England. Guihen l'Orphelin and Jean de l'Ours are authentic Provençal folklore heroes, but their roots in an earlier Celtic or even Proto Indo-European tradition are wholly my own suspicion—yet myths seldom emerge without context. In the sense of *The Sorceress's Tale*, all are valid, because all have shaped perception and, as Breb would say, "Seeing is believing."

Breb and his people, who exist nowhere but on the pages of this book, were created to elucidate that important Medieval absolute: that what we can know of the universe is only what we can see through the door of perception, and that all perceptions are real—which they are, in one sense. The masc who eats amanita mushrooms and nightshade feels like she is flying, and when she arises sober from her bed, her subsequent actions are influenced by what she saw and did when she flew.

The voice of God—heard as crosstalk via the *corpus callosum* between the two halves of a prophet's brain, or as words issuing from a stone, a sacred pool, or a burning bush—are not ignored by history; wars have been fought over them, and great religions have arisen. They have shaped our modern, skeptical world.

Chronology

The Sorceress's Tale may begin a few decades after the Battle of Poitiers in 732 A.D., or just before Harold Bluetooth espoused Christianity, around 965 A.D. The early Middle Age was monotonous in Provence. Common folk little cared who ruled in Aix (Aquae Sextius), Arles, Paris, or Ravenna—and cared little more just who raided, raped, and killed them, whether Saracen, Christian, Magyar, or Viking. The results were the same. Times changed only imperceptibly.

Aam's people painted the chambers of the Grotte Cosquer between 25,000 and 16,000 B.C.; the animal paintings probably date from the later years, the traced hands from the earlier. At present the cave's only entrance lies under 120 feet of water, beneath the Calanque de Sormiou.

Thera's eruption in 1628 B.C. establishes the beginning of Minho's reign. Extensive Minoan ruins have been excavated on the broken island, source of the Atlantis myth. Biblical accounts of pillars of smoke and fire, and shifting seabeds, arguably tectonic phenomena, date from the reign of Sesostris, Rameses II, and thus fall forty-odd years before the radiocarbon-dated destruction of Jericho by soldiers equipped with Egyptian arms. Thus do myth, oral history, and modern science converge, to the detriment of none.

The *apostoli* landed at Saints-Maries-de-la-Mer no later than 40 A.D. Magdalene pursued her mission in Lugdunum (Lyons), then lived in her cave for thirty-three years. Maximinus heard her last confession and buried her, and was himself surely buried—and Lazarus and Martha and Cedonius as well—by 90 A.D.

Places

There is no fortress atop *Cap l'Aigle* (the Eagle's Beak) west of La Ciotat, Roman Citharista, but waves lash the foot of the cliffs, and friable conglomeritic rubble would have crumbled in a hundred years, let alone a thousand. The Roman quays are covered in concrete. The spidery towers of the Black Time loom over La Ciotat, but there is talk of removing them, because the naval yards are closed, and an expanded marina would bring tourist revenue. Will their removal signify that Pierrette has at last won her battle, and the Black Time will never be?

The "Roman fountain" is on Michelin Map 245, but the sacred pool is not; it lies behind a veil of confusion, and you would walk by unknowingly near the shoulder of Highway D3. The unusual occurrence of a wet-climate, northern beech and maple forest among the scrub oaks and pines of Provence is patterned after the Sainte-Baume valley a few miles to the north of the sacred pool, where the towering cliffs that house Magdalen's cave shade the ground, and springs moisten it.

The dragon's bones lie bleached and exposed just north of highway D141, above Le Ciotat. The thousand-foot cliffs Pierrette measured are a few miles further on. Poor Ant'ny's red blanket and cart are (on this side of the Veil) a red automobile blown off the road by the terrible winds.

The loveliest calanques are just east of present-day Cassis; bring lunch, water bottles, and a sturdy hiking stick, because the trail is just as rough and sere as when Pierrette walked it.

In the fifteenth century two bays were added to the fortified church at Saintes-Maries-de-la-Mer, and the newer stone of restoration and addition is lighter and smoother than the old. The Camargue is still magical, though much tamed.

Massalia is buried beneath modern Marseille, and only scattered ruins remain; one can part the veil of years briefly while walking the short stretch of Roman stone road between the gate towers, where Pierrette entered the town.

Maps

I have taken few liberties with mountain ranges, coast-lines, or known human settlements, but I have not shown towns that play no part in the story. The Roman road from Massalia to Aquae Sextiae existed, as did the Via Julia Augusta between Aquae Sextiae and Arelate. I have renamed the Via Domitia Via Tiberia, for reasons that will become apparent in Volume II of *The Sorceress's Tale*, *The Veil of Years*. The east-west road on Map 1 is my whim, but surely existed, at least as a trail.

In recent centuries the rivers of Provence have been con-strained within their defined beds, but that was not always so. The Crau Plain was once the delta of the Druentia (Durance), which emptied directly into the sea. The lower Rhodanus (Rhone) itself has shifted many times within the memory of man; I chose to show it in its present bed, which is no less likely than any other: the very existence of Camargue indicates that at one time or another the river flowed over every hectare of the vast delta, and the "main channel" could have been anywhere, in Pierrette's time. Sea levels were higher once. Arelate had direct access to the sea when it was founded; Marius's canal was an attempt to maintain it as a port, not to create one. Saintes-Maries-de-la-Mer has been an island off and on—but I wanted Pierrette to ride there on a horse.

Languages

Languages shape us, and we shape them. Changes can be confusing. If I say *bhagos* in Proto Indo-European, and you hear *bhergos* in some early Indo-European tongue, the tough beech table I order may be made of brittle birch instead. If I say "Reed Sea" and you say "Red Sea," my Moses will get across, but your Pharaoh will drown.

Provence is rich in languages. Ligures are the first folk whose name survives. They maintained an identity even after successive invasions of Indo-European Celts—Segobrugii, Anatilii, Dexivates, Verucini, Deciates, Ligauni, Salluvii, and others—and may have spoken a Celtic dialect (or a non-Indo-European tongue, as did the Etruscans, and as do the

Basques of today). Latin, Celtic, and Greek had not diverged far from their common Indo-European root in 200 B.C., but were no longer mutually intelligible by Pierrette's time, when French, Italian, Spanish, and Provençal were becoming distinct.

That Aam's Magdalenian or Aurignacian speech was Proto-Ligurian is not much less likely than the known relationship between Lithuanian and Sanskrit, two millennia and thousands of miles apart. The pace of change was slow throughout prehistory.

Written characters (hieroglyphics, syllabaries, or alphabets) are not always consistent with spoken tongues. The Celts used anybody's alphabet—Etruscan, Greek, Latin, and Iberian—so it is not a stretch to write Pierrette's horrible spell (spoken in bastard Proto Indo-European) in Mycenaean syllabic characters.

I played fast and loose with words, because people did so then, and do now. It is impossible to say just when Proto Indo-European *pa* became Latin *pater*, which became French *pere*, Spanish *padre*, English and Italian *papa*. We know that Greek Massilia and Roman Massalia became modern Marseilles, and Aquae Sextiae Calvinorum (122 B.C.) became Aix-en-Provence (1997 A.D.), but what form did a particular name or word take in 1000 A.D.? I have freely used Proto Indo-European, Latin, Gaelic, modern French, and interpolated variations, wherever I wanted to.

Religion

Anthropologist Edward Wilson suspects that the capacity for faith is hardwired; I do not doubt it. I had trouble with Faith until, in a kind of epiphany, I realized it was qualitatively no different from the "willing suspension of disbelief" that writers and editors worry about. "O Lord, I believe. Help thou my unbelief."

The Sorceress's Tale is allegorical; the growth of Satan as "Eater of Gods" parallels his growing role over several millennia of religious thought. In early books of the Old Testament "a satan" is a common noun meaning "adversary"—or "lawyer." In later books, "The Satan" was a title—*The* Adversary. In the New Testament we find Satan, an individual with a proper name, portrayed as attractive and compelling, not ugly or deformed.

When Christianity spread among Gauls and Germans, Satan gained his "modern" appearance when priests told converts their old gods were aspects of the Deceiver. Satan indeed "ate" the older gods, and took on their attributes—Pan's cloven hooves and a satyr's impressive member, Cernunnos's horns and a long, dragonlike tail. The poor chimaera! How far bright Lucifer had fallen!

My assumption that "underground" pagan worship flourished in Provence 750–950 A.D. has two bases. First, a Diana cult survived into the nineteenth century in the hills of the Ligurian coast. It turned to Satan worship when eloquent priests convinced the stubborn folk they had been worshipping the Deceiver all along. Second, Provence has been home to every imaginable cult and heresy, from Albigensians to Zoroastrians—and still is.

That Reikhard, a Burgundian of Germanic descent, might hold beliefs we recognize as Celtic, reflects both the miscibility of traditions and confusion of the two peoples by early historians. Today we think of peoples as concrete entities, but it was not always so. The Ostrogoths, "classic" Germans, arose from Celtic, Germanic, Scandic, and Hun roots, and came to power as kings in Italy.

My portrayal of an easy relationship between Christians and pagans only seems strange in light of the "publicity" that purges and religious conflicts have generated; years or centuries of relative peace lie between the persecution of Christians under Nero and Diocletian, between early purges of Mother-cultists and the American colonial witch trials. I contend that religious persecutions correspond with political and economic polarizations.

Saint Augustine lived during a critical period when great "heresies" threatened to fragment the Pauline Church just as Minho of the Isles wished them to, and when hitherto remote Gothic tribes (and their beliefs) became near and familiar. Needless to say, Augustine is historic; Anselm and the Hermit are not. Muhammad abd' Ullah ibn Saul is loosely based on ibn Battuta and other Arabic-speaking travelling scholars of later centuries.

Fantasies, like "heresies," often avoid theodicy, the question of the *origin* of good and evil, and opt for Gnostic philosophies: a Good force and an Evil one created the universe, and have been squabbling over it ever since. That avoids the paradox of good God having created the world's evils. It puts all the responsibility on us humans to save the day— but doesn't it ultimately mean that both good and evil gods are irrelevant?

Augustine, as Father Otho tells the priests at Saintes-Maries, resolved the paradox by reasoning that God was good, but that by giving us free will, he had no choice but to allow us to sin, and that evil thus stems from human choices. Otho partly confuses Augustine with his archenemy, the druid-influenced Gallic bishop Pelagius, whose Latin name translates to "Myrddin" (Merlin) in Celtic, and whom Pierrette will meet in a future tale.

The point of his confusion is that ordinary Christians often espouse beliefs theologians consider heretical. Does that really matter? The Arian heresy divided nations, but who really understands the distinctions between Father, Son, and Holy Ghost? "In their hearts," said a pastor friend of mine, "I think most of my congregation are Arians."

The Sorceress's Tale need not be a Christian story. Gilles is saved by Grace of a Christian God, Pierrette by her mother—the Mother—and there are pagan stones built into the Christian edifice. If we humans have created Evil, we have done it by drawing lines in the sand with ourselves on one side and Evil on the other, by setting conditions for worship, salvation, redemption, and rebirth, and by making rules about where prayers, spells, and pleas for intercession go, when they are uttered.

Bibliography

It would be impossible to cite all the sources that have flowed into *The Sorceress's Tale*, many of which I no longer own or even remember, but which have shaped my views on history and myth. I have listed only those I referred to during the conception and writing of the *Tale*, and that currently reside on my "working" shelves. They are an adventure in themselves. Have fun.

Andre, Louis J.; *Pour Visitez Entremont*; Association Archéologique Entremont, Aix-en-Provence, undated.

Armstrong, Karen; *Jerusalem: One City, Three Faiths*; Alfred A. Knopf, New York, 1996.

Artz, Frederick B.; *The Mind of the Middle Ages A.D. 200–1500; An Historical Survey*; Third Edition, Alfred A. Knopf, New York, 1962.

Barruol, Guy; *Les Peuples Pre-Romains du Sud-Est de la Gaule: Etude de géographie historique*; Editions E. De Boccard, 1969.

Benoit, Fernand; *Entremont: Capitale celto-ligure des Salyens de Provence*; La Pensée Universitaire, Aix-en-Provence, 1962.

Boissonade, P., *Life and Work in Medieval Europe, the Evolution of Medieval Economy from the Fifth to the Fifteenth Century*; Harper and Row, New York, 1964.

Burton, R.; *The Book of the Sword*; Dover, New York, 1887.

Chadwick, John; *The Decipherment of Linear B, The Key to the Ancient Language and Culture of Crete and Mycenae*; Vintage Books, New York, 1963.

Childe, V. Gordon; *The Dawn of European Civilization*; Vintage Books, New York, 1964.

Clément, Claude; *Contes Traditionnels de Provence*; Editions Milan, Evreux, 1995.

De Camp, L. Sprague; *Lost Continents: the Atlantis Theme in History, Science, and Literature*; Dover, New York, 1970.

Enslin, Morton Scott; *Christian Beginnings, Parts I and II*; Harper and Row, New York, 1938.

Fichtenau, Heinrich; *The Carolingian Empire: The Age of Charlemagne*; Harper and Row, New York and Evanston, 1964.

Fichtenau, Heinrich; *Living in the Tenth Century: Mentalities and Social Orders*; University of Chicago Press, Chicago, 1991.

Flint, Valerie I. J.; *The Rise of Magic in Early Medieval Europe*; Princeton University Press, Princeton, N.J., 1991.

Forsyth, Neil; *The Old Enemy: Satan and the Combat Myth*; Princeton University Press, Princeton, N.J., 1987

Frazer, Sir James George; *The New Golden Bough: A New Abridgement of the Classic Work*; Dr. Theodor H. Gaster, Ed.; New American Library, New York, 1964.

Fustel de Coulanges, Numa Denis; *The Ancient City: A Study on the Religion, Laws, and Institutions of Greece and Rome*, Doubleday, Garden City, N.Y., First English Translation, 1873.

Geanakoplos, Deno John; *Byzantine East and Latin West: Two worlds of Christendom in Middle Ages and Renaissance*; Harper and Row, New York, 1966.

Granier, Jacky; *Water Supply in Antiquity in Provence and Languedoc: the Pont du Gard*; Sté Ajax, Monaco, 1993.

Graves, Robert; *The Greek Myths: Volume 1*; Penguin Books, Baltimore, MD, 1955.

Graves, Robert; *The Greek Myths:Volume 2*; Penguin Books, New York, Revised Edition, 1960.

Graves, Robert; *The White Goddess*, Creative Age Press, New York, 1948.

Guibert of Nogent; *Self and Society in Medieval France: The Memoirs of Abbot Guibert of Nogent*; John F. Benton, Ed.; University of Toronto Press, Toronto, 1984.

Harnack, Adolph; *The Mission and Expansion of Christianity in the First Three Centuries*; Harper and Row, New York, 1962.

Hay, Denys; *The Medieval Centuries*; Harper and Row, New York, 1964.

Humphries, C. J., J. R. Press and D. A. Sutton; *Le Multiguide Nature de tous les Arbres D'Europe*; Bordas, Paris, 1982.

King, John; *The Celtic Druid's Year*; Blandford, London, 1995.

Kung, Hans; *Credo: The Apostles' Creed Explained for Today*; Doubleday, New York, 1993.

Kruta, V., O. H. Frey, H. Raftery, and M. Szabó, Eds; *The Celts*; Rizzoli, New York, 1991.

Lamouroux, René; *The Living Camargue*; Sindicat National des Directeurs de Parcs Zoologiques Français, n.d.

Levi-Strauss, Claude; *Structural Anthropology*; Basic Books, New York, 1963.

Lot, Ferdinand; *The End of the Ancient World and the Beginnings of the Middle Ages*, Harper & Brothers, New York, 1961 edition.

Mallory, J. P.; *In Search of the Indo-Europeans: Language, Archaeology and Myth*; Thames and Hudson Ltd., London, 1989.

Markale, Jean; *Contes Populaires de toutes les Bretagne*; Editions Ouest-France, Rennes, 1993.

Nock, Arthur Darby; *Early Gentile Christianity and its Hellenistic Background*; Harper and Row, New York, 1964.

Oswald's Etymological Dictionary; Key and Biddle, Philadelphia, 1836.

Painter, Sidney; *The Rise of the Feudal Monarchies*; Cornell University Press, Ithaca, N.Y., 1962.

Pendlebury, J. D. S.; *The Archaeology of Crete: an Introduction*; W. W. Norton, New York, 1965.

Poueigh, Jean; *Le folklore des pays d'oc: La tradition occitain*; Editions Payot & Rivages, Paris, 1994.

Russell, Jeffrey Burton; *Witchcraft in the Middle Ages*; Cornell University Press, Ithaca, N.Y., 1972.

Simkins, Michael; *Warriors of Rome: an Illustrated History of the Roman Legions*; Cassell, London, 1988.

Southern, R. W.; *The Making of the Middle Ages*; Yale University Press, New Haven, 1953.

Talbert, Richard J. A., ed; *Atlas of Classical History*; Routledge, London and New York, 1985.

Waddell, Helen; *Beasts and Saints*; Constable, London, 1934.

Waddell, Helen; *The Wandering Scholars*; Constable, London, 1958.

Weiss, Johannes; *Earliest Christianity; a History of the Period A.D. 30–150*; Harper and Row, 1959.

White, Lynn Jr.; *Medieval Technology and Social Change*, Oxford University Press, 1962.